I0666277

THE PROPS MASTER PREQUEL

Behind the
Ivory Veil

Copyright ©2017 by Elder Road LLC
All rights reserved. No part of this publication may be reproduced or transmitted in
any form or by any means, electronic or mechanical, including photocopy, recording,
or any information storage and retrieval system, without permission in writing
from the publisher.

Requests for permission to make copies of any part of the work should be submitted
via e-mail to ElderRoadBooks@outlook.com.
Cover art licensed from Shutterstock.com
Art by Mikhail Bakunovich

First Print Edition
ISBN 978-1-939275-72-1

THE PROPS MASTER PREQUEL

Behind the Ivory Veil

DEVON LAYNE

ELDER ROAD BOOKS
BELLEVUE WA

Contents

Introduction

BEHIND THE IVORY VEIL is an occult fantasy. Much of the story revolves around two pagan cults, one in England and one in Greece, that preserve ancient practices into the modern day (1955). Its underlying assumption is that magic is real, it works, and it is present in our everyday lives—usually unrecognized or passed off as mere coincidence. So the people in this story are all normal folks you'd meet on the street and never imagine were involved in the art and ritual of pagan magic, any more than you would suspect they were Methodist or Catholic.

Famed witch Aleister Crowley is thought to have said that the difference between white magic and black magic is that white magic is poetry and black magic works. As a result, this volume is filled with stories, legends, and poetic rituals. You, like the characters, may be surprised that they work. Many of these rituals have been developed by other practitioners and, although I recognize works that have been influential in my view of paganism, it is not possible for me to identify if specific parts of rituals might have been more heavily influenced by one author or another. I cite *The Spiral Dance* by Starhawk, *A Book of Pagan Rituals* by Herman Slater, *The White Goddess* by Robert Graves, *Mythology* by Edith Hamilton, *Bulfinch's Mythology* by Thomas Bulfinch, and a library filled with other books about mythology and paganism. It is likely that the stories and rituals have influenced my phrasing and even words within the rituals here and I do so with utmost respect, acknowledging that every brother and sister of the craft contributes to the overall knowledge and experience of the others.

For those faint of heart, it is only fair to say that the gods, whether Greek or Hindu or Christian or Pagan, are seldom kind and compassionate. They have their own agendas and humans are an insignificant and sometimes incovenient part of their plans. So, do not be surprised when gods have their way and people are brushed aside. Remember that the story continues in *The Props Master 1: Ritual Reality*.

Now, let us begin the journey. Doc discovers a path to the legendary City of the Gods, their abandoned home on Mount Olympus. He enlists musicologist Wesley Allen to return and interpret the strange musical notations at the site. Wesley's fiancée, Rebecca, goes to the University of Edinburgh to complete her thesis on matriarchal thealogy. She meets Mrs. Weed and is initiated into the ancient Coven Carles. But Doc's one-time protégé, 'The Blade', dogs Rebecca's footsteps, attempting to locate Doc's dig. His intent: to find and claim the lost goddess hidden behind the ivory veil. Myth, magic, and mayhem nearly destroy the coven and place an impenetrable curtain between Rebecca and Wesley.

Names of places and things

LIKE ANY art, pagan ritual has a unique vocabulary that includes words from several sources. Some of the words here are Celtic in origin and others are untraceable. This is not meant to be a definitive list of terms and definitions for the art, but is provided for context as used in this story. Coven Carles might be referred to as *Cobhan Carles* and the members of the coven might be referred to as *cildru*. Occasionally, Greek words and phrases are also used, but they are defined in context.

PAGANS OFTEN NAME each of their tools, but I am only listing here the names of the Four Faces of Carles, the sacred tools of the grand coven.

Athamé: is a knife or sword—a blade—sacred to the workings of magic, and representative of Air and the East. The ritual *Athamé* of Coven Carles is named Creüs and is in the keeping of Ryan McGuire, The Blade.

Wand: may be a short wand (think Harry Potter) or a full staff (think Gandalf), sacred to the workings of magic, and representative of Fire and the South. Usually, but not always, made of wood. The ritual wand of Coven Carles is named Iäpetus and is sometimes referred to as the Staff of the Vagabond Poet. It is in the keeping of Doc Heinrich, The Flame Keeper.

Cup: may be any shape or material, sacred to the workings of magic, and representative of the West and Water. The ritual cup of Coven Carles is named Cottus and was in the keeping of Mrs. Weed, The Water Maiden.

Pentacles: May be a star, star-shaped stone, medicine bag with symbols on it, or a disk, usually also engraved with a pentacle of some sort. Sacred to the workings of magic, and representative of the North and Earth. The ritual pentacles of Coven Carles is named Enceladus and is in the keeping of the high priestess, "Magda".

SPECIAL NOTE: My use of the word *pentacles* may differ slightly from that of other practitioners, but to keep terms straight for readers of fiction, I offer the following. The tool referenced herein is always referred to as a plural. The use of 'is' or 'are' is based entirely on what sounds better in the context, but as much as possible, *pentacles* always refers to the tool, no matter what shape it takes. The singular form, *pentacle*, is the *design* on the tool. The design is not necessarily star-shaped. Of the forty-four known Pentacles of Solomon, only two designs (the second pentacle of Venus and the first pentacle of Mercury) have a five-pointed star. In magical workings, however, a five-pointed star is often drawn on the floor or even in the air. This specific symbol is a *pentagram*. There are many ways of drawing the *pentagram* (forward, backward, upright, inverted) and each has its own use. But all are five-pointed stars.

A ***Book of Shadows*** is a journal kept by a witch, chronicling what he or she has learned, including dreams, rituals, spells, and lore. One witch's *Book of Shadows* may become another witch's grimoire.

A **grimoire** is a book of witchcraft with spells, chants, rituals, and various charm-making recipes. It is usually intended to be copied and/or passed on to another witch.

PAGAN HOLIDAYS FALL at the quarters and cross-quarters of the year, in other words, the four celestial holidays and four between them. They are:

Yule, the winter solstice. This is considered by some traditions to be the start of the pagan year. ~December 21.

Imbolc, in the United States celebrated as Groundhogs' Day and in the Catholic Church is marked as Candlemas. ~February 2.

Oester, the vernal equinox. Originally the feast of Astarte, near Jewish Passover and Christian Easter. ~March 21.

Beltane, or May Day. The first of May has long been celebrated as the great fertility festival.

Litha, the summer solstice. While westerners largely consider the quarters to be the beginning of the season, old references point to the fact that these were considered mid-season, as in *A Midsummer Night's Dream*. Longest day and shortest night of the year. ~June 21.

Lughnasad, also called Lammas or first harvest. This festival celebrates the death of the corn king. ~August 1.

Mabon, autumnal equinox. End of the harvest season and sometimes celebrated with the burning of a wicker man. Current celebrations in the U.S. that arise from the tradition include Burning Man over Labor Day weekend. ~September 20.

Samhain, or All Hallows Eve, Halloween. This celebrates the end of the pagan year as it descends to the darkness of Yule. It is said that on this night, the veil between the worlds (of the living and dead) is thinnest and both humans and spirits may walk between them. October 31.

Greece. The Metéora is a region of Greece located in the Plains of Thessaly and is home to many monasteries built in the 1500s on the tops of great sheer pinnacles of rock. I have tried to be faithful to the spirit of the area, but you would be unable to draw a map from my descriptions.

Indianapolis. As much as possible, the places in and around Indianapolis are real or were real in the '50s, though some names (especially around the college) have been changed.

England. As nearly as I can remember them, the locations in and around Keswick, England are described accurately for the time and the geography is at least nearly the same.

The Grand Coven Carles Castlerigg (*Cobhan Carles*) comprises four smaller circles, named for the landmarks that surround the stone circle, Skiddaw (in the north), Threlkeld (in the east), High Lodore (in the south), and Braithwaite (in the west).

Cast

THIS IS a list of the principal characters in *Behind the Ivory Veil*. When a character is or becomes involved in a pagan circle, he or she is usually given a special name. This name is how the coveners refer to each other as a way of keeping their actual identities secret. The custom originates in the Burning Times. Even older, however, is the practice of adopting or being given a secret name that is shared only with others who are engaged with the practitioner in deep ritual magic. Hence, Rebecca Allen is given the circle name 'The Hart' when she is initiated. But her mentor also gives her a secret, magical name, 'Sadb', which is only used when Rebecca is working deep and intense magic or has fully entered her identity as a practioner of the art. Most people in the coven are commonly referred to by their coven name. Only a few are referred to by their secret name.

Dr. Phillip "Doc" Heinrich, professor of archaeology, Farrington University in Connecticut. Also known as The Flame Keeper, keeper of the Second Face of Carles.

Dr. Margaret Jacobson, former student of Doc's and associate professor of anthropology.

J. Wesley Allen, professor of musicology at Indianapolis City College (ICC).

Rebecca Hart Allen, graduate student in anthropology at ICC and Wesley's fiancée and then wife. In the circle, she becomes The Hart and in magic working, Sadb.

Dr. Ryan "The Blade" McGuire. Scots-English archaeological adventurer and treasure hunter. A thorn in the side of Doc and member of the same coven. Keeper of the First Face of Carles.

Andrew Pariskovopolis, an old man of the Metéora. Keeper of the secret.

Apollo "Pol" Pariskovopolis, Andrew's 12-year-old grandson.

Mrs. Alice "Hebe" Weed, a witch in Scotland who adopts Rebecca. As The Water Maiden, she is keeper of the Third Face of Carles.

William Renton, Doc's valet, friend, and former classmate. A sculptor in wood and stone.

Dr. Benjamin "The Firebrand" Wilton, disgraced archaeological adventurer and former bearer of the Second Face. Doc's mentor. Also wrote fiction as Ben Wills.

Brother El, a monk of one of the monasteries of the Metéora, not identified as such, but may have been Elbert Parker, Wilton's spy contact.

Thea Pariskovopolis, Andrew's wife.

Sophia, Andrew's daughter and Pol's aunt.

Marcos Pariskovopolis, a taxi driver/chauffeur in Greece. Pol's father.

Helen Pariskovopolis, Pol's mother and wife of Marcos.

1
Firebrand

Sunday, 1 August 1937, Northern England

FIRE!

The walking stick held in his hands came to life and flames sprang from tip to tail as he held it over the laid wood. The fire leapt from the walking stick to the dry tinder and it burst into flame. Yet his hands, grasping the staff stayed cool as the flames licked around his fingers then flickered and died.

In a country where witchcraft was classified as an offense of con artistry and vagrancy, young Doctor Phillip Heinrich had just participated in a ritual that made him keeper of a sacred tool of Coven Carles. He was now The Flame Keeper and would never be parted from the walking stick called Iäpetus until he gave it into the hands of a new guardian.

Around him, the naked dancers were caught up in an ecstatic spiral around the burning fire. Doc was passed from dancer to dancer, kissed, fondled, and brought to his own crescendo as the dancers shouted and fell to the ground leaving only the sound of the fire and their gasping breaths in the wake.

And then Doc saw. It was more than his eyesight. His eyes could see the exhausted coveners lying around him, some clasping each other, still lost in their unions. His eyes could see the fire in the pit. His eyes could even see the outline of the stone circle that surrounded them. But his mind could see further.

His mentor, disgraced Professor Benjamin Wilton, stood at the edge of a cliff. Wilton was headed back to Greece—not as a professor this time, but as a renegade. His paper on the lost goddess of Metéora was a subject of ridicule in academia. He was going back to find the proof he needed.

"I'll find her, Phillip," he said. "I may never come back, but I'll leave you a sign. You know now that it is real. You've seen the power manifest in your hands. The establishment may never accept it, but you know the truth."

"Truth? What is truth?" quoted Doc. "Can I believe what my eyes tell me? If the staff was on fire, my hands should be burnt. How can I know the truth?"

"I'll leave you a sign. You'll know it when you see it. When that day comes, your doubts will disappear." With that the professor turned away from Doc and toward the edge of the cliff.

"Wait!" Doc shouted. "What do I do with this stick?"

"Go on a walking tour of the Lakes and Scotland. Listen to people. When they ask if that is not the staff of the Vagabond Poet, respond with the words 'Merry meet.' Then listen. They will tell you stories you could not imagine. Return here at Mabon and you will never again question what to do with the staff. Blessed be, Flame Keeper. Blessed be."

"Blessed be, Firebrand," Doc whispered. "Stay clear of the Germans. They say they are moving into Greece."

Wilton turned back toward the cliff, naked as the day he was born, and dove. A long time later, Doc heard the distant splash.

2

The Metéora

Saturday, 25 September 1954, near Kastraki, Greece

THE STAFF in his hand was still alive, though it had never again burst into flames. Doc felt it vibrate with each step through the canyons of the Metéora, the fire of the Mediterranean sun beating on his back. He'd been back every summer since the war. Though the staff had never again called fire, Doc had found other uses for it and felt it resonate with the land around him.

The goat track that locals called a road was as dusty as the foothills had been. A preternatural awareness of his surroundings prickled at his senses. Turks, communists, still a few Nazi sympathizers, and local city chiefs all vied for the privilege of being the most feared threat. A lack of vigilance could be fatal.

As he stepped through the narrow passage, hands grabbed at him from either side. Doc responded automatically. If it no longer spit fire, the walking stick still moved with a mind of its own. His right hand worked as a fulcrum as he swung the top of the stick down with his left. Its ironclad heel struck one assailant in the groin. Not stopping, Doc spun on the other attacker and struck out with the butt of the stick. A quickly raised hand deflected the blow, but Doc won his freedom.

He turned on his attackers and slipped the pack from his back, the staff grasped firmly in both hands. What he saw made him sick. Children, not more than fourteen or fifteen years old. One already had a knife in his hand. The other gathered up a rock to throw. *God damn this land of misery!* Maybe he already had.

The boy threw his rock and Doc no longer felt sorry for them. He picked it out of the air wielding the staff as a bat and crashed down on the charging knife hand in the same move. The bigger youth screamed in pain but dropped the knife into his other hand and attacked again. Doc parried the knife neatly but failed to dodge the next rock. The missile

3

struck him squarely in the chest. He staggered back a step, tripped over his discarded pack and fell.

The knife-wielding youth yelled in triumph and leapt to a rock above Doc. He brandished his knife ready for the kill. His accomplice shouted above the noise. Doc watched the boy's focus shift as silence fell in the wake of the echo. The boy backed off the rock and joined his companion. Then both ran back the way Doc had come.

The sudden change in behavior piqued Doc to alertness for new danger. A predator abandons prey when faced with a superior predator. Struggling to regain his lost wind, he rolled, planted his staff and pulled himself upright to face whatever challenge might now appear.

A monk.

And an old man leaning on a short cane. Doc breathed a sigh of relief. A coarsely woven robe and pillbox hat identified the religious as a monk of one of the monasteries gracing the pinnacles of Metéora. It was he who spoke first.

"Are you injured, sir?"

"Bruised but not broken," Doc answered in nearly flawless Greek. "Nothing serious."

"An American," laughed the older man, identifying the accent in spite of Doc's facility with the language. "Didn't I tell you, El?"

"Yes, yes," answered the monk. "How you know these things…" Turning his attention back to Doc he continued. "May we help you, sir? We will escort you to the village if that is your destination; or gladly offer hospitality among the brethren if you are not afraid of heights."

The monk raised his hand and pointed to the top of one of the sheer cliffs nearby. It towered at five hundred feet above them. About halfway up, a net swung at the end of a long rope. An unfortunate but long-standing joke restrained Doc from accepting the invitation: *How often do you change the ropes?* asked the tourist. *"Whenever they break,"* answered the monk.

"Thank you. I was on my way to Kalambaka," Doc answered. The monk held Doc's eye for a moment flicking back to his staff.

"Is that not the staff of the Vagabond Poet?" the monk asked in English, so softly that Doc barely heard him.

"Merry meet," Doc whispered.

"Merry part, and merry meet again," the monk intoned. He glanced at the old man and nodded slightly.

What were the odds? He was in the middle of the Plains of Thessaly talking to an old man and a monk and greeted with words from an

English cult. A sign of recognition Doc had not heard outside The Lake District. And this monk was not Greek.

"May I offer my home, Doctor?" the old man broke the silence between Doc and the monk. "It is not so highly exalted as the monastery."

"How did you know I was a doctor?" he asked immediately. In thirty-plus years of not strictly academic work, enough scavengers dogged his footsteps to keep Doc suspicious of any familiarity. First the monk and then the old man.

"Don't ask Andrew how he knows anything," interrupted the monk. "He will probably tell you that he has been expecting you all day."

"All week," the old man confessed.

"You have the advantage of me," Doc said skeptically. "I've only expected to be here for the past three or four hours."

"I have reached that age where I am always expecting a visitor," the old man smiled. "I'm Andrew Pariskovopolis," he said, extending a hand. "You looked like a scholar to me."

"Phillip Heinrich," Doc replied, returning the handshake. "Professor of archaeology at Farrington University. Most folks call me Doc."

"Well then, Doc. My invitation is genuine. If you would share bread with my family this evening, my home is open to you."

"I feel that I already owe you for rescuing me from those young hoodlums." Doc winced as he rubbed the sore spot on his chest and retrieved his pack.

"It's a sad thing," broke in the monk. "They are refugees from their own homes, forced to steal in order to live. The communists raid the villages and kidnap the children they find. To escape, some flee into the hills. They become hungry enough to attack travelers. Finally, they will give themselves up to the communists for the offer of a good meal. We will never see them again."

"You seem to have influence over them, Father," said Doc. "Is there nothing that can be done?"

"Just 'Brother'," the monk corrected him. "Is it a good thing that children should fear the church? I must leave you now, but I leave you in good care, Doctor." The monk turned off down the path after a parting word with the old man. Doc and Andrew were left alone to make a short climb up the edge of the canyon.

"Brother El has tried many times to help our children. He is one of the few monks who do not stay on their mountain tops," the old man told Doc. "But the children fear the monks as much as they do the communists. Nothing is here but confusion these days."

"I must thank you again for your offer of hospitality, then," Doc responded. "It must be dangerous to invite unknown guests into your home."

"Sometimes there is danger," the old man answered looking at Doc carefully. "But Zeus commands and he protects."

Doc's suspicions melted into curiosity. A dozen images swept through his mind. Embodied in that phrase was the heritage of Dionysian sects predating civilization. In Zeus's name, the wayfarer seeking lodging could not be refused. Doc added up the possibilities of such a sect surviving in the relative isolation of Metéora, even among the Christian monasteries. They equaled a treasure. The title for the paper that he would write after this visit was already forming in his mind.

"You keep the ancient ways?" Doc asked tentatively.

"They keep us," the old man affirmed.

They came upon four small dwellings surrounded by a low wall. Here the old man stopped. As soon as he opened the courtyard gate, several children and two yapping dogs descended on them.

"My grandchildren. All except those two," the old man laughed, pointing at the dogs. "Children, tell *yiayia* we have a guest for dinner." The two walked on into the courtyard and the old man drew water from the central well. This is my home, Doctor. Welcome. My wife and I live in the little house. My children and grandchildren occupy the other three. We change places from time to time as our families grow and change."

"All your family lives right here?" Doc asked, trying to tabulate quickly how many people might form the cult he was sure existed here.

"No. I am sorry to say." Andrew paused and drew a pained breath. "I lost my youngest son in the war. It was very hard. My eldest son and his wife moved to Athens some years ago. Where others talk, he charges in to see what will happen. They could not have been happy here. But their son is visiting for the summer. Maybe longer."

A little woman emerged from the first house and bustled across the yard toward them. "He's come?" she asked Andrew with her eyes questioningly intent on Doc. "You found him?"

"And this is my wife, Thea," laughed the old man. "Thea, this is Doctor Heinrich, our guest," he said gently to her.

"Excuse me, sir," she said, critically surveying her guest. Whatever the old man's generosity, Doc was not what she expected. She glanced at her husband and he nodded. "I beg your pardon," she sighed heavily. "I thought... well! I'll put dinner on the table. You will join us."

Behind the Ivory Veil

"Thank you," Doc answered to her back as she retreated.

He joined his host and followed the woman into the house which rapidly filled with the rest of the clan. The dinner was shared in common with all the families. Doc couldn't separate one household from another. They noisily fell to their meal and told stories around the table. Doc was not the expected guest, it seemed, but was certainly not unwelcome. He spun yarns about his travels and adventures, sticking to the ones of his younger years when he adventured as far as China, South America, and Africa.

THE MEAL ENDED and the storytelling grew more spirited. Doc sensed a subtle shift. As he told of an adventure, the old man would turn it into a lesson in the ancient myths. Finally, one of the children was asked to tell a story.

The child was well-versed in mythology, apparently the fruit of his grandfather's teaching, but the story was all his own woven into the fabric of a classical myth. It was a romantic story, though some of the romance was lost in an over-exuberant description of Apollo's glory and in the child's enthusiasm for the magical qualities that the gods exhibited. The boy was especially enthused in his description of the muses.

Following in Apollo's entourage, his heavenly muses
Listen to the sun-god's lyre and fawn over him.
That pleases Apollo.
Polymnia, singing praises to her patron god Apollo.
Calliope, still reciting the epic poem she had composed just last year.
Clio, correcting the historical allusions in her poem.
Thalia, making fun of the proceedings and laughing at
Star-gazing Urania, falling over her own feet.
Melpomene, weeping for a hero lost in battle, fatally flawed.
Erato, reciting a love poem written for Asklepios and his bride.
Behind them all dances Terpsichore, celebrating,
And encouraging the lagging Euterpe to speed up the tempo
with her flute.

But Euterpe, lyric muse, sees not the joy of this occasion
The day on which her one true love will be bound to another.
If only she were as beautiful as Health.

If only she could heal.
What good is music and lyric poetry when people still fall ill.
But fair Asklepios sees her not.
So, as Health is conferred on the new godling,
Euterpe, a mere muse, creeps away.
Far from the celebration she pipes her mournful tune
And from her flute issues gossamer tones weaving a veil
As if of ivory silk between the lyric muse and Olympus.
Unknown, unmissed, the muse weeps for her lost love.

She imagines herself the very picture of Health,
Taking her lover in her arms and welcoming him to her bosom.
As Asklepios consummates his marriage to Health,
Euterpe feels him part her temple gates
And plant within her the seed of their love.

Behind her Ivory Veil,
Euterpe's empathic pregnancy advances apace with Health's.
In the fullness of time, Hygeia is born of Health.
But behind the ivory veil another child gasps her first breath.
Euterpe calls her symbiont child Serepte.

Anon, times change.
An instant as gods measure time.
Men cease offering the sweet scent of burnt flesh.
Starving from neglect, the ancients give way to new gods
And flee Olympus
As the Titans gave way to the Olympians.

Apollo gathers his muses to him and numbers them.
But one is missing.
"Euterpe!" he calls and she must answer his summons.
But behind the ivory veil, the child goddess Serepte is held.
"One day, my child," the muse sings out,
"One day a hero will come. A mortal will release you into the world.
And on that day, you will be the goddess you were born to be."

And here we wait.
Millennia are but an instant to the immortals

But eternity to men.
Her story is forgotten by all but a hand of faithful
Who await the mortal hero to rise
And free the goddess from her prison
Behind the Ivory Veil.

Doc WAS SURPRISED by the frank descriptions of sensuality given by the boy. Even at the University, Doc would take flak if he recited such sexual details. Such was America. The character of the empathically conceived child was left a mystery, but Doc thought it might bear a resemblance to other known goddesses or be a key to a local legend. There was no clue to her special characteristics in the story. Doc found that strange. The pantheon always had function associated with deity. If the goddess was to prove a legitimate piece in mythology, she must have a function. The story ended with the empathically conceived goddess shrouded behind the ivory veil that bound her to old Olympus awaiting a mortal savior as the other gods took flight to the heavens.

Doc applauded with the rest of the family and Andrew hugged the boy. Doc smiled and reached to shake the boy's hand.

"Well, Doctor Heinrich," said the old man, "what do you think of my Apollo and his story?"

"A very talented young man," answered Doc. "It's a beautiful story. May I ask questions? I've never heard anything quite like it and I'm curious. Of course, if it's not appropriate, I certainly understand…?" He left the sentence hanging in an unspoken question that belied his own impatience. The old man laughed.

"There are no secrets to our faith, Doctor. Only the blindness of those who will not ask. Even the priests and monks of the monasteries know. It is that alone that keeps us concealed from the rest of the world. 'Knowing, they know not; Seeing, they see not; Understanding all, they understand nothing.'"

Doc was certain the old man's quotation was not quite scriptural. But it added to the incongruity of the whole setting.

"At the moment, I admit that I am too taken by the story to question the roots of belief. It seemed… incomplete." Doc began. "Why did the story end before the goddess—I assume goddess is an appropriate term for Serepte?—before the goddess was freed from her captivity? What mortal ultimately came along to deliver her and how?"

"Ah, that is the heart of the matter," the old man responded. "The end of the story. We don't know the end of the story, Doctor Heinrich. My family has passed it down from generation to generation in hope of the mortal savior. It is the basis of our faith. For that reason alone, the legend has been preserved."

"You may be isolated and alone, but you have a great faith."

"Well, the time cannot be far off now," he answered.

"What?"

"When I came of age, it was prophesied that the deliverer would come in my lifetime. I am getting old," Andrew chuckled. Apollo wrapped his arms around his grandfather.

"Age is a matter of the heart," Doc assured him. "You strike me as very young of heart."

"I thank you," said the old man. "But there is another reason I believe the time is at hand. No doubt you have seen many religions in your travels, of which our faith is simply an anachronism. You must surely know that this faith can survive only in relative isolation. You and I have twice seen the entire world at war. We have seen manmade acts that exceed all the myths of deities from all the ages. If we have become gods ourselves, what need is there of a pantheon that no longer shows itself to mortals?"

Doc absorbed what the man was saying. His religion was doomed and he addressed the matter as a calm student of his own demise.

"What will happen if—or I should say when—the mortal savior actually reaches the veil and releases the goddess? Is it to be a time of cataclysm? Is she to reestablish the ancient religion? Do you expect a revival? A war? Anything?"

The old man drew a deep breath and for a moment Doc was afraid he had crossed the barrier of good taste. But when the voice reached his ears it was one of sorrow and question.

"Your faith is a faith of answers. Ours is one of questions. Those which you ask are the deepest. I do not know the answers. It may signal the end or beginning of another age. We may loose a power that we do not understand on a world that it cannot comprehend. And it may be that we will simply set at liberty a captive spirit that has no other purpose than to take flight—to reunite with her own. But it will take a mortal not of my family to work the release. This we do know."

"Well, may your gods send you a fine strong young man to do the job."

"We will settle our minds on whomever is sent to us by the gods" nodded the old man.

Doc nodded unconsciously then cocked his head to one side as he realized the weight of the old man's statement. "Certainly, you can't expect that I'm the one you are waiting for? I'm not a keeper of your religion." The old man smiled. Doc continued. "I don't see how I could possibly be of help to you." The last thing he wanted at this stage of his life was to become involved in a mystery rite about which he knew nothing. He had had his share of that.

"Perhaps the name Benjamin Wilton, known also as the Firebrand, means something to you, Doctor Heinrich." The old man leaned forward trying to connect with Doc's averted gaze. *Wilton.* He could not let out the depth of meaning that the name held for him. "You need not answer, the old man continued. "You carry his staff, though your way of using it is different than his."

"I'm afraid that I do not have the same talents that my... he did. How do you know of him?"

"And have you heard of the City of the Gods?"

"If you profess to have a map to the ancient city, Mr. Pariskovopolis, you engage in a cruel and outdated jest. I have purchased no less than twenty such maps over the years. They were elaborate hoaxes. Some I purchased because I thought it might indeed be possible. The rest, simply to get them off the streets. I am a scientist and am no longer prone to wandering around with unchecked pieces of parchment as my only guide." Doc was irritated and close to bidding his host goodnight and returning to the village. Wilton's alleged fraud had marked the end of an illustrious career for Doc's one-time mentor. The old man stopped him with a gesture.

"And what do you think? Was Wilton a liar?"

Doc said nothing for a moment. He had never quite believed the allegations, but couldn't bring himself to believe that Wilton had found a path to Old Olympus.

"I think that Professor Wilton believed in his discovery," he said finally.

"You are pained by the mention of his name for reasons that I do not know. I will share with you my own pain. In 1943, my youngest son was killed fighting the Italians in the North. Two years earlier he made a sacred trip to this fabled city and was followed by a man that I believe to have been Professor Wilton. That man desecrated the holy place. How, I do not know. There are many rules. My son could never say. But he witnessed the gods' revenge and that was more than he could bear. Within a week he ran away to join the army. He was too young, Doctor, but it was believed that a boy was better off in the army than in a reestablishment camp. At 14 the son of my old age was killed. I do not know what Professor Wilton did, but my son is gone."

"That would have been 1941," Doc said. "Wilton disappeared four years before that. I saw him…" The image of his mentor in the firelight was burned into Doc's memory. With fire still rushing in his veins, he watched the professor step to the edge of the cliff and dive off—an impossibly long way to the water. "It simply can't have been him."

"I would like to believe that, Doctor Heinrich, as much as you."

It was late and Doc's exertions of the day were catching up with him. His chest ached from where he'd been struck. He winced as he yawned.

"If Wilton desecrated the holy of holies, why would you share this with me?" Doc was certain none of this would make sense in the morning.

"Doctor Heinrich," the old man smiled at him, "we must have an ending to our story."

"And you will take me there?"

"You will go in the morning. Apollo must be in the city on his twelfth birthday—the day after tomorrow."

"A ritual?"

"A redemption," nodded the patriarch.

Doc rose to retire for the night. At the door Doc turned once again to his host.

"Do you really believe in the ancient gods?"

"Do you believe in stones, Doctor Heinrich?" Doc paused at the question. "You may build with them, throw them, shape them, use them, stumble over them, or ignore them. Or even cast them at your enemies. They are beyond the realm of belief."

Doc slept a short and restless night.

3
City of the Gods

Sunday, 26 September 1954, Metéora, Greece

IN THE before-dawn blush of the next day, Doc sat on the ground with the family. They formed a loosely drawn circle around the well in the center of the courtyard. He had agreed to participate in the ritual without further thought after Andrew explained it. It was not unlike those Doc had participated in over the years in countless cultures, including at the stone circle in Northern England. Silently, they watched the old man in the center as he moved about the circle inscribing it with his gestures. Doc felt a subtle barrier at his back after the old man passed him—an intangible wall that defined the ritual space. It had been years since Doc felt the presence as powerfully as he did this morning. Perhaps he was remembering his own initiation. At last the old man stopped moving just to Doc's left. He turned toward the outside of the circle and faced East. Though the words were in Greek, Doc had no difficulty translating them as they were spoken.

Within this sanctuary cast
Are all the powers of the ancients.
Let the air—
The fire—
The water—
Gaia herself join us
In this circle of power.

The family took up the chant from the old man. "*Symmetochí ston kýklo tis exousías.* Join in the circle of power." The old man raised his hands to the East and continued. While the ritual casting of a circle was similar to the pagan rituals of England in which Doc had participated, the words were cloaked in classic references to the powers of Olympus and had the flavor of a Greek play. The old man was Choragus and the family was the Chorus.

"Open, unlidded eye of golden dawn, and cast upon us your rays of life."

His timing was impeccable. The sun broke over the crest of Metéora glinting into his eyes and filling the courtyard with the sharp light of morning. He turned slowly to his right and stopped with his back to Doc. The family continued the almost sub-vocal chant "Join in the circle of power." The old man raised his arms to the South.

"Flame within us, Hephaestus, volcano of eternal fire."

The eldest daughter held a candle. Doc saw no sign of a match or lighter, but the candle flared to life with a crack that echoed in the courtyard. The chant picked up a little volume as the old man moved to the West and held up his hands.

"Rise Poseidon, tide of the sea; flood us in refreshing waves."

Thea raised a pitcher and a cup and began to pour water. She kept pouring. Doc expected the cup to overflow, but the more she poured, the more water it seemed to hold. She kept pouring as the old man moved to stand in front of Doc and Apollo and raise his hands to the North.

"Demeter, mother of the seasons, dust of our bodies, accept us and fill us with the power of Earth."

Apollo scooped dust from the ground in front of him and let it filter from one hand to the other. A light wind rose and the dust swirled in the palm of his hand. When he held it out, Doc could imagine that he saw the shape of a woman swirling in the dust.

The old man smiled and ran his fingers through Pol's hair. "Now, let's hope this works, eh?" He pointed to Doc's walking stick and asked, "May I borrow this? It's not necessary, but it looks so spectacular." Doc hesitated. Only he and Wilton had used the staff for rituals in at least forty years. It made his hand twitch to present the staff to the old man.

Andrew rapped the staff on the ground setting a rhythm that the clan picked up with soft clapping. When the old man began to chant again, Doc could not understand any of the words but he was able to grasp a sense of it all. It was a summoning. The old man danced and gestured with the staff as he chanted. He swung it above his head and passed it beneath his feet. Doc had seen other summonings in other cultures, but nothing quite like this. It left him with only one concrete image: Laughter. Then he was aware of the laughter of the rest of the family, nearly covering the chant that had been taken up. *"Hanistemi udor oste pino. Hanistemi udor oste pino."* Andrew stopped before the well with Doc's staff held in front of him. Doc felt the chant growing and joined the rest of the group.

How it happened, or even if it happened, Doc could never tell. He saw—or thought he saw—water rise to the edge of the well and brim over. At its edge, the old man resumed dancing, laughing, swinging the stick and splashing water out of the overflowing well at and onto the members of the circle.

At the peak of the excitement, with the well a geyser, the old man shouted and everyone fell silent with a force that knocked them back on the ground. The silence hummed through Doc's mind. For a moment, he could not even hear his own breathing. But the image of the laughing spirit of the well was firmly imprinted in his mind.

He gradually became aware of the sounds around him—his heart beating, his breathing, the rustle of leaves in the breeze, the distant chirp of a bird. Then came the intonations of the old man, still softly chanting above him. Doc rose on an elbow to look around. The sun was well up now. It was later in the morning than Doc liked to begin traveling. They would need to rest in the heat. The other celebrants were also rising and a loaf of bread was passed followed by a plate of cheeses and olives. Thea and Sophia were making the rounds with a pot of tea and cups. Doc's stomach rumbled and he broke bread

When Andrew had completed a circle counter-clockwise, he stopped in front of Doc and helped him to his feet.

"Your staff," the old man said, handing Doc the walking stick. Then he pulled Apollo up to his feet and embraced the boy. "It was very good. Go and travel safely."

Without a further word, Doc and Apollo shouldered their packs and left. Doc paused at the gate for a quizzical look at the old man and the dry courtyard. Andrew smiled and waved.

Doc and Apollo were on the road and moving quickly on the outskirts of Metéora before they spoke to each other. Preparing himself, Doc thought. A memorized ritual must be performed. Doc wondered what his part in the ritual would be this time. *Quiet observer,* he hoped. Perhaps this journey—simply finding one's way to the sacred place— was the entire ritual. There was data to support that among Native American tribes. Perhaps this would be a parallel—a spirit quest. When they stopped for lunch, the conversation was casual and Doc felt free to ask questions of the boy.

"Apollo, are you a believer in the ancient religion?" The boy laughed.

"I believe. But I believe like a child believes in Agios Vassilis—you say Santa Claus. When we grow up, we understand that Agios Vassilis was a saint who lived centuries ago and we commemorate his day the last night of the year by giving gifts. He does not actually visit. So, many of the stories *Papou*—Grandfather—tells are hard to understand. I don't know if they are real or if they represent something. In school, we are told that the myths were teaching stories, but my teachers often don't know what the stories teach. Papou says that when I make my journey, I will understand and will be able to decide for myself what to believe."

"Is your father a believer?"

"No. My father does not believe. He is a good Christian. He taught me the stories of our ancient way."

"He taught you to be a believer but is not one himself? I don't understand."

"Like Papou, he wants me to make my own decision. In kindness to me he has taught me the stories so that I would know the choices."

"In my country, parents teach only what they want their children to believe," Doc grumbled. "As do teachers."

"Oh, he taught me that, too," Apollo laughed. "I had to memorize half the Bible." Doc joined the laughter.

"And if you choose wrong?"

"There is no wrong choice—only different ones. The important thing is to choose."

The words seemed old for a boy so young and Doc reminded himself that though well-schooled, he was dealing with a child. The boy's long black hair and simple clothes would make it impossible for a stranger to tell if he was a boy or a girl.

The way became more rugged as they began to climb gradually and the two lapsed again into silence. For a while, Doc had kept track of the general direction they were headed, but by noon the sky was so unnaturally overcast that he could no longer identify east from west by the sun.

As they traveled, the boy became more reticent about talking. He was carefully checking every landmark. There had been no identifiable trail for several hours. On a slope of rocks, indistinguishable one from another to Doc, Apollo selected one and walked straight toward it. Then he abruptly changed his course just slightly and walked on to another rock. The sound of running water gradually broke in on Doc's senses. He looked up beyond Apollo and saw a broad swath of green as the slope evened off beside a mountain stream. The stream and broad greenway were an oasis in the midst of a rocky terrain. As he stepped onto the soft grass, Doc felt he was on very old ground, like walking through a rain-forest where thick mulched leaves coat the ground for generations. It was springy and almost alive to the touch as they turned upstream. There was one tree, however, which dominated the greenway like a patriarch of nature. Here, Pol stopped and tossed his pack on the ground.

"We'll camp here for the night."

Heinrich tossed his pack down beside the boy and set up camp near the ancient tree. He worried about the threatening sky that grew ever darker, but detected no scent of rain in the air. The tarp made into a hasty lean-to would protect them from any mild rain.

Doc had an irresistible urge to remove his hiking boots, recalling older passages of Exodus concerning holy ground. Yet, here there was no burning bush, no voice of God—only an old gnarled tree and a small boy.

"You've never been to the City of the Gods, yet you know the way so well. You don't have some secret map that someone sold you, do you?" Doc asked.

"It is an ancient holy place," began Apollo. "There are no maps. All the members of my family have made this trip on or about their twelfth birthdays. My father, my aunts and uncle, my grandparents, and as far back as we can tell. When we marry, the new spouses are invited to make the trip with their mates. All receive the blessing of the holy place and all make their choice."

"I'm honored to accompany you on such an important occasion," Doc said. "Why are you willing to show me the way to the holy place? Isn't it a secret?"

"I can take you to *ta hagia hagion*. I cannot show you the way. You will go with me, but even if you found your way back to this spot, you can only enter the city if invited. The dangers are many and stories of those who have tried and failed are also many. That is why we rest now. Tomorrow we will be shown the way to *ta hagia hagion*."

"*Ta hagia hagion*. The holiest of all. Is it so to all people or only to your family?"

"The way was given to us a long time ago by a strange visitor. We have never met others there—at least not others we recognize."

"You mean your family owns this place?"

"No one owns *ta hagia hagion*."

"But all these years your family has passed it on from generation to generation?"

"Over the years, much of the story has been lost," Apollo answered. "It is difficult to live apart and guard the mysteries. We believe and hope but do not understand. May Apollo, my namesake, enlighten us."

With that, Pol pulled off his clothes and dove into the stream. There he swam and bathed as Doc looked on from the shore. It was tempting, but Doc was too reserved to join in. Too old for such a childish pleasure. Ritual bathing was not unknown to Doc. He thought of the stone circle in England and his initiation. Soon Pol brought water out of the stream and bathed Doc's feet. The water was refreshing and the gesture was one of sincere respect and affection.

"Doctor Heinrich, do not be mistaken. Tomorrow, you must also make your choice," Pol said softly.

Doc fell asleep listening to Apollo sing softly a few feet away, a lilting, enchanting hymn.

> *Winter, give me peaceful rest,*
> *Quiet heart within my breast*
> *Yours the gift of solitude,*
> *Grant a silent interlude.*
> *Spring, like dawn, replace my sleeping*
> *Constant ever in your keeping.*
> *Grant that I might turn my face*
> *To worship in your holy place.*
> *Summer baking, heat my soul*
> *And let my mind in pastures roll*
> *Where bitter herbs cannot be found*
> *But passions sweet lie all around.*

Doc slept before he heard the verse about autumn.

Monday, 27 September 1954, City of the Gods

FOG SHROUDED THE camp when Doc awoke to Pol's urgent prodding. He found it difficult to focus his mind where he couldn't focus his eyes. He repeatedly checked to see that his glasses were properly situated.

Pol took Doc's hand and they began moving slowly up the slope. It turned rapidly to scree, but Pol picked out a stable path. Doc was hesitant to proceed in the fog, but it was either go with Pol or stay behind.

Doc tripped over hidden boulders in the scree. Gusts of wind swirled the fog but would not clear it. He pushed at his glasses again with the butt of his walking stick. The fog seemed to hang in his eyes instead of in the air.

And shadows moved there. Just beyond the range of his vision, he could sense the movement. He wanted to ask questions, but could not bring his voice above a whisper, which Pol could not or would not hear. His voice was masked by the fog as much as his eyes.

Beside his own constant mutterings, Doc imagined other voices wandering in the fog like echoes of his own thoughts. But silencing himself to listen sent the echoes fleeing. He became painfully aware of a spot where his pack was rubbing his back raw. Each step of his unsure feet shifted the pack again He reached with his free hand to adjust it, but his walking stick caught in a strap and he had to concentrate on untangling himself while maintaining the steady pace that Apollo set.

Finally, the spot in his back irritated him past his endurance and Doc jerked his hand free from Pol to adjust his pack. He started to move again and felt his foot slipping on the loose scree. The ground beneath him was giving way in a shower of cascading gravel. He shouted as he lost his balance and sent his staff flailing in front of him. He came to a jerking halt, flat on his stomach with his staff stretched out up the hill in front of him. Pol held the other end, wedged behind a rock, pulling him back to safety. Doc regained his footing on the loose rock, took Pol's silently outstretched hand and did not let go again.

The transition came slowly. First Doc sensed singing in the air and recognized Pol's voice. The terrain leveled and the loose shale turned to wide flat areas of rock, almost like broad stairs. The gray half-light of dawn now illumined the way. Pol released Doc's hand and moved ahead in the clearing fog. Heinrich followed.

He could feel the shadows of monoliths not quite seen. Gradually, the shadows took substance, materializing around him as pillars in an ancient temple, so tall he could not see the capitals in the early morning light. He walked on a few steps behind Pol to the forum where a circular rostrum stood isolated in the center. It was this to which Pol walked.

What followed was more solemn and awesome than Doc could anticipate.

Pol went to the far edge of the rostrum before making his ascent. He stood there, facing down the forum toward Doc. Doc fidgeted uneasily for a moment and muttered something about having been inadequately prepared. He shuffled off to one side where a pillar partially hid him. He turned the direction the boy faced and saw a flash of light as the sun burst suddenly into view. Its rays sharply outlined the pillars and isolated the rostrum at the end of the forum. Pol stood in the center of the circle now and began to sing an odd combination of vocal patterns, rhythms, and accents. Sometimes, Doc understood words, and yet there were times when he was sure there were no words at all. It was sound beyond language and music. Images of history and mythology raced through Doc's mind faster than he could comprehend them. Pol sang a message of greeting to the dawn and to all the countless dawns preceding him.

Then the dawn responded.

Someone or something from the depths of the ancient past answered and Doc felt Hyperion's chariot ride through his soul on a flood of music.

Then calm and quiet.

The whole event lasted only minutes—perhaps seconds. When it ended, Pol knelt in the center of the circle and drew a small knife from his belt. With it, he cut his long, black hair. When he was raggedly trimmed all the way around his head, he gathered up the locks, and held them toward the dawn. Then he flung the hair into the air where it was blown away by a wind Doc hadn't felt blowing. Pol left the rostrum.

Heinrich did not move. Eventually, Pol came to him. "I must go to be alone. You are free to explore. Learn what you can of this place. Perhaps you can teach me about it," he said. "All paths lead to the orchestra. We must leave before sunset. I will meet you at the center."

Pol left silently without giving Doc an opportunity to respond. It was not a time for questions. Doc began to examine the architecture and surroundings. The massive pillars formed even avenues extending from the orchestra outward like spokes of a wheel. Doc braced himself for the first test and began walking directly down the eastern avenue, examining the pillars as he went. He checked frequently behind him until the rostrum was out of sight then quickly and resolutely walked onward. Just when he thought he should turn back, the rostrum appeared ahead of him, not quite directly in the avenue down which he walked, but just to the left of it. Doc searched in his pack for a marker of some sort. He laid his staff in the center of the avenue pointing the direction he was traveling. He walked to the rostrum and debated with himself but could not justify laying anything directly on it.

He drew an arrow on a piece of paper and anchored it under a dislodged flagstone near the rostrum.

He returned to the path and walked on, determined to test Apollo's statement to the limit. A short time later, the rostrum appeared again, this time on his right. He marked his place on the path with his staff and approached the rostrum. He put another scrap of paper with an arrow on the ground and then walked around the platform to verify that his original marker was on the other side. Shaking his head, he returned to the path and continued.

This time, the rostrum appeared directly in front of him. As he approached it he made several calculations in his mind but could not map the configuration in his head. He skipped several steps of logic and assumed he must be approaching from the west, opposite the direction he started. He muttered something about having failed to mark his origin. He would have to retrace his entire path to confirm his finding. He'd walked some miles by his calculations and ended up where he started. Yet he'd always walked in a straight line. It was incredibly disorienting and had to be the result of an optical illusion. And if the paths all led back to the rostrum, where was the one he and Apollo had originally entered from?

For the third time, he knelt at the rostrum to mark his place with a slip of paper. He dislodged another flagstone and heard a pebble drop beneath it striking a hollow note below. After a moment's struggle, Doc removed the stone completely from its resting place. A foot beneath the surface lay a thick leather folio. Doc abandoned his attempt to map the avenues and unearthed the folio.

He examined it carefully, observing it was of an ancient design but was not more than 50 years old at the most. The leather cords that tied it were supple and showed no wear. Inside were papers, but not ancient by any means. Across the bottom of the first page was scrawled the signature of Benjamin Wilton. The papers in his hand were his mentor's journal.

I'll leave you a sign. You'll know it when you see it. When that
day comes, your doubts will disappear.

Doc remembered his mentor's words as he sat, mesmerized by the material in his hands. He was so absorbed in the discovery that he did not even notice the sun setting in his eyes as he sat with his back against the rostrum. He heard a sound and turned to see Pol standing on the rostrum leaning on Doc's heavy staff. The boy pushed the stick toward Doc.

"You left this over there," he said. "It is time to leave. We should put the stone you moved back in order."

"This journal… It's my…"

"Yes, it is yours. The price of passage is to leave a part of yourself behind," Pol said. "I left my hair as an offering to my goddess. Perhaps another pilgrim left this book. You will leave your doubt."

"I don't know what to say."

"Let us go. You will need the papers before you return."

"Return?"

"Will you not return to *ta hagia hagion*?"

"Will I be permitted?" Doc had already allowed himself the fantasy of bringing a small and discreet team to the site next summer if he could persuade Pol to guide them. Pol was suggesting the expedition himself.

"You are expected," answered Apollo. His voice seemed to echo in the vast empty forum.

Doc hastily gathered his scraps of paper, and stuffed them along with the journal and portfolio into his pack. As they moved away from the rostrum, a misty fog began to roll in with the sunset. Heinrich took Pol's hand to avoid being separated on the treacherous trip down. He reminded himself constantly.

I will return.

4
Finding Our Boy

Thursday, 17 March 1955, Greenwich, Connecticut

THE DESERT *sun beat down as Doc climbs one dune after another —dunes that were in different places hours ago. That was before the sandstorm buried him and his fellow archaeologists in the Sinai. He has to get help. Any relief from the burning heat. More miles of desert to cross.*

In his Greenwich home, Doc snapped back to reality, staring at a carved wood panel in his library that replayed the event. Each of the eleven panels in the room showed a different expedition. His eye wandered back to the massive blank panel above the fireplace. This year, his visit to the City of the Gods, his crowning achievement, would be carved on that panel.

"Or," he mused, "like Wilton, I will lose my credibility and be accused of an elaborate hoax. The capstone of my career will be an albatross around my neck and I will sink into oblivion."

The very existence of the papers in front of him should be proof enough. But he found them in a dream. *Can I trust my memories? It was all so unreal.* Yet he found himself unable to doubt that it occurred.

He should have investigated further before returning to America, but time was of the essence. Scavengers masquerading as archaeologists still followed the steps of legitimate scholars, stealing from the digs to supply a booming black market in antiquities. At the docks in Athens, Doc excused his hasty departure to such a one with a plea of illness. Ryan McGuire. Doc was sure he would see that particular thorn in his side again. It just showed that sharing a common circle did not mean common ideals. Doc weighed the evidence in support of an expedition against the academic and physical risk involved. He had a week to think during the voyage back to New York. He had scarcely left his cabin on the entire crossing, so intent was he on reading Wilton's journal. There were no mountains near enough to Metéora to have walked to in a day. Geologic maps showed no places within twenty miles that would match the terrain Doc had walked. The whole journey was impossible, yet he had been there.

Doc shuffled the notes and maps on his desk. He had been studying them ever since his return in October. Four months now. He was confident he could find the cluster of houses where his guide would await him, but where they had gone from there he simply could not tell. He was so absorbed in his study that he didn't hear the bell ring and William had spoken twice at the library door before he responded.

"Doctor Jacobsen is here to see you," the steward repeated.

"Oh, thank you, William. Send her in." Doctor Margaret Jacobsen was a dear friend of Heinrich's. Her caring for him extended far beyond his need for a research assistant years ago.

"Phillip, how are you?" she asked, coming into the room and reaching for his hands.

"I'm fine, my dear. What's the news from the outside world? Did you get the references I asked for?" Doc was already reaching past her outstretched hand for the satchel she carried.

"Be patient, Phillip. It's all here."

"You've been telling me that for twenty years, Margaret."

"And it has yet to sink in."

"Well, come. Sit down. Would you like coffee or tea?" Doc asked. William materialized at the door. "Coffee please," Doc said.

"Certainly," William responded.

"Not for me," Margaret said. "I want to show you what I've found."

"A reference?" Doc slapped his hands together and cleared a spot on the desk between them.

"A whole book! But you aren't going to like it." She drew a thin and brightly colored book from the bag and set it in the middle of the desk facing Doc.

"*The Last Gift*? A children's book?" he asked.

"Isn't it beautiful?"

"A children's book?" he repeated. "This is a serious scientific study. We don't need children's books."

"Who led you on your journey, Phillip? Who told you the story? Look at the name. Ben Wills. I've discovered that Benjamin Wilton wrote fiction under that name."

"Wilton? *Writing children's books?*"

"Phillip. Please stop talking in italics. If he couldn't get anyone to believe him with scientific research, why shouldn't he put it down as a children's story and hope some little believer would rise to take up the search?" Margaret calmly reached for the teapot William had brought and poured a cup for each of them.

"Once upon a time," Doc read from the first page and then closed the book. "I can't do this. Could you just give me a synopsis? Didn't I ask for coffee?"

"You know how coffee keeps you awake if you drink it this late in the afternoon. Now drink your tea, dear," Margaret said.

"I thought you weren't having any."

"I wouldn't insult William by not sharing what he brought for us. That would be terrible."

"The story?" Doc motioned at the book.

"The book was published about a year after he disappeared, according to your account, August of 1937. The publishers wouldn't give much information. They said the manuscript was sent to them from overseas. They had a contract for Ben Wills' works and had no reason to believe that it was not his. It came with a cover letter designating a college in Indiana as future recipient of all his royalties, which were apparently not much."

"I don't understand," Doc said. "Wilton never had any connections in Indiana. He was strictly Ivy League."

"How can you be so sure of that? Very little is known about his life in the U.S. Everything is about his travels and scholarly work."

"No. I knew Wilton personally. I was with him the night he disappeared in 1937."

"Oh, Phillip! Who were his parents? Did he have any family? Who else knew him?"

"He was my advisor on my thesis and I worked several digs with him in the early thirties. I know—or I think—he was involved in the gathering of intelligence in Central Europe as Hitler rose to power. Sending things to Indiana simply does not make sense."

"And all I remember is you disciplining a student by shouting out 'Thou shalt not quote Wilton in this class!' We were all terrified."

"In the forties, it could ruin your career to cite Wilton. So, tell me. Here we have his story in a children's book. An unheard of Greek goddess who was left bound to old Olympus behind an ivory veil, abandoned by the gods as they take flight into the heavens. There she awaits a mortal savior."

"Hmm. Sadly, it's a different story," broke in Margaret. "This is a little romance about a magician who falls in love with a gypsy princess. It's set in one of those all-purpose romantic gypsy eras. A forbidden love. Different castes. But the magician frees the leader of the gypsies from a camp where he has been taken prisoner. He is adopted into the clan and marries the princess. They live happily ever after."

Margaret noticed doc's shattered look.

"Phillip!"

"No gods? No ancient myths? No prophecy? No function? No goddess?"

"Well, the story says the princess had found the magician when he was quite ill and tended him until he recovered. She wasn't helpless."

"We already have a goddess Health, and Asklepios is a healer. Heritage is usually important. The lyric muse and the healer and health. Her legitimacy depends on a function. Gaia and Uranus—earth and sky—are the parents of Hyperion or light and watchfulness. Hyperion and Theia, or brightness, become parents of Helios—the sun. Helios is the father of Phaeton of heat and danger. This one is a late parthenogenesis myth and not a common archetype by that time."

"Music? All the spells in Ben Wills' little book are sung. It's a common contrivance in this type of story," Margaret said. "Wait. Parthenogenesis?"

"Conceived in empathy with Health and born in the same hour as Hygeia."

"Hmm. Try this. A goddess of empathy. Maybe one who can heal through her unique gifts of empathy and music. That would bring a wonderful gift to humanity—when we are ready for it."

"Gift?"

"Like Prometheus giving fire to humans. The goddess behind the ivory veil brings the ability to heal ourselves—or each other. It's the title of the book: *The Last Gift*. It has nothing to do with the rest of the story. Perhaps it's the last gift of the gods to humanity."

"Prometheus. He was one of Wilton's contacts. I remember them meeting at a dig in '34. Never knew his real name. Younger than me. After the brief meeting, I never saw him again."

"Perhaps Wilton passed on something besides information," Margaret said.

Margaret's voice was soothing to Doc and she let him drift in the fantasy she wove. For a moment, he forgot they were both pushing retirement—him a little harder than her—and saw her as they had been thirty years earlier, ready to dream and believe.

"Margaret, are you a believer?"

"You know better than that, Phillip. I'm a wisher. I wish it were all true. I wish the goddess was real. I wish we were twenty years younger.

And I wish we were a few more steps ahead of Ryan McGuire." Her last statement broke the spell. Ryan McGuire had been a problem for Doc ever since the young man had joined an expedition eight years ago and stole the most valuable artifacts. Of course, there was no proof of that. The artifacts simply disappeared at the same time McGuire did. They'd never been seen again. McGuire, when confronted, said he'd taken ill and had an emergency appendectomy. He had stitches to prove it. Still, the artifacts were gone.

"He was arriving in Greece when I was embarking. He seems always to be a few steps behind me no matter where I work. Or ahead. It's the affinity."

"Affinity to what?" Margaret asked.

"Oh. His nose is connected to buried treasure. He always seems to know where I am." Doc knew that Margaret dabbled around the edges of the occult, but he had never shared the depth of his own involvement in all their twenty years as companions. Doc bore the Second Face of Carles—the staff of the Vagabond Poet that was said to control fire. Ryan McGuire, known as The Blade in the Great Cobhan Carles, bore the First Face, the *Athamé*. The tools knew each other. "I told him I was ill when he asked why I was leaving. Thought it might be my appendix." Margaret chuckled at the veiled reference to McGuire's excuse eight years ago.

"Well, he's arrived here. I saw him at the library in the city yesterday. He caught me by surprise when he asked about your health."

"What did you say?"

"Oh, I told him that you'd been fevered and unable to leave your home since returning from Greece. I was just picking up some reading material for you. I don't think he saw the book." They both laughed at the incongruity of Margaret bringing a children's book to Doc.

"Margaret, I've done all I can here. We need to mount an expedition," Doc said abruptly. They'd both known this moment was coming. Doc had stated as soon as he arrived home that he would be going back to Greece in the summer. "We need a team."

"Who do you have in mind?"

"No one… but you. But from now on, we need to devote our research to assembling the proper team. I know that I forbade the quoting of Wilton in my classes, but the time has come to dig out everything we can about him. In his journal, he alludes to other papers that he wrote. We need to find them."

"Perhaps we should invite Ryan to become part of the team. We know he's looking for whatever we are. If we had him closer, we could keep an eye on him. It might throw him off the real scent."

"Keep your friends close and your enemies closer? Margaret, you are becoming positively Machiavellian. But Ryan would be as likely to murder us to steal our lunches if he was hungry. He's a grave robber, pure and simple."

"You said there was nothing apparent at the site to be stolen."

"The very existence of the site would be an invitation to Ryan to exploit it or the family who guards it. Andrew told me his son returned from his last trip to the City with Wilton so demoralized by what had happened that he ran away and joined the army. He was only fourteen when he was killed in the war. We can't let the value of this family or this sacred ground be harmed by exploitation. I'm half tempted to simply walk away and never go back."

"Half tempted, but not all the way. I know what you are like, Phillip. Once the puzzle has been presented, you will worry it until there is a solution."

"Perhaps we should sleep on it. Let's make the rounds of the libraries in the morning and see what else we can turn up." Doc paused to pour two glasses of sherry and handed one to Margaret. "Do you think you'll be safe spending the night here? I'll have William make up the guest room."

Margaret sighed. "Still the guest room? When will you learn, you old fool." They finished their sherry and went to their rooms.

Friday, 18 March 1955, Greenwich, Connecticut

YES, THERE IS passion after sixty. It might not burn as brightly as that of youth. It might take a bit longer to kindle the flames. Sometimes taking longer has its own rewards. But for the most part, the equipment is more likely to atrophy than to wear out. And so, Doctors Heinrich and Jacobsen continued the practice secretly as they had when she was his student and a scandal could have destroyed both their careers. Though their relationship in 1955 might have raised some eyebrows, it was unlikely that it would have caused more than a ripple in the world of academia.

Nonetheless, they breakfasted separately in their rooms in the morning, served by Doc's all-knowing companion and steward, William.

Unlike Margaret, William had not been a student of Doc's, but rather a classmate. The two had formed an unlikely friendship during a lively discussion of the romanticization of mythology in art. Doc took the part of the fact-driven archaeologist. William Renton debated from the viewpoint of the artist. A third member of the discussion was Sylvester Dalton, a literature major who was well-versed in the influence of popular mythology on contemporary literature. The three became close friends, but William and Sylvester became much closer.

It was obvious to Doc that their relationship could cause censure and likely arrest. Intercourse sodomy was illegal in the United States, whether between males or between male and female. The law was openly used to persecute homosexuals. Upon graduation, Doc offered a position in his household to William that would allow him both privacy for his personal life and a studio for his professional life. In return, William provided the basic services of a gentleman's gentleman and the role had suited him so well that he never left. Sadly, Sylvester had passed away in the early thirties, victim of a viral infection.

William delivered Margaret's soft-boiled egg, toast, coffee and the most recent issue of *The New York Historical Society Journal*. Then he took Doc his toast and coffee. Doc was sitting at his table with a stack of papers in front of him. He wore a dressing gown and his bed was a mess.

"William, have you seen my latest issue of *Archaeological Digest*?"

William went to the bed and pulled the magazine from beneath the pillow. "I left it there for you last night thinking you might want to read before sleeping." William busied himself at opening the drapes.

"Of course. So tired last night. Probably slept on the other side."

"Yes. You were exhausted. Do you need anything else?"

"That will be sufficient." Doc watched William move toward the door, then muttered under his breath, "I should have asked for the *Linguistics Quarterly*."

"It's under the other pillow," William responded and left the room.

HALF AN HOUR later, Doc was pounding on Margaret's door. "Margaret, I must see you at once!" he said, pushing open the door.

"Phillip! In the morning, no!" Doc was already sitting on the edge of her bed bouncing like a teenager. Margaret hid behind her magazine. "I've not put my face on."

"Come now. Respectable people are already having discreet *tête-à-têtes* in coffee shops all over the city."

"This is not a coffee shop nor anything near discreet."

"I've found something very important. Look at this article." Doc shoved his *Linguistics Quarterly* behind Margaret's raised magazine. Margaret grabbed the issue out of his hand and began to read. "*Music and Language: In Search of the Mother Tongue* by J. Wesley Allen. Bet he's a Methodist." She quickly scanned the article. The symbols used by the writer to translate words into music were identical to those found in Wilton's papers. "Incredible. Where from?"

"Look at the editorial note."

"Indianapolis City College. Of course."

Friday, 18 March 1955, Beech Grove, Indiana

"MR. HART," SAID the extremely nervous young man, "May I... I should like..." He glanced to the kitchen door of the house in Beech Grove home where Rebecca and Mrs. Hart stood watching. Rebecca looked somewhat bemused but smiled encouragingly. "Sir, may I ask your daughter's hand in marriage," Wesley burst out. Once started, he could not stop. "I assure you that I am able to comfortably support a wife and children, though I expect things will improve in the coming year when I receive a full professorship. I have acquired a small but acceptable home just a block from the campus where Miss Hart and I are both affiliated. I am not a wealthy man, but I assure you that I will devote myself to providing for my wife and family. I am, sir, an honorable man and hope you will grant me the privilege of marrying your daughter."

Charles Hart stood from the sofa, crossed the room to the music of "You'll look sharp," and turned off the television.

"That Fuller was never a match for Cason. I don't think we'll have a real matchup until Marciano faces Cockell in May. We won't want to miss that one." Charles reoccupied his seat and waved Wesley into a chair. "Have you discussed this with the lady in question?"

"Uh... Sir... I felt it best to get your permission first, sir. But... We have spoken of our feelings for each other," Wesley stammered.

"Becky!" Rebecca Hart scrambled to her father's side, her mother a step behind her. She was twenty-three years old and didn't even live with her parents, but Wesley had insisted on this meeting. She was blushing furiously as her father held out his arms and she perched on his knee. "It seems the gentleman you brought home to dinner this evening was not really interested in the Friday Night Fights. Is there any reason that I shouldn't grant this young man the privilege of marrying you?"

"He hasn't asked me, yet, Father." Mrs. Hart burst out laughing. Wesley went red.

"Well, that settles it," said Mr. Hart. "Mr. Allen, you have my permission to ask my daughter for her hand, but I simply can't guarantee her answer." Wesley gasped and looked at Rebecca. She grinned at him but was shocked when he fell to his knees in front of her and her father.

"Rebecca Hart, my heart is bursting with love for you. Will you do me the honor of becoming my wife? Becc, will you marry me?"

It was Rebecca's turn to gasp. Her father gave her a gentle shove off his lap and she fell to her knees in front of Wesley, taking his hands in hers. "Yes!" she squeaked. They knelt in front of her parents, lost in each other's eyes.

"I guess that settles it," Mrs. Hart laughed. "You might as well kiss him and seal the deal, Rebecca." Both the young people blushed crimson, but Rebecca leaned forward and placed a soft kiss on Wesley's lips.

"Yes," she whispered again.

5

Hoosier Connection

Sunday, 22 May 1955, Indianapolis, Indiana

DOC AND Margaret boarded a train to Chicago with Milton's notes safely tucked between them. The Chicago tickets, purchased by William the day before their departure, would postpone anyone following them at least a day. If they were lucky, it would send *someone* ahead of them to Chicago. When they arrived in Fort Wayne, Indiana, they got off the train. Wesley Allen was waiting to pick them up. The meeting was warm and cordial.

The three-hour trip from Fort Wayne to Wesley's home in Indianapolis was spent discovering more about each other. Wesley taught courses in piano, music history, and musicology. He was engaged to be married, but they were waiting until Rebecca had finished her Master's in Sociology. Wesley's undergrad minor had been in New Testament Studies and he was reasonably fluent in both Greek and Latin. He was, as Margaret had guessed, a Methodist.

After they defined their goals for the visit in terms of learning about music as it relates to classic literature and Wesley had given them a quick rundown on his work in the area, they retired for the night. Wesley's hospitality was impeccable. He insisted that Doc and Margaret stay with him in spite of their prior hotel arrangements. They would meet again after Wesley finished his instruction in the morning. He would bring Rebecca with him to lunch if they didn't mind.

Monday, 23 May 1955, Indianapolis, Indiana

WHEN DOC AND Margaret arose in the morning they found a continental breakfast had been prepared for them with a note indicating where the nearest restaurants were and what numbers called cabs. After looking at the listings and directions, the two decided to spend the morning preparing for their interview with Wesley.

"How shall we get around to the sources for his research?" Doc asked Margaret. "We need to be discreet. If he knows more than we do, we could be endangering our purpose."

"I suggest that we be totally honest with him. I don't mean to say that we should tell him the entire purpose of our visit up front, but tell him that we are very interested in his method of notation and how he arrived at it. We might even indicate that we had seen some similar notations before. Either he will withdraw, in which case we are better not to attempt to push him, or he will respond with the same candor. He seems to be thoroughly familiar with us and our work."

"That is what I was worried about. Do you suppose that he already knows about the place? Let's go take a look at Wilton's manuscripts to see if he left any notes here that may have been found."

Margaret was agreeable and when they reached the college library, they were led up a back stairway to "the stacks."

"This is where the old papers are kept," the student librarian rambled on. "We don't have as great a facility for keeping things in good condition as we should. This building is newer, though, and it's a lot better than when the library occupied a couple of rooms over in the Administration Building. We really needed the space." She ran on and on, seeming never to get to the point of the papers that Doc and Margaret were after. "The papers came over here in boxes and have never been unpacked. Before that, they just sat in stacks on the shelves. I guess that's why we call this area the stacks. Here we are." She finally came to a steel shelving unit with boxes stacked on it. "Benjamin Wilton. Everything should be in this box. I hope that you find everything that you want. If I can do anything for you, just let me know. There's a new phone system connecting the stacks with the desk. It's right over there. Don't forget to let me know when you are ready to leave. I'll have to come back up and lock the doors." She finally left.

Doc and Margaret went to work immediately. They began sorting and ordering the papers as best they could.

"It looks as if the papers were packed into this box in a hurry. No particular order at all."

"True, but at least they don't appear to have been rifled and repacked," Doc said.

"Do you really suppose they just picked up stacks of paper from shelves and put them in the boxes? There isn't even a catalog number on the papers. Oh, look!" she said, holding up a couple sheets from her stack.

"Music of the Gods?" Doc said. "Look at the notes. The same hieroglyphs that are in Wilton's papers and at the City. He didn't even finish it. Broke off in the middle of a sentence. That's strange."

"Or else a page is missing." Margaret looked at Doc. Both seemed to know already that they would find the missing page or pages in Wesley's possession.

"It's time for our luncheon. We must take a good look at this young man." Heinrich loaded the papers back into the larger box as Margaret called the librarian and she dutifully locked the doors behind them—and talked all the way back downstairs to the main floor.

"That girl should consider a career other than librarian," Margaret laughed as they left the building.

A YOUNG WOMAN was putting dishes on the table when Doc and Margaret reached Wesley's home. They were all startled to see each other when the two came through the door unannounced.

"Excuse me," the young woman said at last. "Wesley said that we would have guests for lunch, but I guess I expected you all to arrive at once. Please come in."

"We arrived last night but went out for a walk this morning. You must be Rebecca. I'm Margaret Jacobsen and this is Phillip Heinrich. You have a look about you that has told me already that we are going to become very good friends."

Rebecca laughed and greeted Margaret warmly. "When Wes told me he was picking up Doctors Heinrich and Jacobsen, I thought you'd both be men. I'm so glad I was wrong."

"If you will excuse me," Doc broke in, "I will go wash up before dinner. You obviously have a great deal in common to talk about."

"Oh, Phillip. You are such a martyr." Doc grinned at the women as he left the room. "Now, Rebecca," Margaret continued, "tell me about your work. What Wesley described was so interesting."

"My master's? It's a sociology degree. I'm all but thesis. It's a study of the Coexistence of Matriarchal Thealogy and Patriarchal Theocracy in Western Societies."

"Do I interpret you correctly in saying 'goddess worship'?"

"Wesley would kill me if I put it that way," responded Rebecca. "But yes. There seems to be quite a lot of evidence that even into modern times some forms of that cult held sway in certain western civilizations long after the people had officially been Christianized. It is difficult here in Indiana to find adequate resources, though."

"You realize, don't you, that most Westerners term that witchcraft? Now it's not so poorly viewed in many Eastern cultures."

"Wesley is nervous enough about my dealing with the subject. Please don't use that term in his presence. He's so conservative. And now…" Rebecca took a deep breath. "I've been awarded a fellowship for the summer at Edinburgh and he's not very happy about my going off alone. It will delay our wedding until fall instead of June as we had planned. I think he's also a little jealous, though he wouldn't admit it."

"Rebecca, I think we might be good news for you—in more ways than one." The front door opened and Wesley hurried into the house as Doc came downstairs.

"Ah, I see you have all met already. I'm sorry to be late at my own dinner party. A student had an urgent problem with Liszt."

"A dedicated teacher. That's a good sign," Doc said. "And it did give at least two of us a chance to get to know each other."

"Well, I'll have lunch on the table in a minute. I have everything we need in the Frigidaire." Wesley returned with a platter that revealed not only salad, but a substantial portion of cold cuts as well. The meal was light and friendly and by the end, all felt much more at ease. There was a short pause in the conversation as each finished coffee or crackers. Rebecca was the first to break the silence.

"Well, I suppose that you have some important matters to discuss. I'll clean up the dishes and make coffee if you'd all like to go into the living room."

"Thank you, Rebecca," Wesley said.

"Nonsense," responded Doc. "Wesley told us some very fascinating things about you in the car yesterday. I'd like to ask you some questions also. Can't we all share a hand in cleaning up and then gather for the mutual benefit of all our educations?"

Margaret winked at Rebecca who smiled back. It was agreed upon over Wesley's objections over asking guests to clean the table.

"One thing I've learned while on digs and expeditions is that everyone needs to contribute to the menial tasks or we can't work together on the major ones," Doc said. "I've become an accomplished dishwasher after nearly forty years in archaeology."

THEY SETTLED INTO comfortable chairs in the living room with a cup of coffee each.

"Now, tell me, Rebecca," started Doc. "You are working on your Master's, isn't that right?"

"She's really got it pretty well under control already," said Wesley. "It won't be long after this summer, will it, darling?"

Rebecca made an effort at a smile. Doc turned to Wesley and raised an eyebrow. It was a look that Wesley had used himself when a student got out of hand. He shrank back in his chair.

"What I wanted to know, Rebecca, was the subject of your thesis. It is in Sociology, is it not?"

"Yes, sir." Doc's glance at Wesley had cowed Rebecca a bit as well. "The subject is the Coexistence of Matriarchal Thealogy and Patriarchal Theocracy in Western Societies."

"Goddess worship," muttered Wesley low enough not to draw a reprimand from Doc.

"Have you explored the origins of this coexistence? You know, total matriarchy versus total patriarchy? The primitive versus the contemporary?"

"Oh yes, Doctor Heinrich. It seems to broaden the subject too much to deal with in one thesis. Much of the available resource material focuses on the supplanting of matriarchy by patriarchy, not their coexistence. Do you agree?"

"I do, but I wanted to make sure that you had explored the subject. Goddess worship, as your fiancé has referred to it, takes many forms and is still practiced in many countries where men sit in parliaments and women practice spells to increase the harvest or keep the children safe. I would like you to visit an acquaintance of mine before you complete your work if it is possible."

"I'm going to Scotland for the summer to finish writing my thesis at the University of Edinburgh. I leave in two weeks."

"Splendid," Doc smiled. He scrawled a name on a piece of paper and handed it to Rebecca. She looked puzzled.

"Mrs. Weed? How do I find her?"

"I will write to her. She is one of the few genuine goddess worshipers that I know. You needn't find her; she'll find you."

"Thank you," Rebecca said hesitantly.

The conversation continued on the discussion of primitive culture until Doc and Margaret had carefully bent it back to Wesley's topic.

"Do I understand from our previous conversation that you can make a literal translation of ancient languages into music?" Margaret asked. She made it sound like Wesley's paper was a natural complement to Rebecca's research.

"Well, Doctor Jacobsen," Wesley began, relieved that it was Margaret asking the questions instead of Doc, "there seems to be a middle ground between translating and interpreting. Usually, when a musician *interprets* a story into music, he *translates* his own feelings about the work rather than letting the language itself speak through the music. I think that I have devised a method of letting language speak through the medium of music, though that was, of course, beyond the scope of my paper."

"Explain a little about the difference between translation and interpretation if you would, Wesley," Doc said.

"Well, a translation would imply that it was like a code and certain notes or combinations of notes meant certain specific things. Music has both dimensions. A above Middle C is a constant of 440 Hertz. It makes no difference what instrument it is played on, the entire orchestra tunes to A440 as played by the concertmaster. But when you stop to think about it, the note sounds different when played on a bassoon versus a violin versus, God forbid, a horn," explained Wesley. "Of course, the human voice is also an instrument and may display an entire range of tonality."

"So, the frequency is the translation and the voice is the interpretation?" Doc asked.

"Somewhat more complicated than that, but it is an illustration. When someone speaks to you, you don't see words in your head. What you see are visual images that are triggered by the words. The entire concept of the musical language, if you call it that, is that it may be *possible* to trigger the same images consistently if the right sounds on the right instruments were played. So, there is not so much a grammar as a conceptualization. Keep in mind that the parameters of experience also govern a person's vocabulary of images just as it governs in part our vocabulary of words. But in the primal area of the mind, the universal consciousness, if you will, there must be a key to language that cuts across experience, culture, and time. It is a return to the Ideal as Plato calls it."

"I take it then," said Margaret, "that there is no direct key for the translation or a direct tonality. A equals A, etc."

"Sequence, rhythm, and pitch all have a bearing on it. For example— and please understand this is strictly a hypothetical situation—if playing the sequence of notes A, C, F, A-prime as quarter notes meant 'I am going to the store,' A, C, F, B-prime might mean 'No man is an island.' And then if you changed from uniform quarter notes to a sequence of quarter, eighth, quarter, sixteenth, rest, you may have changed the meaning to say, 'God is the source of all good gifts.' There may, of course, be another completely different meaning if one changed from playing the notes on the piano to the violin."

"It sounds incredibly complex as a language," said Margaret.

"If you look at the music as a literal tongue, it is. But it is merely a medium for projecting images. It has no grammar as we understand the word in English."

"So how do you make a translation?"

"Just as certain graphologists have succeeded in reading character traits from a person's handwriting, I have attempted to read emotional image from handwriting or whatever text I have in front of me. Those images inspire certain note sequences, if you will, which can be understood on an image-for-image basis. Creating a notational system that would stand independent of both the music and the image was the hardest part."

"Have you tested this?"

"Yes. We've used two test groups. Rebecca is quite fluent in German, a language that I have no familiarity with at all. We enlisted the aid of the German professor here at ICC. Our first experiment was to distribute texts of a German manuscript to two groups of Intermediate German students. The control group was given their normal classroom environment in which to translate the manuscript. The experimental group was assigned a room adjoining the choir rehearsal space in which I was seated at the piano playing my 'interpretation' of the manuscript. Across the board, the students in the experimental class delivered more complete and accurate translations of the work. I say that it was more complete and accurate in that the translation was more as a German would speak the sentences and not that it was more technically perfect. The control group had more perfect word-for-word translations. But the experimental group showed a higher level of interpretive sophistication."

"But can it be repeated?" Doc asked. "The scientific method requires that the same steps be used in multiple experiments to yield the same results."

"We pretty quickly used up our quota of German students here. We're a small school," Wesley laughed. "But I believe you are asking two questions. First, can I repeat the same sequence of musical notes and second, will the result be the same? The answer to the first is that

I have recorded the music and each time I have played it, it has been identical. This is made possible by a form of notation that I devised to match images to music, though it seems to work marginally better if I am playing the music than if the students are listening to the recording. I don't believe that recorded music ever has the quality of a live performance and our equipment is not studio quality. Since we ran out of German students, we repeated the exercise with non-German-speaking students—a senior creative writing class and a freshman English comp class."

"I'm not sure I see the point," Doc said. "You can't have had English students giving the same translations as the German students, can you?"

"No, not at all," Rebecca answered as Wesley drank his tepid coffee. "We're still a little new at setting up control experiments, but I saw an opportunity for a short sociology paper on the effect of music on creativity. It was startling. While out of a group of thirty students we received thirty different subjects and styles, each was marked by the same sequence of visual images."

"And those, as Rebecca pointed out to me, were the same as the major visual images in the translations by the German students."

AFTER SEVERAL HOURS of sharing ideas and seeing some examples of how the method worked Doc was convinced that J. Wesley Allen would be an invaluable aid on the expedition. Doc held a copy of Wesley's notations for the experiment in front of him, the symbols on the sheet looking so familiar from Wilton's writing.

"Wesley, I find your discovery exciting and your evidence, though not completely orthodox or conclusive, is compelling. But you have not mentioned anything about the development of your system of notation as was shown in your published paper and here in your notes. While I am convinced that you have the intelligence to develop the *theory* on your own, a notational system like this must have had some inspiration."

"Doctor Heinrich," Wesley straightened himself to the question. Doc sat back, certain that he was going to hear of a dream of some sort that inspired Wesley to create signs and symbols. "I have never been asked that question before and have always been thankful for that. I am afraid that no one would believe me."

Here it comes, Doc thought.

"When I came to ICC three-and-a-half years ago, I found a scrap of paper stuck to the shelving in my office. Apparently, it had been there for years and was embedded in the shellac. The symbols that I have used were written on it as well as some other notes about language and music. All very short and very cryptic. Something about it fascinated me so much that I just sat and stared at it for hours at a time. The symbols kept burning into my mind as a key to that picture language. I have never known where the paper came from nor who wrote it, so I have never quoted it as a source. It has been more of an inspiration. No one ever thought to ask me about it before now."

"And you never investigated who had the office before you and what work they might have done on it?" asked Margaret.

"Oh, yes. I asked the professor who had the office before me. He said he had never heard of such a thing. He had noticed the scrap of paper stuck to the shelves and went on a diatribe about the inadequate job our maintenance people do at cleaning rooms up. Prior to him the room had been a storeroom."

"Can you show us the mystery shelf?" asked Margaret.

"Oh yes," Rebecca said. "It's still in his office under some books."

"Uh, yes. Of course," stammered Wesley. He seemed reluctant to show them the notes, but agreed. Wesley led them out of the house and back to the campus music department, housed on the third floor of the Administration Building.

"The music department has never been too big here and focuses on training choir directors and church pianists," he explained. "But we are growing."

"This is where the old library was, isn't it?" asked Margaret.

"That was before my time, I'm afraid. I know it was in this building, though. Almost everything was."

He led the way upstairs to his office. After unloading a shelf, he pointed to the paper, embedded in shellac, just has he had said. Doc and Margaret examined it carefully. It was the missing page from Milton's notes. To Doc and Margaret, it made little more sense than the first pages had. But this scrap of paper had been adequate to open an entire vista to Wesley. Doc turned to Margaret and she nodded.

"Wesley, in this city of yours, what would you say was the best restaurant?"

"The what?" Everyone laughed at the sudden change in Doc's tone and attitude.

"The best restaurant in town. When one makes a truly great discovery, one must celebrate in an appropriate fashion. Now surely there is something in this town that will match our level of enthusiasm."

"Do you really think my discovery is that significant?" Wesley was beginning to smile.

"I think that your gift for interpretation is beyond doubt a unique talent. I want to celebrate our discovery of you. We have business to discuss tonight and it will take us a while to get dressed for dinner. I suggest we get started."

"I suppose the best restaurant is The Seville on the Circle. But they do serve alcohol. I don't usually go to restaurants like that." Wesley was almost blushing at the revelation that he was a teetotaler.

"If it's the best, Wesley, it is the best. Because they serve it doesn't mean that you have to drink it." Wesley called for reservations from his office and the four left to change for dinner. Wesley stopped on the steps of the Administration Building to have a word with Rebecca as Doc and Margaret went on ahead.

"What do you make of that?" he asked her, looking after the two doctors.

"Of what?"

"The way they just moved in and took over. They don't want to celebrate my discovery, but theirs."

"Their discovery of *you*, Wesley. What more do you want?" Rebecca was becoming irritated at Wesley's demand for attention.

"I want some answers," he responded.

"Wes, relax. Just go along with them until they're ready to tell you. They're not going to hurt you."

"I don't trust them."

"Did it ever occur to you that they might not trust you, either?" Rebecca turned away and went home to change for dinner. Wesley walked glumly behind Doc and Margaret.

6
Forging a Bond

Monday, 23 May 1955, Indianapolis, Indiana

THEY ARRIVED at The Seville promptly at 8:00, a little late to dine in Indiana, but about right for Doc and Margaret. Doc began the story of what had brought them to Wesley. He was careful to downplay the supernatural elements of the City of the Gods, though Rebecca seemed quickly to comprehend that aspect. They explained that Professor Wilton had disappeared after making the initial discovery and that Wesley's key was a page from Wilton's notes.

"We've been here interviewing you for one purpose, Wesley. We want you to join us on an expedition back to the City of the Gods this summer. To us, your services in translating or interpreting the stories and legends inscribed in the area would be invaluable. For yourself, it would give you the opportunity to gain a primary source for your study on communication and language. Imagine an entire city inscribed with the symbols you have used in your papers. What do you say?"

Everything fell into place in Wesley's mind and he began to feel very foolish about suspecting Doc and Margaret. They were there for his benefit as well as their own. Still, he could not completely turn himself over without losing his pride. He hesitated for a moment.

"I am flattered, but you're sure I'd have ample opportunity to conduct my own studies in communications and music and that I wouldn't just be there to translate for you?" Doc nodded. "I don't know. What do you think, Rebecca?"

"I think we should have a talk. Dr. Heinrich, Dr. Jacobsen. Would you excuse us for a moment?" Rebecca stood and walked away from the table up the steps to the front door. Wesley excused himself and followed.

Doc LOOKED AT Margaret questioningly.

"You can't be serious, Phillip," said Margaret. "There isn't a shred of hard scientific evidence in all his work. They're a charming couple, but why?"

"Because it works. I could feel the story he played for us more concretely than if I had been reading it. Tell me it didn't work for you and I'll call it off."

"It worked," answered Margaret, "but it's not evidence we can produce for scientific purposes. I don't know how he does it."

"And if he knew, he would quit," said Doc. "I look at it as a trance-medium state. There was once a balalaika player that I knew who did something quite similar. Wesley has built his pseudoscientific evidence structure around it because he could never accept himself as a medium. It's a black art and he is a Christian. We can get a translator to work on the material when we get back but it could take years that you and I don't have to construct the literal translation."

"It's really just for us, isn't it, Phillip?"

"I suppose so. Margaret, my dear, Wilton told me in 1937 that when I found his sign, my doubts would disappear. I've looked for it for eighteen years. I'm not getting younger. I don't need to vindicate Wilton or prove his thesis. I simply need to know what he knew."

"I see. What next?"

"Champagne?"

ONCE OUTSIDE THE restaurant, Rebecca began walking around Monument Circle at the center of town. Wesley caught up with her and began to chastise her for leaving the table.

"It was far less rude than to let you sit there and insult people who have just made you the offer of a lifetime. Why can't you just admit that you were wrong for a change and accept what comes your way? Wes, if you turn this down or insult them enough to make them withdraw the offer, you're just a fool."

Wesley stuck both hands in his pockets in a grown-up version of a pout. "Of course, you're right. I'm an idiot."

"You're a good man, Wes. Just don't try to push so hard and let things happen. Something good might turn up."

She leaned toward Wesley to kiss him. He looked around nervously as if expecting the college president to be watching and then responded warmly—perhaps even passionately. They walked back to the restaurant where Doc and Margaret were patiently waiting with champagne glasses filled.

"Doctor Heinrich. Doctor Jacobsen. I hope I have not offended you with my lack of good manners. The truth is that I can't think of anything I would rather do than join in your expedition. Especially... Well, it was going to be a long lonely summer with our marriage delayed by Rebecca's study abroad. If you think you can put up with me, I accept your invitation."

"Hear, hear! A toast to our new partnership," Doc said, raising his glass.

"I... uh... don't..." Wesley hesitated as he caught Rebecca's eye. "Oh well," he said, raising his glass. "To our partnership."

Friday, 27 May 1955, Indianapolis, Indiana

Doc AND MARGARET stayed in Indianapolis for several days, planning the expedition and introducing Wesley to Wilton's other writings. Friday morning, they drafted a list of equipment and supplies they would need. Wesley needed a musical instrument and experimented with a guitar. When he adjusted his notations and added his voice, it worked as well as the piano had.

Nor was Rebecca forgotten. Margaret was a veteran traveler and assisted Rebecca in planning every article she would take to Scotland. Rebecca stacked the folded clothing on her bureau.

"Well, it looks like you have everything you could possibly need except better walking shoes," Margaret said.

"I don't know how I'd have done it without your help. I can hardly believe it's only a week until I leave."

"I shan't be much longer, myself. I'm going to Athens by way of Sweden. The three of us will arrive in Greece at different times and from different places."

"Is it really that dangerous? I worry about Wesley."

"Not so much danger as simply not wanting to draw attention." Margaret looked at Rebecca's bags distractedly. "Rebecca, do you have a walking stick?"

"No. Why?"

"Oh, I just knew something was missing. You can go almost any place in the world on a dollar a day, but you can't walk the hills of Scotland and Northern England without a walking stick."

"Where would I buy one?"

"I recommend you ask Phillip. He hardly goes anywhere without his."

They found the men in Wesley's study and once Margaret explained the situation, Doc suggested a drive in the country. It was just what was needed to conclude the visit in Indiana. Wesley volunteered a location and they packed a lunch.

"We have decided to go by air tomorrow instead of by train, Wesley," Margaret said as they sat watching Doc and Rebecca choosing the right piece of wood a few yards away. Once on the subject, Doc had taken Rebecca aside to explain everything there was to know about choosing a walking stick. He talked about weight, wood, length and thickness, how well seasoned the wood should be and the various benefits of stripping off the bark versus leaving it on.

"It's really no problem to drive you back up to Fort Wayne," Wesley said to Margaret. "Or even Chicago if you'd like."

"It's not a matter of convenience, really. Phillip gets nervous when he's planning an expedition. Without his library and maps he's an absolute child," Margaret laughed.

"I guess that's a side I haven't seen."

"Nor are you likely to when we are in the field. It's a secret between him and me. But he is anxious to get back and finalize things. I leave in just over a week. Flying will cut a day off our time away. And that meant spending today with you and Rebecca instead of trying to get today's train."

"She's sure something special, isn't she?" Wesley smiled. Rebecca turned to come back holding her stick up for them to see.

"Yes, indeed," Margaret agreed.

"Look!" shouted Rebecca. "Isn't she wonderful?"

"She? Is it alive?" asked Wesley.

"Doc says all walking sticks are alive and take on a personality of their own," answered Rebecca. "This is definitely a she."

"Well, you are right. She is beautiful. And so are you."

"Ahem," coughed Doc, breaking up Rebecca and Wesley's spontaneous embrace. Wesley could only think how amazingly free and relaxed he felt when away from campus, even in the presence of the two distinguished professors. This summer would be more fun if he were going to Scotland with Rebecca, but he was more relaxed now that he was going to have his own adventure.

"If I could interrupt for just a moment," Doc continued, "there is still one small item of business that we need to take care of. I think it is appropriate to do so out here in the open where we can't be overheard without knowing it."

"What?" asked Wesley.

"Well, because of the history of the people we are going to see and because of my own history, I believe that we need to consider our expedition confidential."

"Of course. We talked about that," Wesley said.

"No, not about this part. Archaeological sciences have changed a lot in the past twenty-odd years. For the better, I might add. But there are still a few of the old type around. Adventurers, fortune seekers. You never know when they will pop up. Wilton's lost City of the Gods and the missing goddess would be just the kind of thing that would bring them flocking. Especially with me connected with it."

"What are you saying?" asked Rebecca.

"Just this: that the less said the better. Rebecca, that goes even in Scotland. And Wesley, frankly I wish I was taking you with me tomorrow. You must have all the information I can give you and I trust your discretion. I'm just saying," Doc stammered on. "Just be careful. They're a rough lot if they think there could be riches to be had."

"*Are* there riches to be had?" Wesley asked.

"I don't think so. Not of that sort at least. But it would be hard to explain that without showing it and there is too much at stake academically to risk public knowledge in advance. Do you both understand?"

They did, but the announcement took some of the edge off their excitement and the ride back to Indianapolis was a quiet one.

Tuesday, 31 May 1955, Indianapolis, Indiana

AFTER DOC AND Margaret flew home, Wesley spent all of his free hours in the library stacks cataloging Wilton's papers. The field was new to Wesley, but he found that he could date the progression of thought from topic to topic through the papers by changing characteristics in the handwriting. Only in the instance of the page on his office shelf and the two pages preceding it in the file, however, was there anything particularly unusual. Wilton was a concise and accurate writer of both fact and fiction. His journey to Metéora was chronicled only in the papers in the satchel Doc brought from Greece. To Wesley, those writings had been like the work of a lunatic. Even the use of symbology Wesley had adapted for his translations made no sense.

On Tuesday, Wesley made his way to the stacks again.

"Lots of traffic today, Professor Allen," said the student librarian looking at him adoringly. "You must be doing something really important. A man came in from Chicago and asked to see the same file you've been cataloging. He said he's a biographer doing research on the life of Benjamin Wilton. I said I'd never heard of him until your friends came last week. That box has been open every day since then. Hope you don't mind. I gave him your name and telephone number so he could contact you. I figured if you already had the file cataloged there was no sense in him doing it over. That's okay, isn't it Mr. Allen?"

"Yes, of course, Doris," Wesley answered a little absently. "Did he give a name? I'd like to know who it is when he calls me."

"Oh, I don't remember. I'll go look it up for you if you'd like. It's on the sign-in sheet for the stacks. He had an accent. English."

"I'll check it when I'm through. Is he still here?"

"No, he left a little after noon. Said he'd be back. He wanted to know if you'd be in today. I didn't know for sure, of course, but you *have* been coming in around three o'clock each day, so I told him to check in about then. Do you want me to show him up if he comes back, Mr. Allen?"

Wesley thought for a moment. There really wasn't much he could do if the man wanted to come around. But at the same time, he didn't relish meeting someone whose name he didn't even know. And why on earth would anyone be interested in Wilton's life?

"Would you mind giving me a call on the system before you show him up, Doris?" He said at last. "And tell me his name."

"Okay. Let me know when you are ready to leave so I can lock up."

Wesley shivered as his imagination took hold. He just didn't like being surprised. He turned back to find Doris still in the doorway watching him. She turned at once to leave.

"Doris."

"Yes, Mr. Allen?"

"I wonder if you would mind locking the door."

She stammered a moment, visibly blushing.

"It's all right, Doris," Wesley said, trying to make sense of the situation.

"Oh, Mr. Allen," she burst out. "They'd miss me downstairs in no time."

Wesley blushed.

"Doris. With me on the inside and you on the outside. Just lock me in."

Doris caught her breath, stammered again, then slammed the door shut behind her. Wesley stayed by the door until he heard her fleeing footsteps and checked to be sure the door was locked. He felt more secure.

Wesley stood looking at the door. He had to admit that it was a strange request. It almost made more sense the way Doris had taken it. *God forbid!* If there was a fire, though, he wouldn't stand a chance. For a moment, he considered calling down to the desk immediately and having her come back to unlock the door. Then he would feel both strange and foolish. And compromised beyond belief. He was glad she was not one of his students.

AT THE FOOT of the stairs, Doris leaned against the railing with her hand held against her beating heart. That dreamy Mr. Allen. Next term she was definitely taking piano lessons.

WESLEY LOOKED AROUND and noticed the high door that led to the roof. It, too, was locked. But it was not considered a high security access as the stairway door was. His master key might fit that one. He tried it and found to his relief that it did unlock to let in a bit of afternoon sun and breeze. He carefully blocked it open a crack with a wooden block that looked as though it had been used for the purpose many times. That would be better.

He retrieved the box that held Wilton's notes and set about organizing himself. Yes, someone else had been through it. It did not seem damaged, nor should he have expected that, but the papers were not in the same meticulous order that he had disciplined himself to return them to each time he opened the box. His was, after all, an official scientific endeavor. He prided himself on that.

As he scanned the page of his own familiar handwriting and read his notes on each entry, he eventually reached the entry "Music of the Gods," the document that had been his initial contact with Wilton through the page stuck to a shelf in his office. It was neatly scratched off the list with two thin lines as if he had himself edited the catalog.

He quickly checked through the piles of papers for the remaining two pages of the document. They were not there. In their place was a folded piece of notebook paper with Wesley's name written on it in a controlled, crisp handwriting. He unfolded the paper to read the message written on it.

"Dear Professor Allen," began the formal, though hastily written letter.

> Yes, two pages of Wilton's work are presently missing. Perhaps I should say two more pages for, as I know you are aware, at least one additional page was missing already. After I have completed my research, of course, I will return the pages I have taken, so there is no sense in raising an alarm about it—least of all to Dr. Heinrich. He is quite aware of my interest in the matter. It might even be more beneficial to you if we were to strike a business deal ourselves.
>
> I want the missing page or pages, Professor. You have created a pleasant if trivial adaptation of Wilton's work relating the concepts to a universal language. A bit far-fetched, if I may say. It is evident that you are not thoroughly enlightened on the true significance of Wilton's material. Render this task to one who truly understands the mind of the author. There may be a discovery surpassing your imagination awaiting us, Prof. Allen. I have an uncanny ability to find lost idols.
>
> If, by the time you have finished reading this letter, I do not already have the missing pages in my hands, I will expect you to deliver them here in the near future.
>
> Yours sincerely,
> The Blade

Wesley's hands were shaking by the time he finished reading the letter. How dare anyone steal manuscript pages from the library and accuse him of doing the same? And virtually threaten him if he did not turn over his part. He reread the closing of the letter.

> … If, by the time you have finished reading this letter, I do not already have the missing pages…

Wesley ran to the door of the stacks and swore at his stupidity in having himself locked in. He turned to the phone system and dialed the desk. It rang. Eight times it rang and no one picked it up. Wesley slammed down the receiver in half a panic. Then he remembered the roof access door.

He pushed it outward and boosted himself up to the sill. This time, he would take a precaution. He carefully wedged the block back into the sill to keep the door from latching behind him. Just to his left, a library box was tucked into a corner of the roof structure. It was too out of place to be overlooked. He pulled it from its hiding place and opened it. A blanket and pillow were neatly folded in it. No wonder

Doris misunderstood his request. If students were using the roof as a hideaway, there must be other access routes to it. He would take care of that matter later.

He looked across the roof toward his office a block away. He could see the office window from where he stood. It appeared dark. There was not much he could see from here, or do if something was going on. His task now was to get down off the roof.

Modern buildings, he muttered, were not equipped with ladders to the roof. He searched around for other accesses. Forty feet away, he identified the painted black glass of the fire windows above the fly space in the school auditorium. He pulled on the window frame and it reluctantly inched open enough for him to slip through. He searched for footing beneath him and found a beam. Balancing himself as the window slid noiselessly shut and his eyes adjusted to the darkness, he began to identify his surroundings. A series of steel beams three inches wide and six inches apart ran the length of the space around him. Pulley blocks were attached to these at regular intervals with cable stretching in a hazardous pattern across the grid. Some forty-five feet below, the school thespians were rehearsing a playlet. He looked back up to catch his breath and calm his vertigo. He picked his way to the access ladder about fifteen feet away across the obstacle course. As soon as he was off the ladder from the grid, Wesley ran for his office and the precious shelf.

7
The Blade

Tuesday, 31 May 1955, Indianapolis, Indiana

IT WASN'T often that Rebecca could free herself early enough in the day to surprise Wesley with dinner. Lately, though, with Wesley spending his afternoons in the library, she had found time to indulge her culinary whims before he got home. This afternoon, the first time this week, she had stopped at the city market and purchased a rack of ribs, smiling at her own extravagance. When Wesley got home he would be greeted by the smell of barbecue sauce. They would still have a good bit of the evening together before she retired to her own apartment. Time together was precious.

As usual, the kitchen door was unlocked and she dropped the groceries on the table. They would have to get new locks and keys for the doors before they left on their summer trips. The student they had found to housesit for the summer would need a secure place. Rebecca couldn't remember a time when she had ever found the door to Wesley's house locked. She put on an apron and set about preparing dinner.

As if in response to her daydreams, she heard steps in the study upstairs and a loud thump. *Odd,* she thought. *He shouldn't be home yet. Who is surprising whom?*

"Wesley," she called from the foot of the stairs. "Wesley, I'm here." There was no answer nor any other sound. Perhaps he wasn't feeling well. He wouldn't normally be home at this hour. Then fearing that she may have heard him falling, she ran up the stairs to his study and through the door.

Before she could react to the chaos in the room or her own foolishness in rushing in, a hand grabbed her from behind and clamped down hard across her mouth. She raised an arm instinctively to drive her elbow into the attacker but stopped short as she felt the point of a knife poised beneath her left breast.

"Now keep quiet and don't turn your head. No sense losing your life over a messy room. Besides, most of the mess is his own, Miss Hart. If I were you, I'd marry someone with better personal habits." His voice had a British accent. Maybe Scottish. The hand on her mouth released its pressure gradually but the knife pressed threateningly against her ribs.

"What do you want and how did you know my name?" Rebecca asked with her arm still upraised.

"It's a matter of public record. I try to know everyone the old man knows. Traveling to Scotland this summer, are you?"

"That's not public record."

The man carefully straightened her arm down by her side and began lightly stroking it.

"There now, that's better. No, it's in your boyfriend's notes from your meetings with Heinrich. He keeps very thorough notes. Mrs. Weed is supposed to look you up. She's a witch, you know."

"Who are you and what do you want?" Rebecca was near panic. What else might Wesley have written in his notes?

"I just want the code. The rest of it. I want the pages that your fiancé stole from the library before I got there. Did he give them to Heinrich?"

"I don't know what you're talking about. What code?" If she survived, there were things Doc and Margaret would want to know. To her surprise, her attacker did not take the bait.

"No, you wouldn't know, would you? You have your own studies to take care of. Dabble a bit in the black arts? A little kitchen magic? Come now, you can confess to your kindly gatekeeper."

"What gatekeeper?"

"You'll find out soon enough. Let's just say I'm a friend of the family. Now here's a family tip. The best guides in the world can't always get you safely through the gates of hell. You might actually need me." The hand stroked Rebecca's arm again and brushed purposefully against her breast. She stiffened under the caress. "Relax. I don't have time to play right now. We'll have time later. He'll be back soon. So, what am I to do with you?"

"Just leave. I won't look. I won't even turn around."

"You're clever," he laughed, "and I would never trust a woman. Least of all a witch."

"I'm not a witch."

"Think about it in the dark." He pushed her across the room toward the closet and opened the door. "You should be comfortable enough in here. Just settle in and wait for your Wesley Allen."

"I don't know who you are but I'll find out," she screamed as the door shut. He laughed

"No doubt you will. Make sure when you find me that you know where my precious goddess is hidden. I want her. This one is just for myself."

His footsteps retreated and she pushed against the door only to find it blocked. She fought her way through the clothing in the closet to the door at the opposite end and opened it quietly into the adjacent bedroom. She could hear him on the stairs already and when she opened the bedroom door she saw only the top of his short blond hair disappearing down the stairs.

She fell back on the bed and heard the front door close. He was gone.

Her relief was short-lived as she heard the back door slam and then slam again. She ran to the open window to see the blond man turn down the alley and Wesley come off the back porch. She leaned out the window and yelled.

"He has a knife, Wes. Don't chase him!"

Wesley turned and looked up at her in surprise, torn for a moment between whether to pursue the intruder or to be sure that Rebecca was unharmed. In an instant, his priorities were straight and he charged back into the house and up the stairs.

"Becc! Are you all right?" He burst through the door and wrapped her in his arms, nearly knocking them both onto the bed. The sudden release of tension and emotion that she felt had her choked with tears before the single syllable could escape.

"Yes," she sobbed into his shoulder as he smoothed her hair and cradled her in his arms. "He wanted the last page of Wilton's notes."

"I know. But he hasn't got it yet. Why did I check my office before I checked here? Thank God you are all right."

For a long time, they sat on the edge of the bed cradling each other. Then they talked and told their stories. They discussed the situation well into the night, the ribs forgotten on the kitchen counter. Rebecca alternated from passion to cold analysis. It was difficult to support Wesley in his battle when she was so involved in her own, both internal and external battle. At last she stood to leave.

"I'm going home. I'm too tired to deal with this anymore."

"Stay here tonight," Wesley responded. "I don't like you being off and unprotected."

"If I thought that was the invitation I wish it was, I'd stay," Rebecca said, pulling him to his feet to kiss goodnight. "But it is no safer in your spare bedroom than anyplace else. At least my apartment has a lock on the door."

"This place will, too, as soon as I get to a hardware store tomorrow. I know, that doesn't help tonight. Come on. I'll walk you home."

Wesley walked with Rebecca to her apartment. They kissed on her doorstep. He shifted nervously on one foot and then the other, hanging onto her so she wouldn't go in yet.

"Wesley, people are going to see us out here on the steps," Rebecca chided softly.

"I know."

"What is it?"

"I'm…" Wesley faltered. It was harder to say than he expected. But the truth was there, nonetheless. "I'm afraid."

Wednesday, 1 June 1955, Indianapolis, Indiana

WESLEY STARED AT the ceiling in the early morning light. He tried to pray, but thoughts of the events of the preceding day filled his mind. He was so stupid, gullible. What a coward! Downstairs, chairs were propped against doors, wooden sticks were jammed into window frames. He should be trusting in God to keep him safe. Instead, he was cowering in his bed alone and wanted nothing more than to hide beneath the covers.

Wesley had never experienced physical violence. Yes, he knew classmates when he was in school who had been in fights. But none had touched him personally. He was too young to be involved in World War II and was a deferred student in the Korean War. The very idea that someone would attack *his* fiancée in *his* home was earthshaking. For the first time, Wesley found himself thinking violent thoughts. That scared him even more. He prayed again.

Rebecca was so much better than he was at reading people, but Wesley couldn't help questioning his trust in Doctors Heinrich and Jacobsen. They'd just waltzed right in and changed everything about his research and his life. They'd exposed Rebecca and him to danger. He distrusted Rebecca's faith in them, even though she was always right about such things.

His dear, sweet Rebecca. It was his responsibility to protect her. She was such a temptation to his rigid morals. They would be married next fall, delayed from their intended June nuptials. Was it really so wrong to move ahead with their relationship before then? She would have stayed with him last night, but knew that he wouldn't make love to her, even after the horrid attack. *Must keep emotions in check.* It was his duty to protect her, even though she was toying dangerously with this goddess cult. That would pass once she finished her thesis. He was certain of it.

Wesley got up and used the bathroom before standing in the doorway to his home office. It had been ransacked, though he knew a casual observer wouldn't be able to tell the difference between before and after. He was not a tidy man when it came to his creative side. His piano and a dozen other instruments crowded the space along with manuscripts, music, and research. But he knew where everything was. Or did. It was obvious that The Blade knew what he was looking for. He already had two pages.

Stolen from the library!

Forgotten in the excitement of the previous day and ensuing anger, was that he had been locked in the library stacks and was now safe at home. He was supposedly still waiting to be let out. How could he get back into the stacks without arousing suspicion? He had left them a mess in his hurried exit across the roof. Wilton's papers were scattered across a library table. The note from The Blade lay among the papers.

He glanced at his watch. The library would soon open. He could walk in naturally enough and ask to go up to the stacks. That would work fine, assuming Doris was not at the desk. He hoped she only worked afternoons.

The alternative, of course, was to return by way of the roof. He could pretend to have been locked in overnight. If no one had gone up to check on him and found him gone… If someone had, he could be in academic hot water. Pages were missing from material for which he was responsible. Perhaps Rebecca…

No. Better to leave her out of this. Best to take the direct and brave approach. He would march straight in, clean, box, and lock everything, and leave. No one would even know there were pages missing. No one would know he had been locked into the stacks. Doris was so scatterbrained that it wasn't likely she would even remember.

He arrived at the library five minutes before it opened and waited impatiently. He read bulletin board notices about youth groups, the Philaletheis Society, the college thespians, and a half-dozen church notices. For all its intended impact on the new urbanity, this college, plopped down in a cornfield at the edge of the city, still held a resemblance to an evangelical tent meeting and stood as a bastion against all sorts of progress. It was ironic that a school that took its name from the city, was engaged in such a vicious zoning battle that would make its campus part of the city proper.

Wesley quickly scanned the previous day's entries in the register when he signed in. Dr. R. McGuire, PhD. That made things worse. No one gave credence to an Assistant Professor when confronted by a doctor.

Miss Miller, the senior librarian, led him up the stairs, slowly, to the third-floor stacks. Unlike Doris, Miss Miller did not speak at all until she delivered the ritual instructions at the top of the stairs. Even then, the words were whispered because they were, after all, still in the library, she reminded him. Wesley breathed a sigh of relief when she closed the door.

The room was stuffy and Wesley opened the roof access door and blocked it.

Wesley quickly surveyed the papers he had left on the library table the day before. Apparently, no one had been in the room since he left it. The papers looked untouched. He began the tedious task of sorting them back into the order of the catalog numbers he had assigned them. Even this simple work would help him in his PhD defense. It was an academic pursuit and engaging in it gradually slowed his heart. He would simply re-box the papers and report some missing. They would go through the register to see who else had access. Of course, Dr. McGuire would deny that he had even been looking at that file. Wesley would be on the hook again. It was far better to leave the theft undiscovered.

"WELL, PROFESSOR ALLEN? Did you bring me the missing pages of the code?" The steely English voice brought Wesley wheeling around to face a mirror image of himself—almost

Wesley had short dark hair and a stylish pencil thin mustache. This man had equally short blond hair and a face so closely shaven it looked like he might have no facial hair at all. Otherwise—the height, weight, build—they were very similar. Most especially, however, the intense blue eyes that looked into his. Wesley regained his voice.

"Doctor McGuire, I assume? Where is the material you stole from the library? I demand that you return it immediately," Wesley said with considerably more force than he thought his voice was capable of.

"Fast to make accusations, are you not?" the Brit said. "There are more pages missing than what you allege I have taken. Are you prepared to reveal where the rest of the material is? You know I will get it eventually. Why not just hand it over now?"

"I have taken nothing from the library," Wesley stated firmly. He glanced toward the stacks of papers on the heavy oak table.

"Really? Someone did. It's either you or Heinrich. And I think old Doc found you because you already had the notes. You're being used by the old man. Give it up, Allen." The man moved closer and Wesley involuntarily stepped back. There was a threatening hardness in the Brit's voice.

"I have nothing to show you and nothing to tell you," Wesley said. He searched the table behind him with his hand, hoping to find a weapon but coming up empty.

"It's time you find out why I am called The Blade," McGuire spat. A knife appeared in his hand and Wesley dove for the door.

It was too far and McGuire hit him in the stomach to drive him back. Wesley flung a hand at his assailant but it was ineffectual. His first thought was of what it would do to his hands. The hesitation was all McGuire needed for a quick advantage and before Wesley could further respond, he was bent backward over the library table with the point of the knife at his throat.

"I get whatever I want, Professor. And I want the lost goddess of Metéora. Give me the rest of the key."

"It's not a key," Wesley blurted out. "It's just a bunch of drivel about talking to gods with music. And there's no goddess. Just an empty city."

"City? Heinrich actually found Wilton's lost city? I knew it! You see, if you talk to the right god with the right music, all sorts of treasures might appear. A heavenly goddess, perhaps. Now where is it."

"You're insane."

"I'm too rich to be insane. Call me eccentric if you like, but if I don't have the rest of that code, I'll make this table into an altar and spill your blood all over it. And when I'm done with you, I'll sacrifice your virgin bride. How would you like to be sacrificed to a pagan goddess?" Wesley felt the knife bite deeper into his throat and was almost afraid to speak lest it cut.

"Heinrich took it," he choked.

"Idiot! You could have saved yourself so much pain by saying so at once. He took it. Did he sign it out?"

"The same way you did," Wesley cried.

"If you are sending me on a wild goose chase, I will find you in Greece and complete that sacrifice. He must have the key if he actually stooped so low as to steal the manuscript," McGuire said.

"I keep telling you, it's not a code."

"Not in the traditional sense. Wilton was a spy. Spies encode messages. It happens that I intercepted a message some time ago sent to a contact called Prometheus. It contained Wilton's code. But there was no message. Now, I'll have both," he took the knife from Wesley's neck and Wesley gasped air into his lungs. "A musician can't help the good doctor if he can't play, you know. All he wants from you is the music that will open the gates. He'll have no use for you if you can't play."

McGuire spun Wesley around, twisting his right hand flat on the table. At the last instant, Wesley saw the knife coming down toward his fingers and in a burst of adrenalin fueled panic, snatched them into a fist. The knife thudded into the oak tabletop. Wesley threw his weight back into his assailant, feeling his arm wrench even as he did it.

Wesley lowered his head like a goat and rammed McGuire away from the knife stuck in the wood. The two men slammed into a shelving unit, sending it crashing into the next. Wesley saw McGuire's fist a second before it connected with his jaw, sending him into the steel shelves on the opposite side. Falling. One after another like dominos. And then there was nothing.

8
Coupling

Wednesday 1 June 1955, Indianapolis, Indiana

"**P**ROFESSOR ALLEN! Professor Allen! What happened here?"
He had never heard Miss Miller's voice so loud. They were in
the library, after all. Didn't she know? But the hands that touched him
were larger than frail Miss Miller's. And the voice that spoke next had
the deep resonance of a campus security guard.

"Professor. Wake up. Take it easy. Stay still. Where are you hurt?"

Wesley groaned. Hurt? Suddenly, everything hurt. Head, arm, face,
back. He wagged his head left and right and regretted the movement.

"Attacked."

"By whom? No one came down the stairs," Miss Miller declared.

Then Wesley remembered the open roof door.

"Out to the roof," he rasped.

"You just stay calm and don't move," the guard said. "I called for an
ambulance." He left Wesley where he lay with the surprisingly tender
hand of Miss Miller on his.

"There, there. Just rest, dear."

The security guard went to the roof door and fumbled for the right
key before he finally got it open.

"Nothing on the roof but this box of bedding. What's been going on
up here? Something obviously happened to you. Did the attacker have
keys? Can you identify him?"

"Yes. No. I had the roof door propped open for a little fresh air up
here," Wesley said. "I don't know about the box. I know who it was,
though. He had a knife. Stuck in the table." The guard went to investigate.

"No knife here, but there is a big gouge in the wood. Could have
been a knife. I'd better call the sheriff." The security guard went to use
the phone and footsteps on the stairs outside announced the arrival of
EMTs. They had Wesley loaded on a stretcher long before the sheriff
arrived, and bundled Wesley out the door.

"Who is going to clean up this mess?" demanded Miss Miller. "This is not a way to treat a library."

"I'm sure I'm okay, Miss Miller. As soon as they finish checking me out, I'll come back and straighten the room," Wesley said. "Or in the morning first thing. Please don't let anyone up here until I get back. I'll put it back in perfect order. I promise."

WESLEY WAS TREATED and released from the hospital. His face was nastily bruised and he had a bruised rib. Most serious was his twisted shoulder joint that would require rest for several days. Rebecca was frightened and tearful when she arrived at the hospital to take him home.

ONCE THERE, A sheriff's deputy came by the house to question him, but the investigation was perfunctory and slightly insulting.

"Next time you don't want him to do you on the roof, Miss Hart, don't go to the stacks with him. If it wasn't you, don't marry him." The deputy left and Wesley sat stunned looking at Rebecca. She smiled at him.

"I wouldn't have fought you off," she said.

"Rebecca, I didn't…"

"Hush, my darling. I know. I have more faith in you than in all the rest of the world. We need to call Doc Heinrich, though."

"They are an hour ahead of us. It's probably too late to call them tonight," Wesley said. The painkillers had made his head muzzy.

"Darling, it isn't even dinnertime here yet. They are probably having cocktails or something."

"I hate to say it, but that sounds like a great idea," Wesley tried to laugh.

"Not with painkillers," Rebecca admonished. "Doctor's orders. Where is the number?" Wesley winced as he twisted to pull his wallet from his pocket. He handed the card to Rebecca and she dialed.

Doc listened silently as Wesley recapped the events of the day and the previous day's break-in and assault of Rebecca. Finally, when the story had ended and Wesley had spent most of his anger, Doc responded.

"Wesley, I'm sorry," he said. "I didn't expect him to be so near already. I was sure we had covered our tracks in visiting you. His sources of information always baffle me. I… We would never have endangered you and Rebecca intentionally."

"I'm so relieved that you were not more seriously hurt," Margaret said. Rebecca, with her head next to Wesley's listening in, quickly turned to Wesley.

"Dr. Jacobson?" Wesley said.

"I'm sorry. I'm on the extension phone. Isn't Rebecca on with you?"

"We don't have an extension, but we are sharing the phone," Wesley said.

"Hello, Margaret, Doc," Rebecca said.

"Are you all right, dear?" Margaret asked. "That must have been horribly frightening to you."

"Yes. Who is he?" Rebecca asked. "He said he was a friend of the family."

"He is a former student of mine," Doc answered. "A man who scavenges ancient art treasures and sells them to wealthy clients on the black market. Most countries, as you know, have nationalized all ancient art treasures and have made it illegal to transport valuable artifacts beyond their frontiers. With the pillaging of most of Central Europe during and after the war, countries have scrambled to tighten controls, but there are many holes that a skillful smuggler can use and the communists are unwilling to help. They are as suspect as anyone else. It is rumored that one of the rare copies of the Gutenberg Bible was stolen from Germany and is now in Moscow."

"Doc, is there a treasure that we're after?" Wesley finally asked bluntly. "McGuire was convinced that it was a rare idol that he wanted for himself."

"Not that I know of, Wesley," Doc said. "I believe that the value is the city itself and the story that goes with it. We will be taking cameras to photograph the evidence, but there is no certainty that any of us could find the location without the guide. If Ryan has a spy-code of some sort, perhaps Wilton was recording something more than the musical language in his notes."

"He mentioned a contact named Prometheus. Isn't he the god chained to a mountain that the crows peck at?" Wesley asked.

"Yes, but I *can* confirm that Wilton's contact went by the codename Prometheus. There was a great deal of cross-over between, shall we say, occult circles and war spies. It's said that Hitler attempted bizarre satanic rituals to assure his victory in the war."

"Wilton was a Satanist?"

"No, no! Wesley, you must get past the point of considering everything that is not of your one true god to be of Satan. No goddess worshipper would ever bend his or her knee to the Christian god of evil. Ask Rebecca." Wesley looked at his fiancée and she nodded. He sighed.

"What should we do?"

"How soon can you be ready to leave?" Doc asked.

"Classes are out on Friday. Rebecca leaves for the port in New York on Saturday morning," Wesley said. "I'm clear as of my last class on Thursday—day after tomorrow."

"Go with her," Margaret said. "Make the voyage to England your honeymoon and then catch a ferry to France and the train to Athens. We'll meet you there."

"Honeymoon?" Rebecca gasped.

"We, uh… aren't married yet," Wesley said.

"Well you can remedy that, can't you?" Doc said.

"WES, I'M FRIGHTENED," Rebecca said as she hugged him. He groaned aloud from the pain. "Sorry," she said, easing her grip.

"I would endure any pain to hold you." He shifted so he could wrap his left arm around her without stressing the injured right.

"People just don't go around killing people over mythical treasures!" Rebecca shouted. "They don't." Her outburst turned to tears as she gently buried her head against Wesley's good shoulder.

"I've never been in a fight before. I'm still shaking," Wesley said. "I didn't come out of this one in too good a shape." Wesley lifted his right hand enough to stroke Rebecca's hair. He was a musician, not an adventurer. What was he thinking? "Becc, honey, I'm frightened, too," he whispered.

Rebecca squeezed him more tightly and he caught his breath, but didn't move or object. Where hadn't he been hit? Her lips brushed the bruises on his face lightly as she whispered to him.

"What are we going to do?"

Wesley discovered his lips were not bruised as badly as he thought when he pressed them against Rebecca's. She was so beautiful to him. She tasted wonderful as her lips opened to his questing tongue. His good arm pulled her closer as they lost themselves in unaccustomed passion. Wesley's hand slipped from her hair and gently caressed her breast. Both were shaking when they looked into each other's eyes with undisguised desire. At last, Wesley found his voice, though it was no more than a whisper.

"My love, we are going to get married and make love and go on a long honeymoon voyage."

"Do we have to do it in that order?" she asked.

I<small>T WAS GOOD</small>. Nice.

Neither had experience, so they had nothing to compare it with. Once they agreed to sleep together this very night, things got awkward. Rebecca did not have sleepwear at Wesley's house. She knew if she went home to prepare, she wouldn't come back. Wesley gave her a pair of his pajamas.

"You wear this part," Rebecca said, handing the pants back to him. "They'd just fall off me anyway." Wesley took the pajama pants.

"Becc, if you…"

"Hush. We're here, darling. I'll be right back." She slipped into the bathroom and Wesley quickly changed into his pajama pants. He pulled them over his boxers, then quickly stripped and pulled the underwear off before putting on the pants again. He didn't take off his undershirt. He paced around the bed, smoothing out the wrinkles created from lying on it this afternoon. He looked at it and turned the covers back before fluffing the pillows. It wasn't a big bed. If they slept together in it, they would be touching all night. Wesley tried to stop his erection from forming. He didn't want to frighten Rebecca. She shouldn't have to look at it.

He heard the bathroom door open and turned to see Rebecca walk into the room. His heart jumped to his throat. He'd seen Rebecca's legs in summer shorts and even in a swimming suit, but seeing her bare legs sticking out from under his pajama shirt, took his breath away.

"You are so beauti… huhk!" Wesley's heartfelt sentiments were interrupted by a hiccup. He started again and hicked again. Rebecca giggled. Wesley strained to withhold another hiccup. "Water," he gasped.

Rebecca ran into the bathroom and returned with a glass of water. Wesley took the glass, his whole body shaking with the convulsions. He bent himself double, put the glass between his legs and attempted to drink the water while upside down. Of course, that resulted in water up his nose and a coughing fit that hurt his shoulder. Rebecca couldn't contain her laughter as she ran for a towel to clean up the spilled water and wipe Wesley's face.

But the hiccups were gone when she pressed her lips to his and kissed him with months of restrained passion breaking loose. Together, they edged toward the bed and sat on it, still kissing, and eventually, found themselves lying down. Wesley winced as he reached for her with his right hand, the shoulder not cooperating. But then his hand closed on the softness of her unrestrained breast and he pushed the pain away from his consciousness.

He was twenty-seven years old and had never felt a breast that wasn't encased in a brassiere. Even those few occasions that he had dared caress Rebecca in this way had been only in the past few weeks after they'd been engaged and had always been followed by the mixed sensation of arousal and guilt. But this, now, was his wife. Perhaps they were not yet married, but they would be in a few days and there was no need to feel guilty about touching his bride.

The progress from kissing to love-making continued to be awkward, moving forward and then hesitating, not knowing what to do next. She had struggled to get his undershirt off without hurting his shoulder, but was then fascinated with kissing his chest. His hand slipped beneath the pajama shirt and for the first time in her life she felt someone other than herself touching her bare breast. Her hardening nipples spoke of her increasing arousal and preparation for her husband's invasion of her most private places.

At twenty-three, Rebecca was no more experienced than Wesley. It was the way life was supposed to be. Even though her questing mind sought out the myths and legends of the goddess, her upbringing had left no question that she would be a virgin on this, her wedding night.

Their coupling was tentative and embarrassed. He slipped her panties off and she nearly cried from embarrassment when he discovered how wet she was between her legs. She pushed his pants down and he nearly reached his climax when she accidentally brushed against his penis. She snatched her hand back as if it was on fire.

Wesley had never felt anything as overwhelming as the touch of his penis to the wetness between Rebecca's legs.

"Gently, please, darling," she begged. "But please, do it now."

He pressed forward only to have his erection slide up and over her slit and through her hair. She gasped.

"Where...?"

"I'll... I'll help," she said. With that, she reached between them and tentatively grasped his penis. Wesley moaned. "Is it okay?" she asked.

"Yes. Oh, yes. I'm... I don't know if I can hold back," he said. She moved his prick into position and felt it between her lower lips.

"Now. Push slowly." He followed her guidance, discovering the entrance was not easy but pushed more firmly and suddenly broke through. "Ow!" Rebecca cried. "Ow! Stop. Ow!"

She had not expected quite so much pain when her hymen ripped open to allow the invasion of his penis. Wesley started to pull back, but she grasped him firmly and held him. He gasped with the pain in his shoulder and bruised ribs.

"Don't move! Don't move," she cried. "Just give me time. It's lessening. It doesn't hurt as much now. Oh. Oh. Are you all the way in?"

"I don't think so," Wesley gasped. He could feel the growing pressure in his testicles and was not sure he would ever make it all the way in.

"Go ahead. I can stand it now. Push in."

"I'm so sorry I hurt you, my love," he said. "Oh, my lord!" He was also sorry that as he pressed into her depths he felt himself lose control and begin spurting inside her. "Oh! Oh! Rebecca. Oh, my Becc!"

"I love you, Wesley. I love you."

Whether it was the physical exhaustion of their first coupling or the pain in Wesley's shoulder and ribs catching up with him, he collapsed to her side, pulling out before he had fully softened. Rebecca rolled with him and held herself close to him as he struggled to pull his pajama pants back up. In that position, they fell asleep, kissing each other and whispering words of endearment to each other.

To Rebecca, it was nice. She would welcome her husband whenever he desired her. To Wesley, it was nearly enough to make him a goddess worshiper. He knew he would want to make love to his wife as often as she would have him. Neither had ever experienced anything remotely like what had driven them into sleep.

Thursday, 2 June 1955, Indianapolis, Indiana

REBECCA ROSE EARLY, before Wesley had stirred. She kissed him lightly on the head before retrieving her panties and going to the bathroom. She was a woman. She had welcomed her husband into her body and he had taken her maidenhead. But when she bathed, she was disheartened. The blood on her thighs was not dried. She had known it was near her menses, but didn't anticipate right now. *Why now?* She knew that even though her vagina ached with the recent pain of deflowering, she would gladly have welcomed Wesley again tonight. Even this morning if he wanted. Now they would have to wait. She was just glad they had decided to go ahead last night and had not waited a second longer.

"Rebecca! Rebecca! Are you all right?" Wesley pounded on the bathroom door.

"I'm fine, Wes. I'm just in the tub. I'll be out soon," she called.

"There's blood on the sheets! Are you sure you aren't injured?"

"Yes. Yes, it's normal, darling. Women bleed the first time. And... I'm very embarrassed, Wesley. I've started my period. I'm so sorry." Rebecca broke down in tears as she finished rinsing herself in the tub and pulled the plug.

"Oh. Is there... Can I... What should I do?"

"Um... Could you bring me my purse? I need a... napkin."

Wesley brought the purse and used the downstairs bathroom to give himself a sponge bath, carefully pulling on clothes as he winced with the pain. In the kitchen, he found his pain pills and took one as he put water on the stove to boil and got the electric percolator ready to plug in. He was still barefoot because it simply hurt too much bend over and put shoes and socks on.

As he sat contemplating the day to come and what had just passed, Rebecca came into the room, dressed in the clothes she'd been wearing the day before. Wesley jumped up to greet his wife and knocked the kitchen chair over in his excitement.

"Darling Rebecca, I love you so much," he said as he embraced her. She blushed. "You aren't upset with me, are you? Are you... disappointed in me?" he asked.

"Wesley," she whispered. "My husband. How could you ever disappoint me? I know that we are not legally married yet, but I will always celebrate our wedding anniversary on June first. I love you so much, Wesley. Now that I have you I never want to let you go."

"I should just come to Scotland with you," he answered. "I'm really not going to be much good to Doc and Margaret with this arm. And... I just don't want to let you out of my sight."

"You have a class to teach this morning," Rebecca said.

"Final exam in Music Theory," he laughed. "I'll be out at eleven. Let's go get our marriage license. And go to the travel agent and get our tickets on your ship changed. We need to catch a train first thing on Saturday morning and I want to do it with my wife."

9
Marriage

Thursday, 2 June 1955, Indianapolis, Indiana

NOT EVERYTHING went as smoothly as anticipated. Indiana required a blood test before a license would be issued and there was a three-day waiting period after they had a license. Rebecca broke out in tears when the county clerk refused to issue a license.

"We leave on our cruise on Saturday!" she protested.

"Have the ship's captain marry you then," the sympathetic clerk said. "You really should have thought about this before you decided to honeymoon."

A visit to the travel agent Rebecca had used to book her passage to England confirmed that they could get passage together and upgrade to a double room rather than Rebecca's single berth. But there were more problems.

"I was supposed to go to New York and Doc was making my travel arrangements from there," Wesley said. "I don't have enough money in my checking account to cover this ticket."

At Rebecca's urging, Wesley called Doc. Doc sent the funds to the travel agent via Western Union. Saturday morning, Wesley and Rebecca left by train to New York and Sunday afternoon they boarded the S.S. United States for Southampton, England. They were surprised to find that when Doc transferred the funds for Wesley's passage, he had upgraded the two to first class. They watched from the deck as New York faded behind them. They were married at the Captain's Table in international waters before dinner.

Rebecca's menstruation had ended by the end of their second day at sea and for the duration of the four-day crossing, they spent more time in their cabin than on the deck.

Tuesday, 7 June 1955, SS United States at Sea

"YOU ARE SO beautiful, my darling," Wesley breathed. Rebecca blushed. It had been so daring—so naughty—to step out of the head and into their berth without a stitch of clothing on. For a moment, she thought Wesley would have another attack of hiccups.

"I feel terribly wicked, letting you see me naked," she said. Gooseflesh had risen over her entire body and Wesley rushed to fold her in his arms before she could cover herself. "Am I a woman without morals?" she whispered.

"I am your husband," Wesley breathed. "You are mine. And I declare this mode of dress to be acceptable in our marriage bed."

"Then undress, my love. You are mine. And your wife wants to see you naked."

Wesley blushed more deeply than Rebecca had as he slipped out of his pajamas. His erection wilted as his wife let her eyes rove over his body, but it quickly revived as she brought her naked body against his.

This, their second coupling, was easier than the first. Rebecca welcomed her husband into her body as he caressed and sucked on her breasts. Wesley enjoyed a slightly longer residence in her depths before he released his seed. He willingly held his wife in his arms for an hour after they rolled apart. She was happy that he neither rolled over and went to sleep, nor jumped out of bed to dress. She would gladly lie in his arms forever.

"How many children shall we have, Wesley, my love?" she whispered. Wesley sat straight up in bed.

"Children?"

"You do want children, don't you?" Rebecca asked worriedly.

"Well yes, yes. Of course I do. I just… I hadn't thought. Do you think you might be pregnant now?" he asked.

"I've never been very regular," Rebecca said. "Still, I just finished my period, so biologically it is highly unlikely."

"Wow! A baby in you. Here. In this beautiful tummy," he said, holding her against him and stroking her abdomen. It felt heavenly. Rebecca could feel Wesley getting hard again behind her. "At least one. Not more than ten," Wesley said. "Unless you want more."

"Wesley, you are actually excited about putting a baby in me, aren't you? I can feel you."

"Oh dear. It's you that excites me, Becc. Holding you. Being naked with you beneath our sheets. Making love to you," he said as he kissed around her shoulders and up to her ear. His hand moved from her stomach up to her breasts and he caressed her tenderly. "And children. I could be a father."

"Even though it is unlikely today, perhaps you should practice making me pregnant again."

"Yes. Yes, perhaps I should."

Thursday, 16 June 1955, Europe by Rail

IT TOOK FIVE days and nights from Calais, France to Brindisi, Italy by train. Another twenty-four hours elapsed on the cruise ship to Patra, Greece, by way of Corfu. Wesley had been almost too tired to appreciate the beauty of the islands and the villages that hung from cliffs that the ship passed.

He'd changed trains in Paris and Geneva, not understanding a word that was spoken around him and little of what was on the limited signage. He'd nearly missed his connection in Paris, but the porter on the second train spoke passable English and pointed Wesley to the correct train in Geneva. He changed again in Milan and was thankful that his years of Latin helped him at least interpret signs in Italy. The trains, however, had been horrid. Doc had told him a joke when they connected by telephone—an extraordinary extravagance in Wesley's mind.

"In Switzerland, the trains run according to the clock. In Italy, they run by the stomach."

He'd had two more delays changing trains in Florence and Rome and was a day late for the ship he'd originally been scheduled on to Greece. This resulted in a shouted conversation at the ticket window that neither Wesley nor the ticket agent understood, but participated in with great vigor.

"Perhaps I might be of assistance," a voice behind Wesley said. Wesley froze at the sound of the British accent, his thoughts first turning to the vicious attack by Ryan McGuire. He turned, however, to find a short and somewhat stout gentleman in short pants and a pith helmet.

"I don't know," Wesley said. "My train was late and I missed my boat yesterday. I'm trying to get to Athens. I would appreciate any assistance you might offer." The Englishman turned to the ticket agent and quickly explained the situation to him in Italian. When the situation was explained, the agent threw up his hands and nodded. In a few minutes, Wesley's ticket had been changed and he joined his new companion as they walked calmly to embark on the ship.

"Here you are," the Englishman said. "I'm Jeremy Percival, at your service. Had to learn Italian when I was stationed here during the war. Perhaps you would join me for dinner. The galley on this ship serves the best lasagna in the world. You can't get better in Italy."

"Wesley Allen. Pleased to meet you. I'll be happy to join you. Shall we say seven?"

"Excellent."

The two had a lively time at dinner. Wesley was not yet comfortable with telling 'the lie' as he referred to his cover story, but he plunged ahead.

"I'm a musician participating in a summer exchange workshop in Northern Greece," he provided. In his mind, he carefully defined the words to mean the work that he would actually be doing. He would be exchanging musical information with his colleagues. Jeremy accepted the story at face value.

"I'm on holiday," the Englishman said. "Here to Patra and then to Athens where I'll board another ship to take me to Crete. I've three weeks there to do a walking tour of the island. I'll fly back to London, from Athens, but on the way here I flew to Rome so I could have this crossing. Just for the lasagna."

Wesley restrained himself from criticizing the amount his companion drank and thoroughly appreciated the lasagna. At least he was assured that there would be no alcohol on their expedition.

He and Jeremy boarded the same train to Athens. Wesley was surprised by the suspicion with which he was greeted on the train. Jeremy seemed not to be greeted with the same caution.

"Your spies were caught trying to fix the elections here," Jeremy explained. "All Americans are viewed as spies first and tourists second. How about giving us a tune on that instrument you carry across your back? Music soothes the savage beast as they say."

"I'm recovering from an arm injury," Wesley said, "but if you think it will help I'll certainly play." He unstrapped the guitar case and began picking a few chords. His shoulder had mostly healed and he suffered only from lack of practice for the past two weeks. Once he began to play in earnest, however, the people in his car warmed quickly. A man pulled a small concertina from a case and joined Wesley. They made a good duet.

It was a sad occasion when they reached Athens and all parted to go their separate ways.

Behind the Ivory Veil

Friday, 17 June 1955, Athens, Greece

WESLEY DRAGGED HIS suitcase and guitar out of the train station in the glare of the Mediterranean sun. Greece! He was here at last. The Acropolis. Mars Hill. The footsteps of the Apostle Paul. All were waiting for him to see. He set his bag down on the step next to him and a man reached over to pick it up.

"I have it," Wesley shouted, grabbing for his bag.

"It's okay, Wesley," Doc said from the other side. "This is Marcos, our driver."

"Oh! Doc, you both startled me."

"Good trip? Anything we should know about?" Doc asked.

"I don't believe so. I didn't see anything suspicious. Not that I would have understood anything that was said around me," Wesley laughed. "Did you expect that I would be followed?"

"On a journey like this, I expect it at every turning," Doc said. "Marcos, this is Wesley Allen, our colleague."

"Happy to meet you, Mr. Allen," Marcos said. They got into the taxi where Margaret was already waiting. "Do you want to see Athens before you get to the hotel? Just watch!"

The cab swung recklessly down street after street. Some, Wesley was certain were pedestrian walkways, but the cab simply bounced over the steps. Wesley exclaimed at each new vista that Doc, Margaret, or Marcos pointed out. Doc also explained that Marcos would drive them to the Metéora in the morning. Wesley sincerely hoped there were roads. As pleased as he was to see Athens, he was even more pleased at the prospect of a bed for the night and was surprised that the small hostelry where they were housed belonged to Marcos and his wife who greeted him.

Wesley was unable to keep himself awake, even through dinner, and excused himself to go to bed.

Music filled his head and he slept dreamlessly until roused early the next morning.

Saturday, 18 June 1955, Kastraki, Greece

WESLEY LOOKED ONCE more toward the Acropolis as they loaded the Jeep for the trip to Metéora. He had stepped into the past. He would discover the very roots of civilization. Rome conquered the world. Greece civilized it.

As the Jeep rumbled along the open road, Wesley looked out at the foreign countryside. The crystal blue Aegean was just visible off to his right and rugged mountains rose on his left. *At least Rebecca is in a country where they speak English,* he mused. He imagined her in a verdant countryside as the land around him turned arid and desolate. Perhaps, after all, she was closer to civilized roots than he was. But wherever she was, he would be in one way or another. They were married and separated all too soon. The two nights they spent in London filled his mind and he smiled.

Wesley was lost in his thoughts but gradually recognized Margaret smiling at him across the backseat. He realized he'd been humming and singing wordlessly to himself. He had no idea for how long. Margaret reached out to pat him maternally on the leg.

"It will be all right, Wesley," she said. "She will be safe and waiting for you. And you will have gained a new perspective yourself."

"Were my thoughts so obvious?" he asked.

"It seemed to come across in your musical musing," she laughed. Wesley couldn't protest against music communicating. He had simply not considered that it would communicate what he was thinking rather than being an interpretation of something that was written. "We want you to enjoy and learn from this adventure, Wesley," Margaret continued. "Just as Rebecca will learn from hers. You will hear stories and music that you have never encountered before. Once you are exposed to the fullness and beauty of the people we are about to meet, you will allow the experience to be as mystic as your own unusual musical talents."

Wesley looked at Margaret without responding. How could a decent American allow herself the fantasy of mystic pagan experiences? And to imply that his scientific studies were a mystical talent… It was apparent that he would be left to hold the important missionary activities on his own. He would not belabor the point to the extent of interrupting his work here of exploring music and language—music that could speak to the heart—the soul.

Margaret turned back toward the road ahead and left Wesley to his thoughts. Occasionally, Doc or Marcos would point out landmarks where some shrine or other marked an important event. Wesley's mind, however, remained on the distant image of Rebecca.

His first glimpse of the Metéora was breathtaking. Nothing Doc had said or described prepared him adequately for the majesty of what he saw. Wesley had seen cliffs before, in Colorado and Wyoming. There was a wall in Wyoming that stretched for miles. Here, huge pillars of rock jutted up from the floor of the plain, turning their journey into one through canyons. They left Kalambaka, a small town with streets named after Christian saints and priests, and wound over a narrow pass into the village of Kastraki. There was little here. A church with a village well marked the center of the tiny town and there were a few small houses. Across from the well was a taverna.

The stone-paved street at the center of town ended near a walled villa. "That's St. Georgio's Monastery," Doc said. "It's considerably younger than those on the peaks." He pointed ahead and Wesley saw a building that seemed to grow from the top of the rock, nearly a thousand feet above them. Beyond it, on a pinnacle that was higher still, sat another monastery. "There are twenty or thirty of these monasteries in The Metéora. I'm not sure of the exact number as the war and life have taken their toll."

The road turned into a dirt track. The Jeep bounced over ruts and through puddles, once even splashing through a stream, winding to a cluster of buildings too small to be called a village. Marcos pulled into the courtyard shared by the four little houses and their outbuildings.

A mass of children met the travelers at the gate, most passing all but the driver, calling out "Uncle Marcos! Uncle Marcos!" When a tall boy came out of the first house and went to meet the driver, it finally dawned on Wesley that their host of the previous night was related to the clan of heathens.

"Hello, Papa," said Pol as he embraced Marcos. Next the boy turned to Doc Heinrich and they shook hands. An old man stood at the door of the first dwelling and beckoned for all to come inside. A meal was ready and it was apparent that the children had been made to wait for the guests to arrive before they could have lunch. There were too many people for one table and plates were balanced on knees as the eldest and the guests were seated at the table and the rest were left to find their own spots on the floor.

"Doctor Heinrich, it is a joy to renew our friendship over this meal," the old man said.

"As we are friends, please call me Doc or Phillip. May I present my colleagues, Margaret Jacobson and Wesley Allen. Margaret, Wesley, this is the patriarch of the Pariskovopolis family, Andrew," Doc said.

"You're a patriarch now?" another old man said as Andrew shook hands with the guests. "What will Father Dimitri say about that?"

"This young goat is my brother Leo," Andrew said. "He has left the taverna in the village in the care of his wife so he could greet our guests. And here is my sister Demi who has traveled farther, from Kalambaka.

Some of the youngest generation are their grandchildren rather than mine. We will introduce everyone as the day goes on, but with my wife, Thea, and Marcos's son Apollo, we have all that will immediately affect your trip here at the table."

THE AFTERNOON WAS spent playing and singing. Wesley, Doc, and Margaret were caught up in circle games with the children as were even the oldest of the family. As soon as his guitar was unloaded from the jeep, Wesley became instantly popular with the children who sang with him as he played. He taught them songs in English and they taught him Greek folk songs. He quickly improvised new chords on the guitar, even changing the tuning to match the tonality of the local music. He sang gospel songs, which were well-received, much to his surprise. He began to doubt that he was being understood.

Music, however, was the groundwork for the festivities. When other people picked up instruments and began playing Greek music, the adults and even the children began dancing. Wesley was pulled into a circle and taught a dance. He blended well with the group and never imagined that heathens, as he still forced himself to consider them, could be so warm and friendly. Wesley was uncomfortable with the dancing, even when Doc and Margaret joined in. It wasn't a couples' dance, though, so he thought it might not be as sinful as he had been taught. He found himself inadvertently providing music for the dancing as well. A priest, or monk, by the name of Brother El dropped by and joined the festivities. Wesley knew that the Orthodox were accused of idolatry by some conservative Christians, but he considered himself liberal enough to believe in the decorative arts.

He thought of himself for an instant as succumbing to the lower nature that true Christians sought to rise above. A pang of guilt nearly overwhelmed him. Apollo, misinterpreting the sudden look of distress on Wesley's face, brought him a glass of water and warned him that in this climate they must all drink a lot of water.

Food appeared after dark, though the music never really stopped, simply being passed from one person to another. But in the after-dinner glow, with many of the adults enjoying a drink, everyone settled down in the courtyard to listen to stories. Old Mr. Pariskovopolis started things off and told the story of the golden apple and Paris's choice among the goddesses. It was a simple story from the myths and Wesley was vaguely familiar with this forerunner to *The Iliad* and the battle of Troy.

Dr. Jacobson was asked to tell a story. She recited the Norse legend of the death of Balder. Margaret was a captivating storyteller. Wesley was as fascinated as the rest of the tribe. He had not known that such feelings of despair existed in mythology. Doc deferred the honor of the next story, but asked if Wesley might have something he could share.

It was the opportunity that Wesley was waiting for and he used it far better than most men of missionary zeal might have. He pulled his New Testament from his pocket and opened it to the Gospel of John. He left the book in front of him and stared at the page, willing the words to come to life for him.

And then he began to play.

This music was unlike the songs and gospel hymns and folk tunes that had been played earlier. In fact, some might not even call it music. He let the notes and sounds he could coax from the guitar become the message, even retuning strings as he played. The strings, notes, chords, rapping on the instrument—none of this was enough. He added and changed rhythms, and with images of the age-old story playing in his mind, he added his voice.

He handled the guitar, the grandfather later said to Wesley's embarrassment, like Apollo handed the lyre. Words emerged from his vocalizations, but so did pops, clicks low vocal growls, and near howls.

He pulled the entire clan with him into the story. He wrapped his mental arms around them and made them a part of it. They shared his vision of destiny. He ended his music before it became anticlimactic or tiresome. His audience was silent. He raised his eyes to see them staring at him. Tears were in the eyes of the old man, the driver Marcos, and the young Apollo. He saw tears, too, shed by the monk.

"A kindred spirit," said the old man at last. "Welcome to our home. Welcome to our mountain. You are well-brought by these people. Pol, you will answer this man's invitation, will you not?"

Pol stood beside his grandfather and father. For a moment, Wesley thought that he was about to receive a new confession of faith. Instead, Pol answered Wesley's song in as clear and fresh a musical language as his own. Using only his voice, he captured many of the nuances Wesley had achieved with the guitar. It brought something different to the mind of each listener, but Wesley absorbed it. The music spoke to something deep within him. The music was all that existed.

Music had always been special to Wesley. He had mastered the piano and organ in his teens and progressed to stringed instruments— first through the violin family and then the guitar family. In college, he had studied voice and had learned conducting and musicology. Music filled his head and he knew he sometimes sang without realizing it. Perhaps it was the habit of Rebecca to also hum and sing when she was working that attracted the two. Music breathed in him.

Pol's story was sung to his ears alone. Wesley lost himself in the music.

As heartrending as his own music had been, the boy's was peaceful and warm. It flowed with promise. The pitches rose and fell with the swell of mystical tides flooding in upon him. Wesley could see Rebecca in his mind's eye, a windswept beach spread before her, a pen and paper in her hand. He saw himself standing before a painted screen on which Rebecca, like an animation, moved. He saw himself reaching to her as she approached him, reaching also toward him. He tried to reach out—into the painting, but could not quite reach her. He discovered that he could not quite focus upon her face. He looked with all his heart into the painting and could not bring to his eye the features that should be so familiar. The features of his wife! Had he never really looked at her? The features blended and molded into something very much like her, but not her at all. His heart shook as Pol's music broke the barrier between himself and the painting and the figure that was not Rebecca rushed into his arms and was Rebecca.

And then the music faded, and Wesley found himself to be part of the painting, gazing out of the screen at the world beyond himself. Alone.

PEOPLE WERE MOVING toward their beds before Wesley stirred after the singing of Pol's song. It had spoken clearly to him of things he could not understand, but yearned for. It had been in his language—the language that he would bring to the world. He went to sleep with the music still in his head.

10

Journey to the City

Monday, 20 June 1955, Metéora, Greece

AT DAYBREAK on Monday, Marcos, Pol, and the three Americans gathered at the common well to receive instructions from the old man. Besides the six of them, the family remained asleep and the courtyard lifeless. Wesley surprised himself when he realized he no longer considered them heathens. The old man was leader of a tribal sect, he thought. After all, a priest had been in the gathering the night before and had invited him to attend services at the monastery when they returned to the village.

"Dr. Heinrich has been exposed to the rules of our holy place before," said the old man. "Our rules may seem simplistic and we cannot give you logical reasons for them. They have been followed for a thousand, perhaps two thousand years, and no one who broke the rules has ever returned to us. You may stay for as long as you wish, but you may not remain in the holy of holies past nightfall. You may take nothing away that is a part of the city. We have no means of exposing the way to you, but Apollo will guide you on your journey. He is my representative and speaks with my voice while you sojourn."

"Andrew," Doc said, shifting to lean on his walking stick, "is there a ritual this morning? Like when I was here before?"

The old man chuckled.

"I know of no ritual for sending archaeologists to the City of the Gods, Phillip. But you go with my blessing. May you each find your heart's desire, and may your presence on the mountain bring fulfillment at long last to the prophecy we have been given," he said.

The crew loaded into the Jeep with Marcos and Pol and began the confusing and circuitous drive to their starting point. Even as a veteran traveler of Greece, Doc could not keep his bearings as the passengers left Metéora and wound their way first south and then north, east and then west. Marcos explained that he could not navigate the paths that he and Pol had taken on Doc's previous visit with the Jeep.

Pol, Wesley, and Margaret shared the back seat. Packs were strapped to the back of the Jeep. Doc and Marcos rode in the front. Even Margaret joined in the singing in the backseat as Wesley and Pol laughed together. Pol took his turn entertaining Wesley and Margaret with some simple but proficient sleight of hand. He told them that he like magic and was learning how to make things disappear. Wesley laughed and Pol pulled a pencil from his pocket and made it vanish. Wesley found it later restored to his pocket. The boy was very talented.

Doc was focused on the mystery of the vanishing City of the Gods that he had visited but could not locate on a map. Wesley had been promised source material for the Music of the Gods that Wilton had provided the inspiration for. But Margaret quested after information about the goddess hidden behind the ivory veil. Who was Serepte? Wesley listened with interest as Pol told story after story. His father and Doc were obviously pleased. Many of Pol's stories were simple renditions of popular mythology. Occasionally, though, they had strange tidbits added that the Americans had never heard before. When she heard one of these, Margaret would pull out a tablet and try to jot down a note or two, a feat rendered nearly impossible in the bouncing Jeep.

In a few hours, the Jeep was grinding its way up the side of a mountain that had no more than a goat track for a road. When the going was getting very rough, Marcos pulled up and set the brakes.

"From here you must walk," he said, jumping out of the vehicle. "Pol will show you the way. Brother El will drop off more supplies in two weeks. If you decide to leave before that, Pol will guide you back by the footpath to Metéora. I must return and try to make it back to Athens yet tonight. I will stop and tell my father that you are safely on your way."

"Thank you, Marcos," Doc said. "I have every confidence in Pol's ability to lead us. The rest of the journey is in his hands."

They unloaded the Jeep and distributed the packs. Marcos also unloaded an additional store of food and left it in a metal case locked to the foot of a tree. Doc took the key. If they ran short of provisions, they could hike back to the locked case.

Wesley carefully maneuvered Marcos aside and presented him with a Greek New Testament, which he had brought for the purpose of evangelizing the heathens. Marcos smiled at the offer and thanked Wesley profusely. Then, reaching into his own shirt pocket, he pulled out a worn and tattered version of the same book.

"You can see that my copy has seen a great deal of wear. I thank you for this gift which I will use every bit as well. You are a generous man."

Marcos was still smiling as he walked back to the vehicle with the gift in his hand. Wesley watched, perplexed. The Jeep disappeared back down the mountainside.

THE TRAIL TO their base camp was steep. Wesley, though fit, fared the worst on the journey because he was not used to carrying a pack with his guitar swinging at his side. It was, nonetheless, a quiet walk, broken only by the huffing breaths that are normally the mark of beasts of burden. Wesley had a moment of wishing that Doc and Margaret had made him cut a walking stick like they had made for Rebecca. It would have come in handy on this trail, though he wasn't sure how he could use it with a pack on his back and his guitar case in one hand.

After more than two hours of climbing the twisting trail, they came to a long open sward of green grass at the end of which was a gnarled old olive tree. Next to the oasis was a stream running from a spring above them. Pol took off his pack, calling a halt to their journey, and they made camp. Each erected a small tent and Wesley mused that it looked like an old-time army camp. They had a bivouac in which they stored their supplies and packs as there was room in each tent only for a person to slip in and sleep.

Margaret gathered the makings for their simple dinner and instructed Wesley on how to set up and use the small white gas burner that would heat the single pan. Most of the food they carried was dried and water was added to the pan from the stream.

Pol took a swim in the stream as they watched. Wesley considered the possibility of joining him, but, of course, he had not packed a swimming suit and, unlike the boy, was not willing to simply strip to his shorts and dive in. When he had swum, Pol brought water from the stream and washed the feet of each of his companions, as he had done with Doc on his first trip.

This opened an opportunity for Wesley and he began talking to Pol about the way Jesus washed the feet of the disciples. Pol listened respectfully as he finished the story. He smiled at Wesley.

"It is one of my favorite stories from the catechism," Pol said. "It is why I wash your feet when you are tired. It is a good example to follow."

Doc and Margaret had patiently watched Wesley's attempts at evangelism throughout the previous evening and this day without interfering or objecting. Now, they nearly exploded with laughter at Wesley's dumbfounded look. Wesley blushed and finally joined the laughter. It had been too perfect a setup for him to get angry. The people he had forced himself to consider heathen, cultic, and pagan were far better versed in his religion than he in theirs. Not only that, but they accepted his ways, his missionary attempts, and his beliefs.

As evening drew on, Pol sat singing in the quiet camp. Wesley thought to join him at one point, but the words leapt from a simple song to the mystic language that he shared. He let the music wash over him and lull him to sleep. His dreams were filled with questions and Wesley quietly accepted that he simply did not know everything, even about his own faith. From that point, he slept soundly.

Tuesday, 21 June 1955, City of the Gods

WHEN POL WOKE the sleeping partners, fog encompassed the camp. It was Doc who emphasized to Wesley and Margaret the importance of not breaking the chain that joined them to their guide. He had narrowly escaped a dramatic conclusion to his career on the previous visit. This time he had prepared for the ascent with ropes, and they linked together with carabiners on a single line. Doc insisted on going last with Wesley and Margaret between him and Pol. Thus prepared, they began the climb through thick fog up the mountain.

Wesley had always believed that if he were deprived of sight, the hearing faculties would compensate. The acuity of his hearing in this fog, however, came as a surprise. Doc's experience was that his hearing was muffled as much as his eyesight had been obstructed in the fog. Wesley heard everything.

As a child, Wesley had been extraordinarily sensitive to sound patterns, whether or not they were inherently musical. To him, there were always innate rhythms, sequences, and tonality. He could hear them in people's voices, in birdsong, in the purring of a cat, and in what others would consider the general cacophony of life. Sound caressed him with fingers tuning more than his ears to their touch. His entire body bristled with the expectation of whispers hidden in the wind.

In the fog, blindly linked to a child whose outline he could dimly discern ahead of him, Wesley's ears were filled with sound. Music. *They* were singing. Only not singing. It was…

Wesley shook his head to clear his ears. Perhaps it was only his imagination. Or perhaps it was something that happened only inside his own ears like tinnitus. Maybe he was schizophrenic and one side of his personality sang to the other. The fog made it easy to imagine voices.

If only he could see the singers and affirm that they were out there in the fog. The soprano voice was joined by a tenor. Then both faded as a rich contralto assumed the lead. This in turn was replaced by a trio of mournful voices raising the hairs on the back of his neck.

Wesley paused. They were just over there. He could unhook from the safety line and go to them. They were only a few feet away. He felt the tug at his waist as Pol pulled him forward, stumbling slightly. Perhaps the voices were sirens and this was what Odysseus felt when he passed Anthemoessa lashed to the mast of his ship. Voices that tugged so deeply at the heartstrings that one would gladly wreck himself on the rocks to join them.

The fog began to lift and the voices dissipated with it, leaving Wesley searching his surroundings for angels fleeing from sight. But there were only massive pillars in uniform rows that stretched out from a central court. In the center was a low rostrum and Pol went directly to it.

Dawn in the City of the Gods cannot be easily described, but once experienced is never forgotten. In the pre-sunrise light, the pillars seemed to materialize around the visitors. They are so tall that even those viewed from a distance looked like they supported the sky. The air was now crystal clear, all trace of the fog was gone and with it, all trace of the loose gravel mountain path they had traveled.

Wesley sensed a lingering presence—echoes in his ears of the mysterious music, but now without apparent source or direction. This experience of music deep inside him left Wesley with moist eyes. But when Pol mounted the rostrum and faced the rising sun, singing his greeting and being greeted in return, Wesley openly wept.

When the ritual was finished and the sun was clearly above the horizon, burning brightly down the avenue of pillars, Pol rejoined the three. Doc asked him to once again explain the rules of exploration and Pol said they could wander as far as they wished and need not fear becoming lost. All avenues would lead back to the central rostrum.

The crew tried this principle several times, using chalk to mark their paths and making notes and maps as they explored and intersected in different directions. They were frequently out of sight of the rostrum, but no matter which path they chose to follow, it led back to the center.

"Any suggestions?" Doc asked as they compared their first maps. Each had drawn the phenomenon in a different manner. The maps were not recognizable as the same location.

"Optical illusion is the best I can offer," Wesley said. "What is straight is obviously not straight." He pointed to his map which showed a single straight row of pillars with the center point showing up in different locations on the path.

"Wesley, if there is anything I hate, it is the world 'obvious'," Margaret said. "Isn't it equally possible that there could be a ripple in the plane grid negating what we normally view as straight? Einstein suggested such possibilities in his theory of relativity. The path is straight in relation to itself but the plane is wrinkled."

"I'm familiar with Einstein's views on peace and world government, but I couldn't grasp the mathematics of relativity," Wesley admitted.

"That is because we live in a space, time, and mindset that does not allow us to physically model the theories that we profess to live by," Doc said. "Regardless, as difficult as it may be to suspend our disbelief, I think Margaret's theory deserves as much consideration as optical illusion. In fact, it might explain optical illusions. We could be in a physical structure of sorts that transcends the laws of physics that we know."

"I will do my best," Wesley answered, "but it sounds much too impossible for me to believe."

Margaret laughed. "Wesley, if this is *too* impossible to believe, is there something *less* impossible in which you might believe?"

"Now we are playing semantics," argued Wesley.

"Precisely," Doc said. "Words are what we base reality on. We have no other way of classifying experience. That is what is so significant about your musical notation. It transcends words. Now, you agree that if one thing is more *impossible* than another, then the other thing must, by definition be more *possible*. Correct?"

"Of course. But..."

"Then if I can think of something more impossible than my first suggestion, you must accept the first as more possible," Margaret said. "Therefore, I posit that, like Alice, we have stepped through a looking glass and experience this phenomenon because we are actually exploring the cap of a giant mushroom and are jointly hallucinating."

The sweet smile that Margaret gave Wesley made her look years younger than he knew her to be. It captured such impish innocence that Wesley began to laugh. In a moment, Doc and Margaret had joined him, all seeing the absurdity of their situation.

"You've got to do better than that, Margaret," he choked. "That's not impossible, it is simply ridiculous."

"Then consider this," Doc said, catching his breath. "We are exploring a completely self-contained global area. This theory allows for the operation of normal laws of spherical geometry to be in force. If you walk long enough in a straight line, you always end up back where you started."

"Now that," said Wesley soberly, "is *totally* impossible. You can't simply take a walk through the fog and end up on another world, which is what I believe you mean. Albeit a very small world."

"Very well," Margaret said. "Having put an absolute on the term 'impossible', we must consider all other theories possible, no matter how improbable."

"Until proven otherwise," Wesley sighed, conceding the semantics while still considering the whole situation to be absurd.

"Agreed."

The three rejoined Pol at the rostrum where the almost thirteen-year-old was practicing card tricks, and doing so with tremendous skill. Wesley had a glimpse of himself at that age and wondered how an adolescent could possibly endure a week, much less a month, with three adults in an environment where he must entertain himself. He resolved to spend some extra time with the boy whenever he could.

They examined the surface of the rostrum for the first time and discovered that it was covered with the musical notations that Wilton had documented in his papers. As they ate their jerky and dried fruit for lunch, they trod carefully across the surface. It was an ancient structure and certain areas showed wear, as though they were on a well-traveled path. This was true at each of the twelve points around the circle from which the avenues seemed to radiate like the spokes of a wheel. Doc was concerned that they would damage the surface by walking on it, but their careful examination showed that even in the worn spots, the symbols were deeply engraved. There seemed to be no way to investigate without walking on them.

As they analyzed the symbols, they disputed the directions. Wesley insisted the east was in one direction and Doc pointed to an avenue next to it.

"But look," Wesley said. "The sun is moving to the west down that avenue. This is the avenue opposite and therefore must be east."

"You can't prove it by me," Doc said. "My compass is not working at all. Whatever the nature of this place, we must be located in some intensely powerful magnetic field."

"Have you never seen the summer sun in the far north?" Margaret asked. Wesley admitted he had not been farther north than the Sault

Saint Marie as a child. "The sun rises just a few degrees east of due north," she explained. "Its path in our perception is eastward. It is not due east until midmorning and then appears to move south and west, then north and west. Around midafternoon, it appears due west and then travels north and east again until it sets just a few degrees west of due north. If we consider that the rostrum might be the north pole of this region, then the sun would always rise and set in the south because every direction from the north pole is south. Even if we are not at the pole, it *is* summer solstice. The tilt of the axis would be at its farthest north."

Wesley stared at her with glazed eyes.

"Um... What time is it?" he asked.

"I've no idea," Margaret said. "My watch seems to have stopped."

"I never carry a watch in the field. Wesley? How about yours?"

"I think it stopped as well. The hands are all pointing to twelve."

"Well, we know it is later than that," Margaret said. "None of us doubted when it was time to eat our lunch. And the sun, no matter what direction, is definitely moving away. Our shadows are getting longer."

"Pol, how much longer do we have until it is time to leave?"

"Soon," Pol answered. "We should gather our things and follow the sun."

"I think we need a strategy session," Doc said. "We won't accomplish much more today. Lead on, Pol."

As soon as the four had hooked themselves together and started down the avenue, fog rose from the ground around them. It soon closed in and the silent voices guided them down the treacherous path to their campsite. They emerged in the late afternoon. Wesley asked Pol if the fog was always there.

"It is always and never there," Pol said. He pointed back the way they had come into camp and there was no sign of fog. They could see far up the mountain. It was simply one of the mysteries of the City of the Gods.

"I recall that in mythology, the gates of Olympus were always shrouded in fog and one could not pass without the company of the seasons—the four goddesses that guarded the gates. It seems appropriate for a City of the Gods," Doc said.

11

To Become a Witch

Tuesday, 21 June 1955, Northern England

DEAREST HUSBAND WESLEY,
I hope you can read this. I'm on a bus. Such beautiful country here in the north. So unlike London. But then, we really didn't see much of London since we stayed in our hotel room. I'm sorry the time of the month was such that I was likely not fertile on our honeymoon. I doubt there is a child yet in my womb. But, oh, my dear, I long to have you in me again. I want to bear your child.

My adjustment to life in Edinburgh has been chaotic. I was thrust immediately into intense research by my advisor. It is going well and I have discovered several sources I could only dream of in Indianapolis. The library here at the university is fantastic. I could read in the manuscripts room for years and not finish the relevant texts. There are even some that I have put away to save for my PhD. And just walking in the halls gives one such a feeling of history. It is alive.

I am on a tour down to The Lake District of England. Once again, my advisor suggested strongly that I take this tour as it includes an ancient stone circle. It is a rugged and beautiful land. We came through Gretna where couples used to elope across the border. A lovely couple enacted the role of bride and groom in a mock wedding. They said they had been married for thirty years. That will be us one day.

I understand our need for secrecy, but I wish I had a direct address for you instead of depending on this priest, Brother El, to deliver my letters. I received your letter from Brindisi and can only say that I wish I had been in that lovely train carriage with you. I've heard that it is the only way to travel through Europe. I traced your route from Calais to Paris to Geneva to Milan to Rome to Brindisi, Italy, and then by boat to the Peloponnese. Please, Wesley, let us make that trip together! Just the names of the cities in which you changed trains make me feel romantic. I wanted to trace your travels from Patra, but only know that you are in the Plains of Thessaly. Please pass on to our friends that I have seen no sign of our nemesis and hope we have seen the last of him.

My darling, my love, I miss your loving arms so. I felt so safe and secure held in your embrace. I dream of you every night.

I am faithfully your loving wife,

Mrs. Rebecca Hart Allen

THE BUS BOUNCED violently as Rebecca finished her letter and her signature streaked across to the edge of the onionskin paper. She would send it via air mail tomorrow. They would sleep tonight in Keswick and explore the little towns around the lakes before returning tomorrow.

She grabbed her walking stick to keep it from falling and groaned. She squinted her eyes in discomfort. Writing on a bus while navigating the curves and ruts of the Northern English countryside might not have been the best idea. Her stomach rebelled against the tallow of a lunch of lamb and butter sandwiches.

She had almost become used to the meals of lamb and mutton that were served more frequently than beef in this country and in Scotland. For lunch today, though, she would have given anything for a good T-bone and would have been happy with a bologna sandwich. She was just thankful that food was the worst of the problems she had faced so far.

After she and Wesley parted in London, he for Greece and she for Scotland, it had taken no time at all to get settled in and actually begin working on her thesis. Her Scottish advisor, a very crusty old man who sneered at her premise, had immediately directed her to a half-dozen additional texts on Druidism and the various Fairy traditions of the region. Then he had told her that she simply must catch this two-day tour to the Lake District to be grounded in the reality of ancient ritual sites.

She pulled the brochure from her satchel as she put away her writing materials. They had visited Hadrian's Wall after Gretna, Scotland. There was something special about standing at the site that had been built by the Romans to protect the south from invading Picts. The whole place seemed still inhabited by the spirits of those long-dead defenders of civilization. She thought about 'old' buildings in Indiana and could not remember one more than 150 years old. Hadrian's Wall was nearly 2,000 years old. Everything here was ancient.

Another jolt on the bus sent the brochure flying from her hands and her eyes turning to the back of her head. Thank God, the last stop before the evening's end was coming soon. Looking at the brochure just made her sicker to her stomach than she had been. Castlerigg—a stone circle predating the great Stonehenge circle—was next on the tour. She leaned back against her seat and closed her eyes with a soft moan.

"Feeling poorly, sweet?" said the old woman in the seat next to Rebecca. "A little seltzer water would perk you up."

The woman had fallen noisily asleep shortly after Wordsworth's Cottage and Rebecca was surprised to find her awake and chattering as if she had been conversing all along.

"A bit nauseous from the bus ride," Rebecca answered. "I don't usually suffer from motion sickness, but the past few miles have been a little stressful." The past few miles had been along a single-track dirt road that seemed to have ruts in its ruts and had been interrupted only by a herd of sheep moving across ahead of them.

The strange old woman had delivered a running commentary on all aspects of the trip—Hadrian's Wall, The Lake Poets, and even the process of spinning wool. She had apparently taken this tour frequently. And the commentary went on. Now she talked of cures for headache, upset stomach, cramps, and a dozen other pains that Rebecca didn't realize she had until the woman itemized them. Under any other circumstances, Rebecca would have found the information on folk remedies fascinating. But her nausea was mounting, multiplied by the brush scraping along the windows with an irritating screech as the bus lurched along the track that was not wide enough for it.

"People think we didn't get motion sickness in the days of horse and carriage," continued the old woman, oblivious to Rebecca's discomfort. "Not true. I remember one time sitting behind a trotting horse in a buggy tottering back and forth, back and forth, back and forth with that incessant clippity-clop of the hooves in front and the awful smell of wet blankets making me so ill I couldn't walk for an hour after we finally stopped. Oh, I know the motion sickness all right. That day was one that I will never forget. Then there was my first train ride."

"Please," moaned Rebecca.

The old woman's words amplified Rebecca's feelings of nausea. She could hear the pulse pounding in her throat. She swallowed hard at regular intervals. Not since her first ride on a merry-go-round as a child had she felt so dizzy and ill. The memory only made it worse. Images faded in and out of her mind in rapid succession and she found herself unable to focus on anything.

"Of course, airplanes, I understand, are a completely different feeling," continued the old woman, oblivious to Rebecca's discomfort. "Not so much the motion as the altitude, though did you know air can be rough? Imagine! My friend Dorothy rode an airplane to visit her daughter in Canada. She said riding that aircraft was bumpier than the old Winchester rail line. Now *that* I find hard to believe. That is the worst rail line in this country. So, I asked her why she didn't go by ship? Any sensible person would stay as close to the earth as possible. And she said, she always gets seasick. And I said, well, you got sick anyway. And she said, yes, but it was over so much more quickly!"

The old woman laughed and Rebecca choked on the smile she attempted.

"My dear," she said. "You don't look at all well."

The bus lurched again and Rebecca nearly lost control, choking and coughing. Her companion offered a handkerchief, but it smelled of a sickly sweet perfume that doubled the effect of her nausea. Then the bus finally slowed to a stop.

"There is a cure for this sort of thing, dear," went on the old woman as they left the bus.

Rebecca gasped in a deep breath, attempting to inhale the whole out of doors, only to find that she was squarely in the exhaust of the bus. She forced down the bile again, unable to free herself from the tour group and the old woman. She wished she had Wesley to lean on. She felt terrible.

"Of course, it's an old witch cure," the woman continued, "but it won't harm you. Come this way and help me over the stile, dear. That's a good girl. Now just down the hill over here, there is a stream and an herb that grows there will have you feeling better in no time. Just come with me, dear."

Rebecca stumbled along with the old woman down the hill, tears streaming from her eyes. She wanted to tell the woman to just leave her alone and let her sit down, but the words choked in her throat. The old hag kept propelling her along toward the river and away from the group at the stone circle.

At last they reached the edge of the river and the old woman broke a stem from a weed that Rebecca did not recognize, crushed it and held it up to Rebecca's face.

"Here now, dear. Breathe deeply of this and you'll feel better in no time." Rebecca inhaled deeply and when the acrid aroma dawned on her senses, it was too late to shut it out. She threw herself away from the old woman and vomited, choking behind a low bush.

"Yes, dear. Best way to cure a motion sickness is to void yourself."

"What was that?" choked Rebecca, tears brimming into her eyes.

"Why, just what you needed," answered the old woman. "You want to be all clean and fresh. Here, now take a drink of water and clear your mouth. And let's wash your face. You'll feel much better in a few moments."

Rebecca was too weak to resist anything at this point and the old woman easily guided her to the riverbank to wash. She handed Rebecca a canteen. "Don't drink from the streams in the summer," she admonished. Apparently, however, it was fine to wash in it. She remembered the advice of her travel agent to never bathe in anything she couldn't drink. Rebecca could not quit crying. The physical purge was redoubled by an emotional one. *Wesley!* She wanted him. She ached to be near him, to hear his voice, to be one with him. She was so far away. So all alone. *Wesley.*

She lay on the river bank sobbing with her head cradled in the old woman's lap. She was rather a nice grandmotherly type. Rebecca slowly began to feel better. She would just lie here and wait a few more moments and thank the woman for her help. Then they would rejoin the tour group. The treatment had been a little brutal, but it did work. *Just for a minute,* Rebecca thought, *and then I'll be fine.*

She fell asleep, conscious only of the old woman stroking her hair and a voice softly crooning above her.

When Rebecca awoke, she was alone.

She was alone. It was dark. It was silent and a sour taste lingered in her mouth and in her nose.

The bus! The tour must have left without her. Abandoned her! That old hag had led her out of sight, let her go to sleep, and abandoned her! She scrambled to her knees to look at what she could see.

The moon was just cresting above the hill she had come down and she could see figures at the top of the hill. People were there. She beckoned her strength and called out. "Hello!" Her voice sounded muted, the sound not carrying beyond her nose.

"There, you're awake, dearie," said a voice from a few feet away. "I must have dozed off a bit myself. Well, we're all about now."

"You're here?" Rebecca said. She wasn't certain if it was good that the old woman was near or not.

"Well, yes, of course I'm here. Wouldn't go off and leave you to the wolves now, would I?" laughed the woman. Rebecca gasped. "Oh! Don't be frightened. There are no wolves hereabout. That I know of. But I wouldn't abandon you anyway."

"But what about the tour?" Rebecca asked.

"Oh, the bus is long gone. You're right about that. They don't wait and they don't count noses. Yes. From that perspective, we've been abandoned." The old woman crawled to her knees and slowly to her feet.

"I saw people at the top of the hill."

"Oh indeed," her companion said. "That's Carles. The wicked ones. Turned to stone centuries ago. You'd have trouble talking to them." The old woman brushed herself off and continued.

> Scarce images of life, one here, one there,
> Lay vast and edgeways; like a dismal cirque
> Of Druid stones, upon a forlorn moor...

"That's Keats, you know," she finished.

"Why? Why didn't you wake me to go to the bus? Why did you strand us out here? Who are you?" Controlled hysteria. That is the way Wesley would have described it. Well, she had a right to hysteria.

"My! Just a bit offensive, aren't we, dear? Why did you get ill and come down here begging me to get you water? Why did you go to sleep and not wake up no matter how I prodded you? Why did you go and strand us here? And who are you? Just tell me that. I'd like to know." The old woman stamped her feet. "I'll catch my death and you'll go on young and healthy as ever."

"No, I didn't. I didn't mean..." Rebecca stammered. "I mean... I'm sorry." She shook her head trying to comprehend the situation. "I'm confused. I just don't understand how this happened." She took a deep breath of the night air and started over. "I'm Rebecca Allen. I never did get your name."

"Careful who you give your name to, dearie," the old woman responded. "I already know who you are. No one else needs to know. That is your first lesson."

"How do you know...?"

"I've been following you here and there since you got to Edinburgh. As for my name, you'll soon find that you already know."

"Why have you been following me? What do you want?"

"See, there you go again. People do jump from bridge to water. You assume that because I've followed you, it is *me* who wants something. Quite the opposite. Nothing. Nothing could be further from the truth. I want nothing from you."

"Why follow me?" Rebecca had her purse clutched in her hand and glanced up the hill. She could probably walk back the way the bus had come as quickly as it had navigated the narrow track.

"You wish to know the secrets of the goddess, do you not? Of course, you do. Certain books are never drawn from the shelves of the University Library in Edinburgh unless one wants to know the secrets. You've drawn all the mystic texts from their dusty shelves. You've searched and catalogued. But have you found the answers you seek? You want more than idle curiosity demands. More than higher education requires. You want to *know*. Am I right?"

"Yes," Rebecca whispered. "I want to know."

"I am your guide between the worlds. Your sponsor before the goddess. Someone you would know as Mrs. Weed."

"Mrs. Weed that Dr. Heinrich told me about?"

"The same. Dear Phillip," said Mrs. Weed. "The Flame Keeper has sent me such an innocent initiate."

"Oh. I'm not really an initiate. I'm just doing a research paper." Even as she said the words, Rebecca knew that they were a lie. Yes, she was doing a research paper, but deep in her heart she knew she was, indeed, an initiate if this woman would teach her.

"And where has your research led you, child? To the very gateway between the worlds on Midsummer's Eve. You've read the texts, but they have no grounding for you. You want to see the inside of a coven first hand. Am I not right?"

"Will you show me a real coven?" Rebecca asked.

"That depends. You must answer some questions, and I must give you instruction. That is why we are out here alone. You don't see covens in the open. There are still laws that cover spiritual advice as fraud. We can't exactly go about proclaiming ourselves in the public library."

"Where are we?"

"At the foot of the hill beneath the ancient stone circle called Carles. Should you or I decide that it is not right for you to see the coven, a short hour's walk along this path will bring you to Keswick and our hotel."

"Carles? The stone circle we were to visit?"

"Yes, dear. The circle is known as Castlerigg in your tour book. But there is an ancient nickname, almost as old as the stones themselves. Carles means the place where the wicked ones were turned to stone. An act of the goddess, if you will. Of course, the poem of Keats recognized another aspect. He saw the stones as the imprisonment of the ancient Titans." Mrs. Weed had moved closer and Rebecca was surprised to find her so near when her gaze returned from the stones silhouetted in moonlight at the top of the hill.

"Now listen, dear." The old woman whispered, drawing Rebecca down to sit on the ground next to her. "There is only one way to truly know the goddess. If you wish to know her, you must fully *know* her. Otherwise you are no more than the men who write about her without knowing. Look at the moon above. No one understands the moon like a woman. Like you do, Rebecca. I've a story to tell you and when it is done, you must decide how deeply you want to learn the secrets you are seeking."

Rebecca settled down in the grass and calmed her heart. Now that she knew this was the Mrs. Weed Doc had referred her to, she was less nervous. The night was warm and if she had to walk a mile or two along the river beneath this beautiful summer sky, she could do that. In the meantime, she would listen. Doc would not have arranged this if he didn't think it would be worthwhile.

Mrs. Weed began her story.

THE MOON IS not the goddess, but she is represented there. Men seldom understand that unless they have encountered her in all her natural wonder. Even then, they often think of her as 'just a woman.' You may encounter such difficulties with your husband, but I believe you will find him much more willing to see the goddess in you than some men. Man's cycle is different than woman's. It is based on the sun. A woman's cycle is ruled by the moon. For three nights in each cycle, the moon is in darkness as the goddess herself has been.

Once, you see, the fair folk walked the earth. But more than that, they roamed the heavens and ruled the underground. Among those who ran freely across the earth's fertile plains was a queen. Let us call her Cordelia or Mother, as fairy names are strange to our tongue. At the same time, there arose a powerful king among the fair folk, but he knew only the arts of war. When all had been conquered, he and his soldiers fell into disarray. They marauded and stole, bringing goods and slaves into his underworld Castle Sidhe. Thus, all the land Cordelia loved became barren and wasted.

In the depth of winter, Mother, in her anger, pounded against the gates of Castle Sidhe.

The guardian of the gate challenged her saying, "You who assails the gate of the great King Gwyn, the white son of darkness. Have you the courage to pass through these gates? For know that it is better that you fall on my sword and perish than to come before Gwyn with fear in your heart!"

But as Mother, she approached this gate with perfect love and perfect trust in her heart.

She was stripped of all her clothes and jewels, all her royal accoutrements. She was bound hand and foot as all are bound who come before the White Son of Darkness. Thus hobbled, she came before the King.

He saw her and instantly desired her.

"Fairest of all the fair folk," said the king, "tarry with me. I will make you my bride and love you."

"Why do you destroy all that I love?" demanded Mother. "My world turns dark at the point of your sword. Release it and let it bloom!"

"Fair one, it is the nature of all things to die. Here in my castle they find rest and peace. Do not forbid your subjects such rest. But you are my heart's desire. Stay with me and love me."

She was moved by his pleas and stayed with him for three days and three nights and the moon was dark in mourning for her. But Queen Cordelia was not subject to King Gwyn and withheld herself from him. At the end of the third night, Gwyn was distraught for having his heart's desire withheld from him. And that was when Cordelia took the golden circlet from his head and he bowed before her. She worked the magic of the womb upon it and wore it around her neck.

"Now enter into me," she said. "This is the circle of rebirth. Enter into my womb and be born anew. Even death is not eternal. Everything passes, everything changes. My womb is the cauldron of rebirth. Enter into me and be reborn. As life is a journey into death, so death is but a passage into life. And so the wheel turns." And he entered her and lodged in her womb.

She returned to the plains of the earth, for there were none to stop her, and there, she gave birth to the king. And he became Gwythyr, the son of youth and joy, King of the Sun.

To this day, each year the Oak King dies and the Holly King takes his Queen to his castle below. And in the spring, the Oak King rises victorious again and returns his queen to her domain. The circle is ever turning.

REBECCA SAT BESIDE the old woman staring up at the sliver of moon high above the stones at the top of the hill. They seemed to come alive as she watched, shapes shifting in the night and in the shadows cast by the moon. They danced the eternal celebration of the cycle of life, death, and rebirth. She could feel the music and the longing in herself to join the dance. A primal urge.

The light of a fire flared among the stones and Rebecca was certain now that she saw shadowed shapes dancing in its light.

"Do you, Rebecca Allen, seeker, have the courage to assail the gates of Coven Carles? To be stripped of all and be bound hand and foot? To have your measure taken and enter into the circle of rebirth? For know that if you do, you will forever be changed."

12
Initiation

Tuesday, 21 June 1955, Northern England

DO I *have the courage?*
"What must I do?" she whispered. Old Mrs. Weed patted her hand gently.

"There are no observers," she said. "If you would watch, you must join. If you would join, you must come as the goddess entered through the gates of death."

Rebecca caught her breath, torn between her own religious morality and the desire to know. To participate in a surviving witch cult, however, might be more than she wanted to know. She took a deep breath and tried to let it relax her.

"You mean naked?" she asked weakly.

"Naked, bound, and hobbled, led by a true member of the circle," Mrs. Weed answered.

"Who?"

"Why, me, of course!"

Rebecca's heart pounded. She knew in her heart that this was what she wanted, but it was terrifying.

"Only my... husband has ever seen me like that. I don't know." Tears ran from Rebecca's eyes. She licked her lips and chewed upon the lower one. She could see the shadows at the top of the hill dancing and could now hear a drum beating—a rhythm her heart soon matched.

Intellectually, she had no problem with nudity, but she was from Indiana! No one there would ever consider... And it wouldn't just be a bunch of little old ladies like Mrs. Weed who told fortunes in gypsy camps. They could be normal people one might pass on the street, or in the halls of academia.

"I could never cheat on my husband. I would never..."

"Shh. Something that you must learn is that nudity is not an invitation to violation," Mrs. Weed said. "The goddess dwells within you. We of the circle honor the goddess. We would never violate her." Rebecca breathed a sigh of relief. Perhaps she could… "That is not to say that others in the circle will all abstain from sharing with each other. It is Litha, the summer solstice," the old woman continued. "Some might even ask if you are interested. You, however, are always the one in command of your body. No one will press you, even in the ecstasy of raising a cone of power."

That should be enough, Rebecca thought. If she was safe, then there would be no harm in being seen naked when everyone else was naked. She simply wouldn't look at anyone else. Her heart beat more rapidly as excitement quickly overcame reticence. What she had wanted throughout her studies was primary research in her field. If she could not observe, she could—would participate. The decision came through a conscious effort to shut off her nagging conscience.

"All right," she said, laying down her purse and pulling off her earrings. "What do I do? Quickly, before I have a chance to change my mind."

"First we bathe in the river. Yes, sure I will stay with you. I will share secrets with you as we cleanse ourselves."

As Rebecca swam near the shore, Mrs. Weed described the ritual and what would occur. Many of the coveners who were gathered had been on the bus with her all day and had come to welcome her to the circle. There would be representatives of the four lesser circles present for the celestial holiday.

"Precautions were taken centuries ago to conceal the true identities of witches so no one could accuse another of a capital offense. Your name will never be used though many of us socialize outside our gathering. In the circle, I am called The Water Maiden," the old woman said. "This is the name I was given when asked to carry the third of the four Faces of Carles, the cup. You have met another of the sergeants. Doc is called The Flame Keeper and bears the staff of the circle, the second face. It is rare to have all four faces gathered at once—perhaps once in a generation. Tonight, you will meet the keepers of the other two faces. Before we approach the circle, you need a name. I give you back your maiden name as a wild one who has come to the circle. You will be called The Hart."

She handed Rebecca a small towel. When Rebecca was dry, she obediently held out her hands and Mrs. Weed bound them with a light cord. Rebecca was reasonably certain that she could snap the bonds with little effort and breathed more easily. As she looked down, though, she saw that her nipples were hard and erect in the night air.

Rebecca let the name wash over her and discovered that as Mrs. Weed led her up the hill toward the standing stones, she was humming to herself.

THEY WERE VERY close to the great northern gate of the stone circle. Rebecca could see the fire in the center, but the circle appeared to be empty now that she was close enough to see.

"There is only one password that you must now have, Hart," Mrs. Weed said from behind her. "I give you perfect love and perfect trust. Enter with these."

A man's voice suddenly spoke from behind the stone on Rebecca's left. She panicked, ready to run. She knew that voice. He had found her.

"Who comes before the gates," the man demanded as he stepped from behind the stone and deftly placed the point of a long knife between her breasts. He was naked, his pale skin glowing in the darkness. On his head was an eyeless black hood. *It can't be him. It's just another English voice,* Rebecca admonished herself.

"It is I, The Hart, a child of earth and starry heaven," Rebecca said. Her voice quaked. The noise of her heart in her ears almost drowned his next words.

"Who speaks for you?"

"I, The Water Maiden of Carles, vouch for her," said Rebecca's companion. The challenge, however, was not yet over and the sword's point nearly forced Rebecca back a step.

"You are about to enter a vortex of power, a place beyond imagining, where birth and death, dark and light, joy and pain, meet and make one. You are about to step between the worlds, beyond time, outside the realm of your human life. You who stand on the threshold of the dread Mighty Ones, have you the courage to make the attempt? For know that it is better to fall on my blade and perish than to enter here with fear in thine heart!"

In spite of the story she had heard, the ritual phrasing of the challenge, and the careful coaching of Mrs. Weed, Rebecca felt the gatekeeper was in deadly earnest. Words struck her memory: *The best guides in the world cannot always get you safely through the gates of hell.* She summoned up her courage and the passwords that Mrs. Weed had given her.

"I enter the circle with perfect love and perfect trust."

For a moment, the blade bit more deeply into her flesh and she wondered fleetingly if she would be found worthy to enter the circle. Was there more that was expected of her? The polished blade glinted in the firelight. A quick warding gesture came between Rebecca and the Guardian.

"Blade, your duty is finished," Mrs. Weed said.

The pressure against her chest immediately released and the gate-keeper placed the point in the ground. He rose again before her and whipped the hood from his head. His face was smooth and young, shaved so closely you would almost think he had no facial hair beneath the closely cut blond hair on his head. Rebecca gasped. The Blade. He had said he was part of the family. Was this what he meant?

His eyes looked so much like Wesley's that Rebecca caught her breath. He leaned forward and kissed her lightly on the lips, never glancing at her naked body.

"Thus are all first brought into the circle, Hart," he said with a gentleness that belied the violence he had shown in Indiana. He seemed not to note her nakedness, but she had been unable to suppress a glance at his smooth physique. So like Wesley. "The High Priestess awaits at the altar." He stepped aside to allow Mrs. Weed to lead Rebecca to the altar on the east side of the circle.

A dozen people stepped from behind the stones all around the circle and the High Priestess arose from behind the altar stone itself. She was a woman, ten or fifteen years older than Rebecca, she guessed, and beside her stood a small blonde child, not more than nine or ten. Both were naked save a golden circlet around the priestess's head. The priestess took the string from Mrs. Weed and led Rebecca around the circle that had drawn close. All were naked. Most were women. At each of the points of the compass, they paused for an invocation. When they passed The Blade—Rebecca knew this was Ryan McGuire—the little girl rushed to him and he picked her up in his arms. Rebecca felt conspicuously on parade before the coveners and was thankful for the relative dark that at least hid her heightened blush, even if not her naked body.

When they returned to the altar, Rebecca stood facing the fire as the High Priestess knelt in front of her. To Rebecca's surprise, the priestess kissed Rebecca's feet and untied the cord that bound them.

"Blessed are your feet that bring you along the path of the goddess," the priestess said. She pulled Rebecca's hands to her and kissed the palms as she untied them. "Blessed are your hands that offer comfort and kindness in the name of the goddess." Rebecca gasped as the priestess leaned forward and kissed her mound, directly on the pubic hair. "Blessed is your sex, the cauldron of rebirth and gateway of the goddess into this world." The priestess stood and kissed Rebecca's left breast. "Blessed are your breasts that can nourish new life with the love of your heart." Finally, the priestess kissed Rebecca softly on the lips. Rebecca felt tears escape from her eyes as she welcomed the kiss. "Blessed are your lips that speak the sacred names and pass on the knowledge of the goddess."

Mrs. Weed assisted the priestess in using the string to measure Rebecca's height. With the remainder, they measured her head and knotted the length. Finally, they measured her bust and cut the string. The priestess rolled the string into a ball and pressed it into Rebecca's palm. Ryan McGuire stepped up beside the priestess, still carrying the little girl. He handed the priestess a finely engraved knife with an ebony handle. The priestess pricked Rebecca's finger with the tip of the blade and pressed the blood against the string before handing the knife back to McGuire. The little girl clapped.

"Your measure has been taken," said the priestess, "head, height, and heart. We hold this against a day when your witness is needed. Never shall you reveal the name or identity of any person in this circle. So you must swear."

"I so swear," Rebecca said.

She knelt before the assembled coveners and placed one hand beneath her heel and one on top of her head. After the priestess, she repeated, "All between my two hands belongs to the goddess."

For the first time since she had entered the circle the coveners broke their silence, all shouting at once, "So mote it be!"

"So mote it be," Rebecca whispered. She had crossed a threshold. She belonged to the goddess.

Sunday, 26 June 1955, City of the Gods

After a week of daily excursions to the strange city or temple, the group decided on a day of rest. They packed empty food containers and rubbish in a pack and trekked back to the drop-off point to replenish their supplies. Wesley placed a letter to Rebecca in the trunk. He understood that the monk, Brother El, would be by sometime this week to refill the trunk and take any messages to be posted. It was a strange arrangement, but no one else, even Brother El, would be brought to the base camp by the old olive tree.

The group prepared their evening meal and Pol did some sleight of hand for their entertainment. He was working on new tricks and was as absorbed in his magic as the rest of the team was in the City of the Gods.

"Pol," said Doc, "neither Wesley nor Margaret have actually heard the legend of Serepte. I'm afraid my telling of it leaves much to be desired. You did such a good job of telling it the last time I was here. Would you mind telling it again?"

"I will be happy to tell of Serepte," said Paul, "but it will not be the same story. What I told before was what I had heard. What I must tell now is what I have seen."

The first thing Doc noticed was that Pol's storytelling had matured since the last trip. He was surprised that a twelve-year-old's frame of reference could allow for more than a recitation of the romantic tale. It was obvious, though that the boy's love for the story and the characters had only increased.

"The story of Serepte has been passed down through my family for many generations. My father taught it to me as his father taught him. Those who choose not to follow the ancient paths forget. My family alone keeps the mystery of the mountain city alive. I may have been one like my father who chose to depart from the ancient ways, had not the great powers intervened to awaken me with prophecy. It happened like this." With that, Pol's demeanor changed and he spun a tale the captured the hearts of his listeners.

ON MY TWELFTH birthday, I was led to the holy place. One can only come to the holy city by way of revelation. To those who seek without the blessings of the gods, no fulfillment comes. Those who are ready to believe, the gods bring into their presence, even if they seek not. Such a one was I—believing, though I did not understand. I was brought to the holy of holies, into the presence of the principalities of the worlds.

The King brought me into his presence. On his left were cupbearers. On his right a feast was spread. The winds sang in his halls and he floated upon a throne of sunlight. The stars were his crown and all the worlds sat at his feet. The King summoned me to his feet and lightning flashed around him. I was afraid.

Behind the Ivory Veil

"Mortal," spoke the awesome one, "your little belief is the herald of great things. Understanding will burst in upon you like the dawn of a new day when day has truly dawned. Your kindred have waited long. Your service to this shrine nears its end. Nor will the gods neglect your reward, accumulated for generations in these hallowed halls. Answer mortal: Who is this you see before you?"

And I looked and behold I saw a serpent climbing the rod of one who stood in the stars. And I answered and said, "It is Asklepios, the healer." Asklepios was the son of Apollo by the deceitful Koronis. Apollo plucked him from his mother's womb on her funeral pyre. Thus he came to fulfill the prophecy of Chiron the Centaur that he would never be born but would see death twice. Then, as immortal, he took as wife Iasis Epione, the goddess called Health.

"You are instructed well, mortal," spoke the awesome one. "See how your guardians, Cynthia and Cynthius, smile upon you. You are taken as son to Asklepios and your grandfather grants you his name. Rise Apollion and observe both history and prophecy."

And I arose and stood between the Cynthian twins, Apollo and Artemis. And he who was now my grandfather showed me history through his eyes. I knew the pain of Koronis's deception. My fury cursed the white raven black. And as Artemis stretched her bow, my will guided the arrow to the heart of Koronis. Remorse heaped itself upon grief upon anger as I saw the funeral pyre kindled. The flames leaped up to consume the body of my one-time love, her unborn son still locked within her womb. Some pain, a mortal is not made to know. Seeing through Apollo's eyes, blurred with immortal agony, I begged him—no, commanded him—to save some remnant of his love. And so, with hands ablaze in the funeral pyre, we snatched forth the unborn son from the unyielding womb and, without birth, brought him into mortal life. I carried my son-father to the cave of Chiron to raise him and heard the prophecy of the twice dead, mortal and immortal child.

But things mortal are doomed to die. And thus, to appease an angered Hades, Zeus struck down the healer for daring to reclaim a life from the darker god. Thus did Asklepios have death at the beginning and the end of his life.

Then my guardian Artemis guided my eyes through her own, for Apollo's were filled with tears. She showed me how Asklepios was restored to eternal life among the gods and became renowned after his death as a healer greater than before. She feasted me at the wedding that joined Health, Iasis Epione, to Asklepios.

Then the King spoke again and the voice like thunder whispered. "You have seen the pain brought by untrue love. You will see what joy may be yours through the love ordained by the maker of all. Behold your mother." And a sound of singing filled the air. I saw nine sisters dancing in the temple, the music filling all who heard with joy. But one among the sisters pined for love lost. This was the lyric muse whose tones were sweeter and purer than all other living creatures. She it was who loved Asklepios and mourned because he was wed to Health. But unlike jealous gods before her, she forsook the way of Hera and turned her painful love to the service of her rival. She I knew as mother.

Euterpe sang a song of devotion deep and sincere. Its chords were strong as fiber, as pure as ivory. They wove in and through each other like silk. As the mesh of music enclosed about her, she was seen to look after Iasis so longingly, so devotedly, that it was as if a mirror reflected the very image of Health behind the veil of music. I beheld this as if I, too, were behind the ivory veil. All others were held without and could not see in. Behind the veil was a shrine to Health, the veiled goddess. Euterpe cut her hair and laid it upon an altar. In its place grew locks so like Iasis that were it not for the finely woven veil that parted them, one might have thought that Health had passed in and Euterpe disappeared.

But here I found the greater mystery. So complete was this reflection that when Iasis grew with child, Euterpe's body changed as well. Hygiea and Serepte were born within an hour of each other, twin sisters of different wombs. In Euterpe's arms lay a child born of desire, conceived by empathy.

Great Zeus commanded Euterpe's presence and through that veil which she had woven, she passed without a mark. But Serepte, who would join her, found the wall as hard as stone. I was torn, for though mere mortal, I knew that I could follow Euterpe if I so desired. But to look upon that child, born of impossible desire, would bring a man to leave mother, hearth, and home. I was her playfellow and loved her. I stayed to bring her happiness and company as we grew up together.

Our home behind the veil was always as large as we wished, and yet for warmth at night we could draw it in around us like a blanket. Love grew there as flowers in a garden. As we climbed one day to the peak of a mountain to look down at the clouds, my mortality caught up with me and I fell. I knew my time would be short in this land of bliss where my love and I played together. My broken bones cried out from within me as I lay at the foot of the peak. My love, my beautiful Serepte, came and cradled me in her arms. Her hair, taken from the altar where her mother had lain it, adorned her with beauty beyond compare. Her silken gown fell about her in soft folds. Her arms lifted me and in love carried me to her birthplace where first we met. Her tears washed my brow and she bound my wounds with kisses from her lips as she sang to me songs of love. I looked and saw that it was not I alone who had been injured, for her brow bled and bruises were on her delicate arms. The legs with which she carried me were crippled just as mine. And I beheld that my legs were strong and my brow no longer bled.

I lifted my love, my beautiful love, upon that couch where she had laid me and listened as she sang words and music that filled my soul and washed away my fears. We stood in another world and there the pain dissolved and took on new forms in the music that she sang. And her hymn reached the heavens as we wafted back to that place, our marriage bed.

But here my vision ceased. I stood no longer behind the ivory veil, nor did Zeus call me back into his presence. I knew that all had fled to places in the heavens. But in the city remained one with whom I was already bound. Her voice whispered yet across the wind to me and pledged me to her love. I know that even though I may not deliver her, mine will be the reward.

THE STORY AROUSED strong feelings in Wesley as he listened. He lay back enjoying senses that awoke in thinking about Rebecca. When the story ended, it was only he who spoke.

"I would like to see your Serepte, Pol. I would like to meet her very much."

13

Beware the Night

Friday, 8 July 1955, City of the Gods

DURING THE following days, the story haunted Wesley. He questioned Pol more in depth about the story, the promised deliverer, the origins. He wrote songs and poems about the goddess, some of which he included in his weekly letters to Rebecca. She became his own goddess.

The crew continued to meet each day at the central rostrum to strategize their work. A profusion of writing decorated the rostrum and this, Wesley was assigned to copy and begin translating. There was also writing on the base of nearly every pillar in the forest that surrounded the platform. The three examined several of the pillars and with their combined knowledge of Greek and Wesley's linguistic abilities when they encountered the hieroglyphs, they pieced together one or two myths. The stories were told in first person by the character involved. They identified the pillars by the character and event represented in the story. Their first significant discovery was that the twelve pillars closest to the rostrum were named for the twelve principal deities of Greece and corresponded to the twelve signs of the zodiac inscribed on the edge of the rostrum.

Doc and Margaret moved outward, systematically plotting the names and positions of the pillars. Wesley and Pol set to work at the rostrum, Wesley copying the symbols carefully while Pol juggled or practiced magic tricks. The two got along well and frequently laughed at odd little bits of trivia.

The designs on the rostrum were a complex set of geometric designs, overlaid with hieroglyphs, overlaid again with ancient Greek characters. That was Wesley's analysis. There was, however, a constant nagging at the back of his mind that he was missing something. He tried a half-dozen systems for drawing the patterns to scale. On one part of his drawing the figure was barren. On another it was too crowded to read.

Beginning on one side and working inward left him with a funnel of data that got wider as he approached the center instead of smaller. It was plain by this approach that the contents of the circle took up more room than the circle itself.

Wesley sat at the edge of the rostrum with Pol, biting into dried beef strips for lunch and puzzling over the process. So far, he was getting nowhere. He dug into his satchel for inspiration in the name of a sharp pencil, finally dumping the entire contents out on one of the flat stones. Having found a pencil, he began replacing the contents. Candles, matches, gloves, electric torch, spare socks, button thread. He paused, looking at the spool of button thread in his hand.

"Pol," he said, finally, "will you give me a hand for a moment?"

The boy willingly held one end of the thread on the symbol of Aries as Wesley stretched the line across to Libra. Here he cut the thread and they let it lie across the rostrum. Then taking a fresh end, Pol held it on the sign of Cancer as Wesley stretched the line to Capricorn. Once again, he cut the thread and laid it on the rostrum.

"Thank you," said Wesley.

"What did we do?"

"Well, if our ancient architects were at all symmetrically inclined, we have just located the precise center of the rostrum. And even if they were not, we have laid out uniform repeatable quadrants. I can work from the center point out to map the circle, just as Doc and Margaret are doing with the pillars."

Pol was impressed, though Wesley had his doubts whether he understood. At the moment, however, he was more interested in finding what lay precisely at the center of this circle. Pol leaned over Wesley's shoulder to examine the crosshairs.

"What is it?"

"A star," said Wesley. There at the center of the pattern was an incongruous, perfectly proportioned, five-pointed star, so finely etched in the slab that it seemed almost like a mosaic.

"It's even a different color," Pol said.

"Yes. Now that you mention it and we have isolated this one, you can see veins of color running all through the orchestra. Very faint. Blue. Green. See?"

The two stood on the rostrum looking down at the crosshairs formed by the thread. Wesley laid an arm around Pol's shoulders and gave him a squeeze.

"It is important, isn't it?"

"I don't know," answered Wesley. "Doc knows much more about significance as opposed to something being merely pleasing. But it *is*, somehow, inspiring."

Wesley knelt to begin sketching the design once again. This time he sketched the crosshairs vaguely, indicating the signs at each end. Then he carefully penciled in the star at the center. The two talked as Wesley continued drawing, marking off sections within the section with additional pieces of string.

"You drew the string from Spring to Autumn and Summer to Winter," Pol commented, surprising Wesley. "And the star is aligned to those directions." Wesley looked at his sketch and again at the star in the center of the rostrum. He had drawn from a different position, but when he moved to what was obviously the base of the star he saw that the arms definitely stretched parallel to the spring/fall line and the crosshair stretched through the upper point and between the legs of the star from summer to winter.

Thursday, 14 July 1955, City of the Gods

IT WOULD BE a long job to even come close to an accurate mapping of the rostrum. Of course, when Doc and Margaret had joined 'the boys', as they called them, there was a flurry of photography as they photographed the star and each quadrant of the rostrum. They would need more film with Brother El's next delivery.

Pol gladly worked with Wesley, even drawing some of the symbols when he was not juggling. And their discussions took on a depth that was both refreshing and surprising. The boy was not, and did not pretend to be, a theologian, but Wesley attended what he said as if he were the twelve-year-old Jesus teaching in the temple.

"I believe the stories," Pol said, "but I do not understand them. Why are we made guardians of *ta hagia hagion*? When all the gods have flown to the heavens, why do we preserve the mystery of the one left behind?"

"I don't know, Pol. Why don't you make the choice that your father made and become a Christian?"

"But my father taught me the stories. He still believes, even though he embraces the new faith. And there is no one else to give charge of the stories to."

"Maybe that is why you must keep the mystery safe." Wesley had begun to show as much compassion for Pol's beliefs as Pol respected

Wesley's. One thing that he was learning on this journey was that he had a far greater capacity for belief than he was aware of.

As the day drew to a close, Doc and Margaret returned to the rostrum and looked again at Wesley's quadrants, carefully laid out again that morning. Wesley and Pol began rolling up the thread and stowing it in his pack.

"That is an idea we could expand upon," Doc mused. "In a climate as still and dry as this, we could save a lot of re-tracking in the morning if we sectioned off the pillars we have identified by laying a piece of string around them. Ultimately, we would have quadrants laid out throughout the city. Nothing living here to disturb them but ourselves."

"No." Pol's voice was small but commanding. "You see nothing alive here, but it is a living place. Even a thread might bind a god that mortals would break without thought."

"They don't change places, do they, Pol?" Margaret asked.

Wesley laughed. "That's ridiculous."

There was a long pause and Wesley knew he had misspoken. He was drawn back in his mind to the patterning of the rostrum. He was sure there was a connection.

It was Pol who once again broke the silence.

"It is time to go." He marched down the Cancer Avenue. It had been named by the group according to the sign on the rostrum in that direction. They were reasonably certain that this was east. It was the route they entered and exited by. They linked together and followed Pol as fog closed in on them again.

When they emerged from the fog, the sun was still glimmering on the horizon and they had adequate time to locate their gear and light small lanterns before cooking the simple meal at dusk. The skies had stayed reasonably clear at the base camp with occasional wisps of cloud floating overhead.

Wesley sat huddled in silence with the pages of drawings he had made laid one over the other on the ground in front of him. The dim lantern light did not make reading easy when the last light of day faded from the sky. Not far away, Doc and Margaret were huddled in a similar position with papers spread between them, talking in low tones. Pol, it seemed, had gone to sleep shortly after dinner. Wesley, too, was tired enough his eyes were blurring. They played tricks with the symbols, leading him to believe he could see through them, superimposing fragmented lines over one another. His mind painted the colors over the figures that he had seen on the rostrum. In the middle, spun the star.

In the half-awareness brought on by approaching sleep, Wesley's mind slipped into channels he would consciously block. It was like this when he first made the leap from Wilton's notes to musical language. He jerked awake to refocus on the maps in front of him. It was a strange way to draw maps, but if every direction led to the same point, then that point had to lie in every direction from all other points. The rostrum would be represented by the circumference of its circle, the avenues of pillars by the design inside.

He jerked himself awake again to stare at the patterned drawings laid one over the other, wondering what made him think of maps. This was a great mandala—a patterned design that held the secret of ancient faiths. He lost himself in the patterning of the mandala drawn into its rhythm. He was unaware of the fact that he hummed as he worked. His tongue worked against the roof of his mouth, clicking out time as his voice wandered through the maze of the mandala. He was unaware that Doc and Margaret stopped working and stared at him. He did not notice that Pol opened his eyes from sleep to look and listen.

When preparing for the trip, Wesley had carefully explained the use of voice as an instrument when discussing musical language.

"An oscilloscope will show that there is pitch in every sound," he lectured to Doc and Margaret. "When we hold the notes and speak them at different rhythms, we essentially have music. But part of the mystique of the voice is that the notes are not clear. We vibrate with overtones and undertones. It is what separates a folksinger from an opera singer. The opera singer spends years training his voice to hit pure notes, hence the oft-referenced ability to burst a crystal wine glass with a sustained vocal note. It is not just hitting the right note and having the right volume. It is the purity of the note. On the other end of the spectrum, a crooner might have a wide range of overtones that enhance the emotional impact of the music—or that detract from it in some cases. I have heard of a choir in Bulgaria that can actually split their voices into two or more concise tones, though with the communists in control, I suppose I will never get to visit there. The voice is a mysterious instrument and can mimic many different orchestral parts. I find that when the piano is inadequate or the guitar has too little range, adding the voice will enhance the emotional impact of the music."

The voice—Wesley's voice—brought forward the mysteries of the symbols.

HE FOCUSED ON the star at the center. The voices played through him, following one channel until it broke off, then skipping abruptly to another, radiating from the star in primitive skipping patterns—five beats—pentamic syncopation. The primeval voices kept rising within and around him.

Fear. Beware the night. I am captive of the night. Who in his cleanness is pure? Who can face himself in the clear reflection of his mind at midnight? The darkness is unbroken.

The images that flooded their minds were brutal, what Doc later described as Dionysian. There was, pent up in the tones, a ravishing of being, made all the more unpleasant by the shape and eerie light of the waning moon. There was nothing bearing a sign of hope—nothing that permitted the hearers even that small cathartic of a complete act. It was primitive to the root of its character. When it ended, they sat stunned into silence, immersed in the nightmare conjured by Wesley's voice.

Each awoke from the dream as a softer, more plaintive and beautiful lay called them back to reality. As they listened and relaxed, they realized that Pol was singing, perhaps had been singing for a long time. Each found comfort and hope in the soft searing tones. Without discussing the images that each had shared during this bizarre interlude, the group retired to their bedrolls and went off to sleep as Pol continued to sing.

Thursday, 14 July 1955, Edinburgh, Scotland

REBECCA WOKE FROM her sleep with a shiver, certain someone was there. Every sudden occurrence in the past three weeks had sent that foreboding chill across her senses. She could feel the tracery of the knife held against her breast. He was a creature of the night—one with the darkness that surrounded her—a phantom stalking her through her dreams.

No! He was not there. His subtle insinuations were not real. It was a dream. Of course, he was still in Scotland or England, but not here. Not now.

What was it then? What had called her up out of a deep sleep? She could still hear that vague ringing in her ears that all but overpowered the shallow breathing of Mrs. Weed a few feet away. It was almost a melody, almost an agony, too primitive for words. *But the impact!* An involuntary shudder shook her limbs again. This was no mere foreboding, but an outright warning. It called her to awaken, take notice, protect herself with every ounce of her strength.

She had never been afraid of the dark, but now it seemed too close for her. She could scarcely breathe. The room was hot and sweat trickled off her brow as she lay rigidly in bed.

"Alice?" The word forced its way from her mouth with the hope that a whisper would awaken the sleeper with whom Rebecca had shared a room since her initiation into the coven.

"What is it, Becca?" asked Mrs. Weed. Alice Weed was the widow of a Professor Weed at the University, whose writings on goddess worship were primary texts during Rebecca's study in Edinburgh. "I heard you wake, Becca. What did you dream?"

"It wasn't a dream, Alice. It was too real. I heard a warning."

"Yes?" probed her friend. She could feel the effect in the darkened room.

"Why should I fear the night? I've never been frightened of the dark. But Wesley…" Rebecca made the unexpected connection between the primitive music and Wesley's voice. "Wesley warned me to beware the night."

"You are certain it was your husband?"

"Yes. It was Wesley's voice as I have never heard it before. It was as if he was wringing out my lungs when he sang. I couldn't breathe. The dark was suffocating me."

"Could it have been meant for one of his companions?" Mrs. Weed asked.

"I don't know. Can we turn on a light?"

"I've a candle here." Rebecca turned her head away as light flared near Alice's head. She had probably just lit a match, but Rebecca did not want to see. Too many strange things. She turned her head slowly back toward her companion to see the old lady swing her feet out of bed, holding the candle in one hand.

"Stay still, dearie. You needn't move," she said as Rebecca started to rise. Rebecca relaxed back on her pillow and watched as Mrs. Weed, The Water Maiden, silently invoked the guardians of each direction and placed herself into a mild trance. "Now, Hart, just look at the candle. Focus on the flame. It dances a single dance to all music. The flame is the center of all that is. The flame is the heart and soul, now leaping in ecstasy, now quivering in fear. The flame is the center of your being. You see the flame. You are the flame. Let your mind be one with the flame."

Only Rebecca's open, transfixed eyes were a clue to the non-sleep trance she entered. Soon, they, too, slowly slid closed. This time there were no dreams, no nightmares, no warnings. Sleep was deep, opaque, and solemn.

Mrs. Weed turned her own gaze to the candle. For a long time, she stared silently into the dancing flame and then began to intone low syllables. At first, they were scarcely audible, never more than a whisper. She quested deeply into the lingering presence of the warning—felt the intensity of its impact on Rebecca. Yet, deep in the primitive howling of the spell, she found hope. A key to the trusting, the pure, the innocent. There was a throbbing, seductive presence that spoke beneath the booming warning which said, "Come. Come. Come."

She held her right hand above the candle, feeling its heat, not quite close enough to burn. She searched in the candle for the essence of the light. She searched it with her hands and her mind. After several minutes, she lifted her right hand with the candle in her left slowly sinking. As they parted, the flame lengthened, drawn upward by the movement until, at last, it split. A clear ball of light was held in the palm of her right hand.

"Ancient powers of the night, hear thy servant. We have heard thy warning. We stand before you to consecrate within The Hart thine promise as ward against all evil."

Mrs. Weed knelt beside Rebecca and guided the globe of light above the sleeping woman's head.

"May love guide your steps and light your path. May you be a light in the darkness when danger surrounds and dispel the danger as darkness flees. All this may you do to claim promise, hope, and love in the midst of remorse, in the depths of despair."

The light slipped from her hand and came to rest on Rebecca's forehead. Here it paused and was gradually absorbed into the flesh of the sleeping woman. Her face glowed as the light sank deeper within her. Mrs. Weed raised her hands to the sky.

> By all the power of three times three
> This spell bound around shall be
> To do no harm, nor turn on me;
> As I do speak, so mote it be.

Sunday, 1 August 1937, South Whitley, Indiana

WESLEY DREAMED. IT was not the first time in his ten years of life he had this dream. It was one of his earliest memories. Nor would the dream ever seem to release him. But this night it was so real that when he awoke for church in the morning, he thought he was still dreaming.

HE STANDS IN a cornfield with the farmhouse about two hundred yards away over his right shoulder. The corn is high, but it doesn't obstruct his view. He faces east to watch the sunrise. It's good to know the directions. He wouldn't get lost. Every direction has a purpose.

History is in the east. The Revolutionary War, Philadelphia, Washington, DC, and across the ocean, England, the Roman Empire, Jerusalem. East contains all the glorious past of the world—the foundation of history and the origin of humanity. Eden is in the East.

He turns slowly to his right. The south is a strange country of the wild frontier. The slavers of the Confederacy threaten another Civil War. Mountain men with illegal stills feud with one another. The heat of the sun beats down on the South, and beyond lie the Aztec ruins of Mexico and the jungles of the Amazon. South is a hot, wild, threatening place.

Farther to his right he faces the setting sun over the maple grove that parts him from the city. He must have taken a long time in turning, following the sun, to now see it setting. The City. Not just the local business center, but Chicago—the only city he has ever visited. The City holds Christmas where people gather in great crowds to shop in the stores of the Loop. The City had more people than he imagines the rest of the world to have. West is not wild; it is the most civilized place he knows.

Finally, his slowly spinning arc of the compass brings him to face the darkness of the northern skies. But North is not threatening. North is a promise of faith and safety. Michigan is north. He'd visited relatives there. And beyond Michigan is the Yukon. Here, Aurora Borealis ruled. He stands quietly waiting for the flash of brilliance to come. If ever there is trouble, North is the holy place, the direction to run for protection. He would climb the Northern Steps to the holy temple of Aurora Borealis. Vast open gentle steps away from the violence and worry of the world. Ever up the steps. All directions are North now. If only he could reach the temple, he would stay with the three sisters of his dreams, Shirley, Goodness, and Mercy, following him all the days of his life, dwelling in the house of the Lord forever.

And he would never again fear the night.

14
The Cup

Thursday, 28 July 1955, Edinburgh, Scotland

REBECCA AWOKE alert and refreshed. She'd had uncommonly restful nights for the past two weeks, possibly related to the exhaustion she experienced, first through her research and second through the instruction she had been receiving from Mrs. Weed. The sun cracked through the fog that seemed present every morning in this part of Edinburgh, and streamed through her window. The amount of energy she felt this morning crackled up and down her spine. The gift she had received from the woman sleeping in the second bed across the room seemed to lift her up.

Alice Weed, her sponsor and friend and now roommate, slept on noisily into the dawn. Rebecca smiled. In the weeks since her initiation, the woman had become a mother to her.

Friday, 24 June 1955, Edinburgh, Scotland

THREE DAYS AFTER her initiation, Dr. Reston, her advisor, approached Rebecca following his lecture.

"How are you settling in, Mrs. Allen?" he asked.

"Life has been a bit hectic," she admitted. "I spent part of last week at the embassy getting my passport changed to my married name. I didn't anticipate such difficulty. This week... Shall we say I discovered resources I never imagined existed."

"I'm not surprised. All the older legends of the British Isles are heavily dosed with the worship of the goddess. How are your lodgings?" asked the professor.

"I admit the boarding house is a bit stressful," she answered. "Mark it up to my being a spoiled American. We always expect a level of, shall we say, convenience."

"Or to be pandered to," laughed Dr. Reston. Rebecca knew he was at least partly serious. "Sharing a bath with four other women, I assume could be a hardship. That is why I took the liberty of talking to an old friend. She has expressed a willingness to board you in more private quarters for the summer if you'd like."

"I would be interested in speaking with her."

"Her cottage is in Musselburgh, so you might need a bicycle to get to the university, but the opportunity to have quiet while you study will likely be worth the seven miles you need to pedal. I've written down her information for you. She is expecting your call. It is a quick trip by black cab." He handed her a slip of paper and Rebecca started as she read the information.

"Is this…?"

"The widow of Dr. Weed, whose treatise you investigated this week. I told her of your interest and she suggested you visit her. She still has many artifacts from Dr. Weed's illustrious career. You should go today."

REBECCA FOUND HERSELF on the doorstep of a lovely cottage, in sight of the Firth of Forth. When the door opened a smiling Mrs. Weed greeted Rebecca.

"Mrs. Weed…"

"Alice, dearie. We know each other well enough to be first name friends when we are together, don't you think?"

"You can't imagine how happy I am to see you. I was afraid that… I don't know. It seemed almost like a dream."

"Now, Becca, you have adequate evidence, I think, that what has happened has indeed happened. Come in. Come in, girl. You must have a thousand questions."

Rebecca did have questions but scarcely knew where to start. The two women had 'tea' from four in the afternoon to nearly midnight. Rebecca was shown a room with two single beds where she and Mrs. Weed would sleep. It was still better than the five women in the boarding house. Their conversation centered on the craft and thealogy, reflection on the feminine divine.

"You have come one long step, Becca. You have entered inside the circle of the goddess. But that does not necessarily mean that you must go further. Perhaps you already have enough information to write your thesis."

"I certainly have more than enough to satisfy my degree," responded Rebecca. "But I have not begun to satisfy myself. When I entered the circle, there was a feeling of warmth, even overcoming the fear I had. It was a sense of homecoming. It's strange, isn't it? I thought I would feel dirty or sinful, but I don't sense a conflict between being a good Christian and being a good witch. It was like God was there with me."

"That He was, child. Our coven has never denied His presence or workings. We simply accept that there is more to the universe than is revealed in one set of holy writings," Mrs. Weed said.

"How can I learn more?"

"Well, now, since you've asked, I suppose that I can teach you. I wouldn't consider it but what you insist. It's no place for a fine young Christian girl like yourself."

"Alice," laughed Rebecca, "you can't be serious!"

"I'm very serious. I would not consider teaching you the craft if it were not that you asked, and then only because I think it may stand between you and danger."

Rebecca remembered words that continued to haunt her dreams. *The best guides in the world cannot always get you safely through the gates of hell.* She could certainly not be guided unless she devoted herself to learning.

"What do you mean by standing between me and danger," she finally asked.

"I saw a spark of recognition between you and The Blade at the circle. Yes, I know you have had doubts—or perhaps hopes—but it was he. I don't know what is between you, but I dare say it has to do with dear Phillip and the adventure your husband is on. You and The Blade are now members of the same coven, though of different circles. He is of Threlkeld and you are of Braithwaite, my circle. The Flame Keeper, whom you also know, is a coven brother, but he chose not to pursue the craft, only to link in fellowship through the circle at High Lodore. The Blade follows the craft with a vengeance. He might be the best ritual magician I've ever met. I suspect, however, that he dabbles on the dark side. I fear for him."

"What should I do?"

"Do? Why, doing nothing is always the best defense, but not if faced by a demon. The Blade is under the protection of the circle, just as you are, but God knows what he might do if you meet outside our sphere of influence. If you have any talent at all, I can teach you enough arcane wisdom in a fortnight to counteract most of what he might throw at you magically. However, his passion and skill with a knife are unmatched."

"How did he get so attached to knives?"

"That's a fine place to begin your teaching. A witch, which you must know we are still called, uses four tools in the ritual practice of her craft..."

Wednesday, 27 July 1955, Edinburgh, Scotland

"EVERY MEMBER HOLDS responsibility in a coven," Alice instructed. She was preparing Rebecca for the coming ritual at Lughnasad in just ten days. It would be the first time she had returned to the stone circle since her initiation and Rebecca was thrilled. "In Cobhan Carles, the tool keepers are of great significance. They are all brought together only for the working of powerful magic. It has happened during the times when there was open revolt in our country, when a tool needed to be replaced, when danger to the coven arises, and even to help Britain withstand the assault of the Germans."

"You went to war?" Rebecca asked.

"In a manner of speaking. You must understand that magic is a very real thing and Hitler was known to employ his own dark coven to attempt to weaken his enemies. We bound ourselves together with other covens throughout the country and fought the battles on a spiritual plane."

"What are the tools and who keeps them?"

"The First Face of Carles is the *Athamé*, called Creüs, ruler of the air spirits. It is in the keeping of The Blade. You saw him as the gatekeeper of the circle, but that is a position that is delegated for each gathering. The gatekeeper is responsible for the integrity of the wards around our circle—to see that nothing malevolent gets in. The Second Face of Carles is the wand, Iäpetus, ruler of the fire. It is a staff about chin-height in length that you have seen in the care of the one we call The Flame Keeper. The Third Face of Carles is in my keeping. It is the cup called Cottus, ruler of the water. And finally, the Fourth Face of Carles is the pentacles, Enceladus, ruler of earth. It is currently in the keeping of our high priestess, The Earth Mother. While the bearers of the tools may change, it is always a member of the circle charged with its keeping."

"What responsibility will I have in the coven?" Rebecca asked.

"When it is time for you to take responsibility, the coven will direct you. You need time to be instructed in the workings of the circle first. Sometimes it is several years before a member is called to her full charge."

"Would a tool do to me what it has done to The Blade? Take over my personality?"

"Power is neutral. People make such decisions, not the tool. The Blade had a fascination with knives long before he became a keeper. His little girl is much the same way. She is ten years old and is already training as a fencer with Olympic hopes when she is sixteen."

"She seemed so young and innocent. I was surprised to see a child in the circle," Rebecca said.

"Her mother is the high priestess and she was conceived during the raising of power as we fought the Germans. So, you see, she has been part of the circle since conception."

"What is she called?"

"Last time we met she was just The Point. The time before, she called herself Epi. She is young and not fully initiated into the circle, which cannot happen until her first woman's blood flows. Until then, she chooses a name according to her mood at the moment."

Alice rose to retrieve her own sacred tools from a shelf. These she set on the table between them. Then she also brought a pewter goblet, heavily engraved with runes, to the table.

"We need a space in which to work. Follow me and repeat the words I say. As we finish each spell, draw a summoning pentagram in the air. We will begin in the East." Mrs. Weed had often cast a warding circle when she taught Rebecca rituals, so the words and gestures were familiar to Rebecca as they worked from east to south to west to north and finally, back to the east where they closed the circle.

"Now, Hart, we are within our circle of power," she said, switching to their coven names. "May the words of our mouths and the meditations of our hearts be sweet savor to the powers we invoke." She picked up the pewter goblet and caressed it in her hands. It was heavily engraved both inside and out. As Rebecca looked at it, she realized the engravings had been done by hand, not with the popular electric engraving tools. Mrs. Weed smiled at her.

"This was my husband's cup, Hart. He used it as a member of our fellowship for thirty years." The older woman's voice became wistful as she remembered her husband. "The etching is all in his own hand—symbols of spells and rituals that you may find useful in the future. I give this cup into your hands and consecrate it to your good works. With this cup, I give you a secret name that you will not share with others unless you are working deep magic with them. This name is Sadb. You are named for the Celtic goddess of transformation. She herself was transformed into a hind, the female counterpart of the hart that is your name in the circle. You will have the transforming power of both. With your name, I give you mine." The old woman took her knife from its position on the east side of the table and asked for Rebecca's hand. She pricked a tiny spot in the left palm and then did the same to her own. She grasped Rebecca's hand in her own so the two drops of blood would mingle.

"I am Hebe. Your blood now runs in my veins, my blood in yours, Sadb. We will always be bound. Let all that passes between us be sealed in our hearts in trust and friendship," she intoned. "May your cup be always filled with joy. May it work blessings for you ever."

Rebecca was overwhelmed. She whispered the words of acceptance, "So mote it be," and rushed to embrace her friend.

"When you have gathered all your tools, you will be fully in your power, but they shall all come to you from the hands of others. Be careful that you consecrate each to the service of the goddess." Rebecca could see herself gathering the sacred tools of her craft.

"How do I consecrate them?"

"Ah. That is for tomorrow."

Thursday, 28 July 1955, City of the Gods

WESLEY STOOD AT the center of the rostrum slowly turning to his right as he looked out toward the edges. The strings partitioning the surface had been removed for the day a little early. All the explorers were weary after over a month of daily trips to the City of the Gods. Doc and Margaret collapsed next to the rostrum and leaned back against it. Pol watched as Wesley slowly completed one revolution of his languid spin.

"Perhaps we should take a break," Margaret sighed. "We could go down and spend a few days with the family and get re-energized. It would do us all a world of good."

"What do you think, Pol? Could we take a break and then come back to the City?" asked Doc.

"Yes." The answer was simple and unlike Pol's usual gregarious nature. Doc looked over at the boy and saw his gaze fixed on Wesley. Doc and Margaret both turned to look at the man on the rostrum.

WESLEY CONTINUED HIS slow spin, images flaring before him from the symbols on the rostrum. Light and dark were important images, but so also were water and fire, earth and air. They spun around him like horses on a carousel. He felt the dip in his legs as one image receded and another arose. His voice joined the calliope in the joyous spinning of the ride.

Calliope, muse of eloquence and epic poetry with a voice of ecstatic harmony. It seemed the chief of the muses leant her vocal support to Wesley as mixed harmonies seemed to rise from the center of the rostrum.

> *Here rise to life again, dead poetry!*
> *Let it, O holy Muses, for I am yours,*
> *And here Calliope, strike a higher key,*
> *Accompanying my song with that sweet air*
> *which made the wretched Magpies feel a blow*
> *that turned all hope of pardon to despair*

* Dante's *The Divine Comedy* from "Purgatorio", Canto 1, Lines 7-12

His feet picked up a rhythm from what he was singing. The great wheel of the rostrum was like a hopscotch board. The pattern of where to place his feet was as clear as if Terpsichore, muse of dance, were guiding them. To his side, he heard Pol's voice join his in wordless harmony, calling forth a dance that Wesley would never have considered properly Methodist.

> *They're quiet enough in the morning hours,*
> *They're quiet enough in the afternoon,*
> *Reserving their terpsichorean powers*
> *To dance by the light of the Jellicle Moon.*

* T.S. Eliot's "Jellilcle Cats" from *Old Possum's Book of Practical Cats*

Doc and Margaret stood and began to clap in rhythm with Wesley's feet. Pol joined them and they circled the rostrum contretemps to Wesley. Images of lovers entwined together nearly cost Wesley his rhythm as his wife of so few days embraced him and they danced together.

> *Come, tuneful Muse, Erato,*
> *begin the melodious song,*
> *in praise of the lovely Samian youths,*
> *sounding the strings of the delightful lyre.*

* "Rhadine" a lost poem quoted in Strabo's *Geography*

As the four people sang, whistled, and danced around the rostrum, it seemed their voices were joined by others. The pillars around them sang.

On Doc's first visit to the City, Pol had mounted the rostrum and sung. His voice echoed with so many harmonies that Doc thought he had been joined by the gods themselves. Subsequent visits to the City had less ceremony, but the team always seemed to hear faint voices sing-ing as they made their way through the fog at the beginning and end of the day.

Now, it seemed the voices came out of the fog and joined in clarity. Wesley's own voice dissolved to whistling as he mimicked a flute spin-ning to face the setting sun. Standing on the rostrum and facing Libra, Wesley began to raise his hands to the sun in the western aisle. Pol, Doc, and Margaret stopped around him, watching the sun illuminate their musician as all the muses seemed to raise their voices in concert.

> *Kleio, Euterpe, and Thaleia,*
> *Melpomene, Terpsikhore, and Erato,*
> *And Polymnia, Ourania, Kalliope too.*
> *Of them all the most comely Euterpe,*
> *for she gives to those who hear her sing*
> *delight in the blessings of love.*

* Hesiod, *Theogeny* (with great liberties taken)

From beneath Wesley's feet another song arose. It must have been a trick of their ears and their eyes, for as the flute music mounted, the rest fell silent. From Wesley's outstretched arms, light began to flow to meet the setting sun. In his eyes, he could see his beloved Rebecca and feel the outpouring of the spirit of love emanating from his body to hers across the miles.

There was still an echo of the flute as Pol led them down the west-ern aisle and into the fog.

Thursday, 28 July 1955, Edinburgh, Scotland

"First," instructed Mrs. Weed, "you must cast a circle. We will place your cup in the center of our altar and create a safe space in which we can work."

The two women were in the garden of Mrs. Weed's little cottage. It was not large, but a tall hedge shielded it from view of her neighbors. In the center of the garden was a flagstone patio with a circular stone bench in the center. Upon arriving at the open area, Mrs. Weed had wistfully described how she and her husband would often celebrate the lunar cycle in this garden, dancing and loving, praying for a child. That desire had been unfilled during her husband's lifetime, but even after both were well past an age of childbearing, they still came to dance and celebrate beneath the full moon.

In preparing for Lughnasad, Rebecca had sewn herself a deep red robe of the type she'd seen the members of the circle—the cildru, as they were called—wearing when they were not naked. Mrs. Weed had helped her select the fabric and used her own red robe as a pattern. The women wore these robes—and nothing else—into the garden for the consecration of The Hart's cup, the first tool that she would consecrate to the service of the goddess.

"Your tools can enhance any magic that you work, dearie, but they are not *necessary*. The magic comes from within you and is blessed by the powers you invoke. You can raise a cone of power simply dancing alone in the moonlight. You should be able to invoke wards—a circle of protection—with no more than a few gestures and a whispered prayer. You will have doubts. You will wonder if you truly see a glowing dome over you, or if you merely *want* to see it. But that is the magic—when what you want is real to you. So, even when you have doubts, you must respect the powers. When Satan teased Jesus by instructing him to cast himself from the cliff because the angels would not suffer his feet to be bruised, Jesus responded that you should not tempt God. It is a good teaching. Do not *test* the powers of the mighty ones. *Trust* them. Now, you have learned the words for casting a circle. Pour forth your spirit as you say them and believe."

Rebecca was more nervous about this—casting her first circle—than she had been about her initiation. Somehow, it was comforting to know that the gathered coveners had all been through the same thing she had been and witnessed her becoming one of them. Now, however, only Hebe, The Water Maiden, would watch. It was embarrassing to raise her hands and begin speaking. Her voice seemed weak. She concentrated on imagining the circle Hebe instructed her to cast. Imagination. Image. I, Mage. Magic.

> *Guardians of the Watchtowers of the East*
> *Michael, wielder of the sword of God,*
> *Powers of the Air, I invoke your presence.*
> *Guard us with your watchfulness*
> *As we consecrate this tool.*

A brief chill coursed through Sadb's veins. Sadb, the witch. No longer Rebecca in this ritual. She had missed the casting of a circle at her initiation, being an outsider at the time. Of course, she had watched Hebe cast circles during her instruction, but had not understood the feeling of power as she invoked the guardians. Now she moved around the altar to the south.

Guardians of the Watchtowers of the South,
Gabriel, guardian of the gate of Paradise,
Powers of Fire, I invoke your presence.
Guard us in your watchfulness
As we consecrate this tool.

This time, Sadb felt no difference. Perhaps her concentration had faltered. She forced herself deeper—strained to see the light forming around her.

Guardians of the Watchtowers of the West,
Raphael, friend of humanity,
Powers of Water, I invoke your presence.
Guard us in your watchfulness
As we consecrate this tool.

Was this all it was? Her concentration wavered with the doubt Hebe had warned her of. Whether she could see the circle forming or not, Sadb determined that she would act as though it was there.

Guardians of the Watchtowers of the North,
Uriel, Regent of the Sun,
Powers of Earth, I invoke your presence.
Guard us in your watchfulness
As we consecrate this tool.

Tears squeezed between Sadb's tightly closed eyelids. She simply must succeed in her first working of magic. She was trying. Trying too hard, perhaps. She completed the circle turning back toward the East. Sadb emitted a low moan of agony, trying desperately to see the wall of light behind her eyelids.

"Lord! Dearie!" exclaimed Hebe. "We are only warding the circle, not burning down the house. Ease your mind a bit."

Sadb slowly opened her eyes to see the flaring white light that surrounded them on all sides. She wondered if it could be seen like a beacon out at sea. She squinted into the light to see her friend beside her.

"I have not seen so much power displayed in a novice," declared Hebe. "You must promise that you will work no magic when you are alone and unwatched. Such power out of control could take possession of you instead of you possessing it."

"What happened?"

"Why, simply that you have warded our circle as though we were under siege. Take it down a little."

"How?"

"Just picture it dimmer, dearie. It will respond. You control it."

And the light did respond, dimming to a point at which their eyes could function more easily. *It is only imagination,* she thought to herself again. *Vivid, vivid i-magic-ation.*

"Turn to your cup, Sadb. Imagine it filled to overflowing with the light that you have wrapped around us. Charge the cup with your energy."

A peacefulness surrounded her as she turned to the cup on the altar. In her time with the older woman, she had discovered a great deal about the husband who wrote many of the manuscripts she studied at the university. She found he was a gentle and loving man, filled with good humor, sharp in his criticisms as in his witticisms. He had etched each of the symbols in the cup with his own hand. She thought of the gentle man and imagined the cup filled with his spirit. In the midst of her rumination about the man who had once owned the cup, she could see Wesley's shining spirit reaching out to her as well. She had her own love and he supported her, even when his religious teachings discouraged it. He was her husband and he filled her with light.

She picked up the cup from the altar and paraded it around the circle, stopping finally facing the West. She lifted the cup and let the light flow into it.

This is my cup
My cup of life
Charged with my energy
Alive in my hands.
I name this cup Lear, ruler of the sea.
Oh goddess of many names,
May Lear be filled with your love.
In serving me, may he always serve the goddess.
May he be charged
with the power of the air to serve me in the East,
with the power of fire to serve me in the South,
with the power of water to serve me in the West,
with the power of earth to serve me in the North.
By all the powers surrounding here,
So mote it be.

If light could be said to overflow a container, this liquid luminescence spilled over the sides of Sadb's cup and poured down on her hands, climbing her arms like a living being.

"Earth the power, love," prodded the voice of Hebe. "You control it; it does not control you." Gradually, Sadb regained control and the living light receded into the bounds of the pewter goblet. It disappeared completely as she set it back on the altar, placing both hands flat down beside it. She turned toward Hebe and found the older woman kneeling on the ground with tears streaming from her face. Sadb found her own face wet as she sagged next to the woman and embraced her. She was drained of energy after consecration.

"How did you know?" Hebe asked as the two women embraced.

"Know?"

"You named your cup Lear. It was my husband's secret name in the circle. Blessings on you, Sadb. Mine and his."

15
Facing the Devil

Sunday, 31 July 1955, Kastraki, Greece

"I AM HAPPY that you chose to join me on this little jaunt, Brother John," said Brother El.

"I go by Wesley. No one has called me John in many years."

"Precisely why I chose to name you Brother John. Should anyone hear your name spoken, they will not relate it to the American explorers in the village. Are you doing all right?"

Wesley glanced down at the sheer cliff beside him and the narrow stairs cut into it. For a moment, he considered that he might have been better being hauled up the side of the cliff in a basket. That caused a second shudder.

"Fine. Just catching my breath," he said as he continued to climb. It was only another seventy steep steps up the cliff face before they ducked through a low door into the entry of the monastery.

"Welcome to the Monastery of Agios Nikolaos Anapafsas," Brother El said. Wesley caught his breath rather quickly since he had been climbing to the City of the Gods daily for the past month. But the climb was not finished. Inside, stairs continued to wind through the rock with occasional landings that opened onto candlelit rooms with paintings on nearly every surface. They paused in Brother El's personal quarters where Wesley was handed a black robe and small hat.

"I take it my expedition clothing is inappropriate for church," Wesley chuckled as he slipped the robe on. "Am I supposed to keep the hat on throughout the service?"

"Brother John, do you know anything of the art of spying?" Brother El asked, incongruously.

"Ah... no."

"I am putting you in disguise as a monk. Monks and priests always have their heads covered. We are also bearded, at least with a mustache. Thank you for keeping the beard that has grown while you were on the mountain. I assure you that your hair is short enough to pass. Aside from that, just follow me in the service. I have no role to play other than as a respondent."

"So, I'll know when to stand up and when to sit down?"

"I assure you that you will have no difficulty with that. There are no seats."

Wesley followed Brother El into the *katholicon*, the church of the monastery as opposed to the several little chapels and shrines. The room, Wesley estimated, was about thirty feet square, elaborately painted on every surface, including the breathtaking dome above them. Enough candles were lit in the room to see by, but as Brother El had said, there were no pews to sit on. The twenty or so men in the room simply stood silently and waited. Wesley also saw one woman, dressed in black with her head covered in a heavy shawl.

A priest entered the room, assisted by an acolyte who waved a censer. Once the priest had said a blessing, one of the monks began a chant. When he finished, the gathering responded with 'Amen'. This continued. Wesley surreptitiously looked around the room to see what kind of program or hymnal people were using, but discovered none. They simply knew the forms of worship. Finally, Wesley gave up understanding what was happening in the service and simply bowed his head in prayer and let the prayers and chants wash over him. In his peaceful and receptive mind, he felt the similarities with the symbols on the rostrum, and felt the images and icons melt into a uniform language and spirit. It was uplifting.

THE SERVICE WAS long. While Wesley had acquired a reasonable grasp of written New Testament Greek, he missed a lot of the spoken modern language. Nonetheless, he emerged from the service refreshed. Brother El fixed them both a plate of food in the refectory and they carried their plates to the rooftop garden of the monastery. Wesley had noticed how quickly the tower had cleared after the service. They saw only one other monk in the kitchen.

"Where did everyone go?" he asked.

"Home, mostly. There are only four of us who live here. Our priest comes here from Trikala. Next week he will conduct services at Roussanou. They have a larger residency, but we attract more locals and tourists for Sunday service because we are not as high and inaccessible as the other monasteries."

"What brought you to Greece and led you to this solitary life?" Wesley asked. Doc had told him when they first arrived that Brother El had come from America to take up the life of a monk in the Metéora. By appearances, you couldn't tell him from any of the other monks.

"That is part of what I wanted to talk to you about, Brother John. The Lord moves in mysterious ways. So does the United States Government. I was recruited as a student of theology. I had thought of becoming a minister—I wasn't even Orthodox at the time—but I became caught up in the study of the Word and in other ancient texts. My theology studies rapidly morphed into comparative religions. As such, when I graduated, I decided to get firsthand experience with the texts of other religions. I scheduled a journey around the world. I was fascinated with the differences between Hinduism and Buddhism, for example, so I spent a lengthy time studying in monasteries in India and Tibet."

"It must have felt strange as a Christian to participate in pagan practices," Wesley mused, thinking of his own work and changing values in the City of the Gods.

"Indeed, but that came later. I could have made a lifetime study of the two religions, but I wanted to survey the world. That led me from India through Pakistan and into the Middle East where I studied Islam, Judaism, and the roots of Christianity. But I found much in each of the religions—commonly held beliefs and even scriptural passages—that came from other religions as they were absorbed and swept away by the dominant faith. Which brought me to Greece."

"When did you come here?"

"I arrived at the same time Hitler came to power in 1933. It was easy to see war was coming. Italy had already made threatening gestures toward Greece by occupying Albania. That was when life changed for me. The allies needed information. As a student, I was traveling all over Greece. I was given a contact and began filtering out information on troop movements and the attitude of the populace. The Greeks repelled the Italian invasion but were overwhelmed by the Germans a month later. By that time, I had made my way here to the Metéora, directly in the path of the march. In November of 1942, an American in the path of the Nazi Army was a dead American. I joined the local resistance."

Wesley was rapt. Had he been just a few years older, he might have been in this war himself, but he, too, was a theology student and intended to become a minister of music. By the time he changed his major to musicology, and his intent to become a college instructor, the war was over.

"Look there," Brother El pointed east over the low wall around the rooftop garden. "The first rock is where the Church of Agios Giorgio is located. You have passed it going into Kastraki. Just over its shoulder is the Tower of Agia, the tallest of the peaks here in Metéora. It overlooks Kalapaka from 630 meters. It was our point of resistance. From the peak to its right, we snipers picked off those who would plant a Nazi flag over our town. The Germans found out exactly what the Ottomans did. It is impossible to assault the towers. So they bombed us. On fifteen of the peaks of Metéora, there are ruined and abandoned monasteries. A friend in the resistance brought me here to the monastery. I thought it was temporary shelter, but I have been chained to this rock for twelve years. I expect it will be ten more before I am able to extract myself and return to the United States."

"It's a fascinating story," Wesley mused. He scratched at his beard. Now that he was down from the mountain and had fulfilled his obligation to come to the monastery for services, he was anxious to shave.

"It has a purpose," Brother El said. "You are a man of faith, Brother John. Your faith is being challenged at every turning. You are seeing bits of religion that predates your Christianity—even predating Moses. What I have found is that doctrine is a fleeting and temporary truth. What may be true for one community at one time does not make it true for a different time and place. Your search for a universal musical language may leave you chained to your own rock of solitude, just as mine did. It is what is here that you must trust." Brother El put his hand on Wesley's chest. "Now let us go down from the mountain, Moses, and see what your companions are up to."

Wesley and the crew rested and studied for five more days before returning to the mountain.

Saturday, 6 August 1955, Northern England

Lughnasad. Rebecca and Mrs. Weed had joined the circle in time to be there for the initial invocations and immediately became The Hart and The Water Maiden. They had driven down to Keswick in Mrs. Weed's old car and checked into a small hotel earlier in the day. Rebecca wasn't sure but what the bus that had made her so nauseous a few weeks earlier might have been a better choice. Mrs. Weed admitted that she didn't usually drive the auto that had been her husband's, but assured Rebecca that she did have a license to operate it.

With the uncertainty and focus on initiation of her first visit to the stone circle past, Rebecca was able to better appreciate the celebratory ritual of the Feast of Lugh, from the casting of the circle and invocations of the guardians to the dancing that soon ensued. She was caught up in the dancing circle around the fire, joining hands and going first left then right. She was greeted with a kiss by each member of the coven and after having shivered through a kiss from The Blade that confused her, she found herself back by The Water Maiden.

With a shout, the coveners raised their hands and all fell to the ground. The Hart was exhausted and long past her embarrassment. So far the coveners had all kept their red robes on, though she was certain there would come a time when those would fall to the side. The High Priestess arose and began chanting as she walked and danced around the fire inside the circle of seated coveners.

> This is the wake of Lugh.
> This is the Sun King's funary.
> The Corn King dies upon the stalk,
> The Sun is fading to the South.
> The winter winds are gathering—
> Their attack is surely coming
> And our harvest is not in.
> And now we stand 'twixt hope and fear,
> In the waiting time.
> Our labor stands, its fruits are ripe
> But our rewards are not yet certain.
> The days shorten.
> The light goes out.
> The summer passes.
> The harvest calls forth sacrifice.
> Requires sacrifice
> To make the passage safe
> To winter.

When the priestess had finished her chanting, a woman from the other side of the fire rose and brought a basket to her. Together they began the circuit of the coveners. To each person the priestess whispered a question. The answer was picked up immediately by the next person and was chanted around the circle like a wave. With the answer, each was given a small loaf of bread. The wave passed her and the whispered word "Failure" was taken up around the circle. Next, "Vanity." At another covener, "Heights" was whispered and passed around the circle.

At once, the priestess was before The Hart and held a small loaf shaped like a person.

"What do you fear most, Hart?" the priestess asked. Immediately thinking of the warning she had received, Rebecca answered.

"The night."

The word was picked up by the next person and passed around the circle and The Hart could hear the haunting whispers until it reached her again and she was forced by the wave to repeat, "Night."

Her heartrate accelerated as she looked at the breadman in her hands and saw Wesley singing on a mountaintop. "Yea, though I walk through the shadow of death, I will fear no evil," she whispered. "I love you."

Other words passed her with the wave of sound and then a chant was started. She followed the words and joined.

> *In this fire, may it pass, may it pass.*
> *May it pass on the outflowing tide*
> *And burn with the red winter sun.*
> *As the year dies,*
> *As everything fades,*
> *As everything passes,*
> *All fades away.*

With the rest of the cildru, The Hart rose and threw her bread in the fire. Then silently they joined hands and wound around the fire, faster and faster. To her surprise, as she met the eyes of others around the fire, she found them also filled with tears. This time it was a long and mournful sigh that brought the group once again to the ground as the Priestess once again picked up the basket and began her rounds.

The wave of words began to circle the fire once again. Still shaken by the image that had first struck her about fear, The Hart carefully considered what the remedy would be. She was flooded with the images of her honeymoon and the nights spent with Wesley before they parted for the summer. When the priestess held out another bread figure, this one a star, she asked, "What do you hope to harvest, Hart?"

"Love."

The word spun around the circle until she repeated it again. Her eyes were again filled with tears as she whispered, "Love."

"May the star of hope be in us always!" shouted the priestess as she completed the circle. Then she ate her bread star and so did all the coveners. The bread was sweet.

The Blade leapt to his feet on the other side of the fire and suddenly stripped off his robe. His tumescent phallus bounced as he danced and jumped around the fire. The coveners began to clap a rhythm as he clowned and mimed in front of the bread basket. Finally, he drove his hands into the basket and brought out a much larger bread figure of a man. This, he held high over his head in one hand while the other drew forth a bottle of wine that he uncorked with his teeth.

"Behold the grain of life!" he shouted. "Eat of the life that ever dies and ever is reborn!" With that he took an obscene bite out of the center of the bread man and took a long drink from the bottle of wine. He shook his head and shouted, then began his own circuit around the witches who each broke bread from the loaf and drank of the wine. It was like a communion of sorts. But by the time The Blade had brought the bread and wine to The Hart, other food was being distributed as food appeared all around the circle. She realized how long it had been since she last ate and how hungry she was.

OTHER MEMBERS OF the coven had removed their robes, but not all. It was obvious that some were couples who kissed romantically as they ate their picnics. The Blade sprawled naked on the ground at The Hart's side as if he would be her 'date' for the picnic. He thrust the remainder of the bread man out to her with the bottle of wine. In defiance of him, she bared her teeth and bit viciously into the head, then took a long swig of the strong wine.

He caught a chunk of cheese from a passing covener who stopped long enough to hug them both with a blessing. The Blade had produced a smaller knife than the ritual *Athamé*, from where she didn't know. He busily sliced cheese and found a basket with dried meats in it.

"Join me for the feast, won't you Hart?" He pushed more bread and cheese her way. "It is traditional to share food at a ritual."

"Thank you." The Hart looked quickly for The Water Maiden and saw her nearby, talking to the priestess. She pulled her robe more closely around her. The Blade's erection was not so pronounced now, but she was having none of it. "Where is your daughter tonight?"

"Ah. The little hellcat," he laughed. "She is not yet a full member of the circle. The women handle that kind of thing. Something about becoming a woman. As a novice, she is permitted two celebrations each year to attend. This year she has chosen the solstices."

"You must be very proud of her." She was searching for another topic to normalize the conversation. The naked man beside her had attacked her and her husband in Indianapolis. How could he be so calmly sharing food and wine with her in the circle?

He stabbed another piece of cheese and lifted it to The Hart's lips. She opened automatically to receive the offered food. When the cheese was between her lips, he withdrew the knife only enough to extract it from the square. She thought she detected a soft glow in his eyes as if more than The Blade looked out from them. He casually let the flat of the knife touch her chin and dragged it intentionally down her throat and between her breasts. The Hart shook, knowing the gesture as one of intense intimacy. She would have screamed if enough air could have reached her terrified lungs.

"We could be very good together, Hart," he whispered. "I can feel the power in you, begging to be released. Your guide has gotten you through the gates of hell, but I can show you the way across."

"Time to leave, Hart," The Water Keeper said as she pushed the knife casually away from her chest. "Blade, your attentions are neither desired nor appreciated. Depart."

"We've unfinished business, you and I—Rebecca Allen," he whispered. She caught her breath. Real names were never to be used in the circle. "I will be waiting for you. Together we will find the goddess."

He rolled away from her and Rebecca found her teeth chattering as an intense cold swept over her.

16
Violent Gifts

Monday, 8 August 1955, Edinburgh, Scotland

EVEN WITH the shock and daring of The Blade, Rebecca considered her first gathering with the full circle on Lughnasad to have been a high point of her life. There were more celebrations, dancing, and even couples slipping into the shadows of the huge stones to make love.

After the circle had dispersed, Rebecca and Mrs. Weed made their way back to the Bed and Breakfast in Keswick. Breakfast Sunday morning was a typical English affair with boiled sausages, beans, soft boiled eggs, and dry toast. Rebecca looked in vain for a salt and pepper shaker.

The trip back to Edinburgh in Mrs. Weed's old vehicle seemed to take forever, but the two had a lively discussion about Rebecca's impressions of the ritual that kept her from car sickness most of the way. Mrs. Weed had been careful to fill the car's tank on Saturday when they got to Keswick because no petrol would be available on Sunday.

"Study the wheel of the year," Mrs. Weed suggested. "No other place is the combination of male and female so well represented. You will discover that the festivals of the combined circle are based on the solar calendar while the rituals of our smaller circle are based on the lunar cycle."

Rebecca had been to only two rituals of the minor circle of Braithwaite with Mrs. Weed. There was very little to differentiate them from an evening social gathering of friends. In fact, Rebecca thought of the spontaneous card parties her parents hosted or went to while she was growing up. It seemed no one really planned them. Friends simply dropped in for a cup of coffee and ended up at the table with a fistful of pinochle cards. The kids, if there were any in the company, would settle for playing Crazy Eights or Euchre. Later they graduated to Rummy and Canasta. The adults almost always played pinochle.

The gatherings of the lesser circle of Braithwaite were much the same, but getting to them required a bit more planning. Mrs. Weed attended only the Full Moon celebrations as it was quite a drive to get down to Northern England to 'drop in' on the host for the evening.

So, Monday morning, Rebecca was back at work in the library examining various plots of wheels within wheels. It was very difficult to plot on a chart. There were 360 degrees in a circle, but 365 days in a year. She consulted an almanac and discovered thirteen full moons in the year. Yet there were twelve zodiacal signs. And eight pagan holidays. She consulted an ephemeris but even that was only partially helpful. It did, however, show the lunar cycle within the solar cycle.

By the end of six hours in the library, Rebecca's head hurt. The only thing she had conclusively settled on was that her own monthly cycle was roughly in tune with the full moon. She considered the implication as she pedaled her bicycle back to Mrs. Weed's cottage. If she bled on the full moon, then by the standards of women everywhere, she should be fertile on the new moon. She filed this information away, knowing that when she was reunited with her husband, new moons were going to be very active times for them.

REBECCA ARRIVED AT the cottage exhausted and sweaty from her ride. She could think of nothing better than a relaxing bath when she saw the note from Mrs. Weed on the kitchen table indicating her landlady was having tea with a friend. Rebecca would have a pleasant afternoon.

Fixing herself a cup of tea while the bath ran, she hummed to herself light-heartedly. Wesley would love to visit here. It so suited his eclectic tastes. Turning off the water and placing her tea next to the tub, Rebecca stripped off her clothes as she entered the bedroom. She was removing her panties when she glanced at the bureau.

The dresser had been cleared of its normal knickknacks. Instead, a red sweater lay on the surface. On the sweater lay her walking stick. She fondly remembered cutting it with Doc before she left on her trip and his instructions on how to care for it. But the scene was not a pastoral tableau. Instead, a short knife impaled a note on her staff. Next to her pewter chalice, a red candle burned, trailing wax across the note, staff, and sweater. Rebecca moved cautiously, glancing around her to see if the intruder was still present. The sweater was ruined with red wax embedded in the fibers, but that disturbed Rebecca less than the note.

"Unfinished business, Hart of my heart."

The stiletto was easily recognized as the same one The Blade had used to feed her cheese just two nights ago.

Panic gripped her as she stood staring at the tableau, unable to move away. She wanted to run, feeling the presence of the sinister soul who had done this—believing he was still there watching her—still in the room, ready to bend her to his will.

Why? Why did he even care about her? It should be obvious that she did not know where the team was digging for their lost goddess. Somewhere in the middle of Greece. She knew only that her letters were addressed to a monk who delivered them. There could be only one thing he wanted from her and it turned her stomach. She voided herself uncontrollably.

How dare he?

Rebecca rebuked herself for her panic, ignoring the vomit and focusing on the staff and note. Panic receded in the face of a shaking rage. She had been violated! This was worse than the attack in Indiana when he had dared caress her and squeeze her breast. He had handled her cup! He had created a sacrificial altar of her staff and sweater. The thought of having him near her filled her with such anger that the room disappeared from her vision. She could see only the violation. She would not live with this. She would burn it all and wish him in the flames.

Even at the thought of fire, Rebecca could see in her mind the wall of light that had surrounded her at her dedication of her cup. Hebe's words rang in her mind. "The witch's tools are the knife, the wand, the cup, and pentacles. Each of your tools will come to you from the hand of someone else. Dedicate each to the service of the goddess."

Her rage, in its turn, dissolved into something more closely resembling madness. Tools received from others. The Flame Keeper from whom she had received her staff and The Blade from whom she had 'received' this knife were members of her own coven—the great circle of Carles Castlerigg. She would purify them and make them into her *Athamé* and wand. Her dawning resolve outweighed Hebe's admonition against working alone.

Her tools would be the gift of her coven brothers. She hoped they would be pleased when they saw them again. The wand would rule the fire and the *Athamé* would fan it with wind. At the thought, fire flared in her mind and she turned instinctively to the east to invoke the powers and cast a warded circle. She could not remember precisely the words she had used the last time, but she supposed it really didn't matter. It was the mind that counted, not the words, and Rebecca's mind was firmly set. She completed her circuit of the directions seeing a living power in each of the watchtowers and returned once more to the east. The wall of light flared into existence with an intensity that temporarily blinded her. She did not bother, however, to moderate it. She wanted all the protection she could muster.

Now she faced the dresser that would be her altar. She had not and would not touch the items laid out there until her ritual was complete. She was not concerned whether the words that came to her mind were audible, but they rose in pitch as she spun in place gathering power and echoed from the walls of light she had built around herself.

"May you find pleasure in my act, oh most high ones. May you see a tool of good sanctify and purify a tool of evil and turn it to your service. I name this wand Pele! Firerod, flaming beauty, angel of fire, purifier of the unclean. Brigit, goddess of fire, to you be this rod sanctified."

Rebecca, now fully the witch Sadb, raised her hands to the East and began slowly turning clockwise, gathering into her more power as she commanded the blessings of the powers of all the elements on her wand.

"May this wand be consecrated to your service in the East, oh Arianrhod of the air. May this wand be consecrated to your service in the South, oh Brigit of the fire. May this wand be consecrated in your service in the West, oh Mariamne of the water. May this wand be consecrated to your service in the North, oh Rhiannon of the earth."

Sadb stumbled a little as she came back to the East and saw the sacrificial tableau again. She could feel a crackling surge of power all around her and faltered beneath the influence of the assault on her senses. She was filled with strength and power that she was not sure she could control. Her eyes focused on the mock sacrifice, the stiletto still protruding from her sanctified wand. Rage overcame her doubt as she glared at the scene.

"How dare you!" she screamed. "I will not be intimidated by you. You will be pure. You will be free!"

Sadb raised a hand to point at the dagger without touching it. She could feel the force gathering behind her for what she intended. She spun, gathering the powers of the elementals together again and felt another surge in her hands.

For a moment, she lost the object of her focus and set herself adrift on the tidal wave that threatened to wash her away. At the same instant, she felt hot and flushed while still fighting off a chilled shiver that tore through her already wavering concentration.

So, this is power, she thought as she drifted once again around the circle with arms outstretched, collecting more strength as she passed each point. *This is what Phaethon felt when Helios handed him the reins of the Sun Chariot and told him to drive the horses of dawn. No wonder Zeus struck him down. Such power could destroy the earth. And I am the focus of the cone of power. It lives in me. I can do whatever I will.*

The circuit complete, Rebecca forced herself to focus. Her body wanted to keep slowly spinning at the vortex of this awesome cone of power, keep collecting more and more until… Until what? What would happen when she was filled with more power than she could contain. She would burst. Explode. She must finish and return the power to its source.

She focused her eyes on the stiletto and on her wand. She stretched out her hands and began to chant.

"May the fires of Brigit purify you. May Pele rise in the volcanic forge to burn away the dross of your making. May you be lifted ever and only in the service of the goddess. May that hand which wielded you feel and know the force of this power."

The image of a purifying fire leapt into Sadb's mind and she knew instinctively what the final portion of this ritual must be. She bound the image in her mind and felt the power begin to flow as she recited the ancient sealing of her spell.

I bind this spell by three times three;
As I do speak, so mot it be.

As she watched, smoke began to rise from the note. The red wax ran. The sweater began to darken and flame. All around the knife, the fire danced from her wand, licking up the blade of the knife.

"I name thee Elhin. Wind master, air spirit, *Athamé*. May the salt water of Lear and the fires of Pele purify you. Eurus, east wind, bless Elhin and answer his call when I wield him in the East. Notus, south wind, bless Elhin and answer his call when I wield him in the South. Zephyrus, west wind, bless Elhin and answer his call when I wield him in the West. Boreas, north wind, bless Elhin and answer his call when I wield him in the North."

The four winds whipped a cyclone around her. It fanned the flames rising from her wand. The fire had a life of its own, running the length of the wand and licking up the blade. The red candle melted to a mere puddle, the flames hanging like some overripe fruit about to fall. And fall it did, dripping flames back onto the dresser, burning some invisible fuel on the surface. Then they reached deeper into the finish and into the charring wood.

Sadb realized with a sudden fright that she was no longer in control of the fire. It now burned of its own will. She panicked, looking for some means of beating out the flames. Somewhere there was a voice. Someone was alert already to the fire and would call an emergency. She must act but did not know what to do.

"Ground the power!" The shout seemed to be directly in her ear this time, though she could see no one present. Understanding only the concept but not the process, she staggered back toward the burning dresser. In the middle of the fire, still standing erect from the wand like The Blade's tumescent prick, glowed her *Athamé*, Elhin.

She burst into tears at the knowledge of what she must do even before the searing physical pain of the hot knife penetrated the nerves of her hands. She jerked it out of the burning wood and raised it above her head, screaming in agony. Then she drove downward with all her might, burying the knife again, this time into the floorboards. With that act, all her barriers dropped and she released the warding powers that had ensured her privacy.

Mrs. Weed rushed into the room, beating out the last of the flames with a pillow. She cradled Rebecca in her arms as her friend wept.

Monday, 8 August 1955, City of the Gods

"What has you so agitated this morning, Wesley?" Margaret asked as Wesley paced around the rostrum.

The one-week break from their 'dig' with the family of Metéora had been good for all of them. It was filled with discussions, a little sightseeing, and fresh food in plenty. But now that they'd returned to the City of the Gods, refreshed and prepared to work, Wesley was acting as if he'd never seen the rostrum before.

They'd come into the City from the fog with the strange voices around them, just as they had every morning the first five weeks they were there. Wesley had marched directly to the central platform and unshouldered his pack. He pulled out string and set it on the rostrum, arranging a drawing in front of him. Then he had started pacing.

He looked at the drawing and then rushed to the opposite side of the rostrum to compare. He looked at each symbol around the edges and then rushed to the center. On his hands and knees, he searched for the dark star that marked the very center of the circle. At Margaret's words, he crawled across the rostrum with the drawing to face her.

"They've moved," he said flatly. Doc and Pol immediately joined them.

"That's not likely," Doc chuckled. "I'm sure we need to simply get you oriented correctly. There are so many symbols on the orchestra that it is easy to become confused. Margaret and I have fought the same disorientation nearly every time we've explored."

"Do you agree that we come into the City with the sun ready to rise at our backs?" Wesley asked. "And that we leave with it in our faces?"

"I think that has been obvious," Margaret said.

"So, lacking a better term, the direction we arrive from is East and the direction we depart in is West. I'm far beyond determining how it is possible to arrive and leave in different directions and still come out at the same place," he sighed. "But, the symbols on the rostrum no longer align with the directions as we have known them. I fought uncertainty about this before we left because it seemed things in my drawings were subtly off from one day to the next. I credited it to my poor drawing skills and the change was so slight that I didn't think twice about it. But coming back after ten days away, I can see how drastically things have changed."

"How so?"

"The immediate thing that struck me was that Pol and I had made quite a big thing of our discovery that the sun rose in Cancer and set in Capricorn. We charted it the first time that we laid out a piece of string on the rostrum. East to West. But I came straight to the rostrum at sunrise and the symbol on this edge is Leo, not Cancer," Wesley affirmed. Pol looked and nodded. He didn't seem particularly perplexed by it.

"Hmm. It doesn't seem logical that the large and solid stone is somehow rotating," Doc mused. He shoved on the edge to see if he could make it budge and then got on hands and knees to examine the space around the rostrum. He could detect no gap that would indicate machinery was moving the stone platform.

"We stand on this—work on this. I can't detect any motion nor any sound that would indicate that it moves. I recall, however, that there was a subtle shift clockwise. Could the pillars have moved?" asked Wesley. The four approached the nearest pillar and consulted drawings to see what direction that pillar had been plotted in earlier. It seemed to be in its correct orientation to the rostrum.

"If the rostrum doesn't move and the pillars don't move, then the sun must be moving around the center point," Wesley said. "The directions are changing."

"Isn't that the same kind of logic that early man used to determine that the earth was the center of the universe and the sun went around it?" Margaret asked. "I fall back on our earlier conjecture that we are on a self-contained globe that has its own orbit and rotation."

"Wasn't that the one Wesley adamantly claimed was absolutely impossible?" Doc laughed. Wesley blushed. He tossed the ball of string to Pol and held one end on the Leo symbol as Pol circled to lay the string across.

"The symbol?" Wesley asked.

"Aquarius," was the quick response.

Wesley paced to his left until he reached Scorpio. He held another length of string in this position and Pol circled the rostrum opposite.

"Taurus," Pol said. With the geometry seeming to be a variable, Wesley crawled across to the center point to see if the star was still there. He sat with a suddenness that caused Doc and Margaret to rush to him.

"Look," Wesley said. "The star in the center. When we measured east to west the first time we plotted this, the string ran exactly parallel to the arms of the star. North was directly along the vertical axis. Look. The arms are no longer parallel to the east-west axis. They are tilted." The explorers all sat. Pol joined them and looked at the star in the center. He tilted his head toward the sky as if to contemplate a great mystery.

"The stars in the sky all circle Arcus," he said. It was a simple statement. Wesley, Doc, and Margaret scrambled back off the rostrum looking at Pol in the center. They moved to the eastern edge where they had laid their packs.

"Is it... Can it truly be that the symbols themselves... move?" Wesley asked. "Are they a living thing?" He reached out and hesitantly touched the symbol in front of him. He felt cold stone. The very thought of what he was saying struggled with what his brain insisted was logically possible. He looked up at Doc and Margaret.

"I believe we must put that in our list of theories," Doc sighed. "It would be good if you found other relationships among the symbols that have changed. I know there are hundreds of symbols decorating the platform, but surely you have a selection that you can use to see if some symbols have moved in relation to each other rather than simply to the center star. After all, if we are dealing with degrees of the impossible, it might seem just as logical that the star rotates, changing its position relative to the others."

17

Compulsion

Monday, 8 August 1955, Edinburgh, Scotland

THERE WERE not enough tears that could be shed for the pain that laced Rebecca's palm and right arm. Mrs. Weed still held her head in gentle hands, but Rebecca was oblivious to the sterile surroundings of the hospital. At least the salve the nurse applied had begun to numb the pain.

"And how did you manage a burn like this?" asked the nurse.

"I grabbed a hot... pan from the stove," answered Rebecca at last.

"Now what do you suppose they make potholders for?" chided the nurse. "I imagine you won't attempt that again soon." The nurse finished with the salve and turned away. "I'll be back to wrap that for you in just a minute." When she was gone, Rebecca looked up into Mrs. Weed's eyes and tears began to roll again.

"Alice, I'm sorry. I don't know what happened."

"Gently, child. Never mind. You work a powerful magic, but should really not work alone."

"What happened to my wand and my *Athamé*? They didn't burn up, did they?" Rebecca was near panic to think of her new tools being destroyed.

"The *Athamé* is in your handbag, Becca. So watch where you open it. The wand is beside you."

Rebecca reached for her staff with her uninjured hand. She gasped as it came into sight. The rod had been silky white, cut from a white ash at Brown County State Park in Indiana. She had stripped the bark from the staff and carefully sanded it and oiled it, adding a rubber tip from the leg of a card table to the end so hiking would not damage it. Doc's staff had an iron cup on the foot and one day perhaps she would do that as well. But the pale wood of what was now her consecrated wand had been changed. A deep red burnished the wood and seemed to glow from beneath its surface. The fire was contained within the rod. But it was scarred. The Blade had stabbed the knife just below a spot where she had trimmed away a small limb. There was a hard knot in the wood at that point. The gash beneath the knot was a deeper mysterious red dropping to black at the depth of the scar. As Rebecca stared at the gash, it seemed to pulse and her own body responded to the sexual awareness. It was as if her female parts had been engraved on the staff. Far from appearing blemished, however, the rod had taken on an appearance of great depth and intense power. The wood seemed harder, tempered, strengthened. It slid beneath her fingers sensually and she could feel the heat deep inside it, waiting to burst forth.

This shall be my symbol, she thought. *The Sigil of Sadb.*

"It was a foolish thing to have done," Mrs. Weed intruded into her thoughts. "It is a wonder I ever got through to you."

"The power. It was… such… seductive…"

"It was enough to do a fair-sized coven credit. Becca, you must learn to work tandem with someone to draw you back. I almost didn't reach you."

"To tell me to ground the power."

"Aye. So that part did get through to you. Good. So much gift I have never seen in one person in my life." The nurse returned with fresh wraps for Rebecca's hand and cut off Mrs. Weed with her good-natured chattering.

"Well," she said, "there's a rash of empty heads a'loose today. Would you imagine that on the same day someone else would reach to a hot pan without a potholder? Of course, he's a man, but even a bachelor should have common sense." The nurse rambled on as she wrapped Rebecca's hand. The pain subsided to a constant throb. Rebecca closed her eyes and could still see the flames and the hot stiletto she had grabbed so desperately protruding from the gash in her walking stick. When she opened her eyes, the flames faded gradually behind the throbbing. Through the open curtain, she saw a man pulling his jacket over one arm, draping the other side over his shoulder. His short blond hair and fair skin reminded her of some…

…*one!* Rebecca sat straight up with a startled exclamation that drew everyone's instant attention and sent a bowl of water spilling out of the nurse's hands. The nurse left to find a mop for the spill and left Rebecca face-to-face with Ryan McGuire, The Blade. He wore a pained but sadistic smile of recognition and moved toward Rebecca a step.

Rebecca watched the grin fade as comprehension and then apprehension swept across his face. He raised his bandaged hand as he looked at hers.

"You?" he said in consternation.

"Stay away from me!"

For the first time, Rebecca saw a genuine hesitance in the man whose cold confidence had unnerved her so easily. It seemed almost as if someone else... or other... looked out from behind his eyes. He treated her with the same vulnerable respect that she unwillingly felt toward him.

"You don't understand," he whispered. "I won't hurt you."

"Not again," Mrs. Weed interrupted. "You've already done your share."

"It was a mistake." Ryan stepped closer. Rebecca sought and clutched her purse. She could feel the tempting shape of the knife beneath the soft fabric of the bag. "I don't know what came over me. We needn't be enemies. We are *cildru* of the same... of the same Mother. We could be partners."

"I would never be your partner," she snapped.

"You need someone," he answered. "Tell her, Water Maiden. She doesn't know what she's dealing with. Look at this," he finished, holding up his bandaged hand.

"She is beginning to understand," said Mrs. Weed. "I don't think she needs further instruction from you."

"Mrs. Allen... Rebecca. I can help you master the power you hold. I can work tandem with you. Show you ways to raise power you can't imagine. And control it. Power, Hart. Our own coven. You as high priestess."

The pleading seduction in The Blade's eyes threw her. He was a lovely man, very much like Wesley, though harder. She had seen him naked in the coven circle—had been so herself—could still feel the touch of his thigh against her own. Sadb as priestess in a new coven and as priest... what was his name? She had a name she would only use to work magic with one she trusted utterly. Would she give it to him? She felt a heat rising to flush her cheeks. Even the sensitized nerves of her nipples flared to the remembrance of his knife pressed against her chest. The power exceeded flames. It was a seductive vortex calling her to plunge deeper into the source itself. The same power was in The Blade—power to fill, to flame, to burn.

"Blade!" The word cracked across the room from Mrs. Weed's mouth to echo like the sharp snap of a lightning bolt. Rebecca froze. Ryan McGuire's face was inches from her own, motionless, poised at the point of her stiletto beneath his chin. She could not remember how it came to her hand—could not remember Ryan moving so close—could not imagine why. She eased the pressure of the blade and he moved back stiffly.

"Very pretty work, Hart. There is, indeed, a blade between us. You can feel the power. We would make a perfect team." He turned on his heel to leave, but stopped at the edge of the room to turn back. The secondary glint of his eyes faded.

"You should be interested in a bound manuscript in the library archives by a Ben Wills. I'm sure you will make the connection. When you do, I'll be waiting." His casual smile returned. "Waiting for you in Greece."

Wednesday, 10 August 1955, Edinburgh, Scotland

HIDING. WAITING BEHIND one of the great columns that supported the rotunda of the library—Rebecca could feel his sinister presence. Her footsteps echoed in the hollow chamber beneath the great domed ceiling. Some elderly librarian would surely come running up to shush her for disturbing the peace. She didn't mean to be so loud, but the library was so quiet—so empty. And waiting for her in the quiet empty room ahead was the gatekeeper of Carles. Perhaps he was only there to watch her make her discovery—a manuscript by an unknown author. Perhaps he had some other motive. Perhaps it was only her imagination.

The worst was that it didn't make a difference. He was there, even if he wasn't there. His presence filled Rebecca with a mad desire to run and never look back—run until she knew he was no longer behind her. Run to Wesley's arms.

But he would always be behind her—maybe one step, maybe five, maybe a mile or a year. He might precede her and still his presence would haunt her. He seemed always to know where she would be before she did. So, he arrived ahead of her—following nonetheless.

Her hand ached and she paused to hold it close to her breast, biting back a tear that forced its way through the fear and pain. What kind of bond had she forged between the The Hart and The Blade with her ritual? She forced him to feel the pain of purging his own knife. Had his hand spontaneously blistered like hers? Or had he, indeed, coincidentally reached for a hot skillet at the same moment she chanted her curse? How long would their bond last? If the knife between them was pure, what were they?

She concentrated on Wesley's image in her mind and felt the warm calm she always associated with being with him. The rising sense of passion was a more recent addition. The image wavered with the close cropped blond head of Ryan McGuire forcing its way back into her consciousness.

Rebecca was exhausted; that was the trouble. The enormous expenditure of energy Monday coupled with two almost sleepless and pain-filled nights had left her emotionally and physically drained. Mrs. Weed strongly suggested that she stay in bed. For the first day, that had been fine. But on Wednesday, when Mrs. Weed went to market, Rebecca dressed and slipped out. She had found a black cab and made her way to the library. Curiosity drove her to find what was in the manuscript that Ryan had called her attention to.

It was likely a trap and Rebecca fingered the charred handle of the stiletto in the seam pocket Mrs. Weed had sewn for her. He might simply want to get her alone again for god-knew-what reason. Few people at the university are admitted unaccompanied to the archives, but Ryan McGuire held a doctorate in archaeology. He could be sitting up there waiting. She didn't care, *damn him!* Let him try something. She would match him blade to blade.

Rebecca began to chuckle out loud, then caught herself short. This was, after all, a library. But the realization of what she had done sparked hysteria in her that she could scarcely contain. She had neutralized his most deadly weapon against her. The memory of the knife coming to her hand in the clinic burst on her. It jumped to her command involuntarily. It would probably do no good against any other assailant, but Ryan McGuire triggered the response and she could match him move for move with his own weapon. That was the nature of the link she had forged between them. They were unable to oppose each other unequally.

Of course, he would know it, too. That was why the turn from fear to fascination. Rebecca could no longer imagine an attack from him. To attack her would be to attack himself. He would find another, more subtle, more sinister way to get to her. She felt a sexual shiver flood her core. Catching her breath, she strode confidently into the archives.

She expected a bound volume of immense weight and length, like the writings of Professor Weed she had waded through. It would be just as likely for The Blade to have left her a fruitless task that would simply delay her from her research and writing. Instead, she found a folio of papers torn from several loose-leaf notebooks. The folio bore the appropriate catalog numbers and the title, "Assorted Papers by Ben Wills Leading to the Creation of his book, *The Last Gift*."

Fiction, Rebecca thought as she began to read. A child's fairytale, complete with "Once upon a time…" It was a neatly penned manuscript, but rife with line-outs and additions. Occasional margin notes indicated questions and references. She read through the story about a young magician and a Gypsy healer in fifteen minutes. She could see no relationship between the story and her research. Just like Ryan McGuire to send her off on a wild goose chase just to irritate her. She turned to the notes.

At first, there seemed no special order to them. Then Rebecca ran across a page noted in the margins with a number of odd symbols. Symbols like the notations Wesley used for his music language! As she turned to the next leaf, two folded pages slid down. She unfolded the paper to discover the title, "Music of the Gods". In Wesley's neat penciled writing at the upper right corner was the catalog number from the college library in Indianapolis. Rebecca let it soak in. Ben Wills had to be the same as Dr. Benjamin Wilton. No wonder the handwriting was so familiar.

There were too many things to comprehend at once. Rebecca held in her hands a volume of material by the author who had inspired Wesley's work. Why would Ryan McGuire leave the pages in Scotland that he had taken such pain to steal in Indiana? Unless there was something else here that had made them less important as the key he had sought. She could only read on in Wilton's work.

"All the myths of all the lands play upon each other," she read. "To understand one, you must see all as timeless. They are not a paradox, but the natural result of seeing all time as *now*, all places as *here*."

Of all the myths, it is Serepte that haunts my dreams. An old man, I am still subject to the mystic spell that she has cast over me. Once having been so close to her dwelling that I might have entered, had I only the key, I am ever drawn back. But in no way, have I gained access to her secret hiding place. The key is in the center of the εξέδρα, exedra, the dais, but I am unable to dislodge it. The seasons guard access to the City, but by what means, I know not. I will return to that site where once I entered through the Gates of Olympus to ta hagia hagion. I will have no guide, but I will assay the challenge again. May the gods forgive my hubris. I have suffered enough. I would rather die on the slopes of that holy mountain than live on in continued frustration.

And you who read these, my last scribblings, be aware. She has power to reach you. She will affect your life, your loved ones, your very being. Her time is nearing. She will not forever be

*bound behind the ivory veil. In the City of the Gods lies the key,
but you must dare the night to part the veil.*

The night, Rebecca thought. She heard a warning against the night in her dream. Wesley's voice. Was it possible that he would dare the night to gain the treasure that was hidden there? *Of course he would!*

There was no doubt in her mind that there was danger here. If Wesley attempted to unlock an ancient tomb or shrine—whatever it was—he could easily be killed. Stories of the first explorers opening the pyramids were all too popular in fiction and the cinema. There were always carefully laid traps. The unsuspecting treasure hunter was inevitably impaled, beheaded, or crushed. It would be just like Wesley.

Rebecca rocked in her chair, clutching her aching hand. She needed some means of contacting Wesley quickly. Aside from the general description of Metéora in Greece, she really had no idea where the team was. Her only contact was the mysterious Brother El. From Doc and Margaret's description, they didn't know themselves. Perhaps it was like stepping between the worlds in the coven.

She could notify the authorities, but what would she tell them? She believed that three people on an unauthorized archaeological dig were in danger from a metaphysical force because she read an old man's warning written fifteen years ago. No one would pay attention to that. Even Mrs. Weed would not be able to comprehend the force driving at Rebecca now.

She flipped absently through the manuscript one more time, finally allowing the back coverleaf to fall through her fingers. An envelope lay there with her name written on it. She held it in her hands a moment before opening it. There could only be one person who would leave a message for her here. Her hands shook slightly as she fumbled the envelope open. So, this was why she had felt his presence so near. He had been here to leave her a message.

She unfolded the brief note and caught a piece of black silk in her hand.

Thank you for guiding me to Brother El. I will see you in Greece if you dare. And never carry a naked blade.

The black silk was a fine cover cloth, the exact size of Rebecca's stiletto. Black and unadorned. It was the type of gift one would expect only from an intimate friend and Rebecca wavered between feeling the warmth such a gift should bring and anger at his repeated violations of her person. The mixed emotions refused to separate, leaving her shaking with arousal and fear.

Her eyes darted about the room examining the passages and various hiding places. *Damn him!* Where was Ryan McGuire when he could be useful?

REBECCA WENT STRAIGHT to bed when she reached the little flat. She had beaten Mrs. Weed home and there was no sense alerting the older woman to her truancy. When she returned from market, Mrs. Weed bathed and dressed Rebecca's hand and fed her. They sat together on the bed and drank a concoction of herb teas that Mrs. Weed brewed to help healing.

The older woman chattered on about the market, who she had seen and to whom she had spoken. Rebecca was singularly uncommunicative. She sloshed down another cup of tea at Mrs. Weed's insistence, then slowly allowed sleep to claim her as the dishes were cleared.

She slipped in and out of dreams and nightmares and could not tell which was which. Sensual dreams of her husband combined with overtly sexual dreams of Ryan McGuire. And through all, she heard the primitive beating of the warning that had awakened her weeks ago. Wesley's voice. It called them together. Always calling—summoning and yet warning. Beware the night. She could see a misty fog dispersing as she approached her husband, standing on a mountain peak singing the melody. She could not reach him. Still the melody called.

At last she slept soundly.

Thursday, 11 August 1955, Edinburgh, Scotland

Morning broke gradually on Rebecca's slumber. When she finally slept, she had slept as if unconscious and awoke dazed. She could remember only having had dinner with Mrs. Weed and then going to sleep. She robed herself and walked wearily to the kitchen where Mrs. Weed was putting away dishes. What Rebecca wouldn't give for a strong cup of coffee this morning instead of the tea she knew would be waiting.

"Ah, good morning, dearie," said Mrs. Weed cheerily. "How are we doing this morning?"

"I feel like I've been asleep for days," ansered Rebecca.

"Well, you needed a thoroughly good night's sleep. Don't worry, you will be back up to a peak in no time. Here, drink this."

Rebecca savored the hot liquid with a pleasantly bitter aftertaste that reminded her of the longed-for coffee. It was good. She said as much.

"What is it?" she asked.

"Just an herb tea," said Mrs. Weed. "It is rich in caffeine and will get you started quickly."

Rebecca sipped at the cup thoughtfully. "This isn't the same herb tea that you served last night."

"Heavens no, child! That was a brew to make you sleep. This one will wake you up."

"Make me sleep?" Rebecca asked more as an exclamation than a question.

"You were so distraught, Rebecca. And in pain from your hand. I could tell you were planning something and I simply couldn't let you start without a healthy rested body."

Rebecca looked at her bandaged hand and laughed. "This hardly looks healthy."

"Well, let me change your bandage and check your healing, then. You can tell me all about what you are planning as I work."

Rebecca watched Mrs. Weed unwrap her hand, feeling vaguely detached from it, as if she were looking at some bottled specimen in a doctor's laboratory. The palm bore a red blister all the way to her fingertips. The swelling had gone down dramatically, but as the cool air hit her hand she was brought back to the throbbing pain that connected her to reality. Mrs. Weed brought cool water for Rebecca to soak it in and that helped. Then she carefully applied a soothing salve over the burns. Rebecca could once again feel the fire leaving her hand as a slight numbness progressed. With the loss of urgent pain, she flexed her fingers experimentally.

"That is very good. If you can bring yourself to do that frequently from now on, you will not lose much facility with that hand."

"I'll work on it," Promised Rebecca. Then abruptly she asked, "Where does Ryan McGuire live?"

"Now, Becca, how would I know a thing…"

"Alice." Rebecca cut through the sentence. "You know."

"It won't do you any good," sighed Mrs. Weed. "He's not there."

"How do you know?"

"When I arrived home yesterday and found you were out, I could only assume that you had already gone looking for him. I went straight to his rooms and was told he had left the day before. He was not expected back until Samhain."

Rebecca clenched her fingers too tightly and grimaced in pain. "Gone. Where to?"

"Where would he go now, Becca? Surely, you can answer that question as well as I."

To Greece.

Thank you for guiding me to Brother El. I will see you in Greece if you dare.

The answer kept coming back the same. Between Wilton's notes and her mention of Brother El...

"How did Ryan McGuire know about Brother El?" Rebecca shouted, nearly knocking Mrs. Weed over as she rushed to her bureau drawer. Her letters. None from Wesley mentioned Brother El. They'd all been addressed to her and sealed in *Par Avion* envelopes. But the unfinished letter she had begun on Sunday had the envelope addressed in care of Brother El waiting for her to finish the letter. Brother El could lead them both to Wesley.

And somehow, Ryan expected her to find him.

"How am I supposed to find him?"

"I think that you must go to Greece."

"Greece! How would I find anyone there? I haven't the faintest idea how to get there and I don't speak the language. And I don't have money to fly around the world on a whim."

"Perhaps you wouldn't have to speak the language, find Ryan, or pay for the trip," spoke Mrs. Weed calmly. "If you were there, perhaps they would find you. As for money, your fellowship has an extended travel clause should you need research from another source. Dr. Reston mentioned it the day he suggested I rent you a bed."

"How would they find me if I just landed in Greece?" Rebecca asked, objecting as she admitted the possibility of traveling.

"Magic."

"A summoning?" She conjured up images in her mind of yet another ritual that she would have to master.

"Let's not be so dramatic, shall we? There are easier ways."

"How?" Rebecca asked.

"Magic obeys simple laws of the universe. If you can see something in your mind's eye and believe it to be real, you must be brought together. The magic that you practice now is really nothing more than this. See it in your mind's eye and it must come to you. You need only be available."

"If that were really all there was to it," said Rebecca, "I should be able to create the image here and stay put. It would have to come to me."

"So it would. Tell me; are you ready for that responsibility?"

"What sort of responsibility?" asked Rebecca.

"The responsibility of causing whatever event would prompt Ryan McGuire to turn around once he got to Greece and come trekking back here to see you. Think. What are some of the things that could prompt so swift and sudden a return?"

Rebecca thought. Several images came rapidly to mind. Ryan McGuire with the statue of a goddess held triumphantly overhead. Ryan McGuire seeking her out in anger with his knife drawn. Suddenly an image of Wesley, broken, sprawled face down on an ancient altar, a knife raised above his back. Rebecca shook. Any of these quick pictures could bring Ryan McGuire back from Greece to search for her. The more bizarre the circumstance, the more likely it was. No. She was not ready for that type of responsibility.

"You have also been thinking of pursuing Ryan so that he would lead you to Wesley. Put that image aside. It is not healthy," said Mrs. Weed. "Do not think of intermediary steps, think of the desired outcome. Directly visualize that."

Rebecca blushed. Perhaps she had been thinking too much of Ryan. That couldn't be healthy for her relationship with Wesley. What did she really want? She wanted to be held in her husband's arms. To make love to him. To conceive their child. She needed Wesley.

"I'll go to Greece."

18

Invasion

Thursday, 11 August 1995, Edinburgh, Scotland

GETTING OUT of Scotland and to the Metéora proved more complicated than anticipated. Rebecca spent most of Thursday at the embassy retrieving her updated passport with her new name. She ran to the university and explained to Dr. Reston that she would be pursuing a lead in Central Greece where a form of goddess worship was still practiced at the very foot of the Orthodox monasteries. And that while based in the Greek pantheon, it appeared that a single goddess was the object of reverence. This supported Rebecca's thesis that both modern Christianity and ancient goddess worship coexisted in the same space. Reston raised an eyebrow at the rather weak connection.

"And, of course, the fact that your husband is somewhere in that vicinity of Greece is entirely coincidental," he chuckled as he signed the travel voucher.

"I… uh… Dr. Reston," Rebecca started and stopped multiple times, much to the amusement of her advisor.

"Mrs. Allen, I have been friends with Professor and Mrs. Weed for many years," he said. "Alice and I already discussed the likelihood that you would want to engage in this pursuit. Yes, I am aware that your husband is investigating an ancient site with Doctor Heinrich. Heinrich has been a guest lecturer in archaeology here on several occasions. I am also aware that Dr. McGuire has taken off with intents of cashing in on Dr. Heinrich's find. McGuire did his undergraduate work here and then moved to the United States specifically to study under Heinrich a dozen years ago. You pursue the pursuer. Good hunting, Mrs. Allen."

Rebecca left his office somewhat bemused and even a bit confused. Mrs. Weed met her outside the door and took her directly to Waverly train station.

"I packed your bag with everything you should need and expect you to return to me before you return to the United States, dearie," the old woman said.

"It's all happening so fast," said Rebecca. "I hardly know what to do next."

"Things are likely to slow down once you get to London. I have no idea how you will get from there to Athens, nor from Athens to your husband. But I know you will arrive safely. Your circle will pray for your safe and successful journey."

"Thank you, Alice. I don't know how to say it any more heartfelt than that. You have given me both hope and power."

"You will be careful, won't you?"

"Oh, my dear mentor! How could I be anything but? You have taught me well."

"Blessings light and dark, Sadb," Mrs. Weed whispered. "May the goddess smile upon you."

Rebecca boarded the night train for London's King's Cross station. It was not a peaceful journey. The night train made frequent stops for local commuters, even late in the night. With each jarring bounce, Rebecca cradled her tender hand more carefully. She hugged her walking stick, now her wand, as she was bounced into and out of a restless sleep in which visions of Wesley in a vast temple plagued her.

Friday, 12 August 1955, London, England

Rebecca arrived at King's Cross with no other intent at the surface of her mind than finding a cup of coffee. Near the busy train station, she found a café that advertised coffee and ordered a full English breakfast to go with it. It was a typically bland and boiled breakfast, but the café did have salt and pepper that she applied liberally to the entire meal.

On Euston Road, Rebecca found a travel agent, but she was much too early for its posted hours. She wandered on, thinking she might stop at the British Library, but realizing that, too, would still be closed. Near exhaustion from her sleepless night, she stumbled into a small hotel and booked a room. Once there, she collapsed into sleep without bothering to undress.

It was after noon when she roused herself and she panicked at the thought of missing the travel agent. Carrying only her purse and staff, she rushed out of the hotel and the two blocks to the agency.

"How may I help you?" asked a stiff man at the main desk. He wasn't much if any older than Rebecca, but acted as if he were fifty and she a teen. She glanced at her disheveled and travel-weary appearance and laughed at herself.

"I need to book transport to Athens by the fastest route," she said. "I'm afraid I've not had much sleep getting here. It is a family emergency."

"Ah, I see," he responded, loosening a bit. "I understand your condition." She was sure she saw an eyebrow lift at the mention. "London to Athens by fastest route. According to the timetables, it appears that you should fly. There is, however, no direct flight. I could send you via Paris or Rome. No. No. The Rome flight is also via Paris." He busily shuffled through his timetables and belatedly waved Rebecca to a chair. "Ah. I see. You'll be flying London to Paris, Paris to Rome, and Rome to Athens. You can be on the first flight first thing in the morning and change planes in Paris, but I'm afraid you will need lodging in Rome before a morning flight on Sunday to Athens. Should I book lodging in Athens for you as well?"

Rebecca was overwhelmed. She just wanted to reach Wesley. Paris? Rome? And no time to see either one.

"Just book the flights and the overnight in Rome," she finally responded. "I will arrange things… uh… with family… in Athens."

"Of course. And how would you be paying for this Miss…?"

"Mrs. Mrs. Rebecca Allen." She handed the agent her travel voucher from the University.

"Passport?" she handed it over and he copied down details. "I must call to verify the voucher and then call the airlines. If you could return at half past three, I should have everything arranged," he smiled at her. "If I make a suggestion, Mrs. Allen?" She nodded. "You might want fancier dress when you board the aircraft. I understand you've been in the north," he sniffed, "and conditions are different among the Scots. But air travel, you know?"

Rebecca nodded. She might look a bit strange in her hiking gear, but she would need it in Greece. She hoped Mrs. Weed had packed a dress.

Saturday, 13 August 1955, Rome, Italy

NONE OF REBECCA'S destinations were in countries where her limited German could be of help. As a result, the trip was a confusion of different voices and different languages, none of which she understood. A kindly flight attendant had pointed her to the right desk to check in for her flight to Rome. When she arrived at the airport outside of Rome, it was only three in the afternoon, but it seemed to be too great a journey to try to see the Vatican when she couldn't even tell the taxi driver where she wanted to go. She had simply held out the note with the name and address of her hotel and half an hour later was unloaded on Via Fiumara in front of a small hotel. Inside, a very friendly and talkative desk clerk welcomed her.

"You're American!" Rebecca exclaimed.

"Zeke Mosely of Corn Crib, Kansas," he grinned. "Don't bother looking on the map. They call me out of the cellar whenever a reservation is made in English."

"How did you happen to end up here?"

"Compliments of the U.S. Army. Arrived just in time for the end-war occupation. A lot of leisure found me in the clutches of my sweet Luciana. Got married and now I've got three little Dago rug rats running around. They all speak better Italian than English. I think they are conspiring against me!" Zeke jabbered away.

"Fascinating. I wish I could spend more time here. It's lovely," Rebecca said. The hotel was small but filled with a quaint charm.

"It's the only thing I got during the war," he laughed. "My wife's parents owned it. They sent me here to fight the Krauts, but the biggest thing I ever shot was a rabbit." Rebecca laughed. "It's on the menu tonight," he nodded. Rebecca snorted at the admission.

"Before I commit to eating it, what year did you shoot it in?"

"Neither ear. Shot it right in the tail," he rejoined. "Mrs. Allen, I understand you are under some duress in this journey. Let me get your things settled in your room and then please come down to rest in the bar. I will fix you a Bellini. You will sit and watch the people and for a few minutes, you will let your mind rest from your troubles."

"That's very kind of you."

"It's the Italian way. When you stop and think about it, it's the way I was raised in Kansas… except, of course, I wouldn't have served alcohol. I like it much better here."

Rebecca took a short nap before taking advantage of Zeke's offer. It would not do to have any kind of alcoholic drink as tired as she was. *What would Wesley think?* Sleep claimed her rapidly.

SHE WALKS ALONG a moonlit path, her steps ringing in her ears, the only sound in the silence surrounding her. She must hush. Everyone will know she is here.

Deciding she can move more silently without her shoes, Rebecca is suddenly naked, her bare feet moving noiselessly through the dense forest. She is The Hart and The Hind, accustomed to stealth. She is a goddess of transformation, changing in any way she desires.

The baying of hounds breaks through the quiet and she runs. As they close in, her panic mounts. She can see their bared teeth and glowing eyes. They leap for her exposed throat… and freeze in the air. Suddenly, they are puppies, playfully rolling over each other as she rubs their soft bellies.

The one who set these hounds on her trail is a danger to the forest, given to her keeping. Waving the dogs to the fore, she paces through the forest as they pick up the scent of her pursuer and bay in anger. Like Diana, she is no longer the hunted but the huntress. She follows the pack as they race toward the menace.

The stag does not flee when they approach. He turns casually toward her as she stretches her bow. A demon sneers from the beast, changing to a horned man. He waves a hand and the dogs fall to the ground whining, circling in confusion. They look at him and then at her before vanishing in the night.

"You have come to me at last," he laughs.

"I have come for you," she responds.

"It makes no difference. Here in the green we will mate. When we meet on the physical plane you will be mine. Then I will be the hart and you will be my hind."

Rebecca, Sadb, feels moisture gathering at the juncture of her thighs and feels the pressure of her hardening nipples. She is drawn to the evil beast, stepping near enough that he might almost touch her. She might almost touch him. She becomes lost in his hypnotic eyes. Hunter or hunted? Which is which?

Just as their lips are about to touch, a horn sounds. Voices surround them. The hounds return. They are encircled. The confident sneer on the face of the horned man begins to fade. The voices, like music, close in on them and the demon turns to run. Before his first leap a thousand arrows sprout from his hide. Screaming in agony, the demon disappears. The hounds leap into the void after him.

Sadb stands frozen, awaiting her own fate.

The hunter's song softens. He is no longer death stalking her, but is the gamekeeper, protecting his forest from poachers, healing the injured, feeding the hungry. His softly glowing presence emerges from the forest into the clearing, comforting her with his music.

His image resolves and becomes clear. A smile crosses her lips as she looks into the eyes…

Wesley!

Behind the Ivory Veil

Saturday, 13 August 1955, City of the Gods

In Greece, or at some point in the universe which he accessed through Greece, Wesley once again packed his tools—pencil, paper, string, and guitar—to leave the rostrum. The patterns and figures he had recorded spun madly in his head as he attempted to make sense of them. He was certain now that the symbols on the rostrum had moved in relation to each other. His head throbbed at the implications. He was a good Christian. This was deep pagan magic.

If only he could reconcile the two.

That was only one of the wishes that had grown in his mind. The more he hummed and played the soft tunes that came to mind as he sketched the drawings, the more he yearned for Rebecca. Yearned for his wife. He wished for a soft bed with her in his arms. Of course, he also wished for a ham sandwich, an Orange Crush, and a grand piano.

And to be off the mountain by nightfall.

The entire team had been affected by the strange warning that seemed to emanate from the rostrum when Wesley sang there. It was fearful yet seductive. They all left the site well before sundown, traveling into the setting sun and the fog that shrouded them. Their quiet nighttime conversations left Doc and Margaret as disconcerted as Wesley. They had delved much deeper into a mystery than they could fathom. They had seen not only into the past, but into the consciousness of humanity. Their work in the City of the Gods continued with a deeper sense of reverence and a mission that had previously been undiscovered. They were recording the foundation of humanity. The work was urgent and must be completed soon. They were called to do this work, as certainly as young missionaries were called to the service of God.

And yet none of them considered risking the dark to stay on the mountain after nightfall.

The four weary people linked together by their rope, climbed down from the mountain in the dense fog. The music was there. Wesley always heard singing voices in the fog. He was thankful for the silence of his partners who seemed to hear nothing. To Wesley, though, the music was as tangible and present as the tightness of the rope around his waist. It brought him down from the mountain gently. Each night he returned to the camp at peace after hearing the music.

This afternoon, however, the voices were agitated. It chilled Wesley to listen to the music. The soprano was too shrill. It grated on his ears. It was taking too long to get down the mountain. He was becoming more tired instead of less. For the first time, Wesley could feel the looseness of the rocks, the volitility of the ground he was walking on. It seemed like a living thing, heaving, breathing beneath his feet. Something in the air spoke of destruction, devastation. He was sweating beneath his pack and guitar.

A premonition preceded the ground collapsing under him by a fraction of a second. Before his back hit the ground, however, he was out of the fog. It disappeared behind him as quickly as it had closed in. Doc's low curse broke through the air crushing the last echo of the singing voices from Wesley's ears. He started to say he was all right but cut off quickly when he realized that none of the rest of the team had even noticed his fall. They had emerged from the fog ahead of Wesley and dropped the ropes at once. Doc's abrupt curse was joined by a low moan from Wesley as they looked down on the remnants of their camp.

The bivouacs had been slashed and lay scattered. Other supplies had been raided. After a brief inventory, it appeared the only food remaining would be in their packs, or down at their supply point.

The three moved on to assess the notes that they had so carefully compiled. Doc's and Margaret's were intact. Wesley's notes were gone.

"It's McGuire's work," said Doc. "He would take the single item that he thought was valuable—a key to the treasure. The destruction must be intended to drive us away so he has the site to himself."

"No." Wesley held his guitar in his hands. "I won't back down." He strummed a soft chord and a chilling vocal cadence.

"Why only Wesley's drawings?" asked Margaret.

"Maps," answered Wesley as he continued to lose himself in the strumming of his guitar—seeking the calm center music always brought him. The other two stared at him blankly. "It occurred to me a few days ago that the drawings resembled maps if you looked at them correctly. Especially with my notations of the directions on them. If, as you say, he is looking for the key to a treasure, a map would be the first thing to grab."

"That's true," answered Doc. "I am sorry about the loss of your work, Wesley. We will have to attempt to reconstruct it together."

"Not worth our while," he shrugged. "Those were all early attempts. It is a four-tiered guide. If the symbols on the rostrum shift as the days go by, then so do the directions. Given a year of drawings and a few months to study them, it might be possible to predict the movements, just as astronomers predict the movements of the firmament. If he follows the guide, he might come close, but he could never reach the City." Wesley hit a harsher chord on the guitar and lifted his voice in a dissonant complement. Across the greensward Pol snapped his head and locked eyes with Wesley.

The shrill note Pol emitted reminded Wesley of the too-shrill soprano in the fog. An evening wind was rising in the camp and whipped at Pol's hair and loose clothing. He and Wesley moved toward each other, never wavering in their cadence nor their eye contact. They turned to face the westering sun, and as Wesley maintained the underlying rhythm and vocalese, Pol's voice rose in a chant that raised the hairs on Doc's and Margaret's arms.

May your mattress be of thorns.
May your blanket be of storms.
Lie down with scorpions as your bedmates,
And rise with ants as your companions.
May all the gods rise against you at every step
And plunge you headlong into darkness.
As my heart is honest,
May my words be strong!

Pol slapped his hands together, ending the curse. As if an echo, thunder clapped in the northwest and clouds moved quickly from behind the mountain.

Wesley's eyes never wavered from Pol as the boy turned to descend the rock on which he'd been standing. Guitar dropped on the ground, Wesley was in action before conscious thought caught up with his body. Pol lost his footing as a brutal gust of wind hit him from behind. In that second, Wesley found himself exactly beneath the falling boy, catching him in his arms.

Pol wrapped his arms around Wesley's neck and began to sob as the musician carried him back into the camp. Wesley laid the boy down on his own bedroll and whipped the shreds of the bivouac out of the way as Margaret and Doc scurried to get food and water together. He cradled Pol in his arms near the base of the old tree, fed him, and talked to him.

"I'm not injured," Pol said.

"Not in body. Your spirit has been hurt," answered Wesley.

"I have never cursed." Pol's whole body shook. The storm moved to the west and below them. Their greensward remained undisturbed but for a gentle breeze that cooled the night air. Doc brought Wesley his guitar from where it had been dropped and helped Wesley remove the shreds of his bivouac. All four bedrolls were moved closer together and Pol stretched out on his between Wesley and Margaret. As if her mothering instinct took control, she held and soothed the boy.

"Tomorrow is our day of rest," Doc said. "Brother El was to have left us supplies today. We'll hike down and replenish for our last week up here. I trust Marcos will make the journey to retrieve us next Sunday."

"Papa will be here as promised."

"Good. We will defy this attack on our camp by not being moved."

"Pol," whispered Wesley, "we make a good team. Do not fear. In as much as God... all the gods... give me strength, I will protect you, my son."

Wesley once again strummed his guitar. This time, his voice spoke in a plaintive lullaby as the clouds scattered from the night sky. The others fell asleep to the gentle and soothing tones.

Wesley lay awake long after he had laid his guitar aside attempting to come to grips with his sudden acceptance of other gods than the One he had served all his life. In his half-sleep, he stood once again before the Temple of Aurora Borealis, but this time saw the rostrum growing from its floor before him.

Shirley, Goodness, and Mercy would follow him. Even into the night.

19
Chasing a Dream

Sunday, 14 August 1955, Athens, Greece

REBECCA HART Allen, world traveler. She stepped off the plane to the glare of the afternoon sun, much warmer here than in Edinburgh. She shifted beneath the woolen sweater she wore over her plaid pleated skirt. Mrs. Weed had taken her shopping for tartans, a favorite souvenir of Americans who imagined they had some Scottish blood in their veins. Perhaps Rebecca did have Scottish ancestors. They had found a Hart tartan, though it was classified as Clan Urquhart. Nonetheless, Mrs. Weed sewed the skirt for Rebecca. Mid-August in Athens, however, was scarcely the place to be wearing wool.

She looked around as she descended the steps from the airplane, half expecting Wesley to be waiting for her. Or perhaps Ryan McGuire. Her visualizations on the airplane from Rome were mixed. She chanted a spell Mrs. Weed had taught her to put herself into a visualizing trance and settled in to focus on her husband. But images of Ryan kept intruding on her subconscious. The men were locked in combat, spinning on the edge of the world until both slipped and fell into an unending chasm. Spinning, falling. Spinning falling. The image repeated in her dream until she thought she would scream.

The wheels touching the pavement jolted her awake. She was in Greece.

REBECCA TRIED TO come to grips with the utter foreignness of Athens. It was a different world than Edinburgh. Scotland felt like home. Greece was foreign. She was isolated and alone. She had no concept of what time it was and was confused over directions. The travel agent had given her a map, but she was unable to even locate the airport on it.

Worse, she had no idea where she was going. She had told the agent that she would depend on family once she reached Greece. If only she knew where they were.

She finally found a porter who spoke English and he directed her to a taxi stand where she could find an English-speaking driver. She stepped into the cab with her walking stick, and waited while the driver put her bag in the trunk. When he got in the car and pulled away from the curb he asked, "Where to, Miss?"

Rebecca let her head fall back on the seat as she nearly sobbed, "The City of the Gods." The driver looked at her in the mirror, ignoring traffic has he pulled onto the highway. She was intimidated by the intent gaze. He seemed to be looking at something besides her appearance or her face. He was looking deeper.

"Do you have an address?"

Rebecca snorted. Had she really said that aloud? "Please. Take me to the Hotel Athenee." The driver looked at her again and abruptly cut across two lanes of traffic.

"As you wish," he said. Leaving the airport behind, they wound their way into Athens. The driver continually glanced into the rearview mirror—not at traffic, which he seemed to ignore, but at Rebecca. She gradually slumped down in the seat far enough that she could not see the driver's eyes in the mirror. The cab pulled up beside a beautiful hotel near the center of town. Rebecca had seen a glimpse of the Acropolis as they turned in.

"Here it is. Hotel Athenee. One of our finest. Views of the Acropolis and Parthenon from all rooms." He turned to look at Rebecca who was still slumped down in the seat and was making no attempt to move. "Are you ill, Miss? This is where you wanted to come, is it not?" Rebecca sat up slowly.

"Yes. Fine. Just a bit overwhelmed. This is… too big. Is there a smaller hotel you could take me to? Perhaps a bed and breakfast?" she asked plaintively.

"Of course, Miss. There is a small *pensione* not far from here. A bit less expensive, as well, though that might not be a consideration for you. But there is no view. You will have to walk a bit to view the Acropolis." He pulled away from the grand hotel and wound through the narrow streets of Athens. The hotel was so small that it was marked only by a wooden sign on the door.

"This is lovely," she said. It reminded her of the little hotel near the airport in Rome she had stayed at… *Was it just last night?*

"An Italian opened it right after the war. Sadly, after the occupation, Athenians were not kindly disposed toward the Italians. The owner decided to sell out and leave for his homeland before any further damage could be done. To the building or his person." The driver spoke with a note of pride that led Rebecca to believe he might have a vested interest in the property.

"I'm sure it will be fine," she said.

"Not too crowded. Clean," he said as he held the door open for her. "But a long way from the City of the Gods."

Rebecca stumbled through the door, turning to face the driver. She fought down the fear that insisted on rising inside her and half-expected Ryan McGuire to be facing her. During her hour in the taxi, she had nearly convinced herself that her journey was hopeless. Mrs. Weed had told her to visualize and what was real in her mind would come to her. But to have the first person she met in Athens respond to her about the City of the Gods was more than a little uncanny—and frightening.

"What do you know about the City of the Gods?" she demanded. Her voice was more forceful and shrill than she intended.

He reached in his pocket and withdrew a New Testament which he handed to her. She looked at him curiously but opened the cover. Her husband's precise handwriting filled the inside cover. "To my friend, Marcos. May God richly bless you. J. Wesley Allen"

"Wesley!" she cried.

"Are you Mrs. Allen?" a woman's voice spoke from behind her. A lovely Greek woman wiped her hands on a towel as she approached. "Yes. You look exactly like the photo he carried."

"You know my husband?" Rebecca asked.

"The three of them, Wesley, Doctor Heinrich and Doctor Jacobsen stayed with us before Marcos drove them to his father's home in Thessaly," the woman said. "Excuse my rudeness. I am Helen Pariskovopolis. You have already met my husband, Marcos."

"You know how to get there? Can you help me? Please?"

"Of course, Mrs. Allen," Marcos said. "Welcome to our home and our hotel. We will drive to Metéora tomorrow. I planned to go up later in the week to retrieve the campers anyway. Your husband will be quite surprised to see you waiting."

"Pleasantly, I hope. I'm so worried about him." Rebecca's face fell and she looked at the husband and wife before her. Respectfully, she said, "Are you believers? I thought only a select few knew the way."

"We are believers in the true God and his one church," Helen said firmly. Marcos smiled at her and placed a protective arm around her. It was the first look of genuine warmth and affection that Rebecca had seen in Greece.

"I am not a believer as you have phrased the question," Marcos said. "But great is the mystery of godliness. We will talk much this evening and in the morning, I will take you to my father's house."

Rebecca was led to a pleasant room where she changed from the hot woolens into her slacks and a short-sleeved shirt. Refreshed, she returned to the main floor where Helen immediately invited her to the kitchen. Seeing the woman in a modest dress, Rebecca was worried that she might offend with her choice of clothing.

"Helen, am I dressed appropriately? I have very few clothes with me and expected to be hiking, much as I do in Scotland."

"There are differences among people. Women wearing pants is not common in Greece, but is more so in Athens than in smaller villages. We are not as cosmopolitan as large cities like Paris and New York, but there is a great move toward modernization. There is even a part of town where the beats reside."

"Beats?"

"Ahh. Beatniks? Mostly expatriates from various places in Europe and America. Painters, poets, novelists, and wealthy young people who can live wherever they wish as their fathers pay."

"Oh. I see."

"You are dressed for exploring, and that is what you will be doing. I have been to the so-called City myself. Nothing but the ruins of an ancient temple. I suppose, though, that it is of interest to archaeologists. They will have you dusting shards of pottery on your hands and knees, I should think. This manner of dress is most appropriate."

"That isn't the description my husband has sent me." As they worked, Helen opened up a bit.

"I was invited to join in the belief of the ancients," Helen said. "It was as foreign to me as Greece is to you. I was raised here in Athens. We do not believe in an ancient pantheon. Marcos took me to see the ancient site before we were married, but I had already made up my mind. Perhaps if I had not, I would have seen something different. Marcos and I married and moved back here to Athens. We had a bit of a struggle during the occupation, but survived. I think, though, that deep in his heart, my husband still believes. They see something there that pursues them all their lives. Even my son is a believer and is on the mountain with the archaeologists."

There were Wilton's words again. *Pursued all their lives.* Rebecca helped put food on the table and Marcos joined the women for moussaka and a salad. The food was delicious. Rebecca gradually revealed her story and how she had dreamed that Wesley was in danger. The dream had been so compelling that she had flown to Greece.

"If I had enough petrol in the Jeep, we would leave tonight," Marcos said as they discussed the journey north. "But I cannot buy on Sunday and there will be nothing available until after nine o'clock tomorrow but coffee. As soon as I have prepared the Jeep, we will leave."

"I'm worried about Pol," Helen said. "If something has given you a warning that you must search out your husband, it cannot be good for my son, either."

"If one is in danger, all are in danger," Marcos agreed. "Rebecca, I no longer believe there will be a deliverer for an ancient goddess. But I do believe there is a great power on the mountain. I love my son. If he is in danger, I want to be there to help in any way."

Sunday, 14 August 1955, City of the Gods

MORNING DAWNED BRIGHT and clear with no trace of the fog that seemed to surround them in the mornings. The four proceeded to the supply drop-off point and distributed the load for the hike back up the mountain. Doc and Wesley split the burden of carrying the lockbox with them up to the main camp. "Better to be protected than to be exposed," Doc had said. And they had no more supply runs coming. *Locking the henhouse after the fox,* Wesley thought as they struggled up the mountain with the box slung between them.

After supplies were safely back at the base camp and they had eaten lunch, Doc and Margaret decided to take a walk and enjoy nature. Wesley noticed the direction that they chose for their nature walk, which was uphill, and rightly supposed they would look for some clue to the access of the City of the Gods. Pol also went out exploring, planning to see what was on the opposite shore of the stream. Acting responsibly, Wesley asked the boy to stay within earshot in case the previous day's visitor was still about. Pol smiled and said there was not much chance of that, but he would stay close.

Wesley sat in the shade of the old tree and played some relaxing melodies on his guitar, gliding from gospel to classical to flamenco. He intended to read his New Testament and meditate. His eyes fell on the scripture but he could not really focus on any of the words. His mind was filled with as many lines from Greek mythology as from the scripture and they seemed to weave in and out of each other. He thought about the empathic goddess locked behind the ivory veil and considered the parallels with gifts of healing spoken of in Paul's epistles.

Wesley was losing his grip on the reality of his faith. He fought to regain the truth as he knew it.

Why? Why must the truth be limited to what I know? Those who know, know not. Was that scripture or just another myth? Again, the image of the goddess sprang to mind. *No one has lifted my veil.* Another veil came to mind, torn from top to bottom. There must be a way to penetrate the veil and uncloud the mysteries that plagued his spirituality.

As he sat beneath the tree, Wesley sank deeper into his meditative trance. The guitar took on a life of its own beneath his fingers and his voice hummed and popped along with it. Music, words, images. The trance spread until he was no longer conscious of his fingers moving on the frets. He was a thousand years away and removed from the mountainside where only his body remained in touch with the world he knew.

In that other consciousness, Wesley pursued the conflicts of his faith. His mind was full of images of heresy and persecution. Daniel in the fiery furnace. The four horses of Revelation. Christians sent to the Coliseum to be eaten by lions. In every instance, spiritual conflict led to martyrdom. It was apocalyptic. *Why is this so different? There is no enemy to slash at with a sword; only this burning image of a goddess behind the ivory veil.*

His playing morphed into a new chord and cadence, throwing him back to the images of the rostrum admonishing him to beware the night. Yet, in spite of the warning, there was also a challenge to persevere and to conquer. Not only to beware the night, but to dare the night. *Come before me cleansed and clean.* Was that not what his own baptism had been about? To make him clean enough to face God?

God or Goddess? The goddess behind the ivory veil was all that he should love and treasure; not the idol that Ryan McGuire sought, but equally to be sought, to be found. She excited a passion in him that stoked his memories of his wedding night. He could not 'mortify the flesh' in the face of this passion.

She—was it the goddess on the mountain, or the goddess in the flesh of his wife?—was the reason for his being. He could once again be baptized in her.

He was dreaming, he realized as he awoke in the afternoon heat. He was sweating out his fantasy beneath the open skies on a mountainside in Greece, a thousand years away from the goddess and a thousand miles from his wife, yet at the very gate of her private realm.

The sudden rush of water over his face and body tingled and sent a quick awakening into his mind. He swam, as much as one could swim in the rushing shallow water that paused to pool beside the ancient olive tree. No one was around. The water felt better than he ever imagined. So clear and refreshing. Why had no one else—other than Pol—thought of splashing in the stream before this? They had each taken private moments out of sight of the others to wash by the edge of the stream, but none had dared plunge into it.

Wesley was determined to avail himself of the fresh cold water daily from this point forward. He lowered himself below the surface. Once. Twice. Three times. Cleansed by the tide. Baptized in the rushing water. He was one with the lord—all the lords that had ever been.

He crawled onto the bank and lay exhausted in the sun. No one had returned from their various nature hikes. He laughed in embarrassed relief as he realized he was lying naked on the bank, drying in the air. He moved to re-dress and to decide if he should call out to the others. *Olly olly oxen free!* He giggled. He felt so refreshed it was like entering childhood again. He would simply lie on his bedroll and wait for his companions to return. While refreshing, the impromptu swim had also left him tired and perhaps a bit lethargic. He would rest a bit and if they hadn't returned in a few minutes, he would start the evening fire and begin dinner preparations. His bedroll was far more comfortable than it had been on any other night. He relaxed. He would just close his eyes a moment.

Wesley slept deeply through the night.

Monday, 15 August 1955, Kastraki, Greece

Rebecca rode most of the journey clutching her injured hand close to herself in silence. At last the peaks of Metéora arose from the plain ahead. In a few minutes, they rumbled across the cobblestones of a small village Main Street and pulled up in front of a small cluster of houses sharing a common courtyard. It was late in the day as they had not managed to leave Athens before noon. She was hot and tired and unprepared for the family's welcome. Sophia ran to meet them, trailed by children. She gave Marcos a hug and then turned to Rebecca.

"Marcos! We didn't expect you for another week."

"Sophia, this is Rebecca Allen, Wesley's wife. Rebecca, my sister Sophia," Marcos introduced them.

"You look hot and travel-weary," Sophia said. "Tomas! Draw water for our guest." A boy of about ten rushed to the well. "Later we can heat water so you can bathe, but please refresh yourself with water. Just a splash on your face will do wonders for you."

Rebecca was happy to refresh herself from the bucket of cool well-water and surreptitiously used the wet cloth provided to push inside her shirt and wipe her armpits. Marcos entered one of the houses so it was only the two women at the well. Sophia held Rebecca's hair back while the young woman washed her neck. With a sudden thought of warmth and affection, she thought of Mrs. Weed and how like her Marcos's sister was.

As the water dripped from her face, she was caught in a memory of Wesley singing something akin to a hymn in his rich tenor. She swayed as Sophia poured a cup of water over her head, matting Rebecca's auburn hair. The Greek woman then proceeded to towel dry the hair as Rebecca unwrapped her hand and plunged it into the cold water. It was a shock to her senses that soon settled into relief.

Rebecca was caught up in the cooling sensation of dipping her injured hand in the water when a gentle voice behind her startled.

"You have hurt your hand," said the old man.

"Papa, this is Wesley's wife, Rebecca," Sophia said. "Rebecca, my father, Andrew."

"I'm pleased to meet you, sir. Wesley has written to me about your kindness and hospitality. I apologize for my unannounced visit."

"It is nothing," Andrew said. "You are welcome here to our home and to our family. May I see your hand?" Rebecca tentatively reached out her hand, still blistered red.

"I burned it," she explained.

"Yes," the old man said. He held her hand gently in one hand while he passed his fingertips over it with the other. Rebecca could feel the featherlight brush, but her eyes told her that his fingers had not touched at all.

"A very hot fire," he said at last. "I believe that we may have a salve that would soothe you. Sophia, *paidi mou*, will you ask Mama for the special salve I keep in my medicine box?"

"Yes, Papa." Rebecca's new friend departed quickly.

"May I ask how this happened?" he asked.

Rebecca faltered for a moment. This old man whose eyes were so much like those of Marcos would be impossible to lie to. Yet she could hardly tell the truth. Finally, she averted her eyes.

"There was a fire. I grabbed a hot… handle."

The old man looked at her silently until Rebecca raised her eyes to meet his. Then he spoke.

"We are a small village and unusual things are quickly known by all. A few days ago another came to our area, pretending to be a tourist and visiting the monasteries. He, too, carried one hand wrapped in gauze."

Rebecca moaned and lifted her face to the bright Mediterranean sky. He was here. She must get to Wesley before Ryan did.

"A private matter, I see. Are you worried about your husband?"

"Yes," answered Rebecca. "Do you know if everything is all right on their dig?"

"Brother El delivered supplies to their drop point just two days ago for their final week on the mountain. He reported nothing out of the ordinary. Why have you come? What brought you here?"

Rebecca soon found herself telling him the entire story of finding Wilton's last notes, how the haunting image of Wesley had come to her in dreams, and of Ryan's determination to recover the lost goddess. The old man occasionally prodded her with questions as he gently applied the salve Sophia brought, but Rebecca told about her fears freely.

When she was finished and there seemed to be no more to tell, they sat quietly for a few moments.

"Papa, dinner is ready. Will you bring our guest?" Sophia called.

"Come. Let us eat. You need food and rest. We will deal with strange things and you will tell me more," he said.

20
Into the Night

Monday, 15 August 1955, City of the Gods

WHEN WESLEY awoke in the predawn light, he found the air as clear as on those days when they did not go to the city. He felt incredibly refreshed and invigorated. He helped make breakfast and drank of his freshly steeped coffee. He had become accustomed to the Greek method of simply putting the finely ground coffee in the little *briki* and heating it until the foam formed on top, just before the liquid boiled. He would then pour this into his small cup and sip at it until they were ready to leave for the City.

This morning, they went about their preparations, including lashing together on the guide rope as Pol led them up the mountain. Wesley adhered to all the safety precautions they had taken because he had not been up the mountain while the others explored yesterday. Without the morning fog, the way looked clear and open. The gentle greensward continued up the mountain from the olive tree. Wesley vaguely wondered about that and attempted to locate the spot where he'd fallen when they came down two days ago. He couldn't find any loose stones like those that had rolled from under him.

As Pol began the trip up, he looked curiously at his friend. Wesley was smiling and looking around. To Wesley and to Pol, there was no fog. Doc and Margaret continued to stumble blindly up the slope.

The fog receded from Wesley's ears, as well. The chorus of voices were the most beautiful he had ever heard. With nothing around him but the pleasant walk, Wesley could only assume that these were angels singing and he gladly joined his voice with theirs. The musical tongue was so soft and yet so all-encompassing that it did not disturb the natural sounds of the walk. Wesley could see the crest of the hill and pillars visible over the horizon before he realized the voices he heard were not in the air at all, but were centered just inside his ears where no one else would hear. He stepped onto the plateau and took in the truly stunning sight of the pillars and the rostrum in the center of the forum.

The City was tangibly different today. Wesley could "see" more clearly than ever. And what he saw was not the basically monochromatic stone architecture of his previous journeys, but a City that sparkled and glowed like a jeweled crown on the crest of the hill. His entire senses were wrenched out of himself into an ultrasensitivity to the light, sound, smell, taste and feel of the City. Tears drenched his cheeks as he tried futilely to comprehend the scope of his experience. Even Doc and Margaret looked different to him. He could see how much they cared for each other—loved each other.

Doc looked strangely at Wesley and the musician responded before the question was voiced.

"It's okay. I'm fine." A few feet away, Pol waited with a hand outstretched. Wesley took the offered hand and the two ascended the rostrum together, leaving a puzzled Doc and Margaret to stare after them.

The music. First Pol's voice singing his greeting. Then Wesley's own counterpoint in rich tones he did not recognize even as his own voice. The response came antiphonally from every corner of the City as if the pillars themselves were singing the litany. It was more than could be borne standing up. As the sun followed them over the crest of the hill, Wesley sank to his knees in the center of the rostrum. His tears fell on the vivid colors of the dais. The colors themselves rippled with the splash of each tear.

"My tears I leave you, for the price of passage is to leave a part of yourself behind," prayed Wesley. Yes, *prayed*. "I believe. Lord, help my unbelief."

When he regained his composure, Pol knelt beside him. Doc and Margaret had already slipped away to continue their survey of the pillars. Wesley looked at the boy but only said, "It is so beautiful."

Pol smiled and the two set to work with their project, happily chatting about the slight shifts of the symbols and their relationship to the pillars.

It was a very good day.

Tuesday, 16 August 1955, Kastraki, Greece

R<small>EBECCA SLEPT WELL</small> on a bed provided by Sophia and awoke refreshed in the morning. Her hand still throbbed if she moved wrong, but the cooling salve Andrew had used to dress it the day before had helped relieve the pain a little.

"When everyone comes down from the City this weekend, this house will be available," Sophia said as they passed one of the four houses around the courtyard that looked empty. "I thought last night you would prefer not to be isolated and alone. I hope the baby did not wake you."

"Not at all," Rebecca smiled. "I can see why Wesley has fallen so in love with this area. It is majestic." She looked around at the towering pillars of rock that made the Metéora. *Scarce images of life, one here, one there…* The monoliths seemed to be a grown version of her circle of stones at Carles Castlerigg. They joined the others for breakfast in Andrew and Thea's home, the children having already been fed and sent outdoors. Rebecca gratefully accepted dark Greek coffee from her hosts and sipped it lovingly. *If only Scotland had coffee like this.*

As they sat and talked, there was a light rapping at the door and a monk entered.

"Rebecca, Mrs. Allen, please meet our old friend, Brother El. El, this is Wesley's wife."

"I am so pleased to meet you. I have enjoyed my visits with your husband," the monk said.

"Have you any news?" Andrew asked.

"He thinks I'm a spy and always have news to tell him," Brother El laughed to Rebecca. "Well, there is some news. I will be here only another week, my friends. I am told that the good brothers of Mount Athos need my guidance. It seems they have found a manuscript of questionable origin. I have been asked to advise them."

"It will be a sad day when you leave Agios Nikolaos Anapafsas," Andrew said. "We are wondering about the stranger with the injured hand who was in the village this week. Has he, indeed, been visiting the monasteries?"

"Ah, him. I have seen him. It would not surprise me if it was him that attempted to follow me on my supply run Saturday." Brother El looked at Rebecca's hand. "There is a connection between the two of you. Is it you that he seeks or do you seek him?"

"Neither," Rebecca declared, though she asked herself again if she was seeking The Blade. "We are both seeking my husband. I must reach him first."

"And what does he seek?" Andrew asked.

"He has heard there is a goddess of great power there and seeks to plunder her." Andrew stiffened at the words.

"You have the essence of power about you. Is this what binds you to the stranger?" asked Brother El.

"There is a blade between us," Rebecca answered with the words Ryan had used in describing it.

"There was an unusual storm on Saturday evening," Brother El said. "It seemed unnatural. The nuns at Roussanou say a man stumbled in late Saturday night, fevered and haunted. They nursed him, but by lauds, he was gone. I dare say there are mighty powers at work."

"He must not reach them before me. I will stop him!"

"Daughter," Andrew said softly, "we will help. I call you daughter because I have begun to think of your husband as a son. Let us prepare for your journey."

"I will make the circuit of all the orders and see if there is more news," Brother El said. "If he has turned away, there is no need to chase him. If I find he is searching for the base camp, I will inform you." With that the monk took his leave.

"Marcos! Come please," Andrew called to his son. The taxi driver came quickly from the house. "My son, I believe that you must take Mrs. Allen to the City of the Gods. There is more at work than even Brother El comprehends. She must reach her husband at once. You should prepare to go to the mountain."

"But, Papa, it has been many years since I have been to the City. I do not remember the way. Should you not take her yourself?"

"I am too old. The fact that my health is failing tells me that the fulfillment is near. What any of us believes will no longer matter. Go to the drop point. You know how to reach it. From there, let the gods guide you. They never truly let you forget."

"I will go to get supplies," Marcos said softly. "I am sorry you do not have a better guide for this journey, Rebecca. We will reach them."

"We will listen to see if Brother El has additional information this evening and you will leave at first light in the morning."

Wednesday, 17 August 1955, City of the Gods

The City was different today. Expectant. Waiting.

Wesley had taken to swimming in the stream each night after they returned from the City, splashing with Pol and refreshing himself. He could not fathom why he'd been so reluctant to bathe in the stream until Sunday. Now he could not imagine the emerald lawn on which they camped to be any brighter as his vision swept the pathway to the City of the Gods.

Each morning this week, the way had been clear, a pleasant walk up the slope until the green grasses gradually shifted to the paving stones of the City. Pol winked at Wesley conspiratorially as he linked Doc and Margaret to the guide rope. It gradually dawned on Wesley that the fog they had experienced, like the music, was not in their surrounds, but in their minds. The music, he had discovered, was in his ears. The fog was in his eyes. While Wesley's eyes and ears were clear, it was apparent that Doc and Margaret were still operating in the fog.

Wesley wanted to shout at them and tell them to open their eyes! It was so beautiful here that it made his heart sing. But either his mouth was stopped from speaking the words, or their ears were stopped from hearing them. All he could do each night was strum the chords and finger the melodies on his guitar as his voice praised God for this incredible vision.

And this morning, entering the City had special meaning. He greeted the dawn with music as they approached the rostrum and were washed by the breaking light. This was a very special day.

Wesley glanced toward the sun, unable to look that direction for long. It seemed nearer. If the ancients had this view of the fiery orb, it was no wonder that they pictured a shining god driving his chariot across the sky. Hyperion, the last of the Titans to reign supreme. That was the spirit of this blazing globe that tracked directly between the pillars toward the rostrum. Wesley could see it as clearly as the fireball itself, consuming itself and glowing brighter and brighter as it died of its own consumption.

"Have you noticed," Wesley mused to his companions, "that the sun does not track south during the day? Its path is always direct from East to West. At noon, when I stand in the center of the rostrum, my shadow is contained directly below me—the smallest I have ever seen."

"That is curious," Doc said.

"It fits with our theory that this City is a completely self-contained sphere that operates outside the physical laws of our earth," Margaret concluded. Wesley was amazed that they could so blithely accept such a preposterous conclusion. It did not take a new understanding of the universe at all. Why, even Joshua had stopped the sun in the sky to give the Children of Israel longer to fight their battle against the Amorites.

*And the sun stood still, and the moon stayed, until the people had
avenged themselves upon their enemies. Is not this written in
the book of Jasher? So the sun stood still in the midst of heaven,
and hasted not to go down about a whole day.*

It took no bending of the universe in Wesley's mind. This was the
sun of Joshua. Tonight, the new moon would also stand still in the sky.
But darkness would not encompass the City. Even starlight would illuminate the great pillars and the moving colors of the rostrum. For some
reason, he could see all these images in the strange light of Joshua's sun
in the City.

Wesley, himself, had stood still in the center of the rostrum for so
long that the sun was near its zenith when he realized that Doc and
Margaret had taken Pol with them to question him about certain symbols they had found. Rather than laying out his strings and drawings on
the rostrum, Wesley seated himself in the center and began to play his
guitar.

The music today was different than on other days. It was more
intense—crystal tones playing in his ears. His guitar and voice joined
them as he interpreted the symbols around him on the rostrum. He
stood and paced around the dais, almost dancing as he tripped from
symbol to symbol. In his head, he imagined the staves of music before
him and realized that the music of the gods was being limited by this
primitive notation system, confined to octaves and harmonies. Wesley
twisted the pegs of his guitar into new tunings and let his fingers run
across the strings in harmonics, unbounded by the frets.

Paper was scattered on the podium in front of him as he played,
then frantically noted the sequences. This music was so real that it had
to be written down—preserved. It was real in ways that orchestras could
only hope to attain. The staves were too limiting. The only way he could
record the music was to jump into the hieroglyphic notation. Even the
symbols that he wrote refused to follow a linear pattern on the page,
some completely overlapping others as he filled the paper. If it had been
possible, Wesley believed the notes would have leapt off the paper into
three dimensions.

And with that realization, he understood the notation of the rostrum. It was a multidimensional instrumentation. He was looking at
Flatland, as written by Edwin Abbott. He was a square, trying to grasp
a great pyramid while being able to see only a triangle in his plane.

In his ecstatic music—playing, singing, dancing—Wesley grasped
that the rostrum was not flat, but that he was viewing only one side of

a universe stretched by tensions that defined dimensions he could never comprehend. One tension was motion. Two tensions were a connection. Three tensions were a plane. Four tensions were space. Fifth, sixth, seventh, and more tensions might affect the single point that was Wesley Allen, defining him across the universe and moving him in the web of his network. It was a mere coincidence that he was here at this point of the universe. And the possibility of such a coincidence occurring was always 100%, for he was always here now.

It was a window to a new world that he had been able to glimpse as a curtain was pulled aside and then dropped back in place, cutting out the vision. And then he had only the memory of enlightenment.

He could not, however, stop the images as he played, the page of notations forgotten. He fought them, but they came on stronger and he yielded.

The night. Desperate urgency to conquer the night. Trapped and waiting in timeless suspension. Unable to exercise more than patience over the awesome power that was held there. The empath. The goddess was a prisoner of the night.

Free me!

WESLEY COLLAPSED ON the rostrum. Perspiration dripped from his forehead, mixing with his tears as droplets created synchronous waves spreading across the rostrum as if it were not merely stone with runes etched in its surface. He looked up to find Pol sitting nearby. The boy was silent, not having attempted to join in Wesley's ecstatic song. Wesley had a new depth of understanding and a connection with the City. He could envision the position of every pillar and knew precisely how far down which avenue Doc and Margaret were working, oblivious to the meaning that was all around them.

"You heard?" Wesley's dry voice cracked. Pol handed him a canteen and Wesley drank deeply. The two looked at each other with a mutual sharing of experience that transcended the need to speak. At last, however, Pol nodded.

"It rang throughout the City. I think there were times when even Doc and Margaret could hear it. They would pause in the midst of a question and raise their eyes. Touching one of the monoliths, we could feel it reverberate with the music."

"You know then. Pol, I must stay. I must be here in the night. It's in the music."

Tears sprang to the boy's eyes and he embraced Wesley, pushing the guitar aside. For generations, staying in the City past sundown had been forbidden.

"Yes," he finally said. It was such a mixture and outpouring of emotions that flooded them that neither could separate the hope, the love, and the fear. "Be safe, Father Wesley. May our goddess protect you."

Wesley gathered up his pack and handed the guitar to Pol.

"I'll not need this tonight," he said. After thinking a bit, he handed the pack to Pol as well. "I think that I'll not need anything but my presence. Take care of our friends, son."

Wesley turned away and selected a route that led him away from where he sensed Doc and Margaret were approaching. He turned, several yards away from the rostrum, to see Pol still staring after him. When he was over the horizon, he slipped behind a monolith and hid.

There he waited.

Wednesday, 17 August 1955, The Metéora, Greece

THE OLD MAN gave them his blessing and Rebecca climbed into the Jeep with Marcos. Brother El's intelligence, given the night before, was that the stranger was wandering between the great pillars of Metéora, apparently seeking for something. As long as he was seeking, he had not yet found the way. Marcos was wary as they left the cluster of homes, constantly looking to see if they were being followed.

As much as Marcos was vigilant, his demeanor also thawed toward Rebecca. Happy childhood memories flooded his thoughts and he shared them with Rebecca. He related the story of the goddess, Serepte, who was conceived in empathy and left captive behind the ivory veil. He gave different emphasis to the story than Doc had in telling them in Indianapolis. That seemed so long ago. Rebecca allowed herself to listen to him fully, escaping for the moment her fears for Wesley and her dire fascination with Ryan McGuire. It seemed that Marcos drove aimlessly, with random turns. Rebecca was certain there were landmarks they had passed previously and hoped that Marcos was simply avoiding being followed and was not hopelessly lost. At last, just before noon, Marcos pulled the Jeep off to the side of the goat track they had been following.

She groaned and cradled her hand against her chest. She had been thrown around the Jeep relentlessly over the rough terrain, unable to hang on with her right hand. Even so, she had instinctively reached to grab hold of the roll bar as they went over a particularly rough patch and the action set the pain throbbing up her arm.

"We must walk from here. Let us eat our lunch first so we have the energy for the climb. It should not be too difficult if it has not changed from the last time I was up here, but it is uphill."

After eating, they began the walk, which rapidly turned into a hike and thence to a climb. Marcos continued talking to Rebecca and she answered as best she could with her shortness of breath. She was thankful for her walking stick and its non-ritual use. At one point, she asked him again if he was a believer.

"It is not quite as simple as that," he replied. "I will try to explain. When I came here the first time, I was told only to go where my heart led me. The only thing I could think to do was climb, as we are now. I was not a strong boy like my son is. I was just exhausted. There was a stream in my path and I fell into it before I saw it." He paused to chuckle at the memory and for the two to catch their breath a moment. "I crawled out of the stream, sat under a tree, and cried myself to sleep. The next morning, I simply wandered into the City. It was an awesome sight. There was a voice deep inside me that I still hear as clearly as if a person were standing beside me. It said simply, 'Go in peace. Leave this to your son.' I turned and left."

Marcos paused again to take in his surroundings, trying to pick his way.

"I do not remember it being so difficult." He stepped up to the top of a ridge and in one smooth motion dropped back down near Rebecca, motioning her to the ground in one swift gesture. Startled, she started to cry out, but he held a hand against her mouth and she stilled. He explained in a hushed whisper.

"There is a man camped on the other side of the ridge, a few hundred yards away. I do not recognize him. Could it be the stranger that my father mentioned?"

"I must see," said Rebecca, crawling past Marcos to the ridge. He tried in vain to wave her back. Cresting the rise, she looked down on the camp of a lone explorer sitting in front of his fire. It did not take seeing the bandaged hand or blond hair for Rebecca to know that it was Ryan McGuire. As if drawn by a magnet, he turned, catching her eyes with his own. For a moment, they remained locked before she could withdraw, a glowing presence in Ryan's eyes that nearly hypnotized her. She turned and fled past Marcos in the opposite direction. Marcos followed as quickly as he could, hearing movement in the camp behind.

"Rebecca! Rebecca Allen!" The shout behind them echoed in front and returned again so it sounded like it surrounded them. They rounded an outcropping of rock and came to a halt as Marcos cautiously looked back.

"Hart of my Heart!" came the shout again. They were silent. "You can't make it alone. I can show you. Come back to my camp. I'll show you the way tomorrow. I won't chase you, Hart. You know I'm here. Come to me. I will show you the way. Come to me." The echo died away and they listened to the silence.

"We can't get there without passing him," Marcos whispered. "His camp is in our path."

"There must be another way."

"I know of none, unless we can find the Mouth of Vengeance. It's a cave where the stream disappears underground. If we can locate it, we can work our way upstream on the far side."

"What a charming name. Why is it called the Mouth of Vengeance?" asked Rebecca.

"None have ever entered and returned."

"Then we won't enter. Let's just find it."

"You'd better drink," Marcos responded. "We won't dare stop again after we start moving. I hoped we would be there by now. It will be difficult to find the stream in the dark, even if I dare use a torch. Come. It is not safe to stay here."

They climbed on in silence for an hour. The sky was overcast, blocking out the stars and the sunset behind them. It was getting dark and Rebecca stumbled twice. Marcos switched on his torch, but the light seemed to be consumed by the darkness. Finally, they caught the sound of water running not far away. They stumbled toward it and encountered the deep rushing torrent. Marcos threw his pack on the ground.

"I am sorry, Rebecca. We've lost. This is the stream, but we've hit it above the Mouth of Vengeance. We're on the wrong side and the only safe way to cross is to go around the mouth. It could be a mile downhill and treacherous in the dark. We'll have to retrace our steps in the morning and wait at the camp until they come down. I am terribly sorry."

"If they come down," Rebecca answered wearily. She was almost too tired to care. In fact, she was almost relieved. The pain of swinging her hand to keep balance, of straining against her stick to help in the climb, and of absently reaching out to grab rocks with her burn had her sweating more than the exertion of the climb itself. "Don't worry, Marcos. You did your best. We have no choice but to wait until light. If you don't mind, though, I'll wash in the stream before I try to sleep. My hand's killing me. I'm too exhausted to go another step."

Marcos stepped a respectful distance away to set up camp in the dark. Rebecca pulled her cup from her back and dipped it into the stream. She laid her staff beside her and relished the cool water in her mouth. Then she unwrapped the injured hand and plunged it into the stream with a gasp at the shock. The water was so refreshing and cool that it made her want to dive in. A moment's decision and she stripped off her shoes, shirt, and trousers, and was in the water. The current was fast, but she kept hold of the rocks with her left hand as she immersed her body in the water. It was a balm to her body. She dunked again. It was a wonderful feeling. At last she pulled herself out of the water and sprawled on her back on the shore. If she wasn't careful, she would fall asleep right there.

The beam of a bright handheld light blinded her and she heard a deep chuckle on the other side of it.

"Marcos!" she exclaimed.

"Marcos who?" snapped Ryan McGuire.

Rebecca gasped but acted faster than she could think. She clutched her staff and swung it, smashing the light out of his hands. She rolled out of his path, snatching up her clothes with her cup as he dove at where she had just been. A hand caught her ankle. She beat it with her staff and rolled free into the stream. She heard Marcos shouting at Ryan as her head went under and she was caught in the current.

Must get out of the water. Mouth of Vengeance. She would be in it before she could catch her breath. Her feet hit bottom and she thrust upward and powerfully against the current and found herself in a calm backwash. She dragged herself and her clothes with her out of the water. It had happened so fast. She had clung to the few items as if they would save her. Perhaps they had. She felt in the inner pocket of her shirtsleeve and found her *Athamé*. She had survived, losing only her shoes.

She nearly called out to Marcos, but caught herself—fearing to bring on another assault by The Blade. She would sneak up on them. Then… She realized with a start that the current ran to her left rather than her right. She was on the wrong side of the stream! Or the right side. She ran uphill as quickly as she could. Marcos had said the camp would be on this side of the stream. Wesley, Doc, and Margaret. Together they would be safe and could deal with the renegade witch. She must move quickly, however. He might have followed her even here.

REBECCA COULD HEAR voices, but a rising wind scattered the words before they fully reached her ears. There. Or there. Rebecca stumbled toward the sound and thought she saw a flickering light. She continued. Echoing from hill to hill, someone was calling her name. She no longer knew for certain which direction she was going, uncertain as to where the stream had gone or why all directions seemed to be uphill. Always, voices sang her name in the wind.

Rebecca!

21
Goddess Revealed

Wednesday, 17 August 1955, City of the Gods

WESLEY WATCHED from his hiding place as the argument came to an end with Pol leading a reluctant Doc and Margaret away from the rostrum into the West where they seemed to disappear into the sun. Had they realized he was missing earlier, he would never have been able to remain hidden in this small world. But Pol's plea to Doc and Margaret was so insistent, and their memory of the warning against the night so clear, that they disappeared along the Aquarius Avenue with a pang of misgiving.

Wesley was no longer afraid of the superpowers warding the city, nor of ancient curses that warned against the night. Perhaps that was hubris, but he had a clear message that he must brave the night in order to penetrate the veil. His misgivings, what there were, originated in the feeling of being alone in a vast, empty, and foreign space.

Daylight in the City of the Gods breaks almost instantly at dawn. As Wesley watched the setting sun, he realized that nightfall would be equally as sudden. Within an instant of the sun's last rays, the city dissolved. Its presence surrounded him, but it was more felt than seen. The pillars seemed to disperse into the darkness as Wesley made his way back toward the rostrum. Wesley hadn't realized how far down the Leo Avenue he was. It took a long time to reach the rostrum. Too long.

It was vaguely luminescent ahead of him, the colors lifting from the surface into the air. Perhaps it had absorbed the daylight and would glow for some minutes after nightfall. He stumbled on toward his goal. Once he reached it, he would stay there and wait for whatever it was that the night would bring.

He stumbled on one of the paving stones as he shuffled toward the rostrum, losing his balance and going down painfully on one knee. He had never noticed an uneven flagstone during the daylight. He reached in his cargo pocket for his flashlight, but when he turned it on, it flickered and the beam was eaten by the darkness. He slammed it angrily against the heel of his palm and stared into it demanding light.

There was an instant burst of brightness as the light went off in his eyes like a flashbulb, then died completely. Wesley was left in the total darkness with a myriad of colors burned on his retinas by the blinding flash. He had never realized that there were so many colors inherent in darkness. They continued to move and play in his eyes. He could feel his eyelids open and close, but could see no difference in the darkness nor in the patterns of color that lit it.

He continued to half stumble and half crawl toward the distant dais with one hand stretched in front of him to protect against running into one of the massive but invisible pillars. Instead he stumbled again and his outstretched arm crumpled under him as he ran headlong into the ground.

"All avenues lead back to the rostrum at the center," he repeated to himself. "I need only continue forward, no matter how far."

Shaking himself from the daze sent the colors vibrating around him. They no longer seemed to be at a point ahead, but he was within the swirl of colored lights. He could not remember falling, but it seemed he had once again tripped on a step. He was walking along and was suddenly lying on the ground as if he had walked into it like a wall. Beside him was the hard ridge of a step.

He did not remember steps in the City of the Gods.

Yet he stumbled against another. And another. In a flash to his childhood, Wesley thought that he must be ascending the Northern Steps to the Temple of Aurora Borealis and the colors around him were the dancing Northern Lights. He stumbled and fell once more, caught up in the colors that surrounded him.

He felt farther around him and found no wall. Smooth. Not even the small cracks between the closely set paving stones that should be there. Just a surface as smooth as glass for as far as he could reach. Perhaps his sensitive fingertips could also feel small indentations as if delicate characters were softly etched into the cool surface.

He shook his head again and sent the colors swirling about him. If only he could clear his eyes to focus through the darkness on his surroundings. But as far as he could see, there was nothing but the swirling pattern of colors.

Pattern. As Wesley sat, still blinking and rubbing at his eyes, slow realization dawned upon him. These were not the random colors of a flashblinding. These colors moved in defined patterns—the same type of patterns he had discerned in the faint pastels of the rostrum. Now, though nearly invisible in the daylight, the colors were all that he saw in the darkness and they burst into three-dimensionality, springing from the surface to surround him.

He was—must be—on the dais.

He stood regarding the colors with a new sense of fascination. He reached out for them as if they would have some physical presence. He remembered distinctly that first time, at age three, when a photographer snapped a flashbulb in his eyes. The child Wesley had wandered around the room for several seconds with hands outstretched trying to catch one of the balloons that floated before his eyes. Wesley chuckled in mirth at the reminiscence as he once again reached out to touch a visual image that had no physical manifestation.

Here, again, Wesley was surprised as there was a tangible presence. Not exactly shape or texture, but temperature. As he passed a hand through a red presence, he was aware that it was warmer than when he touched a blue presence. Not only was there temperature, but Wesley could smell the hot dryness of the red, the wetness of the blue, the freshness of the green. So intense was his fascination with this new phenomenon that he momentarily forgot the bizarre nature of the experience. He wrapped his hands lightly around a green presence and noted that the color did nothing to illuminate his own body, but the color itself seemed to vibrate and Wesley's ears picked up a childlike giggle. As he held the color in his hands, it brightened perceptibly to a joyful yellow. This color he released and it danced in among its fellows.

No wonder he had so much difficulty mapping the rostrum. It was only a two-dimensional representation of a multidimensional phenomenon. It depicted not only the pattern and color, but also shape, texture, temperature, and movement. *And,* Wesley nodded to himself, *the sound.* As the clarity of the music faded into his consciousness, he was reminded of the choir singing in his ears on the climb to the City. Each presence had a voice of its own and the beings passed him from one to another, moving in such patterns that Wesley could no longer be certain that his feet touched the ground.

Wesley opened his mouth to join the chorus and could not find the note.

Lean against me, said one of the presences. Or Wesley thought the words were said, though his ears did not feel the sound. Wesley leaned into a magenta presence and felt the notes vibrating in his chest. He opened his mouth and his voice resonated with the other, sometimes in unison and sometimes in harmony.

If ever there was truly the possibility of joining heavenly choirs of angels, I have experienced it now.

An increasingly dominant shape captured Wesley's eye as he moved in the pattern, himself no more than one spirit among those who danced. Sometimes the presence was pale white, sometimes almost blue green, Wesley followed the presence among all the rest, whether it was ahead of him, above him, or even beneath him. At last, its shifting form came to rest beneath his feet as he spun clockwise around it, stooping, bending, reaching toward the rich effervescence of this being.

So close was this hypnotic treasure—the end of Wesley's rainbow—yet when he reached toward it, he felt only the solid flat surface on which he stood.

Stood. The illusions began to fade. His traverse of the patterned pathway was ended. The colors began to dissolve and soon Wesley was faced with only the single unreachable form beneath him.

As he watched, a multitude of smaller glimmering lights surrounded the being. They moved slowly from place to place in the dark field of the dais, making patterns and breaking to form new designs. Some of the patterns looked familiar, but he could not decide what they reminded him of.

Wesley lunged forward, having suddenly lost his balance. The surrealism of the colored presences surrounding him made it easy to believe that he was walking on air in some other dimension. As he regained his footing, the realism was too much to bear. Dizziness overcame him and he lurched again. He had never seen such depth and dimension in the sky before. His footing was solid, but his mind would not let him comprehend having the moon and stars beneath his feet.

The moon, that presence that had drawn him through the pattern, ultimately held his eyes. The surface gained additional depth and texture. As if fractured by some kaleidoscopic lens, there were more moons than he could count, in all phases of the lunar cycle. Wesley was plunged back into the dream of his childhood.

ANGRY VOICES ARE outside his window in the attic bedroom. It's a small house that his parents proudly built themselves on the ten acres of land. He rushes to the window and sees people building fires—houses on fire—his own home the next target of the marauding hordes. He rushes down the steep stairway and out the door, unable to find his parents.

"What's happening?" he demands. "Go away from my home!"

"It's the end of the world!" screams a marauder. "Look into the sky and see the sign of the end times. We'll burn the world down!"

He looks to the sky and sees the moon. Not one moon but many. They do not orbit in an orderly fashion, but crisscross the sky in near collisions. Young Wesley waves his Bible in hand.

"No! It is not the end time, but just a sign of God's steadfastness. It says in the Bible, 'Many moons will come and go, but my Word lives on!' Stop trying to burn down the world!"

A small part of his consciousness knows he has misquoted, but it makes no difference. The hordes have turned on him and he flees. North. He must reach the Northern Steps and ascend to the Temple of the Northern Lights.

Wesley runs.

PEOPLE HAVE WATCHED the moon for millennia, imagining shapes within it, but to Wesley it was a new and vivid experience. From the ever-changing moons before him emerged images—presences—beings struggling to escape from the satellite to invade his mind.

His mind was fertile soil for grotesques from his deepest fears. Cyclops, Medusa, Gorgons, The Wicked Witch of the West. All combined in Wesley's mind to take the form born of Wesley's nightmares and nurtured on the dark side of the moon. This figure was the yin of nature; the darker feminine, so named by men who could not comprehend her nature hidden within themselves. She it was whose very repulsiveness attracted him with the fascination held unwillingly in his subconscious for its moment of triumph. Hecate of the dark side— threatening enticement of the fearful unknown. He was petrified as she rose silently from the moon beneath him—rose as his own death arose awaiting him before birth.

Wesley's eyes were torn from their unholy fascination to the molten surface of a moon behind her. It froze and shattered to reveal a second face as beautiful as the first was horrid. An image of marble perfection, or perhaps chiseled from glacial ice. Undeniably feminine, she held him in a trance that bound his emotions before they could take form in his heart and held him transfixed—almost unwilling to breathe in her presence. Selene of the cold a dark moon—the eternal virgin—whispered his name to the night and it froze in the air like crystal.

Beside her chilling presence, another moon, full and ripe, thawed and bloomed. A third and more awesome image separated itself from the orb and rose to face him. The all-encompassing mother—Artemis of the hunt, the fields, the birthing stalls. The nurturing but critical mother goddess, her power ruled over birth and death. Wesley felt faint but could not pass out in the presence of the triple goddess. He hyperventilated, oxygen rich blood rushing to his brain, filling him with dizziness. But consciousness clung tenaciously to him. Nor could he cleanse from his eyes the images that floated toward him, pulsing one after another.

Wesley sang again, this time in the low halting tones of a child singing the alphabet to calm his fears. He would have whistled, but he found his lips suddenly dry and cracked, unable to mold around the slippery air. Nor could his dry cottony tongue make sense of the sounds he struggled to form into words. The sounds dissolved in his mouth and grated on his ears, burning his throat as he sang them. They were hideous animalistic sounds, but natural and beautiful at once. Sounds that in their primeval essence transcended his own picture language by as much as that language transcended mere music.

Wesley could hear the voices of the three images playing in his ears, running counterpoint to his own voice. He found himself supplying the baritone of a four-part harmony that brought him to his knees. In the singing, he picked out the voices of harmony that had played in the fog. The icy beauty was soprano, sometimes whistling a shrill descant to the strange harmony. The hag added an elderly but precise tenor to the chorus. Finally, the dominant maternal image added a rich contralto to the blend.

But just as the colors had cast no light, so the sound broke no silence. His ears rang with the chorus played out on his own vocal cords but he felt a person standing next to him would hear nothing. He was an instrument of the music, no longer controlling even his own voice. It was foreign, but filled his inner ear. And the chorus turned ancient fears to imminent threat. The triple goddess challenged the essence of his being, searching him for motive and means. One after the other, they interrogated him from the inside—exposing every weakness, each fault he strove to conceal—to find if he were worthy.

The gorgon monster, the dark of the moon, the shadow of shadows, Hecate of the night, took first command and sang.

> *I am the summer,*
> > *withering heat within your soul.*
> *Sacrifice your life to me.*
> *Love me.*
> *Cook me a broth of the living*
> > *and speak three times the words*

I give thee:
Dalmaley, Lameck, Cadat, Pancia.
I am the queen,
the sickle bearer of the summer wind
calling you to consuming passion
withering all around you.
I am the ruin.
I am the fall,
harvesting you to the fullness
of your soul.
I demand your all.

Wesley felt cold tendrils wrap around him. He was caught in the grasp of a mythical sea monster. He tore his eyes away from the three images approaching him, only to find the colors had returned to wind a pattern around him, binding him where he stood. He felt the tenor of the fabric taking shape. It was the timbre and tone of the crone's voice. He sought it out with his own—ran counterpoint to the harmony that enveloped him. The pattern broke and the colors flew into a cyclone of sound that tore upward and away from Wesley. His eyes snapped back to the vision of the triple goddess below him.

The face of the crone receded behind the silver-tipped horns of the sullen Selene, the icy beauty, eternal virgin. And again, the words whistled around him as she took command, drawing him ever closer to herself, and sang.

I am the winter,
peaceful rest when life is through.
I am the queen of the palace of ice.
Brave the silent slopes of Borea
to capture my heart
and slip it still
beneath your breast.
I am the goddess of night without end—
the mystery of the eternal
snowcapped sheets of the nuptial couch.
I am the goddess of winter—
Persephone's revenge—
the avenger of lust and greed.
Lie in my icy embrace.
Love me.
I demand your nothingness.

The flesh on Wesley's neck and scalp crawled. Icy fingers wrapped around him and he shivered involuntarily. He could sleep beneath her words as if they were a blanket of snow. The cold goddess wrapped him in her arms. Blue and white colors fell softly around him. The wind whistled lullabies in his ears.

Wesley shook. He was in a snow globe and the flakes spun around him in liquid air. His voice as he sang the fugue was almost inaudible, but soon rose in its own challenge to the icy fingers, sending warmth and sunshine into the voice that surrounded him. The icy crystalline presences melted into air and Wesley turned again to the mocking goddess below him.

The second face made way for the third. The most awesome of all, the mother goddess arose to face him. She commanded a voice outmatching the others combined, and his fear rose to a new pitch as she sang.

I am your mother,
*   the spring and the rain.*
Love me.
Trust yourself to my care.
I am Artemis of the field—
*   Demeter of the earth and corn.*
Lie across my bed of coals
*   till immortality is seared into your soul,*
*   and learn from me the mysteries*
*   of all that grows.*
Find your rest in my bosom—
*   that long final rest*
*   from which only the pure arise*
*   to the newness of life.*
I am the emasculating goddess of fertility.
Give your life to me.
I am she who gives life
*   and demands your life*
*   be paid to me.*

The rich and verdant presences did not merely surround him; they sprang from him as if he were a fertile field in which they might take root and grow as he decomposed. It was his life that gave them life. From life springs life and the rich contralto coaxed the very life from him, sending it twining outward, branching and leafing out into a magnificent growth of tree and vine.

At first, his own voice served as no more than fertilizer, causing riotous blooming of new presences to join the growing garden of Bacchic festivity surrounding him. Here, counterpoint would not avail. He sought the harmony in the voices that these presences brought, blending colors, orchestrating voices into a rich chorale of patterns that had brought him to the juncture to face the moon and its myriad of faces. Each presence took its place and in one last finale ceased to be.

Wesley turned his head and felt the cold hard surface of the rostrum against his forehead and the bridge of his nose. The moon had not been drawing toward him, but he had sunk to his knees on the flat surface and had drawn down closer to it. He struggled to regain a perspective on the single white shining presence beneath him. The goddess was gone. The stars continued to dance on the black field of the sky below as he rose to his knees, stumbled to his feet, still unable to shake his gaze from the vision.

He called for his own vision and rested in his mind as he walked with Rebecca in the quiet park behind Indianapolis City College with the moon and stars spread above them. He looked deep into her eyes and spoke her name, but the word twisted itself around his tongue and the vision of her face faded into the white moon presence below. Another face—not Rebecca's—took her place on the shining surface of the moon. She was familiar to him—gentle, loving, inviting. He was drawn to the face for protection—for the intensity of his desire. The face whispered to him. The words came out of the wind as she sang.

> *I am the soul of the unborn.*
> *I am she who can feel your feelings,*
> > *who knows your heart.*
>
> *I am the captive spirit*
> > *behind the ivory veil.*
>
> *Free me.*
> *Come to me.*
> *I am she whom you willingly obey*
> > *who obeys you willingly.*
>
> *I require only your love.*

She was distant. He could not reach her, but he desired her. He loved her. He reached for her and the voice on the wind called his name. He felt her fingers touch his fingers but he could not hold them. He reached again, overreached himself, fell—off into a vast chasm. He fell through the rostrum into the sky. No footing remained beneath his flailing feet. Air drove itself into his lungs. He screamed without sound, diving into space that he could not fathom.

All the colored presences in all their many voices sprang once again to life, meshing, weaving in and out in a delicate fabric of tangible music. He sang at them desperately, pushing them away, but they merely danced farther off, still weaving and singing their voiceless song.

How wrong! He was not the one. She was not the one. Here was no idol fancied, but more open trusting love than his heart could bear. That love, that goddess, would not contest the love of her whose heart already he bore so closely knit to his own. And plummeting into the chasm he screamed with all the energy that he could put into his voice, "Rebecca!"

The web of colors rose to meet him and dissolved into his own image as he felt the crack of the rostrum against his head and all the stars and all the moons and all the singing dancing faces went black beneath him.

And he floated in empty silent blackness.

22

Goddess Accepted

Thursday, 18 August 1955, City of the Gods

REBECCA!

The voice echoed around her from every direction, but the darkness would not release her as she followed. This was insane. The camp should be right here. It wasn't here. She was lost. She should sit down right where she was and wait for rescue. Every child knew that. But someone kept calling her name just over there. If she could only call out in answer, help would come. But her throat was too dry, her lungs ached, and her heart pounded. She could not answer. So she kept climbing.

The light ahead grew stronger as she came out of the fog at last onto a long flat plateau. The light—starlight. She had never seen so many stars. They seemed so close that she could reach out and touch them. They lit the darkness and scattered it to the winds. On this wide open plain, the stars shone and danced above her, flooding her vision with gentle, pure light. She thanked God that she was safe; the Goddess that she was alive.

A euphoric pleasure in life began to fill her. Suddenly, the fog, the mountain, the danger was very far away. A voice inside told her she had reached a place of safety where she was welcome. She began gently to hum, then to sing, eyes intent on the sky. She dropped her clothes as so much extra baggage and took up her staff and cup in her hands. Her athame, she thrust through the elastic band of her underwear. She rapped time with her staff on the ground, body swaying, head tilting, eyes following the dance of the stars. Her feet left the ground, one after the other, as her body sensed the rhythm of the crystalline ballroom above her. Rebecca had not danced since she was a child, clapping hands to music made up in her head. A feeling of elation welled up inside her and she began to spin—to circle—to spin—to jump—to spin round and round on the wide open plateau, never taking her eyes off the stars dancing above her. She became dizzy and her stomach rose to her throat, but she danced through the dizziness and her heart regained the tempo of the stars.

She sang and pranced and praised and danced. She was filled with a rising sense of power as she had been in her rituals, but it was fueled by pure joy. She created new words and new melodies. She was alive. Her younger self had come out to play. She had survived. She was free. She sang and danced—danced for the goddess of the new moon that watched over her. She sang until she could no longer hold inside her the rushing bursts of pleasure the power sent through her. And she whirled and spun and sang and laughed. Her voice rose and rang out, echoing from unseen surfaces in multiple tones and harmonies. There was an ecstasy in the air that she could not comprehend, but it made her want all the more to dance and sing and laugh.

The plain was flat as far as the eye could see with the single exception of a dome on the horizon. She danced and sang and spun and moved ever closer toward it. This was a sign of habitation. People made domes. She was at home among domes. All the important buildings she knew had domes. Capitol buildings, libraries, museums. All ancient buildings.

But this dome had no building beneath it.

Before her, it rose abruptly from the plain, dark and solid—a voluptuous monument to all that was feminine. It shined darkly beneath the night sky.

She touched it with her foot and found herself upon it. The ground jutted out from its base vertically beside her. She touched the ground and found the dome beside her once again. She laughed. All her childhood laughter, all the booming belly laughs, all the romantic giggles burst out of her in sheets of laughter, cascading through the darkness into the pool of night around her. She danced around the base of the dome, leaping up to its side and then back to the earth—laughing—dancing farther and farther up the sides of the smooth round surface, always flat beneath her feet.

An amazing feat of architectural engineering, she thought to herself with mock sophistication. Her own joke generated new laughter. This was no feat of mere architects. It was magic. No human had engineered this incredible structure with its own gravity field. All around her the world rose like a wall except at the horizon of the dome where all disappeared into the night sky.

She rushed the horizon with a leap and a pirouette and tumbled headlong over the prone body of a man lying across the highest point of the dome. She caught only a glimpse of him as she rolled away, but it was enough to call her instantly back to reality. Ryan McGuire! He had beaten her!

She leapt to her feet and rushed back to the summit, fists clenched in her fury. How dare he violate this treasured sanctuary? How dare he presume to lie across their surface. She would not allow it. The dome was herself, her own full bosom thrust into the air. She would not permit this violation of all that was holy. It must stop.

In an instant, her *Athamé* was in her hand calling out a new pain from her burned hand. She grasped it two-fisted above her head for the sacrificial rite and rushed the man again. But it was the pain blazing in her hand and up her arm that caused her to stumble before she reached her target. The flaming passion was fanned again as she felt the dagger come to rest against her own breast where she had known the bite of his. Even unconscious, he was defended against her blade by the bond she had forged. In rage, she let the sacred tool fall and struggled on toward the man.

All that was woman in her revolted against this conquering beast. She was Bacchante at the Feast of Dionysus. In a frenzy of lust and hatred and love and anger—emotions so tied together she could not separate them—she struck out with her feet, feeling bones crush with the impact. She would purify this place. She would drain his lifeblood on the altar and dance a death dance on his body. She leapt and kicked and sang, deep in her throat a roar of fury. She fell on him and beat him with her fists. He would not move. He lay still. She raked him with her nails and screamed her hatred. He was silent. She bit him and pounded his head. She was all that was holy. He was all that was damned. She would purge herself of the profane. She would drive the curse of man from the world and live at peace.

Exhausted, she fell next to the body that still lay without a sound. The power drained from her in her frenzy. Remorse overwhelmed her. Laughter rose up in her throat but choked there. She was cold. She drew close to the body for warmth, but no warmth embraced her. She was lonely, but there was no companion. She wept, but there were no tears. She sang, but the music had fled.

Slowly, she called her senses home. The dizziness grabbed at her again and she heaved dry, wracking heaves. For an eternity, she lived in that world between waking and the ghastly nightmares of sleep. She could not tell what was real and what was still a bad dream clinging to her mind.

At last the body came into focus. He was familiar, but he was not Ryan McGuire. There was no blonde hair. No bloody *Athamé* held in his hand. She turned him to look at the face and tears flooded her eyes. Wesley! J. Wesley Allen. Her beloved. Her husband. What had she done?

She raised him and cradled him in her arms, whispering his name over and over, unable to believe that she had injured him. Wesley would not awaken. She raised her head to the heavens in accusation and wept. The sound of her voice died in the empty distance without an echo.

Wesley's head fell back on her arm as she gathered him close. She looked into his glazed eyes and he looked back without comprehension. She moved her hand to brush his hair from his face and was arrested by the sparkle of a jewel embedded in his forehead between his eyes. She traced it with her finger and it fell into her hand, leaving a pentagram imprinted on Wesley's forehead.

Her eyes were torn between the imprint on Wesley's forehead and the jewel in her palm. At last, fascination had its way and she stared at the star. It was dark, but unlike the darkness of emptiness, this was a full darkness. Within the darkness of the star were all the colors and all the lights that she could imagine. They were reduced to essential elements and compacted into one darkly shining stone which she held in her hand. She could not believe that the stone could be so lightweight with the immense mass that it contained.

As she focused on the stone held in the palm of her burned hand, the red and blistered flesh began to slowly dry and fall away. Her palm turned pink with new skin. It, in turn, grew to the healthy rich tones of her flesh. It left no scar or imprint of any kind. Then her eyes jerked away from the stone with such a sudden separation that her head snapped back physically. She had not merely stopped looking at it, she had been thrust away.

She found tears in her eyes flowing as freely as the dancing had flowed through her feet, as powerfully as the rage had raced through her mind. The tears fell on the man held in her arms, mixed with the blood on his face, and fell to the surface below. Beneath the two, in the light of the stars, she could see her own reflection in the glassy surface of the dome and the reflection of the new moon and all the stars held steadfast in the sky. She looked from the bleeding surface of the dome to the sky it reflected, then back to the dome.

The moon gazed back at her from the reflected surface. Something was amiss in the way it looked. She checked the reality sky again and was drawn back to the reflection. A small void commanded her attention.

She held the tiny star-shaped stone out over the void and it shrank to the shape and size of the jewel. When she withdrew the stone, the void opened like shutters on a camera lens.

Through her tears, she could see her own reflection in the void, centered in the star. It wept as well, the tears dropping up to meet her own. But the reflection, she realized, was not of herself—at least, not through her own eyes. She saw the image move, independent of herself. Then it moved toward her. Rebecca started back and held Wesley protectively. The image reached toward him. She held him tighter.

A gentle wind came to her from the void, carrying with it a far-away voice and the musical note of a flute. The wind picked up a lock of Rebecca's hair, scattering it on her forehead. The one she saw in the void—who was so much like her, but so apart from her—she was the source of the enchantment that had led Rebecca through the night. Rebecca had found her. The image had not hurt Wesley; Rebecca had.

The Goddess. Serepte of the legends—the myths—was real. She could help Wesley. She *must* help.

"Serepte!" The image seemed so distant, so impenetrable. "Serepte, what must I do?"

She started at her own words, wondering what had inspired them. The image still reached out toward Rebecca through the void. It begged to be accepted. It had no other channel to life. But first they must heal the prophesied one.

Rebecca felt the voice move deep inside her, begging her. Because she loved. Because the goddess yearned for her love. Because through Rebecca, she could love. But there was still more. Rebecca loved her—would love her like no other could. Would love her like the mother she lost an eternity ago when the gods abandoned Olympus. Rebecca had no frame of reference for a love like this. It was overwhelming, filling every possible corner of her being. It was a love that demanded to be consulted before any decision—a love that influenced all of life. And love continued to be its only goal.

Almost. They almost touched. Rebecca almost forgot that it was a reflection—a mere image in a void. She almost forgot Wesley. She shrank back. Tears filled her eyes anew.

"I'm afraid." She almost choked on the words.

The presence of the image moved again. It wavered—for a moment, less of Rebecca than it had been. Then it merged back toward her with such an outpouring of warmth and passion and love that Rebecca was overcome by the intense presence that surrounded her. Emotions without names flowed over them and around them and through them. Rebecca felt that she could gather Wesley and the image up into her arms like little babies and float with them through the air in her all-encompassing, mothering care.

Rebecca reached and found her hand passing through the star-shaped void in the surface of the dome, into the cool depths of its inner chambers. She remembered bathing in the cool stream. The hand of the image rose to meet hers. She could feel soft loving fingers touch and caress her hand. Her heart beat faster at the touch. She dipped deeper, drawing the other to herself. The closer their faces came, the more alike they looked and the more separate they were. Another—created in the image—that looked much like her, but was not her.

The other reached out to Rebecca. The arms were warm, human, loving. They hugged each other in a fluid embrace, suspended in space and time. Rebecca closed her eyes and squeezed the other, the body solid and firm in her arms. She could feel the beating of a second heart against her breast. She felt the breath of the other warm against her cheek. Her skin yielded to the presence of the other.

Rebecca inhaled but could not get enough air. Her body tensed. She pulled with her lungs for more air. The caressing presence was real. She clasped the other tighter, pulling her close to Wesley. Rebecca's head was filled with the sounds of their breathing. Their hearts beat wildly in her ears.

Too much air! She had taken too much air into her lungs and they would soon burst. She had to force herself to breathe. Her body was too tense. She might crush Wesley in this three-way embrace. Still, her arms tightened around the other—squeezed so tightly that they merged. In a burst, the other melted into Rebecca's skin, heart, and brain. The air came rushing out of her lungs and the sound of her own voice split the night air. Her tears were hot on her cheeks as she sobbed. Her entire body was shaking.

Rebecca could still feel the other presence, but they were now one. She rocked Wesley in her arms, bathing him with her tears and singing lullabies to him. She was purged. She was fresh. She was clean.

She was Goddess.

And with that awareness, Rebecca touched her husband and let her awareness sink into him. Every wound that Wesley had, she could feel. And she could feel his trust in her. She could heal him.

She cradled him against her breast and spoke his name softly. The tears from her tightly closed eyes fell across the star-shaped indentation on his head. She had given the wounds that now she received. Her teeth had torn his flesh—her own flesh. She could feel the blood running from her own body where her raking nails had scored his back. She accepted the pain into her body and it flowed out in a wave of music through her tears.

In her heightened state of awareness, Rebecca was suddenly, irrevocably in love. IN love—it danced around her, covered her, lifted her up in a bundle and caught her deftly in strong caring arms. Love rushed over her in torrents of laughter, flicking careless tongues of consuming passion at her fingertips. Love washed her up on a dry sand beach and lapped playfully at her toes. It was all joy and all goodness and beauty, dosed liberally with wicked little touches and hidden glances at her lover. It was all-encompassing with just the slightest hint of fear that it might all be a dream—just imagination. Magic.

It was not fantasy. It was hard fleshly reality that she grasped in her hand. Panic. Lost control. Something was using her mind to satisfy its own carnal lust. Terror as the faces of an unknown power forced their way past her unyielding consciousness. A wall, erected brick by brick around her and in its midst a star-shaped chasm into which she plunged through never ending void.

Rebecca could not comprehend the kaleidoscope of images that assaulted her. It was like walking through the precarious paths of someone else's overwrought mind and having her own mind invaded by an alien force at the same time. So deeply entwined had she become with Wesley's feelings while healing him that she could not separate her own from the torrent of emotions that he felt while rising from his delirium.

In her hand, she could still feel the star stone she had removed from Wesley's forehead. This was her key. Frozen in her position, she reached out with her mind to call the guardians of the watchtowers and create a glowing warded circle around her. In the center of her ring of light was the yawning chasm sucking at her spirit—calling to exchange her soul for that of the goddess.

"No! I shall not relinquish myself. I shall not become the goddess. I am a woman. I love a man—this man. I will not give up my love, my humanity, nor my womanhood. I choose my love." Rebecca felt power flow from her as the star-shaped void was capped and the gaping pit no longer held sway over her.

She was immediately back in her own mind with only her own confusion to deal with. She looked at Wesley's face and saw his open and comprehending eyes. The star-shaped impression was only faintly traced upon his brow.

Rebecca cradled him in her arms and stroked his hair. She kissed his forehead and his lips. She felt a gentle tingling as his hand slipped across her shoulders and down her back, releasing her bra as it went. She felt his strength returning as she pulled his tattered shirt from his shoulders.

"You came for me," he whispered. "My beloved wife, I am yours."

"I love you," she cried as his fingers found her secret place and his lips closed around her turgid nipple. The violence and intensity of the night dissolved into whispered words of love. Her hands floated the length of his body, helping him out of his torn clothes. They were naked beneath the stars and the new moon. Her fingers sought and soothed each spot where her earlier passion had gouged his back. Her lips kissed away the last remnants of the pain inflicted by her teeth. She held him to her breasts and welcomed the life of his lips as he suckled. His strong gentle hands moved along her sides and thighs as the last of her underwear was shed.

She thrilled to his touch. His hands sought her breasts, her hair, her sex, and plunged deeper into her opening. She gasped as she opened her eyes to see his open before her. She let him look deeply into her soul, inviting him to be part of her. She swept him into her heart as she welcomed him into her core, his hardness filling her. She saw herself reflected in his eyes.

They had had only a week of marital bliss before they had to separate, she to Scotland and he to Greece. They had made love as often as their bodies could respond and Rebecca admitted that she enjoyed it. She would welcome him to her body as often as he craved it. But she had been sure there was more. While she enjoyed her husband, she had not felt the instant lubrication that she had when falling under the spell of The Blade.

But on this night, it was a new Wesley. He loved her body as much as he loved her soul. And he seemed to have found in his night on the mountain, not only a new passion but a new understanding of his mate's needs and desires. He explored her with both his hands and his mouth. He sought places of pleasure that even she did not know existed. With his first touch of her wet center, her nerves responded shaking her entire body. When he found the center of her pleasure, she called out her joy to the stars above. When, at last, he fastened his lips to hers, his tongue toying with her own and his penis sliding past the gates of her womanhood, she wept with the joy that overwhelmed her. The orgasm that took her shook her to her core and when she felt his ejaculate in her vagina, her senses overloaded and she passed out.

She awoke, not certain how long she had slept in the arms of her lover. The stars still danced in the sky, but she sensed that dawn was near. She looked at her husband and saw his gaze fixed a few feet away. There, just above the star-shaped void, danced a cyclone of colors. Her heart jumped to her throat as Wesley stood and held out his arms to the presence.

So soon? He would betray her so soon and take, instead, the goddess released from her prison behind the ivory veil?

The presence approached Wesley's arms and coalesced into a lovely young woman, long red hair flowing down her slender and very naked back. She melted into his arms and kissed him.

Tears ran freely from Rebecca's eyes as she watched. But things began to change. The kiss was not one of passion. The nudity was not a prelude to sex.

Wesley lifted the young goddess in his arms and as Rebecca watched, the naked girl began to shrink, reversing the aging process. She became a gangly-legged adolescent, an awkward preteen, a child with missing teeth, a toddler, an infant. At last, Wesley held the tiny, softly glowing presence in the palm of his hand. With this he approached his beloved wife.

Kneeling before her, Wesley kissed Rebecca's stomach, just above the fur of her delta. His hands approached and the tiny flame of life slipped from them and into her womb.

"We will have a beautiful daughter," he whispered.

They made love again, both weeping tears of joy at the seed that had been planted in Rebecca's womb. Beneath the stars they drifted once again to sleep.

Rebecca dreamed of falling past the gentle arms of her sleeping lover, leaving him cradling only himself in his dreams. And she passed through a veil where he could not pass. She saw all the world spread before her and stood alone together with the one who was within her, but was not herself.

"It may be hard, but we will make it," whispered a voice within her. "The price of a rite of passage is to leave a part of you behind."

The voice on the wind was still. The air was cool and made her shiver. She closed her eyes tightly, but could see nothing behind them. Her voice could not call out. Her eyes could not weep. Her lungs could scarcely breathe. As far as she could listen, she strained her ears and all was still.

"Rebecca?"

Behind the Ivory Veil

She opened her eyes. Wesley held her in his arms. They sat on a large flat dais of stone. His hand was held protectively across her womb. The moon and stars were gone in the grey half-light of dawn. Surrounding them was a forest of pillars. Wesley lovingly spoke her name again. There was a flash of light and the sun broke fully into view.

Three figures walked toward them between the rows of pillars.

23

Down from the Mountain

Thursday, 18 August 1955, City of the Gods

DOC AND Margaret ran up the avenue toward the rostrum. Pol moved more cautiously forward at a distance. Rebecca stood to meet them and began pulling her clothes on. Wesley blushed and scrambled into his own tattered clothing.

"Rebecca!" said Margaret. "How did you ever...?"

"Wesley, are you all right?" Doc overlapped in the excitement.

"Did you see them?" Wesley ignored the questions, he was so caught up in the experience. "The pillars arrived just before the sunrise. Did you see them coming?" Doc looked around at the pillars showing a complete lack of understanding.

"Wesley, you're disoriented," he said, taking in his torn clothing. "You must have had quite a night. Here, drink this." Doc held a flask against Wesley's lips and dosed him with pitchy Greek wine. Wesley spluttered helplessly as Doc repeated the dose with Rebecca. She coughed.

"That is not coffee!" she choked. She pushed away the flask away and turned to gather her tools. Her cup, *Athamé*, and staff lay nearby. She still clutched the star stone in her healed hand. She put the knife in her sleeve sheath and carried the cup and staff in one hand.

"Rebecca, how did you get here? Are you all right?" Margaret rushed to her young friend and pushed Doc aside. The older archaeologist took a healthy drink from the flask and nearly choked himself.

"Yes," Rebecca said.

"Isn't it wonderful that my wife arrived in time to celebrate the new moon with me?" Wesley said. He rushed to Rebecca and swung her around. She giggled at him and kissed her lover. "We might be a little shaky from lack of food, but we're fine. Marcos Paris-whatever-it-is brought me. We got separated last night when Ryan McGuire attacked me in the dark."

"McGuire is here?" Doc demanded. "He attacked our camp a few days ago. We weren't there, but he stole most of Wesley's notes."

"I don't know where he is, nor where Marcos is. I assume he walked to your camp as soon as it got light. I've no idea what happened to McGuire. I wandered around in the dark until I ended up here and found Wesley." She looked at her husband's torn clothes. "Um... We had a reunion."

"Oh, my, yes," Wesley agreed. Rebecca wasn't sure how much he would remember about how she greeted him with hands, feet, teeth, and nails. Her eye was caught by the youth who stood several feet away looking at her. She stepped off the dais and walked toward Pol. "It's true, you know," Wesley continued. "The pillars arrive and take their positions just before sunrise. And the symbols on the platform shift through multiple dimensions."

Doc looked again at the pillars and then at Wesley. He took another pull from the flask. This time, Margaret nudged him and took a sip herself.

Rebecca stopped in the avenue facing Pol and the two stared at each other a long moment. Slowly, Rebecca held out her hand with the star stone lying in her open palm.

"The key," Pol whispered. He reached out a tentative hand and touched the stone with his finger. "They are gone. The City is empty. The goddess is free." Rebecca stepped a bit closer and moved Pol's hand to touch her stomach.

"She is free."

A low rumbling filled the air and everyone's attention was drawn to the West. The sky was dark with thick clouds. The night appeared reluctant to retreat from the sacred city. The entire summer investigating the City, the team had never seen a cloud in the sky. Now, a storm raged with the daylight in a war for dominance.

Lightning split the sky a few hundred feet away, striking one of the massive pillars. The five people watched in awestruck fascination as the mammoth pillar crumbled at its base and came crashing to the ground. The earth shook under the impact of the fallen pillar. Doc went into action belying the amount of wine he had just consumed. He looped their guide rope around Wesley and each took hold of the rope.

"Pol! Get us out of here. We'll all be killed!"

Pol looked frantically around as if unable to gain his bearings. Margaret made sure Rebecca had hold of the rope in front of her. Pol stood frozen in place.

"I don't know where. It's all fogged over," Pol said. Rebecca moved to his side and put her arm around the frightened boy. In her other hand she held out the jewel.

"We can find the way," she said softly. The sound of another crashing pillar punctuated her words. Doc, Margaret, and Wesley linked into the chain and the five started down the avenue as the storm raged in the sky above. In seconds, they were encased in fog and pelted with rain. Lightning continued to flash and the sound of falling pillars surrounded them.

Directly in front of Rebecca and Pol, a path appeared and they led the others forward. Ghosts stepped from the blindness to haunt them as they fought their way down the mountain against a wind that would hold them back. Voices screeched out of the fog.

"Back, hag! Back to your fires!" yelled Wesley from the end of the line. His voice rang out in a song that enveloped the travelers and created a bubble of security around them. Encouraged, Pol's voice rang out in harmony. The star stone held in Rebecca's hand cut a path for them to follow and they plunged down the slope.

When one fell, all were taken along, rolling and sliding until they came to a halt on the flat sun-drenched plateau where the old olive tree marked their camp. Marcos rushed to meet them and helped the struggling group to their feet.

"I was afraid that I would not find you at all," he exclaimed. "Is anyone injured? You are wet! Come to the fire."

"Papa!" Pol ran to his father and threw his arms around his neck. "It's all gone! The pillars are falling. The gates are closed."

"It's happened?" Marcos asked his sobbing son. "Don't be sad, son. It was never meant to last forever."

"I don't understand."

"But my dear son, you still believe." Pol looked up at his father. Tears still sparkled in his eyes, but he nodded. "We must attend our friends. One day it will become clear and you will understand."

Margaret took over comforting the distraught boy and Wesley held his wife in his arms as they looked out at the swift-running stream. Marcos and Doc set about preparing as much food as they could eat. After a few minutes, the crew set about striking their camp and packing everything for the journey back to the Jeep. They would not stay longer on the mountain. Wesley and Pol took the water buckets and dipped them in the current, then doused the fire. They covered the firepit and doused it again.

Then they carted all their supplies down the hillside to the waiting vehicle.

Behind the Ivory Veil

Thursday 18 August 1955, Kastraki, Greece

DINNER WAS LIVELY when the explorers returned to the little cluster of cottages. As soon as they arrived, Pol spotted his mother and ran to her arms. She had been too worried to stay in Athens and had taken the train to Trikala and hired a ride from there. She showed that she was made of as sturdy and devoted stock as any of the family when she had walked into the courtyard earlier in the day.

"My husband and my son were here and possibly in danger," Helen declared. "Greek women do not sit at home quietly waiting for word about their brave men." She turned and smiled warmly at Rebecca. "Especially when they have strong women who set an example." The two women hugged.

"I'm so glad everyone is back in one piece."

"It was a near thing," Marcos said. "I fought a demon on the mountain."

"What? Marcos!"

"Rebecca went to the stream to refresh herself while I set up camp. I am afraid that I'd wandered around and did not find the path. When we met the man with the burned hand, we detoured, planning to go over the Mouth of Vengeance. We connected farther upstream and decided not to risk a crossing until morning. As I set up the camp, I heard Rebecca scream. She seemed much farther away than I thought she would be and I rushed to aid her. I called for you, Rebecca. I heard you answer once, but then I was attacked."

"I did answer, but fell into the water and came up on the other side of the stream," Rebecca confirmed.

"The demon struck me from behind. It kicked me. It pushed me. But every time I swung at it, it was just air. A demon that sprang from the night and I could not see it."

"Ryan McGuire is reputed to be an excellent fighter," Doc grumbled.

"I think this was no man. It sprang from the night, striking me. I could not see it, but it could see me, continuing to dart in and out as it punched me. Its eyes blazed like coals. I saw a blade rise to smite me and fell backward into the rocks. I was knocked out. When I awoke... I don't remember having moved... I was in the Jeep and the sun was rising."

"You had no difficulty finding the camp this morning, though?" Doc asked. "No further encounters with McGuire?"

"No. The way was clear and easy. I am so sorry, Rebecca. I did not mean to desert you, but I could not find you. Then when I neared the camp this morning, I found your shoes beside the stream and was sure you had been swept into the Mouth of Vengeance. I was horrified. Thank God you are all safe," Marcos whispered as a prayer.

"Marcos, my son," Andrew spoke at last, "You have needed to face your demons for many years. Last night you purged yourself."

"But I was not victorious," his son sighed.

"We learned in the great war that victory does not always mean defeating the enemy. Sometimes, it simply means surviving."

"Thank you, Papa."

Helen put her arm around her husband's shoulders and kissed his cheek. "You brought our son back safely. You are my hero."

"I'm surprised we didn't hear any of this," Doc said. "You must have stumbled right through our camp, Rebecca."

"With the noises of the night, it is no wonder that we did not hear each other," Margaret said. "I do not know if they were real or waking nightmares, but it is no stretch for me to believe Marcos fought a demon. There were wails in the darkness that would chill the blood. The three of us huddled together under a single blanket all night long."

"I am sorry about the condition of the City when we left, though I don't believe it was anything that we did. Still, I am more than content to let it wash into my memory and not return. I'm glad we have returned, even if a few days early."

"And did you find what you sought?" Andrew asked.

"Yes. And I shall leave it where I found it. Wilton had it right when he wrote a fairytale. It is not the stuff of science." Doc paused and looked at each of the people around the table.

"I am more worried about Ryan McGuire," said Rebecca softly. "He's out there, you know. He will be watching to see if we are carrying a golden idol and will create havoc for us until he is satisfied. He is a dangerous man."

"It sounds as if you have had additional encounters with him, love," Wesley said. "He ransacked our camp a few days ago. Has he been harassing you? I will chase him down." There was a fierce determination in Wesley's voice that filled Rebecca with pride. "He still has some papers stolen from our library."

"Do not worry about that, my darling," Rebecca said. "I have them. He left them in the university library in Edinburgh."

"Are you telling me he was in Scotland and with the circle all this time while we've been looking over our shoulders for him?" Doc exclaimed.

"Until a few days ago. He discovered Wilton's original notes for 'The Last Gift' and maneuvered me into locating them. He left the notes from ICC among them with a letter for me. That was why I had to come to Greece. I believed he'd found you and would work harm."

"I've a feeling you have not told me everything, Becc," Wesley sighed. "But I have faith in you. Great faith."

"I will tell you everything, my husband, but it is a conversation we must have alone and not among friends. There are unbelievable things that have happened."

"You will find me far more capable of believing the unbelievable than I once was."

Friday, 19 August 1955, Kastraki, Greece

EXHAUSTION HAD OVERWHELMED the explorers and they were all led to beds. Doc and Margaret were invited to stay in Andrew's home to clear more space for 'the young ones.' Wesley and Rebecca were shown to a room in the smallest of the cottages while Marcos and Helen took a house between the smallest and his father's house. There, the couple held and listened to Pol all night long.

In the morning, after Wesley had demonstrated to Rebecca his skill at making Greek coffee, among other skills, they joined the rising family in the courtyard. Canopies were hung over the courtyard, shading it from the hot August sun. A table was spread with meats, cheeses, bread, and boiled eggs. As people rose, they helped themselves to the food and sat around the courtyard to eat.

"I believe the demons followed us from the mountain," Doc said casually. "I am sure I heard them howling last night." Rebecca and Wesley both blushed crimson, but so did Marcos and Helen. Sophia looked around innocently, but there was a bit of color in her face as well. Her husband had left at first light for his job in Kalambaka.

When they had eaten and spent some time organizing their day, Wesley took Rebecca's hand and led her out through the gate and toward the towering rocks that rose around them.

"I've not been on it, but Brother El pointed out a path he said was among the most pleasant in Metéora. It winds among three of the monasteries," Wesley said. "I want to be alone with my wife for a bit." They walked half a mile to the trailhead and turned off the narrow road. "Brother El says the monks use this trail as a shortcut down to the village to buy supplies. If their burdens are heavy on the return trip, they take the longer route by road."

"You've changed, Wesley," Rebecca said as she lay her head on his shoulder while they walked. Wesley had not hesitated to put his arm around his wife, not even looking to see if they were being observed.

"For the better, I hope."

"You seem stronger and more confident. I would never hesitate to put my trust in you."

"Marcos talked about battling the demon on the mountain. That night, I had to face my own fears. My own demons. They were all women, you know."

"Goddesses," Rebecca whispered. "Wesley, do you know the walking stick Doc carries?"

"He's never separated from it."

"It's a kind of symbol of office in a… coven… of witches."

"And you with your sturdy walking stick? Is it also a symbol?"

"I joined the coven," she said. "Ryan McGuire is also a member. Wesley, I've committed myself to service to the goddess." Whatever Rebecca's expectations might have been, it was not the laughter that ensued from Wesley's mouth. His whole body shook. Ahead a stone bridge crossed a tiny rivulet and the two sat on it with feet dangling over the edge.

"Becc, my darling," he finally sighed, "I am a Christian. I have always been a Christian. I don't recall a time when I even considered that I might not be a Christian. But I met the goddess in the City of the Gods. I met her in all her various terrible and wonderful forms. I tried to convince myself that I was merely hallucinating. Lucid dreaming. But I can't deny what I saw and felt. I met the triple goddess of the moon. I met the goddess hidden behind the ivory veil. And I awoke in the arms of the goddess of my choice." Wesley leaned in to kiss his wife and she melted against him.

"Wesley, I love you with all my heart."

"You committed yourself to service to the goddess," Wesley said. "Well, so have I. I married her." Rebecca started to object, but Wesley silenced her with a kiss. "I know… I was not dreaming on the mountain when we made love, Becc. I was not dreaming when I released the goddess behind the ivory veil and placed her in your womb." His hand slid over Rebecca's lower abdomen and she was certain that she could already feel the child growing. "I will do all in my power to love and protect both of you until the end of my life. I swear this by the gods and goddesses who have placed this treasure in my hands."

"So mote it be," Rebecca whispered. A wind stirred the leaves around them and a bell rang from one of the monasteries far above.

"Now, tell me what binds you to Ryan McGuire," Wesley whispered. "I've a feeling that he is what I must protect you from." Rebecca pulled the *Athamé* from her sleeve and held it in her open palm.

"There is a blade between us."

"I recognize that knife. He tried to cut my fingers with it. And he's given it to you? How did the hilt get burned?"

Rebecca told Wesley about coming home to find the sacrificial tableau on her bureau and the ritual that ensued. She described how she had grabbed the flaming knife and grounded the power, but had burned her hand in the process. She had then met Ryan in the hospital where he was treated for the same severe burn. Wesley took her hand in his and opened the palm.

"No trace of a burn," he whispered. "No scar. And this was only a week ago?" Rebecca reached in her pocket for the star stone. It glimmered, black with all the colors leaping within it. Wesley stared at it. "The key to the veil," he whispered.

"You used it to free the goddess. She used it to heal my hand."

"Was McGuire healed at the same time?"

"I don't know." Rebecca looked at the stone lying in her hand next to the knife. Her staff was next to her and the cup was in her hiking satchel. "What am I going to do with this? I can't just hold it in my hand forever."

"Let's have a ring made. Then you can wear it."

"I need to dedicate it."

"How can I help?"

Rebecca was uncertain about including Wesley in a pagan ritual of dedication, but… She had married him. Bone of my bone and flesh of my flesh. He had dedicated himself to serving the goddess within her. He might not be part of the circle of Cobhan Carles, but he was in her circle. In fact, he *was* her circle. She stood in the middle of the stone bridge with Wesley in front of her and beckoned him to be still while she placed the four tools around them.

"Powers of the four winds, rulers of the four corners of the earth, champions of the four elements," she intoned as she circled Wesley clockwise while keeping a hand on him. He rotated in place as he followed her. "Attend our ritual. Protect this sacred space. Hold us in your loving care as we consecrate this tool to your service."

Wesley felt more than saw Rebecca's wards flare into place. The power surrounding them was palpable. The guardians were in place around them and they were safe. Without speaking further, Rebecca faced her husband and began slowly and deliberately removing her clothes. Wesley smiled slightly and joined her. Soon they were naked and dancing together in a circle on the stone bridge. Wesley sang as they danced together and his voice seemed to strengthen the glowing field around them and the growing rod between them. They spread their clothing beneath them and Wesley lay stretched out with his head near the star stone.

Rebecca straddled him, looking down at her beloved.

"My sacred tools have been gathered. I am Sadb, known as The Hart. Husband of mine, I name you Deliverer for you have delivered to me this last symbol of my power."

"All that is mine, I deliver into your hands," Wesley said.

"My darling," Rebecca whispered. "May the powers of the north, east, south, and west smile on us and bless this last of my sacred tools to your use. I name this pentacles Key, for she holds the key to a great mystery. I dedicate Key to the power of Earth to bring the elements together. For that use to which the goddess would put her, may I be found worthy to wield her. Now and always. So mote it be."

"Amen," Wesley intoned. Rebecca sank to her knees and directed his shaft into her wet opening.

"Amen," she whispered as she sank down on him.

Their lovemaking might not have been as frantic as on the mountain, nor even as passionate as it had been in the cottage the night before, but it was deep and caring and filled with power. Wesley placed his hands on her waist as she rode him and when he pressed his thumbs into her ovaries, she cried out in ecstasy, certain that the goddess within her would not be the only child of their marriage. He thrust up to meet her need and delivered his seed to her.

24
Death Awaits

Friday, 19 August 1955, Kastraki, Greece

POL MET Rebecca and Wesley at the gate when they returned from their walk late in the afternoon. Even after the exertions of their open air lovemaking, they had continued on up between the two highest of Metéora's monasteries and then followed the road back past yet another. Tourists had begun to arrive for the weekend in Kalambaka to tour the open monasteries on Saturday or attend Divine Liturgy on Sunday.

"Have you been waiting for us, Pol?" Wesley asked. The boy nodded and uncharacteristically gave Wesley a hug. He turned uncertainly to Rebecca but she opened her arms to him as well.

"Mother Rebecca, my grandfather is asking for you. Can you come to him?" Rebecca was thrown at what she assumed was an honorific she would only have thought of in a Catholic sense. Nonetheless, she nodded.

"He is back from his daily walk?" she asked.

"He lay down after breakfast and has not left his bed since. Grandmother is worried. Father Wesley, he will wish to see you as well, but asks for a few minutes with Mother Rebecca first, if you do not object."

"Of course. Perhaps you and I can talk for a few minutes, son." Rebecca noticed, now, the bond that had developed between Wesley and Pol. The titles had not merely been honorifics, Pol considered himself, in a way, a son to the young couple.

"Please do not be angry, Mother, but I told him of our... adventure coming down from the mountain. He has asked to see the stone."

"Pol, I'm not angry. I would never be angry with you for obeying your grandfather." She reached her arms around the boy again and gave him a big hug, which he returned enthusiastically. "My son, I will hurry to your grandfather's side." She turned and kissed Wesley once again and rushed to the old man.

POL AND WESLEY watched her go and then turned to sit on a bench. Pol picked up three stones and began to juggle them, changing patterns as he went. Wesley watched until one of the stones slipped from the boy's hand and he turned suddenly to face his friend.

"You set her free," Pol said. "Truly? She is free now to seek me out? Will the promise of the gods be fulfilled?"

"Pol, I'm not a wise old man like your grandfather. Or even Doc or your father. I'm like a newborn when it comes to the stories your family has been raised with for centuries." Wesley picked up a few pebbles and tossed them one at a time toward a larger rock near the well. "All I've learned is that I can't predict how the powers fulfill their promises. Think. Ryan McGuire believes there is some kind of stone or golden statue that would bring him wealth, fame, or power. You believe in a goddess who will be the love of your life. I admit that I think of the love of my life as a goddess as well."

"May I come to visit you in America?"

"As soon as your parents will allow you to travel to be with us."

The two sat companionably silent for a few minutes. Wesley turned again to Pol.

"There is something else you should know, Pol. I have taken a vow to love and protect her. Them. If I must lay down my life to ensure their safety, I will do that without hesitating."

"Greater love hath no man," Pol recited.

"Faith… Well, we all have it. A lot of people misunderstand it, though. Faith is believing in something for which you have no evidence but the promise. You have a promise and you must have faith, no matter how long it takes, that it will be fulfilled. You will recognize it when it is. Where people go wrong is in having faith in which the evidence is all against them. It is like believing the promise of one who is known to break his promises. Placing faith in that promise is foolishness. But you have seen that the gods are faithful in keeping their promise. Just remember that it has taken them centuries to fulfill this one. Do not be surprised if it takes a few… at least eighteen, I hope… years to fulfill this one."

Pol looked at Wesley curiously and then his mouth dropped open as he looked toward the door of his grandfather's house where Rebecca had entered.

REBECCA ENTERED THE patriarch's home and was invited to sit by his bed. She did not remember him to be so old when she met him just a few days ago. In fact, he seemed to have aged at an alarming rate since breakfast. He seemed withered and frail as if he had been bedridden for weeks. She held his hands between hers. She imagined he might be her own grandfather. Perhaps it was just because she had so much love inside her that she could not help but reach out to him. If he had been a total stranger, she would have loved him and wanted to help make him well and young.

"Rebecca Allen, you are a wonderful sight to my old eyes," he said. "My grandson has told me tales and I want to hear them from you, as well."

For a moment Rebecca found herself absorbed in the aches and pains of the old man's body. She could feel the arthritis that had weakened his hands and swollen his joints. Deep inside, her bones cried out for the pain.

Then it was gone—more quickly than it had come—and she looked at the old man again from the bedside.

"No, goddess. I will not give you my dying," he said. "That is my final special gift. I thank you for easing my pain, but the time is right for my passing. Your promise has kept me alive long since others would have passed."

"You looked no older than my own grandfather just a few days ago. What has happened?" Rebecca asked.

"When I was a boy, I took my journey to the City of the Gods as all in my family had. Each person who goes has his own personal experience with the powers and with the goddess. I was promised that I would live to see her release. That was nearly a hundred years ago. I lost my first family in the Unfortunate War in 1897. Two sons ran off to fight the Turks at Larissa and both fell in battle. Supplies to this area of Thessaly were cut off by war on all sides. A plague carried away my wife, daughter, and mother. I was already 50 years old and looked as young as if I were twenty. My father was also a great believer and looked young. He married a woman much younger than me and soon my brother Leo and sister Demi were born. They have known me only as their older brother, but neither knows how much older. Thea is no older than my little sister, but I waited patiently, knowing that I had been promised the sight of the goddess. I feared for my second family when the Great War embroiled all Europe and I lost my youngest son. But I have never given up hope."

"But why now, Andrew? Why give up hope now?"

"Give up? Oh, no! I have not given up. I have seen the fulfillment of the promise. Show me. Please show me the dark stone that my Pol says cut a void in the mists and gave you firm ground beneath your feet. So glorious was the dark brightness of this jewel that when it appeared all would be lost, you were transported by the stone to land on your feet beneath the holy slopes."

"Pol!" Rebecca snorted. "I think it was not quite as dramatic as that." The old man laughed.

"He does have a slight tendency to exaggerate magical events. Perhaps you merely stumbled down from the mountain of your own accord. It will be a wonderful dream when I sleep tonight." The old man squeezed her hand. "Please, Rebecca. Would you favor an old man's whim and show me this fabled jewel? Perhaps I, too, will find guidance down from my mountain to the netherworlds to which I must travel."

Rebecca fished the stone from her pocket and held it out to the old man. He stared at it for a long while, but it was her hand that held his attention.

"Is this not the hand that was red and blistered when we met?"

"Yes, it healed quickly."

"Gods of thunder!" whispered the old man. "It is indeed the key to the ivory veil." He reached out a bony finger and touched the stone. "Thank you, my goddess." Rebecca placed a hand over her womb, imagining she felt an impossible response from the hours-old fetus. The events of that night were so like a fantasy, yet so real. The images. The lovemaking… The goddess within her.

"She is free," Rebecca answered.

The old man reached out to place his hand over hers.

"Serepte," he whispered. He closed his eyes for a moment and smiled. "I have seen the goddess within you. All is complete. My life is full. It would do no good for me to cling to it longer than Lachesis has measured it. Give me a silver coin for the ferryman and a biscuit for the dog. I will pass the river unafraid, uncomplaining."

They sat a while longer in silence.

"Thea?" Andrew called weakly. His wife hurried in. *She must have been just outside the door listening,* Rebecca thought. "Send someone for Father Dimitri. It is time for an old man to confess his sins. And my precious wife, please come back with Wesley so we may bless them." Thea bent and kissed her husband before she hurried outside. She returned a few moments later with Wesley hurrying behind her.

"Leo and Demi are waiting outside to see you as well," Thea said. "They say they just stopped by."

"A family knows," Andrew said. He reached for Wesley's hand and joined it to Rebecca's. His wife smiled and placed her hands over her husband's as they held the young couple. "Your family is already blessed. You have been married together but have spent much of that time apart. I pray that you will be blessed and that the fruit of your union will bring joy to your lives and to the world she graces. Love and live. Our blessings abide with you."

"Amen," Thea said.

ONCE WESLEY AND Rebecca emerged from the tiny house, Leo and Demi rushed inside to visit their older brother. Rebecca wondered if they had any idea how much older he was. *Why did he trust her with the story of waiting for the goddess?* She found it too hard to believe and wrote it off as an old man's meanderings. Yet, so much was unbelievable in her life. Why not this one thing as well?

By evening, other people in the village had come to pay their respects to Andrew Pariskovopolis before he passed beyond. Each visitor brought food so that Rebecca joined Sophia, Helen, and Sophia's sixteen-year-old daughter Anna in putting out the food and seeing that everyone had eaten. Wesley sat in a corner behind the buffet and strummed his guitar. Pol joined him and the two sang quietly. The music tugged at Rebecca's heart. While it was not particularly sad, it had a peaceful calming effect on the family and friends who gathered.

The priest, Father Dimitri, arrived shortly after sundown and once he had a full plate of food, he joined Wesley and Pol. It seemed an odd combination on the bench. Her husband, having been encouraged not to shave his beard until they were ready to leave Metéora, was a Methodist from birth who now espoused a special commitment to the goddess. Pol had been raised in the combined culture and teaching of Greek Orthodoxy and ancient mythology. A heavily-bearded priest, Dimitri took large swallows of wine to wash down each bite of the plentiful food. And herself. She'd changed to a long skirt and blouse out of respect for the local customs, but knew she would be more comfortable dancing naked around a fire to raise the power of her own pagan coven. Yet, here they all were, celebrating the life and awaiting the death of the old man.

Eventually, the crowd drifted off to their homes and beds. The priest staggered home. Wesley put away his guitar and led his wife to bed where they celebrated the life of the old man by making gentle love and fell asleep in each other's arms.

At some time in her dreams, or at some other level of consciousness, she was aware of the presence of the old man bidding a last farewell to his family, his dreams, and his beloved Metéora. She felt a feather touch on her womb as he blessed her child and left a message of hope and fulfillment.

Saturday, 20 August 1955, Kastraki, Greece

In America, a professional embalmer would be called, the body carted away and made up to 'look natural' for two or three days while friends and relatives traveled hundreds of miles across the country to pay their respects. In this little village, a runner was sent out to tell everyone in Kastraki, Kalambaka, and at the monasteries of the passing of Andrew Pariskovopolis. Breakfast had scarcely been finished when three old women dressed in black arrived to help Thea bathe and dress her husband for burial. The activity took the rest of the morning with other women arriving to prepare food, take care of children, and to clean—not just Andrew and Thea's house, but all four of the cottages around the courtyard.

There had been a minor dispute when Father Dimitri arrived, a bit hung over, about the same time the women went in to prepare the body. He had attempted to take charge and have the body interred in the churchyard with the ritual to take place on Monday. Leo, now the titular head of the family, had put his foot down.

"Andrew lived in the presence of the old ones and he shall pass to Hades as one of their own," Leo declared. Had it not been for Dimitri's headache and the volume of Leo's voice, the argument may have lasted longer. But Dimitri won a small concession in that the body would not lie in state over the sabbath. Therefore, it was agreed that the funerary would be concluded yet that night.

Brother El arrived with three other monks. He persuaded Leo to let them carry the bier to its final resting place on the top of the Tower of Agia. The name was whispered and Sophia told Rebecca that neither the priest nor the regional magistrate in Kalambaka knew the destination for the bier. But in their own way, the monks of the monasteries on the pinnacles of Metéora guarded the heights. The brothers would be sure the way was clear. Andrew had been a benefactor to several of the orders over the years.

Rebecca was given a black skirt and shawl to wear over her clothes. Brother El pulled Wesley aside and handed him a dark robe and hat. "During the circling of the body, slip this on and join me at the bier, Brother John," the monk suggested. "You will carry the pall with us as Andrew would have wished." He glanced over at Rebecca. "You may walk with the women." Rebecca shook her head and resolved not to join the two-mile march and climb to the Tower of Agia. She was tired and would simply wait for Wesley to return, sans habit. He would certainly fit in with the rows of men in black pillbox hats and long straight robes.

The monks erected a platform beside the well. People brought flowers to scatter on and around the platform. Others brought gifts of food, oil, wine, and spices which were appropriately displayed before the homes around the courtyard. Since the cremation would not take place until sunset, the food was kept indoors and would be brought out when the crowd returned about ten or eleven o'clock. Rebecca had joined the fast for the day and was not sure she could wait that late to eat again.

Late in the afternoon, Rebecca and Wesley went into their cottage and she dressed him in his robe.

"You're wearing slacks under the habit? Is that allowed?" she giggled.

"I think they all wear pants," Wesley spluttered. "Do you think not?"

"I thought perhaps the monk's robe was like a Scottish kilt."

"They don't wear anything under those?"

"If they wore underwear, apparently, it would be called a skirt."

"I don't know..."

"Wesley, I'm teasing," she said.

"I know, darling. I'm an easy mark. It makes me nervous to impersonate a monk. At least it's not the first time. And I won't be the only one."

"You are my anchor in a storm of trouble," Rebecca sighed. "I've been exposed to so many new things this summer that I am exhausted."

"I have as well, and I'm sorry to say that I'm not looking forward to the two-mile hike, but we've done worse this summer. Listen." The buzz from the courtyard suddenly hushed and they went to the window. Everyone had risen and was facing the door of Andrew's house. Father Dimitri, still posing some semblance of control, emerged first with a censer waving in front of him. Then Marcos, Sophia, Thea, Leo, and Demi followed. Four monks squeezed out of the opening bearing a pallet with the body stretched upon it. At the sight of the body, the crowded courtyard broke into mournful chants. The monks circled the well three times counterclockwise as dust filled the air. People tossed the dust into the air and onto the body, but as the parade passed beneath the window again, they could see and smell that mixed with the dust were spices that scented the air—cinnamon, basil, tarragon, clove, and others she could not readily identify.

At last the parade came to a halt and the pallet was set on the stand near the well. No makeup had been applied to Andrew's face and he looked every bit the 110 years he professed to be. Still, he looked calm and peaceful. A coin sealed his lips and a flower was held in his hand.

"I think that's my cue," Wesley whispered. He kissed his wife, settled his hat firmly on his head, and slipped out to blend in with the other monks. Rebecca smiled as she watched him go.

Father Dimitri chanted a prayer that was responded to by the crowd, and then retreated. The monks sang hymns and choruses, chanted prayers, and responded. Somehow, Rebecca did not think all the chants were strictly approved by the Orthodox Church. She did not understand Greek, but observing the actions of the monks reminded her more of her own pagan celebrations than of church ritual. She arranged her sacred tools on the bed and began her own invocation of the powers to watch over the funeral, her husband, and the old man's spirit.

Her suspicions were confirmed some time later, as Pol's voice rose out of the music and the rest fell silent. She looked out the window again and saw the boy at the head of the bier. His voice was sharp and clear, resonating within the houses and the yard. He slipped into the ancient musical language she had heard Wesley studying for so long. And then she recognized Wesley's voice joining Pol's. The crowd in the courtyard bowed their heads as the music washed over them and Rebecca realized she was witnessing the funeral of *megalos kai kalos*—a great and good man. In the impromptu duet by Pol and Wesley, she saw the respect of the ancients for the old man of Metéora as they bore him to his place among the stars.

The music was soft and gentle, then rose to heart-throbbing heights. It rippled like the stream in which they had bathed. The images brought by that ancient tongue spoke to each hearer differently. But each image was overwrought with the boy's grief and loss. It was deeper than just the loss of a grandfather, but spoke of the end of an era, of a dream. It wove about them, speaking of tragedies and sorrows just beginning.

Rebecca could not stay within the cottage for this ritual. Wesley and Pol were not alone and she would not let them stand alone. As Pol's voice grew softer, a new voice sang as if borne on the wind. Even though it came from Rebecca's mouth, even she felt it originated on another plane. It was gentle and loving, so completely other-worldly that, for an instant, no one recognized it as a voice at all. It tugged at their ears and drew their eyes toward the heavens. The stars were brighter and more fiery than they had ever seen them. But the music did not come from the stars or the sliver of moonlight rising above them.

Rebecca emerged as a shadow in the gathering dusk, moving toward Pol and Wesley, yet it did not seem like Rebecca at all. She bore an other-worldly presence that matched her voice as she sang in answer to Pol and Wesley. They responded and the blending of their voices rose to a height of beautiful music, without words and without melody.

The mourners shielded their eyes against looking at the intimacy of this cluster of voices. The song brought them all their own images of love and beauty and hope. It rose to a climactic height and as if orchestrated by a great conductor, suddenly ceased. Rebecca smiled at Pol and pulled his hand to her womb. Then she slipped back into the shadows.

Torches were lit. The monks, including Wesley, lifted the pallet and placed it on a cart that moved slowly forward. The priest had disappeared during the music, but the monks and mourners filed out of the courtyard following the cart. The family followed first, then the other mourners, including Doc and Margaret. They stretched out in a column singing hymns as they walked through the village to the foot of the Tower of Agia. Rebecca watched the torches as they ascended the steep trail to the peak. Rebecca brought her sacred tools out to the well, placing them beside her as she looked out toward the peak and saw the sudden flare of fire that indicated the pyre had been lit.

"The price of a rite of passage is to leave a bit of yourself behind," she whispered the words that the goddess had used on the mountain and wondered what she had left behind. The old man would leave his ashes as he made his way to the netherworld.

She filled her cup with water from the well and shed her own silent tear for the departed hero. Already the events of the past few days were being reduced to dreams in her mind. The fantasy and terror dissolving into loneliness and lovemaking; the magic changed to accident and coincidence. She faded in and out of sleep as she sat at the well, losing track of time in the dance of her dreams.

25

Dance with the Devil

Saturday, 20 August 1955, Kastraki, Greece

A SOFT STEP on the gravel near Rebecca began to rouse her out of her sleep. She leaned back against the strong hand that lifted her hair to caress her neck.

"Ah, Wes, you're back," she sighed.

His lips irresistibly pressed against hers and she was locked in the embrace before she was fully awake. She opened her lips to accept the invitation of his tongue and their kiss rose in passion. How odd for Wesley to make such an open demonstration in the courtyard. He took her so much by surprise while she was still in her half-waking state that she could not help responding to the intimacy.

He lifted her, dancing around the courtyard... dancing like they had on the mountain, still lost in that intimate kiss. Flickering images behind her tightly closed eyelids reminded her first of the dance on the mountain and then of the dances around the fire at Carles. Naked dancing bodies circling the fire. The intimacy of the spiral dance, of feather caresses against each of the coven dancers. Her lover was even more passionate than he had been in the City of the Gods, in their bed, on the bridge.

She felt her body lifted in the air as if she weighed nothing—perhaps supported only by the passionate kiss. She was raised and lowered horizontally to their bed, yet so much higher than the bed in their cottage. Still, the breeze began to play beneath the buttons of her blouse and she felt the fabric fall away from her. She felt his soft caress of her breasts and moaned into his mouth.

When a sharp point began caressing her flesh, dreaming fled from her head. She'd felt the bite of this knife at the stone circle when she was initiated. It traced a familiar pattern between her breasts and then slid beneath the front of her bra, slicing through the fabric and letting it spring away from her tender breasts. A sickening sensuality mixed liberally with fear and revulsion as she pushed away from her lover. He held fast to her lips with a hand clenched in her hair and the knife continuing to trace patterns on her bare torso. It generated a pain in her stomach—a sickness that made her revolt from the continued passion. She drew into the sickness and exploded outward, thrusting her sadistic would-be lover away from her, and opening her eyes to see Ryan McGuire grinning above her.

She lay stretched out on the platform that had been built to hold the old man's funeral pallet, her breasts bare to the sky. Surrounding herself and the entire well was the shimmering light of a warded circle through which she could scarcely define the shapes of the surrounding cottages. Beside her, stood The Blade, a black leather-gloved hand still stretched out to touch her with the ritual *Athamé* of Cobhan Carles.

"What is this?" she demanded, taking control and pushing his gloved hand away from her. "Are you afraid to leave fingerprints in your criminal activity?" The arousal and passion had fled from her as soon as she opened her eyes. She could stand naked before this man and have no response.

He grabbed her healed hand and looked at it, then held his gloved hand up next to it.

"I am not as quick to heal as you, Hart. Or were you faking an injury at the hospital?"

"There is no faking the power of the goddess," intoned Rebecca. "Let me help you—heal you."

"Oh, you will help me. You will help me raise the power that I need to open the veil. Your friends failed to bring down the goddess. I will not."

"There was no failure. You seek something that is not there."

"I have already searched and have found nothing, but your husband's notes. They will be helpful in opening the gates."

"It doesn't help to know how to search if you have no idea what you are looking for. You will find nothing on the mountain either. There is nothing there. And I've no interest in helping you raise power."

"You are past choosing," Ryan answered, pushing Rebecca back down on the pallet. "I want the goddess and you have the power. There may be more pleasant ways to raise it than under a sacrificial blade."

"Forget it, Blade. You are not who I thought you were. Not who I ever thought you were. You are far too late for a virgin sacrifice." Her hands darted out and clasped his gloved fist. She squeezed the injured hand with all her might, remembering the pain in her hand that she had suffered. The tender burned flesh beneath the glove tightened around the hilt of the *Athamé* and he yelled in anger and pain. The back of his good hand connected with her face, knocking her back down on the bier. The knife changed hands and Ryan's anger turned to laughter. There was a manic glow in his eyes.

"So, you like pain, do you? I'm very good at that." He moved toward her again with the knife poised, confident in his superior size and strength. This time the steel was met with her own blade and she rose upon the platform again, swinging her feet over the edge.

"A blade between us, as you told me," she said. "I'll leave now. I think you should, too."

He laughed. "Leave? You have missed the point. This is my warded circle. You cannot walk through someone else's wards. You can't leave me. We are locked here until love or death sets us free." Rebecca looked critically at the wards as she circled the well, staying on the opposite side from Ryan.

"Where are your pentacles, Blade?" Rebecca asked. She flicked her knife back and forth. A worn engraving caught her eye. "Did you give me something more than your Athamé when you attacked me? You did, didn't you? You combined your *Athamé* and your pentacles into a single tool and now they are in my possession."

"What difference does it make? Don't believe all that rubbish about witch's tools. They are merely symbols of the power held within. Magic is all in your head. The more powerful your mind the more powerful your magic."

"I see. And is the power of your mind supposed to make me fear your wards?" He lunged at her but she slipped beneath his guard in a feinted lunge. He spun on her and tripped her. Rebecca rolled away and placed herself between Ryan and the shimmering wall of light that surrounded the well.

"You are a pretty fighter, Hart. Circle now. The power is rising. Power is neutral. It is as strong in anger as it is in sex. You can feel it swirling around you in a vortex—yours to raise, mine to command."

"It's about to end," whispered Rebecca. "You don't understand the powers you have been playing with. I can see from here that the lust for power has consumed you and controls you." Rebecca lifted the star stone from her pocket and held it between her fingers. "Have you looked deeply into your heart? Look at my pentacles, Blade. A hungry star-shaped void in space." The jewel sparkled in an odd way, as if the rays of light that missed it were more pronounced because of those that hit it and disappeared. She placed her stone against the engraving on the knife and could hear it hiss as the image on the blade disappeared. "It likes you, Blade. I like you, too. If we had met under other circumstances… Well, never mind about that."

She reached toward the warded wall of light with the black shimmering jewel in her fingers. Where it touched, the light ceased to be. The empty space in the ward grew until the entire shimmering wall of light was absorbed—sucked into the jewel—and was gone.

Ryan sank to his knees and dropped the *Athamé*. Both hands came to the sides of his head. "Stop it, Hart! For the Goddess's sake, please stop it!"

Rebecca placed the black void stone in her pocket. Ryan still knelt with his hands clutched against his forehead.

"My head. It tried… Battering my head." The man choked on his own words and Rebecca was at once caught up in mothering her wayward child. She reached out a tentative hand, half expecting him to grab it in a feint. He was passive as it rested on his head. She could feel the pain—a minor thing—but the terror that accompanied it was irrational—otherworldly. It was a living being, feeding on his soul. She could do nothing about that. Ryan McGuire's inner demons were his own to deal with. She sought deeper and found the damaged flesh and nerve endings in his hand. She could feel the burning, itching flesh beneath the glove—the heat almost soothing in comparison to the cold fear. She felt the stone in her pocket search through her for the fire in his hand and let it go. The pain of the injured hand fled as well. She opened her eyes to find Ryan staring up at her.

"What did you do?" he croaked.

"Ryan," she said and caressed his head as he laid it against her thigh. "Take off your glove."

"My glove?" He obediently pulled the black leather glove from his hand. The dried, burned flesh fell away and beneath it was a wholly healed hand. He flexed it as he looked in awe. "You and I could… As you say, never mind that. Still…" He picked up the *Athamé*, slid it into his belt sheath, and stood.

"As you said, the magic is all in your head."

"I have never needed a tool to work magic since the time I received Creüs as guardian of the First Face of Carles. It is a good thing. You hold three of my tools in your hand. If you ever find my cup, keep it safe for me."

"You made this knife your wand as well?" asked an astonished Rebecca. "Where did you leave your cup?"

"I don't remember. In a desert. Or an ocean. It never seemed important." They looked at each other and Ryan bent forward just enough to place a kiss against her unresponsive lips. "You know, I will have her eventually. I know now how to open the gates of Olympus. Together we could rule the world."

"You'd better go now, Blade."

"I suppose I'll have to do it without you."

"I suppose you will."

Ryan bent to kiss her again, then turned to scoop up a backpack near the entrance to the courtyard. Rebecca heard voices from the village as the mourners returned from the funeral pyre.

"Here's till next time, Hart." He turned on his heel and left before the first of the torchbearers came in sight. Rebecca hurried to her cottage with her tools and cut the remains of her bra off her shoulders. She flung it into a corner and lay on the bed sobbing as the adrenaline ran out of her.

Sunday, 21 August 1955, Kastraki, Greece

WESLEY HELD HIS beloved wife in his arms. She had been stretched on the bed when he returned with the mourners the night before. He ate from the food they brought, but felt uneasy about the crowd in the courtyard. As quickly as possible he'd entered the cottage to divest himself of the monk's habit. He took the time to help Rebecca out of the rest of her clothes wondering that she had been so exhausted that she fell asleep before finishing undressing. He handed her a nightgown. She let it fall to the floor and held out her arms.

While the wake went on in the courtyard, Wesley and Rebecca had made love. Dawn had come before the mourners stopped singing and dancing and before Rebecca had finally slept in her husband's arms.

It was quiet outside after the churches and monasteries had finished pealing their Sunday morning calls to worship. Through partially lidded eyes, he watched his wife sleeping and thought of the funeral and wake. Poor Father Dimitri would have a somnambulant congregation this morning.

But Wesley had noted another presence slipping away from the cluster of houses as he returned from the funeral. He was certain he had seen his and Rebecca's nemesis. He wondered now where he had gone and what mischief he had played. Rebecca had been alone. Should he have been concerned about her virtue? Her health?

Wesley was yet attempting to resolve his internal conflict, thinking that perhaps he should have risen with the church bells to stand in the village church and recite the liturgy. But when he had made love to Rebecca in the night, he was filled with images of the goddess that commanded his loyalty. And he had the strong feeling that goddess lay here in his arms, able to sleep because he was watchful. He would protect her.

As he watched over her, sleep claimed him again and he was one with her dreams.

REBECCA BIT BACK tears of frustration, alternately exploding in tears of rage. Something happened in the encounter with Ryan McGuire that was of great import. Something she needed to know. But the raw emotional outpourings in the wake of the encounter kept her memory at bay. She had taken out her frustrations on her husband, giving him the passion Ryan had aroused. Had she known it was Ryan all along? Had she really believed it was Wesley's lips that held her—that it was Wesley's arms that had lifted her to the bier? And once she had known, what kept her from giving herself to him? She could not deny that even the cold bite of his knife had aroused her. Was it only his dominance that set her on fire? If not, then in her victory over him, why had she not claimed him as her spoils? She could have bent him to her cold will.

Yet, she had not been cold in her farewell. She might, even then, have fallen into his arms. But he had no fire left in him. He was cold in his passion, those demon-lit eyes boring into her.

When she healed his hand, she had carefully left what she called his inner demon alone, but now the image tracked in her mind with horror. Was it merely the inner demons that all people carried and were haunted by, or had The Blade raised a different kind of power in his quest for the goddess?

Her dark star stone that she called pentacles—received from the hand of the goddess and embedded in her husband's forehead—had eaten away Ryan's wards as if they did not exist at all. And then they had turned to the gatekeeper himself, sucking at the fire within him. Sucking at the demon he had raised.

And she had stopped.

She had carefully left the demon alone as she had sucked the fire out of Ryan's burned hand and let it return to the presence in his soul.

The passion and drive to find and possess the goddess did not come from Ryan, but from the demon.

For the first time, Rebecca realized she was truly in danger. The child within her was in danger. It was not a man, but a demon that sought her.

THE ORIGINAL SCHEDULE had been for Marcos to arrive on Sunday and return with the explorers and his son to Athens on Monday. With Rebecca's arrival, the rush to Metéora, and the death and burial of his father, however, plans were in chaos. Seven people would scarcely fit in Marcos's Jeep with their luggage and acquisitions. Marcos felt obligated to stay with his mother and sister a bit longer, but Helen worried about leaving the inn tended only by her one assistant.

"I suggest that we make our departure by rail in the next day or two," Doc said. "Let us leave Marcos and his family to their grieving."

"Most of our gear can stay here," Margaret agreed. "The family can always use more camping gear and aside from that, we have only our personal items and notes."

Wesley uncharacteristically laughed at that. His wife and companions looked at him.

"I've no notes," he sighed. "I thought to look them over this morning, but they are gone. I assume with us all at the funerary last night, it was no problem for Ryan McGuire to search our belongings." He looked at Rebecca. "I am surprised you slept through his invasion and am thankful you were not molested, darling."

Rebecca heaved a sigh and tears sprang to her eyes. Wesley pulled her rapidly into his arms.

"You were," he said angrily. "I will utterly destroy him." Rebecca clutched him tightly.

"I prevailed. This time," she said.

"We need to check to see if our notes are also missing," Doc said, standing. "We'll leave you to talk, but right now, I am in full agreement with Wesley. I've put up with that arrogant graverobber for fifteen years. It's time to put a stop to it." Doc and Margaret left the two lovers to check their packs and precious notes from the City of the Gods.

"Wes, my love, I need to tell you... There is more that you do not understand."

"Is he your lover, Becc?"

"No! But there is a bond of sorts between us. A bond I must sever but I don't know how."

"Perhaps it will be severed when I separate his head from his body," Wesley raved. Of course, he had no ability to carry out his threat in a face-to-face confrontation, and would undoubtedly come out the worse, but his head was spilling over with thoughts of his wife being molested. His wife and daughter. A sudden cold calmness swept over him. The wife and daughter he had sworn to protect. Whatever else was between Rebecca and Ryan would have to wait. The important thing was to protect his wife and child. With Wesley's notes, Ryan would know how to access the City of the Gods, in whatever state of chaos it currently resided. He and Rebecca had freed the goddess, but the veil was still there.

Wesley spun to look at Rebecca, grasping her shoulders in his hands. She met his eyes steadily. "You know how to sever the bond," he whispered. "I know how to eliminate the threat. What must we do?"

"I'm afraid, Wesley. Please, love me. Take me. Possess me. Tonight, we will break the spell."

THE SUN HAD sunk beyond the pillars of Metéora as the family and a few friends continued to sit together in the courtyard. Wesley had taken his guitar outside and played a background of music as Pol juggled and did little magic tricks. Margaret sat with Thea Pariskovopolis, chatting in the meaningless way that comforts the bereaved, listening to tales of when Thea was young and so in love with the older brother of her friend Demi. Andrew's sister joined the conversation to say that Thea was set to go off with Leo until she met Andrew. The storytelling and camaraderie continued well into the darkness of night.

Inside the small cottage, Rebecca explained to Doc what was needed.

"I forged a bond of fire with The Blade," she explained. "I believe, in doing so, that I may have actually created the demon that resides in him. It is hungry and is as fixed on me as on the goddess he desires."

"The Blade has been known to practice the dark arts," Doc replied. "It would not surprise me to find he had raised a demon in himself. Nonetheless, it is completely possible that your ritual binding him could also have strengthened the presence. But I don't know what I can do to help you here." He smiled at her and she maintained silence as he observed her. Finally, she looked squarely into his eyes.

"When I work magic with a sister or brother of the coven, I give my true name. I give it to you. I am called Sadb."

"I was once given a magical name by my mentor. I have not used it in many years. I am called Brand," Doc said. "How can I help?"

"The Blade…"

"If we are to work a deep magic, you should know that his true name is Janus, the two-faced guardian of the gates," Doc interrupted her. It was not completely in keeping with the coven protocols to reveal another witch's name without his permission, but the entire ritual would be focused on this other.

"Janus. How appropriate. He attempted to intimidate me by creating a sacrifice, plunging his *Athamé* into the heart of my staff. He has very little respect for his tools, considering Creüs to be the only thing he needs. He doesn't even know where his cup is." Rebecca interrupted her story when Doc laughed.

"He was at a revel some seven years ago and after drinking a salute to his host, he flung his cup in the fireplace and it shattered. He has had only three tools since then."

"Then he has none," Rebecca said. "He had embodied all his other tools in this one knife—*Athamé*, pentacles, and wand. If he had been able to conceal a flask in the handle, he probably would have made it his cup as well."

"He's always considered the *Athamé* of Carles to be his own."

"I stripped him of his own *Athamé* in my ritual. It nearly killed me and created such a strong bond that his hand was burned as badly as mine."

"Burned?" Rebecca held her right hand out to Doc.

"When I arrived here a week ago, my hand was blistered and red. On the mountain, I was shown how to heal it. I worked the same cure on Janus last night." Doc swallowed hard, wondering what kind of witch Rebecca had become. "But also, last night, I stripped the pentacles from the blade. It frightened him. It frightened the demon within him."

"The wand. The source of the fire. That is what you want to strip away now."

"And break forever the bond between us." Rebecca looked at Doc's staff. "Is that not the staff of the Vagabond Poet?" she asked quietly.

"Yes, though I fear that in my hand it is merely a walking stick."

"It will do. We are *cildru* of the same circle. Just be in the same circle with me. If I lose control, stop me. Ground me. Break the spell. I do not dare to work alone." She prepared her circle and for the first time, Doc saw the black void of the star stone in her hand. It seemed to have a life of its own, sucking at him until he turned away.

Outside, Pol's clear high voice was joined by Wesley's and several others as they sang a hymn, a kind of Vesper. The tones rose and fell, gradually slipping into the ancient music language. Wesley seemed to know the song—if that was what it was—as well as Pol and it reinforced the circle as she cast it. She went to the East and lit a candle from the one on her altar. She moved behind Doc to pick up the candle in the South. Doc closed his eyes to center himself and relax. He could feel the presence of the wards, but had never succeeded in casting a circle. His knowledge was in combat with his faith.

As Sadb moved to the final candle, Doc saw the shimmering glow take shape all around the room. She was pleased. She had not told Doc that she had never managed to cast a circle that was completely controlled. "Hold out your wand, Brand," she commanded softly. Sadb presented the star stone to the altar candle and the flame shrank noticeably, sucked into the void. She then reached out to touch the iron heel of Doc's staff. In a moment, he felt a numbness creeping into his fingertips. He flexed his fingers for a better grip and Sadb moved away with the stone.

"If anything should happen, like I lose control or pass out or something, touch your wand to the wards and blow out the altar candle. It should ground the power and get us to safety. I hope."

With her instructions given, she turned away from Doc and he knew his role now was simply to watch and wait.

Pol and Wesley continued to sing into the night air as Rebecca picked up their rhythm, swaying, spinning, and clapping as she moved. With a sidelong glance toward Doc, she began stripping off her clothes until she danced skyclad around the room. She hummed and subvocalized with the music from outside. A force like an electrical field filled the room and raised the hairs on their necks and arms. The air crackled with power.

Sadb approached the altar, hardly able to stand for the dizziness that swept over her. She focused on the star stone jewel that had come from the center of the dais in the City of the Gods. Her words were scarcely audible, reflecting years of study and research.

"Solomon gave me pentacles, but the goddess gave them to him. Now, power of the earth, arise and hear Sadb's blessing." She spun around once more and collected the power in the room to focus on the stone.

"I charge you, pentacles, with earth. Take power from the air, the fire, the water, and the earth. Glow with passion deep inside. For passion is the life—a flame that burns within the soul. When the flame dies, the body cools. The soul is lost in darkness. The eyes no longer see. The tremors of the loving touch dispelled by fervent plea."

Oh thief!
Return, return, oh Shulamite,
Place the joy back in my heart.
Return the love and pleasure
That has driven us apart.
Return. Return.
Return.

Rebecca reached out her hand so deftly that the stone seemed to jump into her palm. She turned away from Doc so that he could not see the stone. In her other hand, she took up her *Athamé.*

"The purity of this tool must be restored. Let the power of the South recede from this blade and its fire pass into my wand, Pele. Let the fire that bound Sadb and Janus be quenched. Everything passes. Everything changes."

As she spoke, she pointed the *Athamé* at her staff, lying on the altar with her cup. Flame erupted from the point of the knife and struck the wounded heart carved in its wood. As the flame threatened higher, Sadb touched the dark star stone to the handle of the blade and the fire drained out of it. Instead, a continued small flame flickered in the wounded wood and then was absorbed.

Sadb spun rapidly like a dervish, snatching her other tools up as she passed the altar and clasping all four tools to her bare breasts as she danced. She found herself once again caught in the vortex of her own cone of power and slowly drifted again around the spiral chanting an ancient spellbinding that Hebe had taught her.

By all the powers surrounding me
This spell tied and bound shall be
To do no harm nor turn on we
Who work it here. So mote it be.

She made four full circuits around her tiny altar placing each of her tools in their respective quadrants. When she reached the North, she raised the stone above her hand and slapped it down hard beneath her palm, grounding the power. The slap stung her fingers, but the retort knocked both Rebecca and Doc off their feet. Rebecca fell back on the bed. Doc went to the floor. His walking stick, thrust out beside him, touched the wards and he felt them sucked up and dissolved in an instant. His ears rang as he stumbled to the altar on his knees and blew out the candle with as much breath as he could muster. It took two tries before it sputtered out. Only then did he realize that the surrounding candles had gone out with the wards and left them in darkness.

Doc managed to get to the shuttered window and opened it for the light that was in the courtyard. Pol and Wesley continued to sing by the well. The rest of the family and friends all seemed to have wandered off.

Rebecca rolled over and began to collect her clothes as she listened to the surreal music. She identified the pictures of the song with deep emotions and drew strength from her partner. As a finale to her performance, it washed away the footprints on the sand.

She might not be out of danger, but she was at least free.

26
The Northern Steps

Monday, 22 August 1955, Kastraki, Greece

DREAMS. THERE were always dreams. He had just awakened to find Rebecca draped across him, having not stirred from where they ended their lovemaking the night before. His dream had been so real and so familiar in the afterglow. He was married. His wife and, in her womb, their daughter were the world to him and he would guard and protect them for eternity. But the dream had revealed something. Eternity might be a very long time.

HE LOOKS OUT at his dream world through watery eyes. An empty world—light, but with no light source—warm, but without heat. Everything around him is bare and barren. In this plain flatness, he cannot determine his own size. Is he large or small? There is nothing to compare himself to. The ground is hard and flat as far as he can see. The sky is invisible above him.

In despair, he sits and sings softly to himself, rocking back and forth with arms clenched around his knees.

A figure appears. It emerges from a horizon he had not seen before. He flattens himself on his stomach and crawls backward, away from the figure, yet it continues to grow larger—approaching. Perhaps it is a giant. He dares not hope for another human being. He is naked. Yet, he is alone and his alone-ness reverberates in him and emerges as song. Even naked, he cannot stay forever alone. He slows and allows the figure to approach, circling him as he stays flat against the ground.

The woman—it is a woman!—is naked as well. With a wave of her hand, she beckons him to stand. Bile clogs his throat as he rises, and with him his shame. She is tall and graceful—taller than any woman he has known. Her body, proportioned with her height, is a tower of strength and beauty. He cannot make it past his knees as this goddess nearly passes by him, head held high. She turns over her shoulder to speak to him.

Behind the Ivory Veil

"Why do you kneel?" Her words are abrupt, shaking him. He would like to say he was kneeling to royalty and could not rise in her presence, for surely this is as close to royalty as he has ever come. But truth flushes like heat within him.

"I am naked."

"Does not the air clothe you?"

"The air?"

"You have much to learn. Come with me." She continues her stately walk and he hesitates only a moment before he follows. When fully erect in body and spirit, he sees that he is as tall as she. Yet following her shapely back keeps him hesitant in his stride. After a few steps, she turns to him.

"I did not ask to be followed."

"You said to come with you," he chokes. He is like a child and she is all of womanhood before him.

"With me is not behind me. With me is beside me. You have much to learn."

He quickly catches up and walks beside her, not daring to look left or right or to speak. Her path is straight, but there is no sign of any change in their surroundings. They walk on through nothing, yet he is somehow comforted that he is not alone.

He glances at her and sees her from every angle, causing him to stumble and then regain his footing. Her auburn hair falls to her shoulders. Her eyes are deep set and sparkle so that he cannot grasp their color—sometimes blue, sometimes green, sometimes brown. They catch and break down whatever light strikes them. Her jaw is firm but relaxed. She glides in her walk like a cat, all her muscles working together so that none seem to work at all. In spite of the tremendous power in her limbs, she has the ability to expend no energy in using them. She breathes deeply, regularly, slowly. He watches her bosom rise and fall, taut nipples proudly displayed at the crescent of full breasts. He sees that her pulse is slower than his own and rebukes his rising passion. Unable to remain silent any longer, he speaks.

"Where are we going?"

"Going? We are not going anywhere."

"But we are walking."

"Yet we are still here."

"Who are you?"

"I am who I appear to be."

"What are you?"

"I will be what I will be."

Her answers to his many questions only confuse him more. He phrases his next question carefully, afraid he is merely playing a game in his mind.

"If you can offer more information than simply the word 'here,' I would like to know where I am." He adds, *"Please,"* as an afterthought. She stops to turn to him.

"Where in all the cosmos would you like most to be?"

"Home."

"Then why did you leave?"

"I'm dreaming. This isn't real."

"What is real?" She walks again and he hastens to catch up with her. Distance seems only to be relative to their positions and he does not like to be separated from her. *"You are still confused. You wish to protect your loved ones, but do not know how. Where in all the cosmos, in all your dreams, are the answers you seek?"*

He puzzles over the question as they walk. She directed him to his own dreams. Where would he find all the answers? He envisions the City of the Gods, but it was at night in that City that he found his answer. The palace toward which he endlessly climbed.

"The palace of light. All questions are answered there. Perfect safety and peace are there. I go to the palace of light."

"Be in the palace of light. It is your longing. It is here."

He trips over the step in front of him—a step so perfectly the same non-color as the long plain that he had not seen it. A few feet farther, he finds another step. His companion continues to glide next to him. He mimics her walk and breathes in time with her breaths. They rise, step after step, though seeming to get no higher.

"These are the steps of my dreams? The Northern Steps? Where are we?"

"We are still here, where you have always been."

"I've had this dream before."

"This dream?"

"You were never there before. I don't know you."

He looks ahead as the steps draw closer together, steeper. A brilliant flaring of light at the top sets the sky aflame, blinding him. He shuts his eyes and hides his head in his hands. *"No!"* he moans. The flame dies. There are no more steps.

She reaches for him and strokes his hair. He is more acutely aware of the nature of the touch and his own undeniable response to it. She draws his head to her breasts and he suckles greedily as she moans her pleasure. They are soft and warm and solid beneath his lips and hands—unlike any dream he has had before. He loses himself utterly in the unbridled sensuality of her caress. He feels her breath on his cheek, the close warm scent of her arousal. His passion explodes past his sensibilities and he find her lips pressed against his, muffling his roar of pleasure.

WESLEY'S ORGASM AND the pressing reality of Rebecca's lips against his own brought him instantly across the threshold between sleep and wakefulness. He opened his eyes to stare into Rebecca's. He pushed up, but she bore him back down under the weight of her own desires. He responded to her demands with new vigor. Both rose to the heights of another climax, collapsing into their embrace.

"I thought I was asleep and dreaming," Wesley whispered.

"You must have some terrific dreams," Rebecca giggled. "What are you like when you are awake?"

"Wasn't I awake last night?"

"Oh, you certainly were."

"Rebecca Hart Allen, you are the love of my life."

Tuesday, 23 August 1955, Kastraki, Greece

IT SEEMED HE had hardly slept when Wesley awoke. Dawn was graying the sky and he knew the family would be up and about soon. They planned to leave for Athens today and Marcos would make a trip shuttling the Americans to the train station and then returning for his wife and son.

He looked at his wife, still sleeping in his arms. They had made love most of the night and he still reveled in the fact that they were married and so in love. His life had changed over the summer—not only his love life, but his entire faith. He could honestly say he was still a Christian, but there was another dimension to his faith that ran parallel to his old beliefs. And here next to him lay a woman who could work magic, not only on him, but within a circle of witches. And it didn't bother him. In fact, he found great joy in his wife's fulfillment.

He wanted to immerse himself again in her warmth and she stirred as he reached for her.

"Wesley! Rebecca!" Marcos called from outside the door. "It is time to rise so we can leave. Is Pol with you?"

Wesley arrested his caress and went to the door. Rebecca sat up behind him.

"He's not here," Wesley said. "Is he missing?"

"I thought he was with Sophia's children, but none of them have seen him," Marcos said. "It's unlike him to simply wander off in the night."

"Let us dress and we'll be right out to help look."

Rebecca was already out of bed and pulling her expedition clothes on. Even in the sturdy slacks and safari shirt she looked wonderful in his eyes. He hastened into his boots, kissed his wife, and left the cottage. Family was gathering in the courtyard and Doc and Margaret emerged from the cottage shared with the widow, Thea. Off in the distance, Wesley heard the yelp of a dog, suddenly silenced. He headed out of the courtyard and toward the sound, Rebecca following with her sturdy staff clicking on the cobbles. When they reached the town square, Wesley stopped and looked in all directions.

"Which way?" he asked Rebecca as Margaret and Doc caught up. Rebecca looked first to Doc and then to her husband. She dug into her pocket for the star stone and gazed into its depths as the other three shielded her from view of any curious early risers. She looked up in a trance and turned downhill. At the bridge, she left the road and followed the running water upstream, pushing brush aside with her staff. Just above the falls, she stopped and the four looked in horror at the site of what had been a ritual sacrifice.

"McGuire," Doc whispered. "This is a demon appeasement. He had to feed."

"It's worse," Wesley said. He knelt just outside the carefully laid out circle containing the dog's carcass. He rose with a playing card in his hand.

"What is that?" Rebecca asked.

"One of Pol's magic tricks," Margaret said. "Phillip brought him a new deck of playing cards when we arrived."

Turning their backs on the gruesome sight, they hurried back to the road in time to hear the grinding of gears as Marcos pulled to a stop at the bridge. Doc hurriedly explained what they had found, leaving out some of the more gruesome aspects.

"I think Pol's been kidnapped," Doc concluded. "Ryan McGuire will do anything to get his hands on the goddess."

"You think he'll hold Pol for ransom?" Rebecca asked.

"No," Wesley said. "Marcos, you need to take me to the base camp. I'll go alone from there."

"Wesley? What are you talking about?" Rebecca demanded.

"He'll try to use Pol to open the gates to the City of the Gods."

In the courtyard, they held a hurried counsel with Marcos's wife and sister. The clouds in the northern sky erupted in a lightning display and soon the low rumblings of thunder in the distance reached their ears. All stood silently for a moment so that the air was still when a piercing scream of unhuman quality shattered the stillness. Every eye was startled upward to the height of a great dead tree a hundred yards to the north. In its uppermost branches, an eagle danced with wings spread to a magnificent breadth, trying to find a secure spot on the limb to rest. Behind the incredible creature, the entire northern sky lit up in a sheet of lightning. The group braced themselves against the crack of thunder that followed seconds later. The eagle, the lightning, and the thunder were all much bigger than life. They stood wondering where the beautiful life and the bright day they woke to had gone.

The eagle sat perched on the treetop for some moments as the gathering of tiny people watched in silence. It rose to its full height again with wings spread wide and repeated the ghastly shriek that had drawn their attention. Then it plunged toward the earth, disappearing for seconds behind the hedgerow before rising again to wheel overhead and turn to the north. It turned so close overhead that everyone could see that it clutched in one great claw a field mouse, and in the other a young rabbit. Then it climbed into the sky and continued toward the storm in the north. Rebecca became suddenly aware of the pounding of her heart against her chest and the tears streaming hotly down her cheeks.

They stood facing each other, so shaken by the events of the past hour that they could not speak. Thea was nearly to them, bustling across the courtyard, when they heard her frenzied shouting.

"Go! Go! You must follow! You are summoned!"

She hurried them to the Jeep. Wesley piled in the front next to Marcos with Rebecca, Doc, and Margaret in the back. Thea stood defiantly between the vehicle and her daughter-in-law. Marcos did not hesitate to start out.

"I only know the long way," Marcos said. "There are no maps to the City."

"I don't think we'll need one," said Rebecca pointing up. The great eagle had swooped back around as if to gather them up to follow. Then it headed north into the coming storm.

REBECCA LEANED HER head back as the vehicle carried its cargo higher into the mountains. She knew that geographically whatever mountain they were headed to was not within the quick drive Marcos was making to it.

The gods. If they want you someplace, they make it so you get there. But what do they want with me here? Or with Wesley or Pol?

It's all so seductive. They awaken power in you and then they throw you into one absurd mission after another. They sweep up all you love and throw it just out of your reach. Like Odysseus, we'll be shipwrecked on one island after another until we've appeased whatever angry spirit it is that pursues us. Why did I think of him? He was gone for twenty years! Why didn't the Greek heroes just quit and go home? One choice. You get one choice in your life and the rest of your course is set and established.

She fingered the star stone in her pocket and wondered why she ever got involved in this. The landscape was dark and golden under the lightning. It had not begun to rain, but a fog was rising, faint at the moment, but climbing to meet the lowering clouds. She had a stab of pain in her stomach that made her want to run away from this place forever. She had been captive here for too long.

Marcos forced the old car past the previous drop-off point. She felt every jolt in the path and heard the grinding gears and whine of the overworked engine. The mountain above them was aflame with lightning, and still they climbed, following the eagle. Cresting a rise that the Jeep scarcely made it over, they saw the stream that would guide them to the base camp. Only it was a stream no longer. The banks barely contained the torrent of the rushing river.

"It's flooding!" shouted Marcos as the vehicle ground to a halt and they all jumped out. "Stick to the ridge and stay as close together as possible." Rebecca grasped Wesley's hand and felt him squeeze hers as the fog closed in. She released his hand to find her star stone. *Perhaps it will cut through the fog and guide us like it did from the mountain.*

When she reached again for Wesley's hand, she could not find it.

Tuesday, 23 August 1955, The Mountain

WESLEY WAS NO tracker, but the urgency of the situation drove him on. Rebecca released his hand and he panicked, calling out to her. Flailing, he could feel the ground giving out beneath him as he fell toward the sound of the rushing current.

And then he was out of the fog.

He looked at the ridge above and saw no sign of Rebecca or Marcos. He was torn between climbing back to the ridge and just waiting for help to arrive. But he could see the path ahead clearly now and pressed onward.

Thunder brought his head up to look at the gathering storm above him. Incongruously, the sun struck him fully in the back from where there was no cloud cover. It was obvious that Ryan McGuire thought Pol could open the gates to the City of the Gods and was attempting to force him. But he would find nothing there. The goddess was already gone.

Marcos had growled in unison with the engine on their way.

"He has my son! I will find him and make him pay!"

"We will work together, my friend. I can find him."

"How?"

"You are his father, Marcos. But I am a believer." Marcos snapped his head toward Wesley and nearly ran over a large boulder. Wesley nodded. "I can open the gates of the City."

Wesley scrambled over rocks and boulders now with his heart pounding in his throat and his tongue stuck to the roof of his mouth. Thunder cracked much closer. He wanted to wait for Marcos and Rebecca but as he eyed the greensward stretched out before him, what he saw filled him with so much anger he forgot his weariness.

At the base of the old tree, Ryan had thrown Pol down. The boy was tied hand and foot, stretched out much as the dog had been by the river. McGuire knelt in front of the boy with knife drawn and threatening him. Pol tried to cover his eyes, but Ryan angrily jerked the boy's head back by the hair with one hand as he brought the knife to point at his throat with the other.

The scene was brutal, sacrificial, satanic. A hundred expletives were on Wesley's lips, but he bore down on the two at full tilt before one finally broke the air accompanied by another burst of thunder. Ryan looked up to see Wesley only a few feet away and dropped Pol to defend himself before the musician's onslaught. The impact of the two men meeting shook the ground with the thunder as rain began to pelt out of the sky.

Had it not been for the element of surprise, Wesley would have stood no chance. As it was, Ryan was a skilled and brutal fighter, especially with a knife. Wesley saw the flashing point, ignored it and swung high. He felt the double impact of his fist closing on Ryan's face and the knife biting into his side. He fell to the ground clutching his wound with the knife still protruding and saw the dazed shock on Ryan's face as he hit the ground.

Wesley had the knife in hand, hoping he had not done more damage pulling it out of his side. Its razor-sharp blade made short work of the ropes binding Pol.

"Look out!" Pol shouted as a strong arm wrapped tightly around Wesley's neck, dragging him to his feet.

"Give me the *Athamé*!" growled McGuire in Wesley's ear. He swung Wesley around and gave Pol a swift kick as he did so. "The knife! Drop it!" Wesley held the knife out in front of him as Ryan's arm tightened, his free hand reaching for the withheld weapon. With a flick of his wrist, Wesley sent the knife sailing into the waters of the raging river. He drove an elbow back into Ryan, a move that would have meant nothing had Pol not attacked from behind. Ryan suddenly released Wesley and screamed at the disappearing knife.

Wesley turned in Ryan's loosened grip to swing again at his midsection. Pol beat on his back attempting to rescue Wesley. Ryan's rage and new direction completely baffled Wesley's momentary advantage. He uttered a phrase Wesley could not understand and bellowed denial. The force that he threw at Wesley sent him sprawling against the tree. Ryan charged toward the torrent to retrieve the sacred tool. Wesley dragged himself to his feet clutching his bleeding side. Pol struck Ryan as he bent over the bank to search for the knife and both went headlong into the rushing torrent.

"Pol! Don't!" he screamed as he raced to the bank. Wesley kicked off his shoes and shirt as he paced along the bank searching for a sign of either the boy or his nemesis.

Pol's head came up in midstream with Ryan struggling a few feet away. Without another thought, Wesley dove into the water.

The current, swifter than he remembered, caught him at once. He struggled to touch bottom and drive himself back to the surface. He felt a hand clutch at him as he rose, reached for it and went down again, thrashing and struggling to keep his own life and balance in the water. Silence surrounded him as he sank deeper. The water got blacker, but as black as the depth became, he could see through it like an owl in the night. He could see Pol, still plunging a few feet ahead of him while the hand that gripped him continued to drag him down. His lungs ached as he struggled after the boy.

27

Behind the Veil

REBECCA RECOGNIZED all the players as she emerged from the fog. She screamed for Wesley as he dove into the river but her words were ripped away by the wind. Rebecca ran hard for the tree with Marcos slipping on the rocks behind her as the rain increased. They vaulted the near-side stream onto what was now an island in the midst of which the old olive stood unmoving. At the river bank, they could see nothing but rushing water; then, far downstream, Pol's head and hand emerged. Rebecca ran down the embankment after Pol. Without removing her boots or clothes, she was in water up to her knees when Marcos grabbed her from behind and dragged her back to shore.

"You can't do it, Rebecca. He's past the fork and we're cut off!"

"They'll be lost!"

"Look." Rebecca followed Marcos's hand and saw Doc and Margaret moving downstream after Pol on the far side of the river.

"I can't do nothing! Where is Wesley?" she screamed at Marcos. They ran back along the river hoping to see the adult men clinging to a rock. There was nothing.

"Pray!" Marcos yelled as he fell to his knees, nearly dragging Rebecca with him.

"Yes, Pray," whispered the frightened woman, shedding his hand and turning to the old tree. Somehow this was the embodiment of all their problems, a sentinel that watched over the victims of the gods. It made perfect sense in Rebecca's addled mind. The tree represented the mystery that had captured them all with its eagle still soaring above in the pelting rain. Her hand was in her pocket, pulling forth the star stone and *Athamé* as she scooped up her staff and faced the tree.

She held the stone between herself and the tree and held the tip of the tiny dagger to the stone. Ignoring proper warding of her circle, she simply concentrated on seeing the tree through the black void of the stone she called Key. Soon she could see it and poured herself through the stone at the tree. It began to glow and take shape. The shape that emerged was a person in a long robe, human in form but not identifiable as male or female. Rebecca's stomach knotted up as she took in the shape of the specter—a dark reaper—the jailer—the gatekeeper of a circle without end. It had imprisoned her before—no, not her; her daughter. It threatened to claim Wesley and Pol, sucking them into its darkness.

"No! I forbid them to die. Go you down to their grave instead!" she commanded. With all the force she could manage, she swung her staff out toward the tree. "Burn, damn it!"

POL SAW PEOPLE on the shore but the water was around him even when he struggled to the surface for air. He reached a hand above the tide toward them. *Papa!* He would be saved. Rocks in the riverbed loomed up before him and he struck against several as he rushed farther and farther, clutching at each passing rock for safety. His hand grasped at nothing, finding only pebbles in the water, worn smooth by the current.

There were stories—people swept up in streams in Greece that surfaced in Italy. One was rumored to come up in Sicily. He plunged beneath the surface into a dark place. There was no surface to find. He could not tell which direction it should be. In the darkness, he sank into the depths of the earth. *My mortality caught up with me and I fell. I knew my time would be short in this land of bliss where my love and I played together.*

Pol's limited experience of the world played before him at once, transporting him from heights to depths without end. He died a hundred times. He was reborn a thousand. *I will disappear from the face of the earth.* His mind reprimanded him. *Nothing ever disappears. It just moves to a different place. It changes forms.*

Perhaps he would emerge in a new form, a different place. He would have a new life in a new world. He would have a new name; no longer would he be... What was that name he'd had? He no longer remembered his birthright or the family that lived... somewhere. He had been so many things and so many people. If only he could collect them all together. What a person he would be. He would become *megalos kai kalos*—a great and good man. Or simply a fool, broken down to miniscule parts and divided among the generations that followed—recombined and separated—ground to dust and scattered across the generations.

No wonder there were no longer great men and women. They were past. They lived on, but in mere bits of their ancient glory, parceled out among all living beings. And of all those generations and ages that lived before him, who was he? Only a foolish child who believed in fairytales and ancient stories of magic. What magic could he bring to the world now? He would disappear and rise again in another age as another person, divided again and less than before.

Oh, Papa! I understand. I understand and I cannot believe!

WESLEY STRUGGLED WITH the current after Pol, but the weight that clung to his arm in a death grip dragged him down. The water brightened and Wesley could see Pol disappear through the bottom of the riverbed. He drove harder and with one good kick met the gravel and sand of the riverbed. His neck snapped back with the force of the impact and the air was jolted from his lungs. Water filled his nose, his mouth, and his lungs.

Then all went black.

Tuesday, 23 August 1955, City of the Gods

WHEN HE AWOKE, Wesley recognized the fallen and crumpled pillars—the ruins of the City of the Gods. Perhaps he, himself, had brought destruction on the City when he released the goddess from her prison. He struggled to stand up, but a weight clung to his leg. Ryan McGuire had refused to release him, even in death. Or perhaps it was not death as a gasp and lungful of air animated the body in front of him. Wesley frantically looked for a weapon with which to defend himself but there was only a broken fragment of a great pillar.

Ryan McGuire's eyes burned with hatred when they locked on Wesley. They seemed lit from the inside.

"You!" he gasped. "What have you done? You have lost the First Face of the Cobhan Carles, the *Athamé*. I will kill you. I will hunt down every living soul you have known and destroy them. I will..." Wesley cut off the stream of invective by clubbing Ryan in the head with the rock. Kicking himself free of the demon-possessed man, Wesley stood to assess his position. A few hundred yards up the rubble strewn former avenue was the rostrum on which he had spent so much time. It called to him with its seductive music and he could see the dancing lights above it, even in the neutral light of the sunless sky. Hyperion's chariot had been driven off to light some other world.

Wesley nodded as he joined his voice to the tuneless chorus beckoning him. He grabbed the collar of Ryan's shirt and dragged him along the avenue, over broken pillars and dislodged paving stones. Wesley kept the rock fragment in his hand in case he needed to subdue the man again.

At last he reached the dais and rolled the unconscious man onto it. The ivory veil was a time-proven impenetrable prison. He saw the colors dancing in the center that showed where the opening in the veil had been torn. Ryan groaned and Wesley wrestled the man to his feet, locking him in a painful armlock and marching him to the center where the colors whirled.

"What is this?" Ryan demanded. "What are you doing to me?"

"You wanted to know what was behind the ivory veil," Wesley growled. "This is your opportunity to find out. This is the entrance. Go. Go and never return." He pushed Ryan into the colors and they swirled about him. Then, as if sucked down a drain, the colors, complete with their prisoner, disappeared down the star-shaped aperture.

"Seal it," whispered voices from all around. "Seal it so he cannot escape." Whether it was a command to him or about him, Wesley did not know. An ache began behind his eyes and centered in his forehead. He remembered now how he had freed the goddess, crashing into the center of the dais and freeing the keystone embedded in his forehead. The stone was gone, held now in his wife's hands. But his head held the imprint. He knew the passage and sang it with fury as he spun around the rostrum on which he and Pol had spent so much time. Faster and faster. Dizziness overwhelmed him and he wavered, stumbled, and fell. The star-shaped imprint between his eyes meshed with the tiny hole in the rostrum and locked it shut.

Tuesday, 23 August 1955, The Mountain

REBECCA HELD STEADY, all her focus on the robed figure standing in place of the tree. The figure raised a hand toward her staff and the other toward the sky. Twin bolts of lightning hit his hands, one from the sky and one from the tip of Rebecca's staff. The instant clap of thunder knocked her companions to the ground, even as far away as Doc and Margaret were, but Rebecca held steady, eyes locked on the figure. It wavered and faded. All that was left was the old tree, split in half and blazing in flames.

A voice surrounded them.

"It is finished. Your hubris has sealed the gateway. That which is within is within. That which is without is without."

Rebecca dropped her staff to the ground and lowered the star stone. All she could see was the burning tree, but the voice continued as if it grew inside her ear.

"You wished for freedom, child, but the price of a rite of passage is to leave a part of yourself behind. It has been done. This gate is forever sealed. But prophecy must yet be fulfilled. You will open the gate when you understand your gift and first exercise it, not in need or obligation, but in love. When the goddess has learned this truth, the captive may be freed."

Rebecca reeled at the words. She sank to her knees as the vision of Wesley dancing on the rostrum filled her eyes. As the lightning split the tree and sealed the gates, Wesley fell—captive in the City of the Gods.

"Damn you!" Rebecca cried. "Damn your divine trickery! I forswear my powers and lay them to rest. You'll not use me again. Damn you!"

Tuesday, 23 August 1955, Behind the Ivory Veil

I'VE BEEN HERE before.

Wesley looked around at the featureless gray plain. No sensation. No texture. Naked. Simply gray. Gray to the sight, gray to the touch, gray to the smell. Gray.

No. It was a dream. This must also be a dream.

Music stirred him. He turned and saw the powerful and beautiful woman of his former dream.

"You're here. Then I will wake up in Rebecca's arms."

"So, you have returned," she answered. "I hoped you would. You must never leave me again."

"That's a lot for a dream to demand. Everything I love is in the real world." He was not as shy as he had been on their first encounter. He was more than a little upset.

"You will find all things here and when you cannot accept what you have found, you will find nothing."

"Nothing? Am I dead?"

"Life and death have no meaning here. What you desire, you can draw forth from yourself. You will collect many secrets and know many things. But when your knowledge fails you, you will have only your faith to sustain you. That is when you will find freedom."

"Nothing. Alone. Rebecca… I cannot bear it."

"You are not alone. I am with you."

"You are not going to leave me? I'm poor company."

The woman reached toward him again. He felt her hand on his hand, his shoulder. He watched as their arms melted into each other. He felt her thigh against his thigh and watched her move into his body.

"How can I forsake myself?" she asked when they were almost completely united. "And how can you? When you wish me to be separate, I will be separate. When you have reached completeness, we will no longer be separate. I will be always and forever at one with you. You will be whole and we shall travel together to the Temple of Light."

She pulled away again and stood beside him, her hand now resting gently on his own.

"Who are you?" he croaked.

"I am your soul. Come. All creation is waiting to spring from us."

Wesley stood and she put her arm around him to support him. Together, they began to walk.

August 1955, The Sea

Mesh ensnared the boy and he broke the surface of the water. Creaking boards were under him with the smell of fish out of water. Perhaps the smell was his own. Perhaps in this life he would die a fish, trapped in a net. Hands were on his body as voices he did not understand babbled urgently around him. Lips were on his lips. He felt the fast hard rush of a man's breath into his lungs and remembered no more.

28 New Life

Tuesday, 15 May 1956, Greenwich, Connecticut

"IT'S REMARKABLE, William. It captures so much." Margaret, Doc, and William stood in the doorway of the study looking at the panel over the fireplace. William had finished the installation late the previous night and had kept the door locked all morning as he polished and cleaned the room. At last, he was ready to unveil the wood relief. Doc and Margaret accepted filled champagne glasses, ready to toast the artist's most recent work. Looking at it, however, the champagne was forgotten as the two relived the passion and the pain of Doc's last adventure. He had retired at once when they had returned last fall.

"Tell us about it, won't you, William?" asked Doc. His steward friend took a deep breath before he began.

"If Wesley were here, he would play and there would be nothing more to be said," he began. "The City, as you described it, is far more than I could hope to capture on one simple panel. Yet the pillars themselves form a dominant background. I could not include all you described, so you will forgive me for having placed you as a mere shadow in the foreground."

"Three shadows," murmured Doc.

"You and Pol and Me, Phillip," said Margaret. "It feels so real."

"And the center?" Doc asked.

"I could only feel that there was a mystique that permeated what you saw and that you were unable to put into words. Perhaps the shadow of multiple futures played out before your eyes," William continued. "Therefore, I have chosen for the figures at the center of the rostrum, not the lovers that you thought you saw, but a Pieta—weeping Madonna with her crucified son. The positioning is the same as Michelangelo's famous work, but the figures are those of Wesley and Rebecca. The motto flourish beneath is in New Testament Greek."

"Greater love hath no man," Doc translated. He paused to polish his glasses with a handkerchief. They had inexplicably steamed over. He noticed that Margaret was dabbing at her glasses with a napkin as well. "It does embody the spirit of it all."

"Are my eyes playing tricks on me?" asked Margaret. "It's a little hard to tell with tears in them. It seems like there is a shadow brooding in the background?"

"Out of grief, hope must arise or it would all be for nothing. And you went there not only to exonerate your mentor, but because of the legend of the goddess hidden behind the ivory veil. If that spirit was not released, then it was all for naught."

"I somehow think the prophecy has not been completed yet," Doc said. "We shall have to wait and see. Perhaps in another lifetime, I don't know." Doc retrieved the champagne glasses from his desk and handed them around. "William, it is indeed a masterpiece. I salute you." They toasted the artist and drank in silence.

"How many panels are there total, William?" The artist had been creating panels of Doc's adventures since the two were in college together. Not all were on the walls of the study.

"Twenty-one. I believe this will be the last."

"It will be if you insist on limiting your art to my adventures. I am through. I don't believe I will even write the paper. I've not been able to focus on it, and really, it was Wesley's work that was most important. That is lost to us with Ryan McGuire."

"It's a pity, though," said Margaret, "that there is not a suitable venue for this that is open to the public. More people should see your work. You can't even put them all in this room."

"There will be one day," William responded. "But no need to rush. These twelve will be for our private enjoyment."

"And what is this?" Doc turned to survey the other panels in the room and his eyes came to rest on the piano he had purchased in case Wesley had wanted to work with him after the expedition. Next to the music rack was an object covered with a cloth of white silk.

"It's a companion piece of sorts. A gift, I think. What would one expect to find behind the ivory veil but a goddess?" He lifted the cover but the marble beneath appeared to still be veiled. "It's an old technique. Raffaelo Monti was famous for his veiled ladies in the last century. The veil is sculpted into the artwork. Only brief glimpses of the figure are seen beneath it."

The sculpture, done in white marble, was the figure of a woman reclining on a rock. She was playing an *aulos*, or double flute, the instrument of the muse Euterpe. Doc and Margaret could see different views through the marble veil as they looked at the sculpture from different angles. The illusion was magnificent.

The chimes rang and William slipped away to answer the door, leaving the two absorbed in the sculpture and in their memories. In a moment, William returned, adopting his secondary role as steward.

"You have mail. I believe you may be interested in this one right away."

"Well, now. What is this?" Doc smiled. "We've a letter addressed to the Doctors Heinrich and Jacobsen, postmarked in Indiana." Doc and Margaret had abandoned the conceit of maintaining separate dwellings after their return from Greece.

"Oh, good. Rebecca is writing," responded Margaret. "What does she say?"

"Here, you read it. Your voice always does better justice to her letters than mine."

"My dear friends," began Margaret.

It is so kind of you to express continued concern for me. I am happy to report that since my last correspondence things have been quite well. There has been a great deal of work preparing for the baby, but as I told you before, Wesley's life was in perfect order. He could not have left me better provided for. It seems funny, doesn't it, that even if he had known he was not coming back, he could scarcely have left things better organized against that end.

It has been scarcely a year since I first met you and in that short time my life has changed so much that I look in a mirror with a sense of surprise at the image that stares back at me. Even more than having received my degree, I am not what I was a year ago. I can never be again.

You will probably become tired of hearing me talk of this, but I am certain that Wesley is not dead. Perhaps none of them are. When I meditate, I can hear his voice singing, often in that odd accompaniment to Pol. I have dreams of him that are so real that I can feel his heart beating next to my own. The sense of loss when I awake is almost unbearable.

I so hope you will come to visit this summer. Compared to what we went through a year ago, everything seems terribly flat and colorless in Indiana.

I love you both very much, Rebecca

Doc and Margaret let out a unison sigh.

"Such pain," said Margaret.

"I wish there was something we could do. Shall we go visit?"

"Of course. I wouldn't miss seeing the baby," said Margaret.

"When you go, would you mind terribly taking this with you?" asked William from next to the statue. "I said it was a gift, you know."

"The Last Gift," Margaret sighed. "For Rebecca?"

"No. For her daughter."

"Yes, William," said Doc, placing an arm around his steward's shoulders. "That is indeed perfect. Look at this." Doc held out a small card pulled from the envelope.

Rebecca Allen
is pleased to announce
the birth of her daughter
SEREPTE HART ALLEN
Born May 1, 1956

The End

The story continues in

The Props Master 1: Ritual Reality.

www.ingramcontent.com/pod-product-compliance
Lightning Source LLC
Chambersburg PA
CBHW060908250626
47159CB00008B/2913